The BABEL Effect

The **BABEL Effect**

A Novel

DANIEL HECHT

CROWN PUBLISHERS  NEW YORK

Published by Crown Publishers, New York, New York.
Member of the Crown Publishing Group.

Random House, Inc. New York, Toronto, London, Sydney, Auckland
www.randomhouse.com

CROWN is a trademark and the Crown colophon is
a registered trademark of Random House, Inc.

Grateful acknowledgment is made to the following previously published material:
The lines from "In the Wake of Home," from *Your Native Land, Your Life: Poems by
Adrienne Rich,* copyright © 1986 by Adrienne Rich. Used by permission of the author
and W. W. Norton & Company, Inc.

Excerpt from "Syndrome E" by Dr. Itzhak Fried from *The Lancet,* 350: 9094, 12/20/97,
p. 1845. Used by permission of the author and The Lancet, Ltd.

Leonard Cohen for the line from "The Future," from the album *The Future,*
copyright © 1992 Leonard Cohen Stranger Music, Inc. (BMI)
and Sony Music Entertainment, Inc.

Printed in the United States of America

DESIGN BY KAREN MINSTER

Library of Congress Cataloging-in-Publication Data
Hecht, Daniel.
The Babel effect / by Daniel Hecht.—1st ed.
1. Violent crimes—Psychological aspects—Fiction.   2. Epidemics—Fiction.   3.
Conspiracies—Fiction.
4. Kidnapping—Fiction.   I. Title.
PS3558.E284 B33   2001
813'.54—dc21   00-055480

ISBN: 0-609-60729-4

10   9   8   7   6   5   4   3   2   1

First Edition

Acknowledgments

This book recounts a real conceptual odyssey, and neither book nor journey could have been accomplished without the assistance of many brilliant and patient individuals. Thanks are due to my intrepid research assistants, Sheila Boland Chira, Hilton Dier III, and Kathy Hentcy—regular Einsteins all—who constituted my own real-life Genesis crew. Likewise, thanks to Kevin Boland and Geoff Greene for their technical expertise on computers and the e-world. I am also deeply indebted to Helen Butterfield for her insightful reflections on Roman Catholicism, to Bruce Chalmer and Ezra Tishman for their comments on Judaism, and to Professor Richard Hathaway, my resident Baptist. Thanks, too, to Special Agent Peter Ginieres of the Boston FBI field office for sharing his time and knowledge.

The general premises of this book owe their inspiration and articulation to many people. Special thanks to Irene Wainwright, Ph.D., and Dr. Itzhak Fried at U.C.L.A. Medical School Division of Neurosurgery for their discussion of Syndrome E. Thanks to Paul Brodeur for detailed commentary on the health effects of electromagnetic frequencies; to Professor Tony Whedon for helpful literary criticism; to Matt Ridley for discussion of the biological origins of values and for supportive feedback; to Professor Richard Dawkins for making modern evolutionary theory accessible; to Robert O. Becker, Leslie Brothers, Fritjof Capra, Howard Gardner, Theodore Gaster, Stephen Jay Gould, Dorothy Otnow Lewis, C. J. Peters, Stephen Pinker, Oliver Sacks, and Edward O. Wilson, whose honorifics are many but omitted here for the sake of concision.

Finally, thanks to my editors, Bob Mecoy at Crown and Mari Evans at Macmillan, for their patience, vision, and support at crucial moments. As always to Nicole Aragi for keeping the faith. And to Stella Hovis for gracefully holding chaos at arm's length while I wrote this book.

Part ONE

I will give you a name for the sickness of our age. And you shall know it to be true, for it is the name of everything you most fear and abhor, the source of all suffering and confusion.
—REVEREND JARED CONSTANTINE, *PROPHECIES*, VOL. 1

And the Lord said, Behold, the people is one, and they have all one language. . . . And now nothing will be restrained from them, which they imagined to do. Come, let us go down there and confuse their speech, so that they will not understand what they say to one another.

So the Lord scattered them abroad from thence upon the face of the earth: and they left off to build the city.
—GENESIS 11

**Interview with Samuel Frederic Oakes,
May 4, Willowdale Penitentiary:**

Preliminary interview with the goal of securing his consent to be tested.

Crimes: Killed nine children, mixed genders, no sex. assault. Extensive pre- or peri-mortem biting of all victims.

CV: 34 yrs. old, formerly delivery driver for uniform laundry service company. High school dropout. Insanity defense, unsuccessf. No appeals rem., due to be executed May 14.

Appearance: Small, wiry, red hair, gangly arms, a stereotypical "hillbilly" look reinforced by his accent. ????: Began killing after relocating to Connecticut from central south—emigrant psychology, role as "outsider" pushing him over the edge?

Affect: Extreme emotional lability (alternately raging, sullen, confronting, retreating, self-aggrandizing, self-pitying, etc.) w/violent kinesis. Claims no remorse, but self-inflicted pain during interview (throwing himself at glass partition, real injury resulting) suggests subconscious desire to receive punishment, to "atone."

From birth records, early history, one good guess as to contributing neuropathology would be prenatal alcohol syndrome. ????: In utero developmental impairments to which neural loci?

????: Brain damage from workplace exposures to toxins? Uniform services use industrial cleaners, solvents. Look into former employers, neurotoxic effects of chemicals used, exposure levels.

Professes hatred of blacks, Jews, homosexuals, but choice of victims (all white) doesn't reflect racial basis. Ryan very responsive to the racial insults, "protecting" me (and Dagan). Oakes also dislikes X-rays, which prison psych. Dr. Palmer says reflects paranoid schiz., a fear of "intrusion" into or observation of his mind, fear of external influences on thoughts.

All moot. Declined to give us consent.

Our first prelim. int., very disturbing. Given my pregnancy, it's not surprising I found his victimization of children particularly upsetting, but the session affected me more than anticipated. My taking lead big mistake, given Oakes's claimed racial issues. May have cost us Oakes as a subject. Brought it on myself, trying to be tough & "face into" the problem of what moves such a man. Must watch my own emotional needs as biasing factors, try to retain impartiality. Ry's right that I'm not doing well at keeping personal issues separate.

Disappointed by failure to get access to Oakes. But got a frisson of insight when I was explaining the testing protocol & he interrupted me to say something like "Now I want to see the other one (Dagan was standing far in back), I've seen enough of the nigger." Left me wondering whom he had been talking to. Objectification, it occurred to me—I wasn't really there, wasn't real to him. ????: Because I'm black? Because I'm a woman? Or just because I'm another person?(!) Objectification also apparent in his use of his victims—not seeing them as human, he can treat them as objects. Surely an element common to all serial killers. For that matter, to all the injuries & miseries human beings inflict on each other. Much to think about here. Already the project has become for me something far larger than a study of the minds of murderers.

Would like to ask Ry his take on this, but know he'll see it as product of my emotional fragility now, my irrational hunger for encompassing explanations. And he may be right. For now, my instinct is to protect him from seeing full extent of my desperation, imbalance.

Chapter 1

FRIDAY, MAY 3, 2001

Jess had been born with a hole in her heart—a ventricular septal defect. It had been surgically repaired when she was two years old, but Ryan often thought that in some ways it had never really closed: Thirty-six years later, she seemed to carry an opening in her heart, both a wound and a window. He could feel it in her now, as she came up behind him and wrapped her arms around his chest. In the pressure of her body against his back he could feel the deep gentle beat, an unexpected intimacy.

"All set," Leap announced happily. He rolled his chair over, bringing a wireless keyboard and mouse.

Marshall came to stand next to Jess, along with Silvia Sorbanelli and her colleagues from the American Forensic Psychology Association. Leap tapped a command. On the big monitor, what looked like a single raindrop fell onto a smooth surface, sending decaying ripples out from the center of the screen. Beautiful, tranquil, almost hypnotic.

"This is the most basic stage," Leap explained. "We started with a simple energy dispersion pattern, a ripple of energy moving outward from an epicenter."

Dr. Sorbanelli nodded appreciatively. "Nice graphics," she said. "Has this…system…got a name?"

"RAINDROP." Leap was looking happy, a proud father showing off his baby. "Not an acronym, just a little poetic license."

They were in the windowless control room of Leap's data-processing lab, back under the bluff at Genesis headquarters. Through a glass wall, they could see the RAID cabinets and other rack-mounted hardware of Argus, Leap's computer, LEDs blinking erratically. The air in the control room had a zoo smell because Leap kept his ferret, Sneaky Pete, in a cage on one of the counters.

Marshall had flown in from Stanford to join the Genesis people and Dr. Sorbanelli for the first of the death-row interviews and some further discussion of the forensic neuropsychology project. It was a good chance for the AFPA to get to know the Genesis organization on a more informal basis, so Jess had played hostess, walking Dr. Sorbanelli and her colleagues through the house and then down the long outside stairs to the offices. Finally they had come back here to Leap's subterranean lair to show off RAINDROP, now entering the wrap-up stage.

Silvia Sorbanelli had graying hair and patrician features appropriate to her towering reputation in neuropsychology. She had come with two associates: a pretty Asian woman with a quiet, self-effacing manner, and a man in his late fifties with penetrating eyes and a sharp little smile. Though Ryan hadn't caught his name, he kept thinking he should recognize that slab-cheeked face, more like a big-city ward boss or a Kremlin heavy than a scientist.

On the screen another drop fell, this time causing some splashes nearby as droplets flew and set up their own rings of ripples.

"The plot thickens." Leap leaned forward to point out the secondary splashes, chewing his gum rapidly. Nicotine gum, Ryan knew, and not because Leap had ever smoked—he just liked the buzz.

Jess explained: "The commission is from a consortium of state health departments—Utah, Colorado, Arizona, and New Mexico. Really, the impetus for the project came from the first incident, back in 1993—you remember, a mysterious disease outbreak in New Mexico, in the Four Corners region? Very high fatality rates?"

"Sure," Silvia Sorbanelli said. "The 'Navajo flu.'"

"Not very flattering to the Navajos, but yes, that's the one. Ultimately the bug was called the Sin Nombre virus—'No Name.' A previously unknown hantavirus that caused fever, swelling of the heart lining, and acute fluid buildup in the lungs."

"Didn't the CDC eventually trace the virus to mice?"

"Exactly—the southwestern deermouse. The virus was transmitted to humans through evaporated mouse urine. Another epidemic of the same bug cropped up in Argentina in 1996. Then the really bad one in Arizona, in '99—two hundred fatalities in two weeks. Still the rodent reservoir, but this time a form of the virus that could be transmitted from person to person—much more dangerous. There was real danger of nationwide dispersion."

Leap took his show to the next level. On the screen, the surface of the virtual water began to change. A map emerged, showing the lines of highways, wandering veins of rivers, blocks of city streets.

Ryan took up the role of tour guide: "So, after the '99 outbreak, the Four Corners states came to us and said, 'Give us a predictive tool, a way to model dispersion patterns for disease outbreaks—*fast.*' When the next epidemic comes, they want a way to jump all over the first few cases and predict the disease's spread with real accuracy. Something that'll give health departments the chance to take rapid response measures—inoculation, sanitation, quarantine, whatever."

On the screen, a drop fell onto the city map. This time, instead of neat rings, the ripples spread out in an irregular star-shaped pattern, drawn down the lines of streets, filling in blocks as they came to densely populated areas. Secondary droplets spattered here and there, setting off their own ripples.

"Jesus," the slab-cheeked man exclaimed. "Looks like a, a giant amoeba, eating—"

"Eating Phoenix, Arizona," Leap told him. "Yeah. But even this is still very rudimentary."

The AFPA people were unlikely to know the systems math, so Ryan explained. "The analogy to fluid dynamics works only to a point. Ultimately, to model it right, you've got to factor in anything that puts people into contact with each other or with the source of the virus. That means we have to plug in public transportation routes, commuting patterns, workplace contacts, school districts, church attendance, air service to other cities, product shipments—you name it. Thousands of variables."

Ryan covertly watched Marshall's response. RAINDROP was the product of a collaboration between Marsh's people and the Genesis team, but this was his first glimpse of the graphics. Now Marsh adjusted his wire-rimmed glasses, swept his hair back, leaned in eagerly, all indications he was pleased. A good sign—as director of research at the world-renowned Brandt Institute, Marshall Fahey wasn't easily impressed.

Dr. Sorbanelli nodded appreciatively, and her red-faced colleague looked impressed, too. Seeing his shark's grin, half-familiar, Ryan wondered again, *Who the hell is this guy?*

"Wouldn't have been possible only a few years ago," Leap said. "But now we've got the math and the demographic databases. Most of all, the computing capacity. Even my rig isn't up to the heavy stuff. We're designing this program for the national defense supercomputers at Sandia. But here we go—this is our re-creation of the actual outbreak of 1999."

Leap pecked around and the map expanded to include the whole central section of Arizona. The first drop fell on Phoenix, and the amoeba began grabbing the region with arms of different lengths and thicknesses.

Abruptly, secondary splashes of different colors dimpled the map, also expanding until the screen became a scintillating mass of overlapping waves and rings in rainbow hues. Red dots began to speckle the scene: fatalities. They were all silent for a moment, drawn into the mesmerizing complexity of movement and color.

"By this point, we've entered the domain of chaos theory," Ryan said. "Can you bring in the phase-space graphics, Leap?"

Leap tinkered briefly, and the screen changed. Now a geometric figure danced in space, like a hollow wire sculpture made of thousands of graceful loops and curves. It rotated slowly, each strand representing another iteration of the fractal formula.

"Chaos math allows us to create another kind of 'map,'" Ryan explained. "What you're seeing now is called a 'chaotic attractor'—basically it's a graphic mathematical portrait of the disease's movement within the population. Using RAINDROP, we've demonstrated that epidemics have predictable system dynamics—a mathematical 'signature.' Put that signature together with the geographic and demographic mapping, we can not only predict an epidemic's spread very accurately, but also work backwards to source vectors."

They watched the rainbow sculpture for a moment longer, and then Leap cut back to the mapping graphics. The amoeba had expanded, a fluid glob absorbing Phoenix. Ryan was feeling the familiar thrill that came with seeing a complex pattern whole. A design, a mandala. Not to minimize Leap's contribution, but this was only a visualization tool. The real job had been to determine a way to perceive and analyze a vastly complex system—a project that had taken the combined Brandt Institute and Genesis research teams almost two years and was still not finished. But the graphics did put it together nicely, let your mind encompass the system intuitively.

The flush of pleasure lasted until Jess stood back and Ryan looked up to see her eyes, the trouble there.

"That first 'drop' falling on the outskirts of Phoenix, the index case, was a man named Juan Arguello," she reminded them. "Father of three kids, air-conditioner repairman, sci-fi movie fan. That secondary splash up near Flagstaff was Juan's sister-in-law—a plump, cheery waitress who had been saving her tips to get caps on her teeth. The first red dots, the fatalities? Juan's kids."

There was only the smallest reproach in the glance she gave Ryan. *Of course she's right,* he thought. What Jess saw on the screen was not a cool high-tech toy, not even a dynamic system of alluring mystery and beauty. Rather, the record of real human misery, the trail of pain and loss left by the disease. She was right to remind him.

Sobered, they observed for a few more minutes. Then Marshall pointed out the time, and Leap began to close out RAINDROP. Jess gave Ryan's shoulders a quick squeeze and led them out of the lab. Time for the drive to Willowdale Penitentiary.

Chapter **2**

Samuel Frederick Oakes lunged at the Lexan partition, drove his face into the floor-to-ceiling transparent wall, and fell to the floor. He crabbed backwards, stood up, and leaped again, arms outstretched and fingers clawed until his hands exploded, his face and body flattened against the clear plastic. Again he collapsed and rolled away, this time leaving a smear of blood behind. Coming through a pair of small speakers, the thud of impact and his injured whimpering had an enclosed, metallic ring.

Dr. Palmer, the prison psychologist, explained dryly: "Samuel doesn't receive many visitors. It stimulates him considerably."

"Oh, he'll calm down. He's just showing off for you," Oakes's lawyer said. Nikos Amanitidis was a small man with a black toupee and a round belly that bulged between red suspenders. "C'mon, Sam, quit goofing."

Ryan stood with Jess, Dagan, and Marshall, along with the prison psychologist and the lawyer, in the observation room. Silvia Sorbanelli and the other AFPA people had chosen to watch from behind a one-way mirror at the back, letting Genesis take the lead and get a close look at what the proposed commission entailed. Marshall and his people at Brandt Institute had jumped at the job when Dr. Sorbanelli first proposed it—as had the Genesis crew, even Jess. Ryan alone had rebelled. He'd agreed to come this far only because doing this interview would show Jess and the others what they would be getting into if they did take it on.

Oakes was scheduled for execution in just ten days. Owing to the cycle of legal appeals since the death penalty had been reinstated, Dr. Sorbanelli had explained, there was a wave of executions coming, and if Genesis or Brandt Institute wanted to study the brains of murderers, they should do it before this bumper crop of test subjects was "no longer accessible." Oakes was on death row because he'd murdered nine children, mostly little girls. Once caught, he'd been easily convicted when forensic odontologists demonstrated that the bite marks on the bodies, as many as fifty, matched his large, uneven teeth. His lawyer had offered the insanity defense, but the jury hadn't bought it—or, more likely, hadn't cared, given the savagery of his crimes. Ryan didn't blame them.

Oakes attacked the glass again, this time trying to bite and claw and kick his way through it. His garbled shrieks and grunts sounded like a pair of hogs fighting. Sickened, none of the Genesis people said anything for several minutes.

At last the killer got unsteadily to his feet again. He was thirty-four years old, a smallish, red-headed man with sloping narrow shoulders and long arms. Blood trickled from his pug nose and the corner of his lip, spattering onto his blue prison jumpsuit. Seeing their shocked expressions, he smiled and revealed his famous dentition, then sat on the metal chair bolted to the floor of the containment room.

"What y'all want?" Oakes said. An Appalachian twang: he'd lived most of his life in Tennessee before moving to New York State and beginning his career as a killer.

"Hello, Samuel," Jess said. "I'm Dr. Jessamine McCloud, and this is—"

"It's *Mister* Oakes. Niggers got to call me 'Mister.'" He went off on an impromptu exposition on racial characteristics, and Ryan thought, *Good boy, Sam. Let her see the nasty side, right up front.* Hopefully Jess would find Oakes distressing enough to rethink her determination to accept the job.

AFPA wanted Brandt Institute and Genesis to conduct a comprehensive assessment of the neuropsychological origins of violent behavior. Their general objective would be to expand scientific understanding of this difficult area of human psychology, but there were more immediate goals, too: to devise tools for social welfare agencies, psychiatric hospitals, and the legal and penal systems to cope with violence. To give police departments scientific tools to catch violent offenders and give the criminal justice system objective criteria by which to determine a perpetrator's culpability and chances of rehabilitation. To identify possible cures for violence-related disorders, ways to rehabilitate perpetrators while still guaranteeing the public's safety. Maybe, best of all, to find ways to *prevent* the medical conditions that precipitated violence disorders and violent crimes.

All laudable goals, Ryan agreed. Great mission, no argument there, very attractive to a bunch of idealists like the Genesis team. Dr. Sorbanelli had made a great pitch: The time was right for such a project. A paradigm shift had occurred in the last twenty years, as psychology moved away from traditional views of personality and behavior and toward the neuroscientific perspective. Addiction, depression, schizo-phrenia, obesity, obsession, and anxiety were now seen not as "character traits" but as medical conditions, and were successfully treated as such. The change in perspective had been augmented by the development of such sophisticated diagnostic technologies as CT scans, magnetic reso-nance imaging, and electrocorticograms, which let researchers observe the brain in action. Advances in biochemistry and pharmacology had revealed the chemistry of thought and emotion. Progress in microbiology and evolutionary theory had opened a window into the genetic origins of behavior. Yes, there had been studies of certain violent offender or psy-chiatric populations, but never a *comprehensive* study that used the latest techniques and technologies to put together all the parts of the puzzle. They'd be pioneers.

Yeah, Ryan thought, that was the way to nail 'em: good mission, the allure of the mystery itself, the promise of being first.

And the crew had gone for it, even Jess. Particularly Jess. They'd been fighting about it ever since. Logistical and scientific and ethical argu-ments aside, his most urgent objection was Jess herself, how this was the worst possible time for her to be involved in a study like this.

And yet, Ryan had to admit, right now she didn't seem particularly fragile or desperate. Just focused, determined. She was wearing a blue skirt and jacket, heels, hoop earrings, and even in this environment Ryan couldn't help admiring her: a tall woman with chocolate-brown skin, fine cheekbones, a figure like a konk in the head. *My Jessie.*

Jess waited out Oakes's racist tirade, and when he finished she just went on calmly: "Thank you, Mr. Oakes. Now I'd like to introduce you to my husband, Dr. Ryan McCloud, and our associate, Dr. Dagan Rabin-ovitch—"

"Amanitidis says you ain't real doctors."

"Not medical doctors, no. We're scientists who—"

"Y'all want to look at my brain. Why dontcha just wait till I'm dead?" Oakes said sulkily. "Only got ten more days."

"With your permission, we'd like to do that, yes," Jess agreed. "But we'd learn a lot more from studying your brain's activities *now.* If you're at all open to the idea, I can explain what the tests—"

"What'll I get out of it?" Oakes grinned widely, teeth like worn piano keys in his freckled face. One hand moved in his lap. At first Ryan had thought he was scratching himself, but the movement was too sustained and rhythmic. "You gonna get me off death row? No. Gonna give me a last fuck? No. Maybe a special dessert for the last meal?"

"Sam, please behave," Dr. Palmer put in. "You agreed to see these people, so—"

But Oakes was approaching the glass again, one hand still searching his crotch. "What you gonna do for me?" He lifted his chin and bit the air softly, bringing the big teeth together, his eyes on Jess's face.

To Ryan's surprise, Jess took a step closer to the partition, too. "We can't do much, it's true," she said evenly. "But you've got ten days to live, and you're locked down now. You can either spend the time with nothing to do but think about what's going to happen to you, or you can be distracted by some people who're silly enough to treat you with respect and consideration. You can sit there feeling bad about what you've done, or feeling a little better that at least you've helped someone understand why you did it."

"Don't feel bad about what I done," Oakes lied. But his psych evaluations did show he was capable of remorse, and Jess had pushed the right buttons. Now he backed away, as if repelled by her calm, her balanced compassion. He went back to the chair and sat, pouting.

Jess explained the protocol for the tests. The first phase was standard profiling: talking interviews with psychologists and a spectrum of evaluatory tests designed for violent personalities. Ryan doubted these would reveal anything new: Oakes's profile was typical of many serial killers. He'd been born to an alcoholic mother and probably sustained brain damage in the womb. His family environment had been abusive, and as a child he'd shown the classic triad of telltale symptoms: bedwetting, fire-starting, and killing small animals.

But what had actually happened to his brain? The other tests, not available when he'd first been evaluated, would help them zero in on specific impairments.

"We have four main medical tests," Jess said. "The first is just to take samples from you—we'll draw blood, and cut some hair. Our goal will be to look at your body's chemistry, especially the chemicals that work inside your brain." She deliberately avoided mentioning their desire to take spinal fluid, because it would probably discourage Oakes's consent; they'd ask him later. "Next we'd like to give you a PET scan, which is basically a way of taking a picture, a 3-D snapshot, of your brain."

"Like X-ray? Don't know as I'd like that," Oakes said.

"It doesn't hurt at all. The whole process takes only about ten minutes. I've had it done twice, myself."

Oakes put his chin on his chest, scowling. His feet began making a peculiar sideways shuffling.

"Then we get to the EEG—the electroencephalogram. We put electrodes—little wires—on your scalp, and the machine can sense electrical activity in your brain. While the EEG is hooked up, we'll ask you to do certain things, like look at pictures and answer questions. That way we can see how your brain behaves when stimulated in certain ways, creating what we call 'evoked potentials.'"

"What kind of pictures?"

"People doing things. Your family. Your victims. Our goal is to observe how your brain functions when you feel certain emotions or solve certain types of problems."

"Don't know as I'd like that," Oakes mumbled again. One of his shoulders had begun hitching up and down.

Dr. Palmer frowned, and bent to whisper in Jess's ear: "His kinetic signs point to some anxiety here. Usually precedes an aggressive episode."

Jess nodded without taking her eyes off Oakes. "The last test is called magnetic resonance imaging, or MRI for short. It's basically a doughnut or a tube you slide into, that puts out a magnetic field and then measures the radio signals your brain cells give off. Once again, we'd like to use evoked reactions. The functional MRI actually *films* your brain in action, microsecond by microsecond, tells us what parts of your brain you're using, how, and when. And that's all there is to our tests, Mr. Oakes. If you think you'd like to consent, I—"

"Now I want to see the other one," Oakes interrupted. He flipped one hand sideways as if sweeping something out of the way.

"I'm sorry—?"

"The other girl. The one standing in back. Seen enough of the nigger." Suddenly, Oakes was at the glass again, leaning against it with hands upraised, craning to see Dagan. "She's a *kike,* isn't she! Fuck a duck, you brought in a *kike* and a *nigger* and you expect me to go along with this shit!?"

Dagan had been standing partly behind Ryan, but now she moved into full view of Oakes. Yes, she was dark-haired, dark-eyed, her features unmistakably Semitic. She faced the murderer defiantly, her mouth set in a grim line.

Oakes was leering and shaking his head. "Oh my fucking god, a kike and a nigger, and I'm supposed to, you think I'm gonna—what, are you fucking *nuts?* I suppose the big guy's a *homo,* too, and I'm supposed to—"

"Sam, come on, we know you're just showing off," Amanitidis said.

Oakes ignored him and went on raving. Ryan was thinking that maybe Palmer and the others might be inured to these guys, but it was not easy for an outsider to confront them in the flesh knowing what their hands had done, what their eyes had seen. To feel, near at hand, the terrible twist or kink in their psyches, the pathology in their heads. The sense of danger near them—not the risk of physical attack, but more the feeling you got attending a deathbed, that almost superstitious fear of contagion.

He had instinctively taken a step forward, wanting to do something to shut the little psycho up. Jess put a hand on his arm.

Oakes threw himself at the partition again, smashing himself against it, falling, leaping back, spraying saliva and blood. The worst part was the sound: the battering of his skull and elbows, the squeak of his skin as he slid down the glass. The choking, slaughtered-hog squeals he made, the clash of his teeth.

Dr. Palmer was talking hurriedly into the wall phone. Jess turned away, eyebrows high, one hand on her chest as if struggling for breath. She gripped Ryan's arm hard, pulling him toward the door at the back of the room. Dagan was already there, fumbling with the knob. As Ryan went, he glanced back to see a pair of prison guards burst into the containment room and start subduing Oakes. Oakes's laughter rang through the speakers, tinny and cracked.

Out in the hallway, Jess leaned hard against the closed door. For a moment she just stood, both hands over her stomach as if unconsciously protecting or reassuring the growing baby inside her. Then she turned to Dr. Palmer. "I assume this is his way of implying he won't consent?"

Chapter 3

Two hours later their little caravan pulled into the lower parking lot at Genesis headquarters. It was just after three, the sun still bright on the water of the bay. Inside, Jess asked Dolores to let the rest of the team know they were back, and then brought the visitors into the conference room, where they took seats around the big oval table.

The crew filtered in from the offices. In contrast with Silvia Sorbanelli and her associates, so serious and corporate, the Genesis team looked younger, more alert, casual yet as clear-eyed as wolves on the hunt. Even Bates, at fifty-three the oldest of them, carried that air of relaxed vitality: loosened tie at odds with a charcoal suit tailored to a greyhound-lean physique, white-blond hair, laser-blue eyes. Logan sat at her ease in a flowered dress, a small woman with short blond hair, a delicate face, a Mona Lisa smile. Leap was sitting with one leg over the arm of his chair, wearing a tired-out tweed jacket over his T-shirt and faded jeans. Dagan: dark hair framing a heart-shaped face, attentive eyes, stylish raw-silk jacket over jeans, the youngest of them at twenty-five, yet completely self-possessed.

Ryan felt a flash of pride: definitely a special team. So much intelligence, so much heart.

And of course Jessie: stunning. One of the tall, east-facing windows framed her as she sat straight-backed at the conference table, giving her a halo of wave-reflected sunlight. The visit to Oakes had clearly upset her, but she had rallied with determination, was covering well. Her left hand lay in her lap, relaxed, fingers upcurled, but with her right hand she gave Marshall a mischievous pinch: *Hello, Marsh.* Her smile appeared, vanished demurely behind her hand.

From across the table, Logan was giving Ryan a quizzical look, tipping her head toward Dr. Sorbanelli's colleague: *What's he doing here?* Ryan looked him over again, trying to place the taut, smug smile, still not making the connection.

Dr. Sorbanelli cleared her throat. "It's wonderful to meet all of you, and to get an informal glimpse of the McCloud household and the famous Genesis think tank. I look forward to talking about some of the details of our commission, but first I know my companion wants to say a few words. For those of you who haven't already recognized him, I'd like to introduce Jason Ridder, of Ridder Global Corporation. We are grateful for his generous sponsorship of this study, and for his deep personal interest in the project."

The Genesis crew stirred, moving their chairs closer to the table, five pairs of keen eyes looking him over with heightened interest. Ryan was thinking, *Of course!* He should have recognized the sadistic smile and heavy cheeks from newspaper articles and the TV news. Somehow the guy looked different at close range, especially without his trademark cigar. But Jason Ridder, billionaire CEO of one of the world's largest transnational corporations—that explained the stranger's air of authority, the odd charisma of power. Ryan felt himself bristling at Ridder's unannounced invasion of Genesis until Jess sensed his reaction and put a calming hand on his thigh.

Ridder stood up, obviously enjoying the disturbance his introduction had created. "I hope you'll all forgive my incognito foray onto your turf. I know this is a little irregular, but taking a close look at things, on the sly, is an old habit of mine—you gotta understand, it's sometimes the only way for a guy in my position to see what's really going down. Let me just say, you've impressed me a great deal, and I'm confident I made the right choice when I asked Silvia to bring you in on this job." He shot a grin to Ryan, then got serious. "I'm gonna cut straight to the chase here, tell you why I'm bankrolling this project. This is the gritty side of the deal, but I always say you gotta look straight at the ugly stuff."

Ridder reached down into his briefcase, pulled out a stack of newspapers, held up one for his audience to see. *"Chicago Tribune,* two days ago: 'School Shooting Kills Seven.' Here's last week's *New York Times:* 'Hospital Rampage Kills Four, Wounds Six.' Sunday's *Washington Post:* 'Violent Crime, Hate Crimes on Rise After a Decade of Decline.' *St. Louis Dispatch:* 'Road Rage Death Toll Hits Five.'" He frowned as he tossed the papers aside and leaned forward to put his knuckles on the table. "We all know that during the mid-1990s, certain crime statistics fell. But let me remind you, that was only after forty years of skyrocketing numbers—a dip in a rising graph. And, point of fact, many categories of violence are still rising. Serial murder, for example. Rampage killing. Spouse and child abuse. Infanticide. Homicides *by* juveniles are up by *one thousand* percent in the last ten years! Right now, over *four hundred thousand people* are in jail for violent crimes. On the mental health side, psychiatric hospital admissions for violence-related disorders have skyrocketed—again, up *one thousand percent* in the last decade."

Ridder stood back, arms out to each side, an appalled look on his big face. The theatrical touch struck Ryan as overdone, but it still seemed to affect the Genesis crew. Bates had begun staring thoughtfully out at the bay, Logan was nodding her head minutely and her smile was gone, Leap was picking at a hangnail and jiggling not one but both legs. Jess moved uncomfortably in her seat, her face guarded, as Ridder's take on it obviously found a nerve.

"Okay," Ridder said. "Now, Dr. Sorbanelli and Dr. Fahey tell me that some of you still have reservations about taking the commission—I have to tell you, Ryan, I got a big kick out of observing *you* from behind the mirror at Willowdale! So let me add a word of persuasion." His woolly eyebrows rose on his forehead as he leaned forward and put his knuckles on the table again. "People, for the first time in history we have the scientific tools to look into whatever crack or crevice in our heads this stuff comes from. To understand and conquer it. I don't want to overstate the case, but on one level what we're asking is for you to *get to the root of man's inhumanity to man.* Whether we're talking a recent trend or why Cain offed Abel, I want you to identify what breaks in us and drives us to hurt each other. I'm hoping that's a challenge you guys can't walk away from."

Ridder observed their reactions with a satisfied look. From the body language of his audience, Ryan thought, he knew he'd made a good pitch.

Jess was the first to speak: "I think you've been frank with us, Mr. Ridder, and I'd like to be frank with you in return. I'd like to know why you want to support this research. You're not exactly known as a humanitarian, and a research project of this scale will cost you millions—why should you *care?*" There was the light of challenge in her eyes. Another side of Jess. At one point during their research on the Gulf War syndrome, when the Pentagon's bullshit level had gotten particularly deep, she had customized a screen saver for her computer that said *Take No Shit.*

Ridder grinned and shoved his hands into his jacket pockets. "I'm glad you asked that, Jessamine. Three good reasons. First, I've got something like a conscience—I don't take any pleasure from human suffering and would like to feel I'm doing my bit to fix it. Now, if you don't buy that," he went on, scanning their faces, enjoying his own dubious reputation, "I'll give you a more practical motive—profit. Ridder Global may be best known for consumer products and information technology, but we also own Lyden Pharmaceuticals, the world's largest producer of neuroleptic medications such as antidepressants. Another of our subsidiaries is General Medical, a leader in high-tech medical diagnostics. Point being that if your research points us to specific medical origins of violence and effective treatments for even a fraction of violent offenders, our medical divisions stand to make a fortune. Finally, we were among the first to invest in private penal industries, and are now the largest private prison system in the country. Meaning if we can provide better and more cost-effective ways to process violent offenders, we'll make out like bandits. Reason enough?"

Jess nodded, not entirely convinced, obviously not much liking the idea of "processing" human beings. "I take it," she said, "that your arrangement with AFPA gives you some rights to the information the study turns up?"

The question clearly made Dr. Sorbanelli uncomfortable, but Ridder was oblivious to Jess's understated irony. "You betcha. My main purpose here is pure philanthropy, but as you said, hey, this project will cost many millions. I can only justify the expense by thinking of it as a kind of research and development outlay."

Naturally, Ryan thought: Ridder hadn't made it to the top by giving anything away.

Ryan straightened out of his slump. "You mentioned that you particularly wanted us to work with Brandt Institute on this. Why? Why Genesis when you are already hiring the most prestigious research firm in business?"

Ridder nodded as if he'd expected the question. "Well, obviously, there's your collaboration on this Four Corners job, we know the two organizations work well together. Number two, everybody I talk to agrees you're the best. I've read your books and your CV, Ryan, I've seen the TV specials, I know nobody else can put together the different scientific disciplines and give us the systems analysis we'll need for this job. I also like your independence, your comparative newness." He glanced briefly at Marshall. "Not to put you Brandt people down—I respect that your outfit has been around for fifty years, and I want that proven ability on this project. But I've also learned to trust the contribution of the outsider, the young Turk, the cowboy. And that's where the Genesis people come in."

He looked back to Ryan. "But most important, you've got the crusader mentality. I know something about your style, enough to know you'll take risks, you'll make enemies if need be, you'll stick your professional necks out. I'll be paying you well, but you won't be in it for the money. You'll be in it to save this world's sorry ass, which is what you've been trying to do anyway."

Ryan had to smile, and even Jess chuckled: The man had them pegged pretty well.

One of the others asked a question about funding, and Ryan found himself spinning away from the discussion, multitasking. For the hundredth time he enumerated to himself the pros and cons. The project certainly had some allure: good mission, good pay. Good organizational partner: Marshall Fahey had been a close friend since the Project Alpha days, and it had been great to work with him on the Four Corners job. Plus, it had been years since he and Jess had done any research on their supposed field of expertise, the human brain—it might be nice to do some work on the old gray matter, the real final frontier.

But there were a lot of reasons to skip this. Not the least of which was that studying violent criminals and psychotics, probing their actions and urges, analyzing their crimes and pathologies in detail, could be awful. As Oakes had shown them: Turn over a rock, better be prepared to cope with what's under it. And Ridder was yet another reason to turn this one down. From the way Silvia Sorbanelli was taking a backseat here, it was clear that while AFPA was technically the sponsor, Ridder would be the one calling the shots. A guy famously hard to work with, rapacious, controlling.

Framed in the window, a distant jetliner sparked in the afternoon sun and drew Ryan's eyes to the long view of the southern coastline. For a moment he wanted desperately to be outside, up on the deck taking the first taste of three fingers of good whiskey. The May air would be cool and sweet, he'd take Abi on his knee and forget about anything even remotely like the origins of man's inhumanity to man, the root of all evil, the minds of murderers. But then, despite his resistance, he found his thoughts returning to the issue at hand, starting to touch and rearrange the pieces, playing with the mandalas of pattern and possibility.

Chapter 4

An hour later, Dr. Sorbanelli had gone, Ridder had been whisked away by a black Mercedes and a pair of bodyguards, the Genesis crew were back in their offices. The sun was still up, but the shadow of the bluff had begun to creep across the shore as Ryan followed Marshall and Jess up the long outside stairway that connected the office building with the house.

The complex had originally been built in the 1930s as a U.S. Navy marine research station, with the upper building poised at the top of the bluff and the lower one forty feet below, nestled into the rocks at the water's edge. When the realtor had first brought Ryan and Jess to the abandoned station, ten years ago, it had struck them as perfect: less than an hour's drive north of Boston, a splendid view of Massachusetts Bay and its rocky shore, secluded enough to protect them from their own fame, spacious enough to house both a residence and a small private research firm. The name of the indented coastline here had clinched it: Heart Cove. Buying and renovating the place had cost more than they could afford, but they'd never once regretted it.

They paused at the landing to look out at the view of bay, seaweed-matted rocks, scraggy trees overhanging the bluff. Straight east, the line of sky and water was broken only by a distant cargo ship, moving almost imperceptibly out to sea. Far to the south, the skyscrapers of Boston were just visible, standing like tiny chessmen at the horizon.

"Million-dollar view," Marshall said. "It must be fun, huh, being the young Turks, the cowboys?" When Ryan swore, Marshall just laughed. "So what do you think, Ry? Did Ridder's arm-twisting help? Listen, you'll like the way I'm thinking of setting it up. What I want is what Ridder wants and what you'll want—you guys'll be the Skunk Works."

"Hm," Ryan grunted. "I like it better already. The Skunk Works—the independent shop, where long-odds, high-payoff experiments can be made. Where the stranger but more intriguing ideas are pursued."

"Yep," Marshall agreed, glad to hear something like enthusiasm.

"A place where raw creativity is given license. Where the breakthroughs so often happen."

"Exactly!"

Ryan continued in a rhapsodic tone: "A place independent enough that the stink of embarrassing mistakes can be kept away from the rest of the organization—"

"Ry, this is *Marsh,* right? Be semi-human at least," Jess scolded. "Forgive him, Marshall, he's still got his hackles up about Ridder's visit. Plus he's got a big TV talk show coming up, which always plunges him into savage introspection."

"I think Ridder also likes your star power," Marshall went on. "If we need to go public on something, you'd be our spokesman—with your media profile, it makes sense. One other role I'd suggest, given that Ridder's your big fan and that you're here in Boston, is that you'd be our liaison to him. Save us flying somebody out from Stanford to give him progress reports, which he's told me he'll want."

Jess had been staring thoughtfully out to sea, distant again. "A strange man," she mused. "Think his talk was rehearsed?"

"A control freak," Ryan agreed darkly.

"It was just a prank!" Jess chided him. "I'm going to head up now— Abi's due home. Don't be too long—we've got to get ready for tonight." She continued up the stairs with lithe strides.

When she was gone, Marshall took a moment to lean against the railing, appraising the house above them. "Place looks great, Ry. I guess I haven't been here since—what, Allison's funeral. Just about two years now. How's Jessie doing?"

"Better. Really, she's terrific." In fact, she was too bright. Trying too hard, compensating too much. Of course, you had to know her very well to see it.

"And the pregnancy's coming along okay? She's not showing at all. Remind me when she's due—?"

"She's about three months now. Due first week or so of November. So far, everything's great."

"She seems good," Marshall agreed, just a little doubtful. Good old Marsh: He'd zeroed in on the problem and left unsaid, *But I can see why this job might not be the best thing right now.*

"She wants it, Marsh. The team wants it. I'm the holdout."

"I noticed," Marshall said with gentle irony. Then he saw the lingering frown on Ryan's face. "You mad at me because I didn't tell you Ridder would be joining us today? Come on, Ry! I figured, hey, you should know who's going to be pulling the strings. How the bastard operates."

Ryan nodded, grudgingly forgiving him. He'd never been able to hold anything against Marsh. Anyway, he was right, it was good to know of Ridder's involvement right away. Something else to talk to Jess about.

They started up the last flight of stairs, and then, as if reading his thoughts, Marshall called back, "Really, though, she looks terrific. You sure you're not underestimating her, Ry?"

They came through the deck doors to find a trail of clothes, lunch box, shoes, and books running through the big room: Abi was home from school. Jess stood at the kitchen counter, trying to put together a chicken sandwich while Abi jabbered at her and tugged on her skirt and picked at the meat with her fingers. Abi was a physical kid, bone-skinny because she burnt off every calorie she ate before the food even hit the bottom of her stomach—you had to feed her fast when she got home.

When Abi saw Marshall, she ran across the room and launched herself through the air at him with complete trust that he'd react in time. Marsh managed, barely, catching her with a grunt.

Not what you'd call a shy kid, Ryan thought. "'Beb, give Marshall a chance to—"

"It's all right," Marshall cut in. He returned Abi's hug, set her down to look at her. "Hi, Abebi. You've gotten so tall I didn't recognize you!"

"Yep. I'm in first grade!" she said proudly. She went on with the news of her life until Jess called her over to the counter. Marshall joined her there, while across the room Ryan slumped onto the couch and watched the three of them. After the events of the day, the sight was soothing: basic harmony, family, things working as they should. Very nice.

Certainly Jess looked pretty solid now, leaning against the counter, one hand on her outthrust hip. A woman with deep brown skin, flashing eyes, a ready but fleeting ivory smile. Abi wolfed the sandwich, yammering at Marshall when she came up for air. Marshall stage-whispered something into Jess's ear, a joke intended for Abi's benefit. Jess smiled broadly, and then her hand came up to cover her mouth.

Ryan had often thought about the gesture. It had mystified him when they'd first met, but only until he'd gotten to know her father, Judge Henry Maywood. Now he saw the eclipsed smile as left over from a little girl's shame at her own expressiveness, an unconscious way of hiding it from a stern father's disapproval. But that was Jess: a ready, radiant smile covered quickly by a prim hand. A girlish and self-conscious gesture seemingly paradoxical in such a forceful person. And yet it also made the smile a little bit *astonished,* and that was nice. *Sexy,* too, as if the things she most enjoyed were a little scandalous, or—

"Ryan!" Jess called over. "We don't have time for you to mope! You've lost the phone again. Find it! Call the Davidsons, let them know when we'll bring Abi. And then help me get this place cleaned up." She frowned and clapped her hands twice, *chop chop,* to rouse him.

Ryan obediently heaved himself out of the couch, stacked the spill of magazines on the coffee table, collected some empty glasses and carried them to the kitchen. Abi had finished her sandwich and now was leading Marshall around the house, showing him everything of importance: "And these are my fish. And this is my rabbit." The fish were real, darting around their aquarium like tiny aquatic meteorites, the rabbit a worn-out stuffed toy. "And this is a drawing I did of Ma. And this—"

Maybe the damned phone was out on the deck, Ryan thought. From the doorway he looked back, just savoring the scene. Jess throwing plates into the dishwasher, wiping down the counters, and quietly growing their second child inside her. Himself on one of his proverbial quests for the phone. Marshall following Abi: an airport-rumpled, sheepish-looking guy with gray-streaked brown hair a little too long, led by a chocolate-skinned, stick-legged girl in a frilly school dress.

Beautiful, Ryan thought. *Vital, dynamic. By such things does a man measure his fortune.* He went out, shaking his head in astonishment at his good luck.

Chapter 5

A Genesis brainstorming session, a mental reconnaissance into the forensic neuropsych proposal.

Ryan stood in front of a large easel pad, a marker ready to record the group's ideas. Abebi was spending the night at a friend's house, a sleepover they'd arranged as much to leave the house quiet as to keep the topic from Abi's ears. Now Marshall and the Genesis core research team lounged in a semicircle of couches and soft chairs in the big living room. Two stories tall, the room had floor-to-ceiling windows opening to a deck that faced the bay. The kitchen was back against the inland wall, overhung by a balcony that opened from the upstairs bedrooms, separated from the big room only by a counter. Ryan liked to think that the spacious room and high ceilings invited expansive thinking, lofty ideas. Outside, lights of distant ships winked on a vague evening horizon, and the sea worked gently at the shore.

Marshall opened up by summarizing some of the neurological issues the forensic psychology people particularly wanted them to focus upon. Research in the last twenty years had determined two factors to be generally responsible for violent behaviors. One was early injury to the brain through trauma, disease, oxygen deprivation, malnutrition, or exposure to neurotoxic chemicals such as lead. The second was an abusive family environment that not only set a precedent for violence but actually shaped the plastic, growing brain of the future offender: Emotional trauma, Marshall reminded them, affected not only the psyche of the individual, but altered the physical development of the brain as well. But despite all the progress, some big questions remained. What exactly did these injuries do to the brain? Why did one person become violent while another, with the same set of afflictions, didn't?

Just the sort of thing Genesis liked, Ryan thought: the missing element. The mystery with the clues invisible but probably right in front of your face. He jotted notes with his squeaky felt-tip, making a mental note as well: *Invent a permanent marker that doesn't stink.*

They tossed it back and forth, speculating freely, the Skunk Works in action. Two issues came to the fore immediately. One was the issue of acute brain trauma—oxygen deprivation at birth, say, or head injuries in infancy—versus long-term, low-level exposures to stressors. Both could radically affect the brain, but while acute trauma was fairly easy to pinpoint, the database on long-term and low-level stressors was spotty at best, despite a long list of neurotoxins known to cause brain damage.

Acute cranial trauma vs. long-term, low-level stressors, Ryan jotted.

Another big one was the question of stimulus versus inhibition. Did violent behavior result from the overstimulation of parts of the brain that triggered violent urges, or from the underactivation of neuromodules responsible for positive social behaviors? It was the same question cops would ask when investigating a fatal car accident: Did the car go over the cliff because the brakes failed, or because the accelerator stuck?

Ryan scrawled, *Stimulus or inhibition? Accelerator or brakes?*

From there it was only a short step to instinctive drives and the genetic programs that caused them. The basic principle was simple: Evolution selected social behaviors just as it did physical characteristics. Getting along with your fellow humans conferred a survival advantage at least as great as opposable thumbs.

Dagan being the youngest, Ryan was thinking, she'd observe for a time, then come in tentatively, respectfully, with well-considered questions and comments, leading by induction. Logan would likewise hold back at first, processing this on five levels, but when she came in she'd clear your sinuses, hit you hard with dazzling insight. Leap would be the one to throw the first real knuckleball, Ryan decided, open it up wide with something mischievous but worth considering, creating ripples and dissonances that would energize the others.

"Not my discipline," Leap said innocently, "but if we're looking at crime trends, how about population pressure? Suppose we've got a latent sociopathic tendency built into our genes. Genetic population regulator, like lemmings. A lethal gene, triggered by stressors associated with high population—noise pollution, environmental degradation, and so on."

Genetic program? Population regulator? Ryan jotted.

"Here we go with the big view, huh?" Marshall griped good-naturedly. But he went on with some genetics-related ideas of his own, falling easily into the Skunk Works mode, the unabashedly open-minded thinking Genesis did so well. It was probably fun for him to speculate freely, outside the cautious confines of Brandt.

Bates, Ryan was thinking, Bates likes the devil's advocate. He'll challenge and confront soft ideas, the wolf culling the sick and weak from the herd. He'll demand legitimacy of method, rigor of logic and scholarship. And what about Jess? Probably the best intellect in the bunch, but hard to tell how she'd think and work on this one. This subject was affecting her powerfully, that much was clear, but Ryan wasn't sure just how.

Sure enough, Bates jumped in, looking disgusted with them all. "What's to learn about genetic origins of violent behavior? Prehuman and early human males made coalitions to go on raids against rival bands, whom they killed if they could—usually for access to females. Lethal raiding coalitions are well documented among chimpanzees, our closest primate relatives."

Marshall gently lobbed it back at him: "But even if we accept that we've got lethal raiding instincts, don't we have to learn which parts of the brain activate them? And how our hypothetical environmental stressors impair those parts of the brain?"

"You don't *need* environmental stressors," Bates snapped. "Toobey and Cosmides have shown that breeding-access raids pay off. The improved chance of leaving your genes in the gene stream is greater than your risk of being killed. Meaning we've all inherited a propensity to kill each other. It's all in the evolutionary math." Bates had taught them all anthro at Harvard, and he'd never completely relinquished the professorial posture.

"That's prehistory," Marshall said. "Think it's applicable to modern times?"

"Of course. Look at Mequida and Wiener's analysis of the last two centuries of wars and atrocities. When young males, pre-breeding age, exceed thirty-five percent of the male population, you get a critical level of competition for goods and status and mates. Resulting in crime waves and war, every time."

"Bates," Jess burst in, "that's embarrassingly simplistic!" She looked startled by her own intensity, but rushed ahead: "Look, when it comes to basic, biologically derived drives, you have to agree that parental bonding and protectiveness, and prohibition against injury to children are some of the strongest, right?"

Bates nodded cautiously, aware it was a leading question.

"So I did a little Web-surfing this afternoon, looking for indicators related to children. And what I found was *frightening*. Ridder touched on one, briefly, infanticide—the World Health Organization says that worldwide incidence of killing babies has gone up *four hundred percent* in the last ten years." Jess checked some jotted notes and went on, her mouth grim: "From Interpol, I got statistics on children sold into sex slavery or, God help me, for *organ harvesting.* Seems that as transplant techniques have improved, the demand for healthy organs has out-stripped voluntary donation. So a black market has grown up that buys or steals kids, usually in third-world countries, and *sells* the kids, thou-sands of them, to have their kidneys and hearts and eyes and other organs removed. Mainly to buyers in Europe, Japan, and the United States. You going to tell me *that's* business as usual for our genetic behav-ioral programs?"

Her acid tone surprised everyone. Jess could be forceful, but seldom so combative. She was clearly off balance.

"I ran into other indicators related to kids," Jess went on. "Worldwide population of orphanages is at its highest in history, even higher than the post–World War II era. Oh, and another little oddity: homicides *by* juve-niles. In 1990, in the U.S., one thousand murders were committed *by* kids. By 1996, that number had risen four hundred percent. As of last year, *that* number had tripled. What, Bates—*children* are genetically pro-grammed for lethal competition over reproductive access and status? *Bullshit.*" She sat back, breathing hard, looking astonished at herself.

The silence that followed felt awkward. And when they finally began again, the tone of the debate had changed. Bates got into an argument with Dagan, Logan bickered over some nuance with Marshall. Unchar-acteristic all the way around. Partly it was low blood sugars, Ryan was sure, but mainly it was the topic at hand. So many possibilities, such a huge research problem. And a very scary basic premise: *Something gone wrong inside us. Something that makes us kill.*

They mustered on for two more hours until at last Jess caught Ryan's eye and glanced pointedly at her watch. She was right: it had been a long stretch, and the crew was starting to tire. He put down his marker and waved his hands as if flagging a train to stop. "Time out," he told them. "Time for booze and food. Drink and eat. Now."

Jess ordered them to talk about anything but the project, and they seemed relieved to be out from under it, setting to wine and cheese and cold cuts with enthusiasm. For a while Ryan drifted from kitchen to living room, bringing napkins, then mustard, and then he found him-self just watching them. Dagan had made herself at home with the stereo, putting on a disk of an a cappella group that soothed the air with voices like honey and molasses pouring together. As she adjusted the sound, Marshall moved lazily to the music, a glass of wine in one hand. Jess and Logan and Bates were bent over the coffee table, where Leap was scribbling something that made them laugh. A rhythm of voices and movements, a pattern indicating basic harmoniousness. Despite their differences.

Longing for a breath of sea air, Ryan let himself out the kitchen door into the chilly darkness. A raw, sea-smelling wind came off the water, and the waves agitated against the shore. He went down the steps to the beach, enjoying the cold and the fishy salt smell. Behind him, the windows of the living room glowed yellow, silhouettes of Genesis, Inc., moving inside.

At the water's edge, the pebbled beach sagged beneath his feet and a fine spray came in on the breeze. Massachusetts Bay stretched away into the darkness, its waves nearest the shore vaguely lit by the house lights, then dimming into barely differentiated grays, patterns in constant motion stretching out into blackness until somewhere the night sky began. To the south, the red glow of the Marblehead lighthouse anchored the horizon line.

There was space for thought here, good space right at the juncture between the warmth and human camaraderie inside and the cold and solitude outside. Ryan savored his equipoise between the two, the energized mental state he always found at the point of convergence between very different systems or contexts—*bisociation,* Koestler had called it, a kind of psychic stereo.

A life in the Skunk Works, yes, that was about right.

The media had focused on Ryan early, the big brain of his own maverick research group, handing him national press even before he and Jess had left Harvard. Which press, Ryan knew, he owed as much to luck as to any genius he might lay claim to. But in the aftermath of the feature on National Public Radio, the *Smithsonian* article, the feature in *Time, Larry King Live,* and the rest of the media's first feeding frenzy, there had come a steady stream of clients, some obscure and some famous but most of them going away with the answers they needed.

Eighteen years later, an increasingly impressive portfolio, maybe only now living up to the hype that had launched them.

It began at Project Alpha, Harvard's elite research program in cognitive neurosciences. Although Ryan had always tried to discount his assigned role as head honcho or main genius, he couldn't deny there was a germ of truth there. But if the think tank that made so many waves at Project Alpha had a center, it was both Ryan and Jess, and not because they were the smartest, but because they formed a sort of psychosocial backbone for the evolving collection of brilliant minds, big egos, and unstable personalities that made up that original group. The two of them were a rare fluke that amused and fascinated the others: high-school sweethearts whose relationship had survived the perils of interracial love affairs and even the divorce mill of graduate school. And then they actually got married, and actually got along and enjoyed each other a good percentage of the time, in so doing constituting an anomaly that baffled the others and so kept them near. *Ballast* was what he and Jess had provided, Ryan thought, as much as brains.

A wave lapped his shoes, but he barely noticed the sudden grip of cold water around his ankles.

Yes, and it was also true that it was his stubbornness that had started the professional phase of their collaboration. It was 1984, and he was beginning work on a second Ph.D. and was broke. Jess's well-off parents offered to lend their likely son-in-law money, but Ryan couldn't see accepting handouts. Instead he put an ad in the *Globe* and the student papers: GENIUS FOR HIRE, the headline read, and then some gush about innovative problem-solving. It seemed a little brash even at the time, but he was only twenty-two, and besides, he figured Jess would bail him out if he had trouble with the "genius" end of his advertising.

To his surprise, among the crank calls and pleas from undergraduates wanting him to ghost-write term papers, he got a client right away, an old woman who wanted a cure for her granddaughter's crossed eyes. Ryan apologized, explained that he had no medical background, told her she should consult a specialist. Over the phone, she scolded him with a dry, Boston Brahmin voice: "We have already consulted the very best ophthalmologists. I am not looking for a specialist. What I am looking for is, let me see . . . 'whole systems analysis, original and interdisciplinary thinking.'" Quoting his idiot ad.

He took it to heart, accepting that his best assets were an open mind, the ability to learn adaptively, and the desire to find the encompassing outlook. After two weeks of burrowing like a mole in the stacks of the Harvard Medical Library, he stumbled onto literature that suggested a cure. It began with discovering that aminoglycoside antibiotics sometimes caused symptomatic blocks of neuromuscular transmission, temporary myasthenias in the ocular muscles. That led by a series of improbable associative steps to Ryan's building a pair of mechanical glasses that alternately blocked the view of each eye, exhausting the granddaughter's ocular adductor muscles while encouraging her brain to integrate images from both eyes. It was the first time he'd witnessed first-hand the human brain's plasticity—its amazing ability to adapt its circuitry to compensate for disability or injury.

Staring out at the wave-striped dark, vaguely aware of the cold coming up his wet legs, Ryan had to laugh. Even back then, he'd realized it was sheer naïveté that had allowed him to succeed—so he vowed never to lose his naïveté. He and Jess took on more odd problems and puzzles. Eventually they incorporated Genesis legally, sometimes calling on friends like Marshall and others at Project Alpha to help out, establishing an enduring network of collaborators.

Bates was the first. He had served in Vietnam, had come back to earn a Ph.D. and a professorship at Harvard. He'd taken a special interest in Jess and Marshall and Ryan, guiding them through some of the difficulties that came with being too smart for their own good. Later he lost his position because he'd had a love affair with one of his students, a brilliant, delicate woman half his age. When he went before the tenure review committee, he never denied his love for Mai-ling, nor claimed special circumstances to justify his actions. After his removal, he married her and cared for her lovingly until she died of liver cancer four months later. By then Genesis was taking off, and Jess and Ryan gladly offered him a job.

And that was Bates. So much more than brilliant, and so much more than "staff."

The most recent core staff addition came two years ago, when a breathtakingly lovely young woman had walked into Ryan's office and announced that she was going to work for him now. He had laughed uncomfortably and told her there weren't really any openings, what had made her think of joining such an odd outfit, did she have any particular qualifications—?

From her purse she took the little mechanical glasses he'd built, and fixed him with a pair of perfectly straight, striking dark eyes. "I've been wanting to do this kind of work since I was six," she told him. "As for qualifications, I have only one, the same as you—I see poetry and possibility in everything."

It was a profound observation, not to mention flattering. And that's how they found Dagan, now nominally a head research assistant but in so many ways so much more. When the press asked how he and Jess selected their staff, how they found the best and brightest, the only answer was simply that they didn't choose them at all. The whole thing grew organically, less like a company than a tree, a family.

Fortunately, many of their cases were spared press inquiry because they were secret, by contract. Like their Secret Service job, six years ago, where by applying aspects of chaos theory to crowd management Genesis had demonstrated that the perceptual and protective grid the Service maintained for senior government officials had certain holes in it. They had gone on to design a vastly improved crowd-scanning, motion-variable analysis, and threat-assessment and -response system for the Service. And though maintaining complete secrecy was burdensome at the time, it was worth it in the long run: The job didn't invite inane questions about creativity or innovation or whatever from the press.

Once in a while a sensitive interviewer would ask something like "Did your parents encourage you when you were a child?" Another can of worms, best evaded. Yes, Ma had been very bright, and had given him the mental habit of turning things upside down or sideways to get a new perspective on them, but it never got her anywhere or revealed to her a way to cope with a difficult marriage. As for Pa, who was an uneven man, Ma had said it best: "Who's the man I married? An Irish gentleman named Seamus O'ccasionally, I'm sorry to say," referring to his intermittent drunks and troubles with the police. The funny and sad pun on the pronunciation of "shame-us" would be lost in print or on talk shows, too cumbersome to explain.

And yet he could not deny he'd learned a great deal from Pa. Daniel McCloud had worked as a sorting clerk for the U.S. Post Office and never advanced in his position. While he was not a regular drinker, he overdid it when he was frustrated with life or angry at himself, and that's when he'd get into fights. Ryan first saw Pa fight when he was seven years old and had gone down to The Boar's Head to bring Pa home for dinner, only to find him angry drunk and fighting with a man much larger and younger than himself. Daniel McCloud had a paunch and a receding hairline, and he wore a clerk's clothes. While Ryan stood paralyzed with fear and humiliation, the younger man easily pushed Pa down and went back to his drink. Pa got up and pulled the younger man off his stool and in return received a terrifying punch in the gut. But somehow Pa still managed to land a good clop on the young man's nose. That got the guy mad at last, and he began using Pa as a punching bag, swearing as Pa covered up and crouched and fell, and then some more as Pa got up and came at him again. Amazingly, every time Pa went down he came back with a little more, each blow sharpening his anger, fanning the embers of his discontents, and the younger man had a little less until the fight began to go the other way. Finally the young man went to the floor, where Pa worked on him with his post-office-issue shoes, pausing now and again to take a swallow of Guinness, until the police arrived. Ryan never forgot the look of pure triumph Pa had given him as they led him out. "You never give up, Ry," Pa had said, grinning wide with blood-filmed teeth. "Never. You take it and you come back fighting."

Never give up: the best advice, Pa's biggest gift to him. Somehow the principle became a symbol to Ryan, the one way a desperate son could see something like nobility and strength in such a weak man, the one virtue he could hold aloft and above the sadness and shame he felt for his father, and he'd internalized it as a personal credo. Applied to scientific research, the trait became what cognitive theorists and creativity psychologists called "the ability to pursue a thesis despite a period of disconfirmation." *But how it feels, Larry, how it feels, Oprah, is like taking it on the chin and being willing to keep on coming.*

Ryan had to chuckle at the chin-thrusting and fist-clenching he unconsciously did whenever he remembered it, a bit of the old man's personality coming up in him. Probably all this retrospection could be blamed on the impending talk show. That and a virulent strain of unrepentant native cynicism. *Misanthrope,* Jess sometimes called him. Only partly true. Part of him despaired of the human race, was resigned to its cruelty and stupidity. But another part of him took on quest after quest to understand, to heal, to make things better. The same urge, probably, that was responsible for Jess's compulsion to take this new job.

"Ry!" Jess's voice.

He turned and became aware of the weight of his pants, the cold against his skin. The tide had been coming in, and now the waves were foaming around his shins, his pants were wet to the crotch. On the shore, Jess was a graceful dark silhouette against the house lights, the wind tugging at her dress. She bent and put her hands on her knees, and he knew she was laughing at him. "Time to come on in, Ahab," she said. He waded back toward her, shoes heavy with sea water.

"I was thinking about wave dynamics," he explained, and it was true, all the while a part of his mind had been watching the humping water and diagramming the compression of wave-length as the waveform rode up the slope of the shore, as the proportion of height to depth increased and caused the water-hungry crests to form bores and curl forward and fall foaming as fractal systems, deteriorating yet endlessly replenished by wind and air pressure and lunar gravity, a beautiful dance accompanied by its own hypnotizing, rhythmic music:

$$L/t = \sqrt{g(h_1 + h_2)\, h_1/2h_2}$$

"And other stuff," he added.

"We ended up having a nice party," Jess told him as they held hands and began walking back to the house. She added almost shyly, "I apologized to Bates and the others. I didn't mean to sound so...accusatory. I'm okay now."

Another few steps in silence, just the wave noise. "So after seeing Oakes today—you still want to do this?" he asked.

She lost only a short beat. "Yes."

But, but, but, he was thinking. After another moment he couldn't help himself, and asked, "Really think we're up for saving this world's sorry ass?"

Jess just shrugged and swayed away from his side. "Tough job," she said, "but, hey, somebody's got to do it." Trying for a hard, flippant tone, not quite making it, a way of telling him not to probe, not just now.

Chapter 6

Ryan stepped into Ridder's office to find him dressed in a sleeveless undershirt, using his teeth to pull on a pair of light boxing gloves. Despite skin beginning to go loose with age, Ridder's sweat-slicked body looked strong: thick waist, shoulders, and chest heavy with fat and muscle. It was Wednesday, six days since the billionaire's impromptu visit to Heart Cove.

"Listen, don't take offense at my informality here," Ridder said. "The kind of schedule I've got, if I can't sometimes kill two birds with one stone, I'll never get in a workout. Hey, my last appointment was Senator Boseman, who had the dubious pleasure of discussing his business while I rode the bike. Have a seat." He gestured to an armchair that faced a corner of his office set aside as a personal gym: a stationary bicycle, a Stairmaster, a multifunction weight machine, a small free-weight rack. For boxing work, a canvas heavy bag and a leather speed bag.

The office was a huge room on the fiftieth floor of the Ridder Global building. Floor-to-ceiling windows showed a vertiginous drop and a stunning view of Boston's Inner Harbor and the tops of other Hub buildings. A massive desk, conference table, clusters of couches and soft chairs, a wet bar, the gym: The furnishings were modern, elegant yet somewhat functional, spartan. The only exceptions were a battered desk and canvas camp chair arranged beneath a portrait of General George Patton, bathed in a glow of track lighting, almost like an altar. Ryan remembered the antiques from some magazine article: They had belonged to Old Blood and Guts himself. Ridder had a thing for Patton.

Ryan took a chair and watched as the billionaire shot a jab at the speed bag, then stopped to adjust his gloves. "Used to want to be a fighter," Ridder explained. "When I was a kid. Never got around to it, but I like keeping in shape. You ever box?"

"My father started me at Lloyd's Gym when I was nine."

"Gotta be a Southie boy!" Ridder seemed to enjoy their common origins in the rough-and-tumble. "Ever have to use it?"

"Not recently. Mainly it's a way of keeping physically alert. My, uh, my mental processes can get pretty diffuse—it's a good focusing exercise."

Ridder turned back to the speed bag, tapped it with the side of one fist, began the accelerating rhythm, *bappita-bappita,* rolling his shoulders. He had quick hands for a guy his age, Ryan decided.

"I hear you're going to be on the Diana Reese Show tomorrow night. Been after me for an interview for years, always turned her down. Tough cookie, huh? Good lookin', though. Let me know how it goes." *Bappita-bappita-bappita.*

Ryan had to raise his voice to be heard over the drumming of Ridder's fists. "I'd like to get to business here." It was intended as an invitation to stop punching.

Ridder just kept at it, *bappita-bappita.* "Okay. So are you guys gonna join Brandt or what? Why do I get the sense that everybody else at Genesis is hot to trot, but Ryan McCloud is dubious?"

Ryan ignored the probe. "If we're going to do this, certain conditions have to be met."

"Let's hear 'em." Ridder frowned but continued working the bag, sometimes tipping his head from side to side as if dodging incoming punches.

"Number one: We're in charge of our own shop." Ryan stood up, irritated and yet a little envious, wishing he had something to do with his hands, too. *Bappita-bappita.* This had to be deliberate, some kind of one-upmanship body language. Ryan hardened his tone accordingly: "We do it our way. If you or Dr. Sorbanelli have opinions about our methodology, that's tough. Our ways of working strike some people as unorthodox, but our methods are based on sound theory, and they've been proven to work. To guarantee our independence, we need two years' fee up front. We don't want our pay conditional upon your approval of what we're doing. Or what we're finding."

"I like this," Ridder said. He caught the bag in both gloves, turned to face Ryan. With his shark smile and red skin, bulky shoulders and hard breathing, he looked menacing. "You're still pissed about me dropping in on you guys like that, aren't you? But, listen, I like your macho style here, Ryan. I'm usually the guy talking like that. I'd be tempted to probe your commitment to the tough-guy performance, but in this case it gives me confidence that you've got the *cojones* to get the job done. Okay. Complete independence and pay in advance. Done. Proceed." He resumed punching.

"Two: The data this project turns up—all of it, Brandt's, ours—becomes public domain. If we're in on it, you don't own the information, you don't control it. Suppose we turn up evidence that some violent neuropathologies are caused by toxic effects from a product or pollutant—maybe something produced by Ridder Global? We don't want you to be tempted to hush up our findings to protect your profit margins."

Ridder caught the bag again, turned toward Ryan, and beat his gloves together sharply. "This one's tricky, Ryan."

"Not negotiable, if you want us in on this job."

"Whoa, whoa, whoa! I have every intention of letting everybody know what you find. But I'm the one investing in this project, and I can't just forget about the opportunity to profit from the investment. If I can be ahead of the curve, I can invest in alternative industries, services, technologies, whatever. Or get Ridder Global's labs going on producing the remedy. Hey, all it means is giving me first shot at the information, a little lead time to adapt my position before you go public."

Ryan thought about it. On one level it was reasonable. On another, it could be Ridder's foot in the door, an opening wedge for meddling, conflicts of authority. "How much time?"

"A year."

"Three months." Ryan had to grin. They were bargaining like merchants at a flea market.

"Call it six and we're there." Ridder was enjoying this, too. He turned to a heavy bag, which was the size and shape of a water heater, set his stance, swung a punch that rattled its chain.

"Four months, during which you'll position your companies to make a killing. After which anything we've got becomes public domain."

Ridder feinted at the heavy bag, and then the muscles in his shoulders bunched and he hit it with a flurry of hard punches. Ryan pointedly waited him out. At last Ridder stopped, nodded. "Okay. Agreed. Other conditions?"

"Access to Ridder Global's databases."

The pleasure on Ridder's face dried and cracked, and he turned from the bag, breathing hard. "Why?"

This was going to be a tough one, Ryan knew. It was time to ease off, become a little conciliatory. "We'll be looking for neurological impairments in selected populations, right? Acute cranial trauma is relatively easy to assess, but there are many other ways that the brain can sustain injury—medicines taken, exposure to neurotoxic chemicals in food or the environment or consumer goods, certain diseases in pregnant mothers or young children. Problem is, there's a gaping hole in our disease-surveillance systems—data isn't often available for tracking health problems resulting from long-term or low-dose toxic exposures. Especially when it comes to assessing behavioral effects. The effects and the symptoms can be very subtle, the amounts of toxic agent microscopic. The long-term, low-dose issue will be our biggest problem, lack of data on it our biggest obstacle."

Ridder grabbed a towel and worked it over his body. "So why do you need access to my databases?"

"Because we'll need to establish parallels between symptoms and exposures to possible agents. And no other firm your size is going to give us access to the chemical formulas that go into manufacturing various products. To production and sales histories for various goods—plastics, medicines, pesticides, industrial chemicals, food additives—that might prove to be the culprit. To employee health records that might show trends resulting from high workplace exposure levels. Believe me, we're not looking for Ridder Global to become a martyr here—the environmental toxin is only one of many avenues we'll be looking into."

Ridder beat his fists together again and then abruptly turned to stare out over Boston. For a moment the reflection of his face in the glass was superimposed over the gleaming buildings of his domain like the secret, hard soul of the place. At last he gestured for Ryan to come stand with him.

"You know why I put our headquarters here? We considered New York. But I had my reasons for Boston."

"Which were—?"

"The view from this corner." Ridder jutted his chin toward the expansive view of the Hub below, then the Fort Point Channel, and finally the rumpled-looking streets of South Boston. "I wanted to remind myself of where I came from. Something you and I have in common, huh?" He chucked Ryan's arm. "How far I've come, and yet how close I still am."

Ridder's determined ascent from an impoverished childhood was a familiar theme in the mythology of corporate America. Of course, the legend was somewhat tarnished by rumors that he'd begun his climb as a minor crime boss in South Boston.

Ridder grunted at something in his mind's eye. "I didn't tell your wife when she asked, but I have some personal reasons for wanting to bankroll this project. Keep this under your hat, huh? One night about three years ago, I went to the Jazz Train to see a sextet I'd heard good reports about—

been a jazz fancier since forever—and when I came out I was walking down the street and this guy came unexpectedly out of a doorway. Not a great neighborhood, I reacted suddenly, my body language got aggressive, probably I scared him as much as he scared me. And the guy pulls out a gun and shoots me in the fucking chest, then runs away. The bullet rips along the pectoral muscle, glances off a rib, and tips the shoulder on its way out. Knocked me flat on my ass. Hurt like a sonofabitch."

Ridder had traced the bullet's path on his meaty chest, and now his big face pouted as if he were remembering it all too clearly. Ryan made a sympathetic sound in his throat. Standing closer to him now, Ryan could see the age around his eyes, the tiredness that underlay his vitality, kept in check by a powerful will.

"The funny thing was? I sat there and didn't even feel mad at the guy!" Ridder chuckled with wry astonishment. "I thought maybe he'd killed me, blood was pouring out right over my heart, I had all this pain. But what I felt was *sad.* I sat there, trying to hold the blood in with my hands, wondering where this crap came from, my reactions and his, you know? Wondering what would have happened if we lived in a society where this stuff was understood better. Where we understood ourselves better. But we don't."

Ridder shook his head wearily. "After a while, when I figured I was going to live, I got mad at the guy, you can bet. But I'd had a little revelation. I'm no saint, maybe I was just in shock, but at that moment I realized that it *wasn't necessary.* That we could do better."

He stopped, eyebrows rising as if he were surprised at himself. Then his confessional mood evaporated, his face hardened again. "Well. You want me to pay for this session now, *Herr* Freud? Or can I just put it on the tab?" He chuckled humorlessly, strode to his desk, and punched the intercom with the thumb of his glove. "Darion," he growled, "would you mind stepping down here for a moment?"

He lingered at the desk for a moment longer, and when he came back, his eyes were opaque. "Ryan, your insistence on access to our databases concerns me. Corporate security is extremely important to us, I don't have to tell you. We have to be careful about competitors getting wind of new product designs or growth strategies or tactical positions. And frankly there's a certain amount of dirty laundry in every house—"

"We'll make sure your proprietary data stays out of the public-domain reports. And we're accustomed to high-security jobs and strict confidentiality. Many of our clients—"

"Like the Secret Service? Not good enough security, I'm afraid." When Ryan gaped, Ridder smiled again. "Hey—I told you, I do my homework. I was very impressed with your confidential client list, another reason I wanted you for this job. Relax, Ryan, not too many people have my resources. But you get some idea of the problem. Ah—here's Darion."

An inner door opened, and a narrow-shouldered man entered. His movements were fluid, but the angles of his immobile face were as sharp as the facets of a paleolithic spearhead as he crossed the room, eyes on Ryan. "You wanted me, Mr. Ridder?"

"Dr. Ryan McCloud, this is Darion Gable. Mr. Gable is a longtime associate of mine. An indispensable member of our organization."

Gable wore a dark suit jacket and black shirt, a gold cross on a heavy chain around his neck. Ryan wondered if the mafioso look was deliberately cultivated or came naturally. When he shook Gable's hand, one quick, cool squeeze, he was startled by the feel of it: narrow, hard as obsidian. And when his eyes met Gable's, he got another shock. The man's gaze stabbed like a switchblade. He seemed to look straight to the life-force in Ryan's body, coldly assessing what it would take to divest him of it. It was the kind of knowledgeable look that could only be acquired through experience, Ryan thought.

Ridder went back to the heavy bag, set his stance, took a tentative swing and then a hard follow-up. "Dr. McCloud runs a highly regarded independent research firm, and I hope we'll be working closely with him in the near future. I just wanted you two to catch a glimpse of each other, as he gets to know our organization."

Gable nodded as if he'd understood something else in Ridder's words, his long face expressionless.

"In fact, Darion," Ridder went on, "we were just discussing information security. If Dr. McCloud does come on board, I'd like you to acquaint yourself with his outfit and with Brandt Institute—maybe visit their offices and labs, give us an appraisal of their security arrangements. That be okay with you, Ryan? Darion is quite knowledgeable about that kind of thing."

Ryan shrugged an acquiescence. "What do you do here at Ridder Global?" he asked, for lack of something better to bridge the silence.

"I don't have a formal title." Gable's lips tensed slightly, and Ryan wondered if that was his version of a smile. "I suppose you could say I'm a troubleshooter. I solve intractable problems."

"Problems like—?"

"Thanks for coming in, Darion," Ridder said, dismissing him.

Gable nodded. "A pleasure, Dr. McCloud," he said. "I look forward to working with you." Again the metal gaze, a little too long. Then he turned and left through the side door.

Ridder bludgeoned the heavy bag viciously. "Like yourself, although in an entirely different field, Mr. Gable is a very talented man. Head of a very talented team."

"Internal security."

"Oh, no. We have a security section, but Gable is in a, uh, separate division. Less formal, more independent." Now Ridder held the heavy bag's chain in one glove, leaned on it, watching Ryan closely. "Terrifying, isn't he?"

"I'm not sure I want to work with you, Mr. Ridder."

Ridder chuckled and held up a conciliatory hand. "Hold on, hold on." He used his teeth to loosen the Velcro at his wrists, pulled the gloves off, then grabbed a folded towel and wiped his forehead and armpits. "You're absolutely right, Gable has a face that makes Dr. Mengele look like Saint Francis, and he's got a heart like a chip of flint. His job is to do things I don't even want to mention. But you gotta understand, Ridder Global is a massive organization, right, bigger and more complex than most nation states in the history of the world. We live in an era when the nation state is dying, the corporate state is where the decisions are made and actions taken that shape the world. Right? The U.S. government has its CIA and NSA and ten other elite security organizations nobody ever heard of, who do the dirty work that policy or expediency requires. So does every other government. Why shouldn't the corporate state have the same resources? Hey, Ridder Global doesn't play any differently from any firm of its size—if anything, we're the good guys. The Boy Scouts."

"I'm touched. Were you going to make a point?"

"Yeah, I'm going to make a couple of points. First, I wasn't threatening you with Gable. On the contrary, think of it as a demonstration of trust! Because people who are likely to receive his professional attention don't even learn of his existence. Okay? I simply wanted to underline a point: This is the big leagues. Your request for access to our corporate information is very, very serious stuff."

Ridder had started pacing in the big room, tossing his hands out to the sides and bringing them together as he stretched his chest and shoulder muscles. "The second point is that I'm gonna be handing out, what, sixty million bucks? On the gamble you guys're ever going to come up with anything. And I'm gonna be making this expensive information public domain. And yes, I'm gonna agree to give you access to Ridder Global data. All of which means you've got my balls in your hands. I don't like that feeling, Ryan, okay? I haven't gotten where I am by letting that happen, unless I've got a firm grip on the other guy's balls as well. I thought I'd let you know."

"A grotesque image, Mr. Ridder, but I see the point. Complete access?" They were bargaining again.

"Keys to the city. As long as you accept that access means certain responsibilities—like no leaks of information. Like monitoring from our security people. You use our security protocols, and you recognize that if there are mistakes, Mr. Gable will be very interested in who let information slip and who received it. Not a threat—just a fact of corporate life at this level."

Ryan thought about that. "Which brings up a related issue we need to talk about."

"Uh-oh." Ridder grinned.

"How did you know about our work for the Secret Service? If you want us to be secure with your data, you've got to tell me where we leaked."

Ridder waved the concern away, his grin broadening. "Easy. Turns out you and I have a friend in common—Alex Shipley. Old Army buddy of mine. I was telling him about the forensic psych project, maybe bringing Genesis aboard. So he told me a little about his work with you. Had nothing but praise, by the way."

Hardly a friend, Ryan felt like telling him. Shipley was a spook they'd met six years ago, an administrator in the National Security Agency who had consulted with them on various applications of their Secret Service work. About Ridder's age, late fifties, Shipley was a soft-spoken, bland, balding man, with narrow shoulders and mushroom-smooth, gray-white skin. His job was "black acquisitions"—going to private-sector labs and buying or commissioning development of technologies with weapons potential.

Ryan just shrugged, nodded. Ridder no doubt had all kinds of surprising contacts. But whatever their relationship, Shipley had no business talking about what was supposed to be a secret project. Something to think about there.

But Ridder was watching him expectantly: *Decision time.*

It was Ryan's turn to walk through the office. He went to the windows and looked out at the familiar Hub buildings, the knotted traffic, the harbor dotted with ships, the jets sliding in toward Logan. From this height he could almost see it whole, the marvelous ornate system of a human city in the early twenty-first century, in so many ways just like a single, vastly complex organism.

Ridder took a cigar from a humidor on his desk, sliced the end with a platinum clipper, lit up. He settled against the edge of the desk, drawing thoughtfully, content to simply observe Ryan. To his credit, Ryan thought. In fact, his appreciation for the project, for Ryan personally, did seem genuine. He had truly savored the surprising aspects of their confrontation, Ryan's combativeness and frustration. A complex man— almost, Ryan hated to admit, a likable man.

Also, he reminded himself, a man who wouldn't hesitate to exploit his personal charm to have things his way.

The crew had voted to accept the commission. Ridder had agreed to all the conditions. It was a good mission, the money was good. Yet for reasons he couldn't identify, he felt in his bones that this was a watershed decision, a turning point. A little buzz of warning nagged at him. Without thinking about it, Ryan walked back to the gym area, conscious only of his body's ache for some kinetic expression, some way of venting the tension he felt. He put his hands on the speed bag, testing the short chain that anchored the head-sized leather ball. Suddenly pissed at everything, he stepped back and fired a hard punch at it. It was a good clop. The bag tore loose from its tether, hit the Universal machine, and bounced to the floor.

He adjusted his collar and calmed himself down as he walked back to the desk. "Tell you what, Mr. Ridder. We both get Oscars, okay? Now let's drop our acts for a while. We've got serious things to talk about. Sorry about the speed bag. Take it out of our fee."

Ridder grinned, hearing his acceptance, and socked him softly on the arm. "I like this," he said. "I like your moxie here, Ryan."

Chapter 7

It was late by the time he got back to the house, and the big room was dark except for an island of light in the kitchen. He had stopped off for a few drinks at a pub in South Boston, pondering whiskey and marriage and murder, until he'd felt a pang of homesickness and driven through the dark back to Heart Cove. His heart bounded when he saw that Jess was still up. The most welcome of sights. *Homo domesticus, that's me,* Ryan thought. She was at the sink, her back to him, still in her teaching clothes, gorgeous and sexy.

She turned to give him a small smile. "How'd it go?"

"He agreed to our conditions. I said we'd do it."

"And you're thrilled."

"I'm okay," he lied.

"Mmmm." She nodded skeptically.

"All right, I'm not okay," he said. He felt loosened by drunkenness, a little reckless. "I don't like this project. I don't like the way I can't talk to you since this came up. I don't really understand why you're so into it, or—"

"I don't think that's true. I think you just don't trust the reasons for my interest and commitment."

"Do *you?*"

Jess's eyes widened. "You're being condescending, Ry."

"No, babe, I'm trying to—"

"Protect me. Fine. But from what? From myself! And that's not condescending? Goddamn it, Ry!"

Her anger made him falter, but he plugged ahead: "Not from yourself. From things that have hurt you in the past. Jess, this family went through a lot after Allison. Yeah, I'm trying to protect you, Abi, *me,* from that."

She started to speak, caught herself, then went back to cleaning out the coffeepot, motions brusque and hurried. Ryan waited, not sure what to do or say.

Yes: Allison. Two years ago, Jess's little sister, Allison, had fulfilled a lifelong dream of going to Egypt. She'd been in love with the ancient, mysterious desert realm since she was a kid. But she'd had bad luck. She was one of fifty-three tourists slaughtered by Islamic militants at Ghiza, just like the earlier massacre at Luxor. Shot, pursued, and hacked, stabbed, beaten to death. Senseless, sick. Ryan could remember that day too clearly: Jess looking eagerly through the mail for a postcard, so happy for her sister.

No postcard. Then turning on the evening news.

Jess's grief had scared the crap out of Ryan. Sometime during the weeks that followed, he had come home to find her curled on the bedroom floor, face tear-streaked, staring blindly at the wall, unable to talk. It had taken a long time to get her on her feet again. She'd gone to grief counseling and to church, she'd thrown herself into her work, but in some ways she had never come all the way back.

One reason was that as bad as the grief was, the murder had hurt Jess in another way, maybe worse. Faced with Allison's death, her foundation for living had been knocked out from under her. Consciously or otherwise, Ryan believed, everybody relied on some faith or belief to sustain them. True, scratch an altruist you'll see a hypocrite bleed, but Jess's core belief really had been something like *Human beings are basically good.* This was important because its corollary was *It is good to be a human being. I am of a good tribe. I am good.* Or maybe it was *My life has meaning because I work in service to the goodness of humanity.* Something everyone yearned to believe. A reason for being, for trying.

And she had done splendidly with that all her life—until Allison's murder.

Jess had seen Allison's wrecked body. She had read the reports of what happened. It was damned hard to believe in anything like "the goodness of man" after that. So without that, what moved her? What was there to live for? To work toward? Jess was getting wounded by her own irresolution. Obviously, Ridder's quest for the root of man's inhumanity to man would bear directly on her pain, her uncertainty.

"You going to talk to me?" he asked. It sounded gruff. She had shut off the water and was just standing there.

"I don't like fighting with you," she said quietly. "You're right about some of this, but you've also got to trust me to sort things out on my own terms. Ryan, it's okay for people to go different ways once in a while. To have different professional opinions and different personal agendas. A marriage can accommodate that, can't it?"

Go different ways sounded a little scary, and he couldn't answer right away. Just how different? For a breath he hovered behind her, uncertain, then walked away.

But his route was like a wandering comet, out and away and then irresistibly back. Something in her posture, still unmoving at the sink, some wordless communication. Without thinking, he came up behind her and put his hands on her hips, and immediately she covered them with her own hands. The contact dizzied him. Wordless questions and welcome answers. He'd thought the booze had mostly worn off, but now he felt suddenly drunk again. He slid his hands around her, placing both palms against the sweet curve of her belly. For a moment he stopped, stunned by her fertile geometry, and then his body awoke as she backed against him and he felt the gentle pressure against him.

The miracle of one's wife, he was thinking dazedly. How she knows you. How desire and the yearning for solace merged into a great warm irresistible gravity. Her body was saying to him something like *In our pleasure let us banish all pain and fear.* Ancient wisdom.

She had spent the day with her graduate students at Harvard, and was still wearing her blue skirt, white blouse, and nylons. Paradoxically, the costume of professional authority only amplified her sexuality: the violation of that distance and formality. Ryan tugged her blouse out of her waistband and his hands found their way to her warm skin. They rocked together, just feeling the current that ran between them and not needing it to go any further, not yet.

It had been this way since their junior year in high school. He'd been intimidated by her brilliance, and only the even greater attraction of her body had given him the courage to approach her. Sitting in biochemistry class one day, the shape of her legs unexpectedly hit him—that strength and grace in her thighs, the way her hips made that beautiful shape, a heart or a dove's breast. And *bam,* he was gone.

At the counter, Jess murmured. She leaned her head back, cheek against his chin, then lips against his jaw. His hands moved up under her blouse and for a long moment he touched her breasts lightly, awed, just tracing their curves: Her stomach hadn't gotten bigger yet, but her breasts had begun to swell. After another moment he found the clasp and opened her brassiere so that her breasts swung full into his cupped hands. A new wave of desire washed through him, Jess made a sound like the wind.

"Abi's door is shut," she panted. "But we still have to be quiet."

Yes, Abi. Another stage of wonder, she had gotten pregnant with Abebi and he had worshiped her fecund body, breasts turned into turgid cones, belly swollen first into a subtle hemisphere and then a preposterous but sexy ball, smoky skin stretched taut over their child. They had discovered new dimensions of sexuality then, when she was most burdened by her pregnancy, lust tempered by tenderness and the need for caution. And in the years since, Jess the mom, the hardworking woman in jeans and sweatshirt, hair tied back, sleeves rolled up to deal with some kid mess, handling the disordered logistics of domestic life with competence and weary humor. A woman who had borne a child, whose body had bled and healed, whose milk he had tasted. Jess coming up from the water's edge carrying Abebi on one hip, a bucket of beach toys in her hand, pants wet to the knee, hair blown crazy: as sexy as it gets.

Now he could feel the heat of her body, her dark skin smoother than silk. His hand glided down from her hipbone, and their urgency crescendoed until the touch of hands wasn't enough. Jess turned away from the counter and they undressed each other, and then moved to kneel together on the rug, where she rolled him back and straddled him. Somehow the need to be silent amplified the urgency, the pressure. For a moment she drew herself along him, and at last arched her body so that he entered her. The contact of her body resonated like thunder.

Jess rode him, abandoned. He let her lead, and after a time her breathing crescendoed, her body clenched, shuddered, faltered. And then again. But still he reserved himself. Only when her sudden softening told him her hunger was satisfied did he allow the pressure inside him to grow toward release. When he mounted her he felt as wild and lordly as a lion, claiming his lioness, taking her completely and giving himself utterly to the hunger, the pleasure, the heat.

He spun out of the void to see Jess lying near, head on one arm, eyes closed as she floated in the empty aftermath. Her skin was shadow against the white kitchen rug. He restrained the urge to stroke her shoulder, not wanting to startle her from her drowse. His cooling body felt perfectly comfortable, his thoughts spacious. The exquisite freedom, the letting go.

The marriage bed, he thought. *Which is mightier, the pen or the sword? Neither: it's the marriage bed.* The most basic and intimate alliance, foundation of peace and stability. The kings and queens of old, marrying daughters of one clan with sons of another, relying on the mingling of bloodlines and the bonds of love and desire to unite whole peoples. Similarly, so much of the cohesion and collaborative harmony of Project Alpha and later Genesis depended on their marriage being solid. Amazing. Nice. The universe endlessly surprising. Always bringing you back to basics. The current difficulties were just the little bumps any marriage could expect.

Again he repressed the urge to stroke the smooth, shadowed sweep of her skin. When they'd first gotten together, he had only vaguely noticed her blackness—until he had at last seen the whole length of her naked, skin so much darker than his own pale hide. It had struck a chord of uncertainty in him: *So different.* But that lasted only until desire lashed him onward and they'd coupled ineptly and laughed and shivered together. Though his unexpected consciousness of her color when they made love was strange, he soon began to savor it. Sometimes, as he breathed her scent, it seemed he smelled the African savannahs, the jungles, the long coasts. Yes, her darkness was the dark earth of Africa, infinitely exciting and nurturing, he couldn't help feel that in coming to her he came home to himself and to the beginning place of humankind. Coming to an ancient home, a root place.

Lost in his thoughts, he inadvertently drew his hand along the line from her shoulders to side and waist and hips, the hilly horizon of some African landscape. She stirred.

"Oh," she said. Her eyes opened and she gazed at him. "Mm. Hi. A long way to come back."

"Time to go to bed."

"I can't move. Let's bring the bed down here."

"C'mon." But not moving himself.

Jess groaned, shutting her eyes again. "You know what I was thinking?"

"What?" *Please,* he unexpectedly found himself thinking, *not about people killing each other, about violent drives and pathologies. Not anything complex.*

"I was thinking that you're *damn* well hung. For a white guy. Wow." She opened her eyes and smiled broadly at his scandalized expression. "I missed you all day. No way was I going to let you go down to New York and get anywhere near Diana Reese without...this...first." She laughed out loud, and then her prim hand came up, eclipsing her smile.

They helped each other up, gathered their clothes, cut the lights. Following her up the stairs in the dark, he loved her intensely and could no longer feel the sharp edge of anxiety. Her form moved gracefully in front of him, shadow within shadow, guiding him to their bed, while through the windows he could see the distant light at Marblehead, guiding ships safe to harbor.

Paradoxically, neither of them fell asleep right away. For a while Ryan lay with his hands behind his head, staring at the ceiling and listening to the beat of the waves outside. Jess lay next to him like his reflection in a darkened mirror, also watching the subtle play of reflected light.

"I keep thinking," she said after a while, "that if you're going to make a case for humanity, you have an obligation to look straight at evil. Don't you think? If you haven't witnessed and—and come to grips with the worst about human beings, how could you make an argument we're any good?" She didn't sound too confident.

True, but, Ryan thought. *But, but.*

"Maybe Dagan's right, 'Everybody's half something and half something else.'" A sleepy voice. Her body was shutting down, getting on with baby-building.

Dagan was half Viennese Jew, half Boston Episcopalian, and she often joked cynically about the mix. But it was a good observation: Most people were born with something at odds inside, feet in two worlds. He wasn't sure what Jess was saying, precisely. Maybe that she was half mourning the death of Allison, half celebrating the impending life inside her? One foot in death, one in life. Only one of many oppositions inside her. Living in the flux of such juxtapositions made you vulnerable, but it was also a place where insight came, a place of power. Maybe that's what she was saying.

His mind dipped into wandering half-dreams where things merged with equations that rounded into concepts and became things again, shape-shifted. *The way lovemaking brings you close,* he was thinking. *Finding your common animal selves, ancient mammal family feelings and procreative longings.* But then he looked over at the faint sheen of Jess's cheek, turned half away from him, and she seemed remote in her gathering drowse, her body abandoned. *And then how you become strangers again as you drift off into worlds utterly mysterious and solitary. How you can never really know the one you love.*

He felt himself spinning away, too, dreams darkened by that last thought, the anxiety awakening again.

Chapter 8

Ryan watched from the wings as Diana Reese opened her show with the usual humorous commentary on current events. He couldn't see the auditorium, but the sea of crowd noises gave him a sense of its size. Behind him, a stagehand wearing a headset watched too, one hand on Ryan's back to cue or restrain him.

He shut his eyes, glad for a moment to charge up his batteries. Thursday night, 8:00 P.M., and it had been a big day: the morning staff meeting, packing for the overnight in New York, the rush to the airport, Manhattan traffic, the hotel, the studio, an interminable hour sitting in a chair as a makeup artist worked over his face and hair. And even the show wasn't the end of it: He had arranged to meet Karl Alexander for a drink afterwards—maybe not such a good idea.

The techie held up a finger, then pointed it to Diana, who had begun her introduction: "Our guest tonight is America's favorite bona fide genius, the man who at an early age took the academic establishment by storm and who now spends his time solving some of the most intriguing and puzzling scientific mysteries. He's the author of three important and controversial books, and he's the best-known scientific personality since the late Carl Sagan. Let's give a big welcome to Dr. Ryan McCloud!"

At the roar of applause, Ryan's handler gave him a little shove, and then he was out in the brilliant lights. Crowded, half-lit auditorium stretching away. Robotic forms of several TV cameras, silently pivoting to follow him. Diana Reese, standing to receive the obligatory kiss on each cheek, her famous mane of honey-colored hair afire in the lights.

He took the seat across from her, feeling cramped in the chair, trying to look as if he were enjoying himself. Diana crossed her exquisite legs, showing a good length of glistening thigh.

"You know, Ryan," she said as the applause subsided, "when we met backstage a little while ago, I have to admit I was unprepared for the way you look. I mean, for a guy who's supposed to be so, so *cerebral,* there's an awful lot of the *physical* you!" She made a *big* gesture with both arms at his body.

"Yeah, well, we cerebral types come in all shapes and sizes," he said.

Diana faced her audience. "In fact, he's quite a hunk, isn't he, ladies? I'm tempted to ask him to make that entrance again!" With her shoulders she mimed a macho, big-guy walk, and the women in the audience hooted approvingly. "Wotta hunk, huh?"

This was one of her signature techniques: sexualize her encounters, catch her guests off balance early on and keep them that way.

Diana glanced at her notes and continued: "In fact, there's a lot about you that defies stereotypes. You had a hard childhood—you grew up in a tough neighborhood in South Boston, son of an alcoholic father, became quite a street fighter, had some serious family troubles, worked all kinds of blue-collar jobs. But then you went on to be a *wunderkind* at Harvard, to win big honors, to start a wildly successful independent research firm, and to achieve considerable celebrity. I guess my question for you is, how does it feel to be a tough Irish kid from a poor family, and to rise so suddenly into respectability—into the limelight?"

Ryan forced a wooden smile. "Well, first of all, a few corrections. I'm not just Irish. Half Polish, on my mother's side. Also, it never occurred to me that I was having a 'hard' childhood—I look back at it as a hell of a lot of fun. Our neighborhood wasn't all that tough—it seemed pretty normal at the time. Finally, my father wasn't an alcoholic—"

"If that's the case," Diana broke in, "why do Boston police records show several arrests of Daniel McCloud for drunk and disorderly conduct, assault and battery, disturbing the peace?"

That's right, the other aspect of *The Diana Reese Show:* the sudden pounce—the provocations, armed with considerable background research, that put her guests on the defensive. In person, she was even more beautiful than she appeared on screen, and the sexual shock of her body in its revealing sheath was a distraction that she used well, another weapon in her arsenal.

"Well," he said, "it's true my father would get drunk a couple of times a year, but he didn't drink regularly. Didn't even keep alcohol in the house. Honestly. I'm not trying to look pretty here—I drink regularly myself, maybe too much, but—"

"Don't you just love that South Boston accent?" Diana asked her audience mischievously. "'Hahd childhood.' 'My fah-thuh.' Love it!"

"As for street-fighting, every kid in South Boston gets into a few fights. Actually, I've been pretty committed to nonviolence since I was sixteen."

"Does that mean you were *born* with that incredibly sexy nose? You didn't get it from some swashbuckling punch-up?" She looked at the crowd for approval. The women loved it. The camera to Ryan's right seemed to bore in, looking for the revealing close-up, of the rugged nose or his reaction.

Ryan plugged ahead, feeling like a wet blanket: "It's not from a fight. I, uh, managed to run face-first into a windowsill when I was a teenager."

"Sounds like a regular Einstein, doesn't he?" She waited for the laughter to subside. "So Ryan, for those of us who need a map to find the Mr. Coffee machine in the morning, tell us what it's like to be a genius. Do you have special mental techniques? I guess this is a backwards way of asking, to what do you attribute your phenomenal success at solving difficult scientific puzzles, despite the fact that you're not a specialist? Wait, wait, stop!" She waved her hands, as if flustered by her own enthusiasm. "Looks like I've got several questions here. *Do* you have a special discipline? What would you call yourself?"

"Let me start with the last question first. At Harvard I mainly studied cognitive neuroscience and dynamical systems theory, but I, uh, I've branched out quite a bit. I guess you could say I gave up on studying my own brain and decided to *use* the damned thing. So now I think of myself as a generalist. Interdisciplinary." He recrossed his legs and wondered how many times he had done so already.

"At 'Hah-vuhd,' you helped found the famous Project Alpha. I've always wondered who was studying whom at Project Alpha—it sounds almost like the researchers were the guinea pigs in their own experiments."

"Yeah, it was a bunch of exceptionally bright people, and we did look at our own mental processes a lot. We also did tests on both 'normal' populations and special populations like autistic people, mentally retarded and gifted kids, brain-damaged people. To put it in perspective, a lot of my colleagues had me in the latter category."

The audience chuckled, and Diana gave him a grin. "So how about your secret, genius mental techniques?"

"No secrets. Mainly I just give myself time to think. You might say I go fishing—I put down the line, and I've gotten very good at sensing when something's nibbling at the hook, when some unconscious process is working. Anybody can do the same thing." Diana just waited, so he offered more: "Oh—and I often exploit what my wife calls 'the doughnut principle.' The most obvious thing about a doughnut is its hole, right, the part that's not there. If you're trying to solve a scientific mystery, you're always starting out missing some data, or it wouldn't be a mystery. The principle is just that from the shape of the hole, you can often infer a lot about the shape of the doughnut."

Ryan had put his thumb and forefinger together and traced the resulting negative space with his other index finger. Diana turned it into a lewd joke, holding up her hands: "I think I get the general idea—be still, my heart!" She let the laughter die and checked her notes again. "So let's look at a specific project you've gotten considerable press for in recent months. As I understand it, you're wrapping up an epidemiology study—tell me, why is this so important? And why should it require the combined genius of Ryan McCloud's crack team *and* a research group from the famous Brandt Institute in Stanford?"

Ryan decided he'd better skip explaining the math of RAINDROP and give the audience something more dramatic. "Not to sound like an alarmist, but there are three new factors that put us much more at risk than we were in, say, the Middle Ages from the Black Plague, or even in 1927, the great flu epidemic. One is simply the density of the human population nowadays, which means that a disease can do an enormous amount of damage in a very short time. Second, we're vastly more interconnected now, with air travel, highways, public transportation, and so on. Our global lifestyle puts people in contact and facilitates disease transmission—diseases can't easily be contained geographically anymore. Third, we've accelerated the mutation of bacteria and viruses by saturating their environments with chemicals and radiation. Ironically, it's *antibiotics* that have done the most to create these new disease strains. It all adds up to a kind of a powder-keg situation—it's not a matter of *if* we have a global epidemic, it's only a matter of *when, what disease,* and *how bad.* The need for a predictive tool like RAINDROP is very urgent indeed."

Diana had put on a look of theatrical alarm, but when he was done her grin came back. "All I can say is, it's reassuring to know we've got Ryan McCloud looking out for us, huh?" More applause.

They moved on, sparring over one topic or another, Diana alternately flirtatious and confrontational. Her dress continued to ride up that endless length of perfect thigh. For a time he found himself trying to explain the idea of emergent properties, until Diana held up her hand.

"I want to get personal again," she warned him. This was predictable: After any theoretical stuff, she rotated perspectives, kept her

audience entertained. "You're married to Dr. Jessamine Maywood, also
a Project Alpha alum, and the daughter of Judge Henry Maywood, a
prominent African-American federal judge. Has that ever been difficult? I mean, how has being in an interracial marriage affected your life
and career?"

"I've never paid a lot of attention to my wife's race," Ryan snapped,
"and I always feel a little sorry for those who feel obliged to do so."

Ooooh, said the audience.

"Okay, then, how was it for a poor, blue-collar, South Boston kid to
marry into a well-off, intellectual, Back Bay family?"

"Hey, I forgot to mention another of my secret 'genius' techniques,
Diana. One of the best: I avoid thinking in clichés and stereotypes."

He'd tried to say it with elbow-in-the-ribs irony, but it came off as
nasty. The audience *oooh*ed again, smelling blood now. Suddenly the sea
of expectant faces looked to him like a single, sadistic organism, eager to
prey on someone else's discomfort.

Diana just pressed on: "You have an older brother, Thomas McCloud.
What's he like? Does high intelligence run in the family?"

Ryan sensed what was coming, but couldn't figure how to forestall it.
"Tommy's very bright, yeah," he hedged. "In a different way."

"You downplay your family's disadvantages, but I always get the sense
you're holding something back. For example, Tommy was severely
injured in a motorcycle accident when you were a teenager. How did that
affect you?"

"I was devastated. But I don't usually talk about this stuff. I don't think
it serves a constructive purpose, and it's really nobody's business."

Again the audience murmured, moved not by compassion for a family
tragedy but by lust for spectacle.

Diana kept her cool completely: "I sense that there's a lot of feeling
there, and you're evading me."

Abruptly he'd had it with her. "You want an honest reaction? My real
feelings? I'll tell you. Making a crowd react feels good, and it therefore
constitutes a dangerous form of behavioral conditioning. Like Pavlov's
dogs, Diana, you've become conditioned to offer them titillations, sound
bites, little dirty revelations, but never anything of substance. Looking at
you now, what I feel is sympathy for a beautiful, vibrant, intelligent person who's been led down that path—at the sacrifice of a lot of potential."

Whoooaaaa! the crowd gasped.

Just the slightest twinge touched her face, and then she came back. "Just trying to give our audience the inside picture of a *very* evasive guest."

There was a tense moment when it seemed there was nothing to say, and Ryan felt a pang of genuine sympathy for her. Fuck. He *was* being difficult, he *did* get touchy about the Tommy thing, he *was* preoccupied with forensic neuropsych job—

"Okay," he said, relenting. "I'm really thinking and feeling that you've got a terrific pair of legs, but if that skirt rides up any more even *you* are probably going to be embarrassed."

The audience cooed, and Diana looked pleased, taking it as it was intended, a peace offering: *Okay, I'll help you entertain them.* She made a show of tugging her skirt down an inch or two, and got a good laugh that turned into sustained applause. Ryan did a few "genius" tricks like explaining his sweating under the spotlights by quoting formulae for heat transmission in light:

$$F\,A_1, A_2 = \frac{1}{A_1} \int A_1 \int A_2 \frac{\cos\varnothing_1, \cos\varnothing_2}{\pi\,r^2}\,\ell A_1\,\ell A_2$$

"With, what, twenty-four one-kilowatt bulbs at about eight meters, at absorption rates for my size, that's, uh, that's about 96.7 watts," he concluded. "About the same as if I'd swallowed a hundred-watt lightbulb." Typical trained-monkey stuff.

————

After the show, Ryan went gratefully back to the dressing room, took a shower, changed into street clothes for his meeting with Karl Alexander. He was toweling his hair one last time when he heard a light knock at the door.

He opened it to see Diana, wearing jeans, a simple blue silk blouse, and a tweed jacket. Her hair was tied loosely behind her head, and she wore almost no makeup. Without her stage costume, she was even more attractive, more human and accessible.

"So how was it?" she asked. She leaned against the door frame, one fine hip cocked. Outside, the studio was quieting down.

"You're a tough lady. I didn't like the prying. Or was that goading?"

"Neither. I figure if we can give the audience some of what they want, and slip something of substance in with it, we've done a good job. Isn't that why you agreed to come on the show?"

"Yeah, more or less." Ryan tossed the towel onto the dressing table. In the opposing mirrors he saw an army of Ryans, stretching away into dimming glassy corridors. He was sick of his own face.

"You're tough, too," Diana said. "Did you mean what you said? When you were embarrassing me in front of twenty million viewers?" She moved into the room and leaned against the wall, arms folded across her chest. "The 'beautiful, vibrant, intelligent' part?"

"Of course." Ryan zipped up his suit bag, checked the room for his things.

"Would you like to have a drink with me? Now?"

The invitation was clear in her eyes, and looking at her, he felt his body responding to hers. He hesitated, momentarily confused by desire and fatigue. Then he stepped closer to her, touched her cheek. "I'm married, Diana. You're beautiful, and you're talented, and you're sexy. But no."

She pulled away from his touch, and her eyes hardened. "I really *hate* rejection, Dr. McCloud. It's a great way to make enemies." But then abruptly she leaned to kiss him. Her mouth was luscious but disconcertingly foreign.

After a moment he stepped away, feeling dizzy, clumsy. He managed a grin. "You…you take my breath away, Diana. But I've got a wife I love and have been with for a long time, and I'm pretty old-fashioned about marriage stuff. I'm sorry. Anyway, I'm meeting a friend, got business to talk about."

"Male friend or female friend?"

"Male. But that's beside the point."

She pursed her lips, frustrated, looking suddenly very tired. Ryan could imagine how hard it would be to do what she did, to reliably generate so much wit and vibrancy, to sustain so much public scrutiny.

They locked eyes for several long seconds, until he broke the gaze. "Want to walk me out of here?" he asked. "This place is a maze—I'd probably get lost."

"You're a strange son of a bitch, Ryan," she said, shaking her golden head.

She smiled minutely, took his arm, led him down the hall. Outside, they waited arm in arm, not talking, as her driver brought her Mercedes up, followed shortly by his cab. Paradoxically, their formal courtesy felt surprisingly affectionate, almost intimate. They said good night with a handshake.

Chapter 9

"I watched the show," Karl said. "So—did you screw her afterwards?"

Ryan glanced uncomfortably at the people who sat nearest them. "You're such a goddamned deviant, Karl. Christ!"

"Always," Karl agreed, smiling. "Hey, she's a good-looking woman. Don't be such a prude, Ry—it'll give you prostate cancer." He tucked into his drink with relish. Karl thrived upon the kind of big, fruity concoction that Ryan had always considered an abuse of good alcohol. Now he set the glass down and licked his foamy mustache. "You seemed especially mulish, even for you. Combative."

Ryan tasted his own drink. *Vodka tonight,* he'd decided earlier, feeling more than usually Polish. They sat across from each other in deep leather chairs in the cavernous bar of the Hotel Royalton. For half a block in all directions, stylish Manhattanites sat or stood, laughing, arguing, smoking, flirting, sulking. With its coffee tables and clusters of soft chairs and couches, done in grays and burgundies, the interior seemed less like a bar than like someone's enormous, opulent living room. Back in Boston, Ryan tended to favor workingmen's bars, the more dark and cramped the better.

Karl looked like a plump Oscar Wilde: dark hair in a cut that seemed somehow nineteenth-century, floppy tie, jacket with wide lapels. His coal-black eyes glowed with a lethally cynical intelligence. He was now director of Montgomery Laboratories, one of the leading centers for human genome research, and chaired an elite genetics advisory panel for the Surgeon General's office. Despite his stature in the scientific community, he maintained the bad-boy persona that had distinguished him at Project Alpha: bad attitudes, bad friends, complete scorn for anything bearing the slightest perfume of political correctness. Also the habits of blunt candor and conceptual playfulness that made him a good source of feedback for the Skunk Works.

"You're right, I was a lousy guest," Ryan admitted. "I was preoccupied, Karl."

Karl turned a priestly ear and mimed drawing aside a confessional screen. As Ryan gave him an outline of the AFPA proposal, he sat with hands on his knees, staring at a young couple who leaned against a pillar fifteen feet away, their heads bent close. The woman wore a dress cut low in back, and the man's hand caressed the supple curve at her waist.

"That's beautiful," Karl said at last. "Go'geous."

Ryan followed his gaze. "She's pretty, yes."

"No—your project. It's lovely. What fun. What ghoulish fun." Karl's eyes were doing that spinning thing, like the rollers on a slot machine, the tumblers inside his head turning fast.

"Anything on your radar that ties in? From a genetics perspective?"

Karl sucked down his drink and flagged a passing waiter for a refill, then turned back to Ryan, frowning. "Ah, you know where I stand on this 'gene-for' business. About once a month, some hotshot announces he's discovered the gene 'for' anxiety, or curiosity, or homosexuality. Demonstrating that the genetics community is full of media whores! All anybody discovers is a weak leak in a chain of genetic programming instructions. There's no single gene 'for' any goddamned thing, let alone behavior. Skip *human* behaviors, we couldn't tell you how genes code for a peacock's mating dance, or why a swallow builds one kind of nest and a sparrow another. You know how these hucksters' grandstanding distorts public perception of genetics issues? I'm telling you, Ry, at night I lie awake fantasizing tortures for these sons of bitches—seriously, we're talking creative uses for superglue and corkscrews here." Clearly there was some genuine agitation mixed in with Karl's hyperbole.

Ryan allowed himself a small smile. "So I shouldn't ask you if anybody's discovered the gene for murder?"

Karl rolled his eyes. When the waiter arrived with Karl's preposterous drink, he grabbed it and gulped it half down. Ryan ordered another vodka martini.

But once he got out of his dudgeon, Karl had a number of useful insights to offer. Since most of the research on the human genome focused on finding cures for inheritable diseases, his position required a broad general knowledge of medicine. Ryan spent several minutes elaborating on the problems of assessing the role of low-dose, long-term exposures. He finished up, waited for reply.

Karl was jiggling his leg furiously and watching a passing group with disapproval. "Jesus, has she got an ass like a bag of hammers, or what?" he said loudly.

"Karl—"

"Okay. You want neurotoxic agents? I'd say three main suspects. One's pretty obvious—viral infections that have few physical symptoms but attack parts of the brain. Main culprits would be small viruses, like the Bornaviridae, or rabies-like viruses that can travel through the neurons of the brain. Then there're EDs, endocrine disruptors—environmental chemicals that resemble our body's own hormones enough that they can be absorbed and screw up health and behavior. These babies are everywhere. The EPA is working on a study of some *fifteen thousand* sources, mostly man-made pollutants and consumer products. Then there's the perennial bugaboo of electromagnetic fields, which have thousands of sources, too. Again, mostly man-made but some natural. The World Health Organization is working on a five-year study on the adverse health effects of exposure to EMFs."

When Ryan asked for names and citations, Karl pulled a palm computer out of his disheveled jacket. "What day is today? Wednesday?"

Ryan glanced at his watch. "Technically, it's Thursday morning."

"I'll be out of town for a week. But I'll make a note to have my assistant get something to you ASAP." He jotted quickly with the computer's stylus. For all that he affected a negligent persona, Karl was supremely organized—a fact he did his best to conceal.

It had always been hard for Ryan to draw a bead on Karl's personal life. Back in Project Alpha days, Karl's shady lifestyle had provided fuel for endless rumor: He had a lover who was a prostitute; he had a lover who was actually a transvestite. He was a pedophile. He was secretly working for the CIA as a scout for promising avenues of mind-control research or recruitable high-IQ talent. He was experimenting on himself with exotic drugs like K and ayahuasca. Karl had denied nothing—as far as Ryan could tell, he relished the gossip and did his best to encourage it. But once when he was visiting Karl's apartment, a run-down flat tucked back in one of Cambridge's public alleys, he had gotten a different perspective. He'd absently pulled a high-school yearbook from the shelves, and found Karl's photo: a sad-faced, chubby boy with heavy, black-framed glasses. He had realized with a start that if you stripped away the deliberate overlay of decadence, you'd still see that kid in Karl. Given what he was, the negligent, slightly dangerous bad-boy persona was probably this brainy nerd's best shot at anything resembling glamour and mystique.

Under the mirrors along the side wall, an argument had turned noisy, and a few heads turned. Two red-faced, well-dressed men shoved at each other until friends interceded.

Karl observed it with satisfaction for a moment, then turned back to Ryan. "So are you jumping right in on this job?"

Ryan shook his head. "We're participating in the initial death-row studies, but we won't be able to start full-time for another few months—we're still wrapping up the Four Corners project."

"So there's still time for me to offer some advice?" Karl had gotten abruptly serious, a disquieting transformation. "There are areas here into which you don't want to stick your nose. This is potentially dangerous turf."

"Dangerous because—?"

There was a flash of impatience in Karl's eyes. "Ah, yes. Ryan McCloud's famous cognitive proclivity—the always-open mind, the tabula rasa. The unbiased and thus infinitely adaptive learner. We worked on each other's heads so thoroughly back then, Ry—I know you've thought of this stuff, but I know you'll ask me anyway because you're the consummate synthesist, withholding your own analysis until all the data's in! But I'll play along."

"If you wouldn't mind," Ryan said dryly. You always felt a little exposed in talking to fellow Project Alpha alums.

"I'll start with the most obvious. First: field work among dangerous populations. Like mass murderers, institutionalized sociopaths. Where you going to draw the line, Ry? Maybe you decide you've got to look at hate groups, urban gangs, Mafia hitmen—I'd say that qualifies as high-risk field research. A good way to make enemies."

"Sounds right." Ryan felt a sudden, irrational concern for Jess and Abi, an acute awareness of the distance from New York City to Heart Cove, Massachusetts.

"Other enemies? Bigger, badder gorillas? Corporations who don't like you looking into the skeletons in their closets. Suppose your findings suggest the neurotoxicity of a pollutant, or some widely used consumer product made by one of our nice new-world-order corporations? Hey—remember Karen Silkwood? I still believe she was murdered by the nuclear power industry. Or Mannie Skovanik, killed by electric utility corporate security." Karl stopped, glanced past Ryan again. "What the *fuck* is with these guys, anyway?"

Across the room, the two men were at it again. One shoved the other so that he tripped over a coffee table and hit the floor hard, shouting. Several waitstaff stood uneasily nearby as the man who had fallen lurched upright, grabbed a pedestal ashtray, and brandished it at his—what? Friend? Lover? Rival?

Karl turned back to Ryan, his eyes black holes in a humorless face. "Go ahead, Ry. There are your test subjects. Go get your blood samples. Ask 'em to submit to cranial imaging."

"Point taken, Karl. You got something more?"

"You bet I do. More enemies? Governments. What if your pollutant or product is manufactured by a state-run industry? Or suppose—" Suddenly Karl's eyes wandered and he stopped, as if he'd said more than he intended.

"Go on."

Karl shifted uncomfortably on his chair, leaned closer to Ryan. When he continued, his voice was lower. "Let's just say governments have all kinds of reasons to frown on people prying into this stuff. Let's just say I'm speaking from experience here."

Ryan stared at him for a moment. Karl's sudden awkwardness suggested this wasn't just his usual self-dramatization. "And here I always thought your fabled CIA connection was a bunch of hot air. Or was it the Defense Intelligence Agency?"

"Dammit, I'm feeling exposed here, Ry, I'm trying to make a point to a guy who's been a pretty good friend—"

"Are you going to tell me something useful, or do we have to do some elaborate tango first?"

Karl's eyes flared, subsided. "What the hell. You guys'll come across this stuff anyway when you start digging. You ever hear the term 'torpedo'?"

"You mean, as in submarine warfare?"

"Wouldn't that be nice." Karl's face puckered, as if he'd tasted something sour. "No. A human being who's been psychologically programmed to kill. It's an industry term."

Ryan held his eyes. "What industry would that be?"

"I'll overlook the tone of condescension and accusation, Ry, because I'm trying to help you. Remember MKULTRA? The LSD experiments were the tip of the iceberg. The overall goal was to use behavioral modification as a weapon. Mind control. One of the main thrusts was to produce guys who could be programmed to become assassins, controlled and targeted like torpedoes or cruise missiles."

Ryan looked at him, uncertain what he was hearing or why. *Turning people into weapons.* It had a sick sound to it, somehow bleakly credible. *Always the worst horrors are the ones we visit upon ourselves.* "You're bull-shitting me, right?" he mustered at last.

"Oh, come on, Ry! I'm not revealing state secrets here. It's a matter of public record that the U.S. tried them during the Vietnam era. Didn't work very well, because the guinea pigs tended to go on the fritz in various ways. There were articles in all the papers, back in the 1980s. If you'd get your head out of the clouds once in a while, you might notice these things!" Karl had always ridiculed what he considered Ryan's naïve idealism. Now, mad at having to spell it all out, at being ignored when he tried to flag a waiter for a refill, Karl raised his empty glass above his head and held it there like Liberty's torch. Mute protest at shoddy service.

"Okay," Ryan said. "So how would that pose a problem for us?"

Still holding his glass aloft, Karl let his head fall forward, his face sag, as if positively *martyred* by Ryan's obtusity. "Let's see. Suppose you start poking around the science they used? I mean, these guys' brains were altered to make them violent. Probably by surgery, followed by posthypnotic suggestion and behavioral conditioning—but what're the specifics? Somebody, somewhere, knows enough about the neuropsychology of violence to accomplish that, and you'll want to know what they know. Or suppose, when you're doing your death-row interviews, you come across one of these former guinea pigs? One of those guys who came home from Vietnam, but never successfully 'reintegrated' into society? Or you might even find—" But again Karl stopped, looking suddenly uncertain. He took his glass down and looked at it despondently. "I'm fucking loaded. How many of these have I had?"

"What else, Karl? We might find—what?"

Another clamor of voices broke out, and Ryan turned to see the man with the pedestal ashtray swinging it wildly at the other. A woman screamed as a lamp fell and the bulb popped in a flash of white light.

"My point is," Karl said quietly, "Ry—you think the powers that be are going to *welcome* your interest?"

"Just a minute, Karl." Sick of interruptions, Ryan stood up and walked back through the long, crowded room. When he got to the standoff, he went straight to the man with the ashtray. The guy glowered at him and raised it like a baseball bat.

Ryan loomed over him and snatched the ashtray out of his hands. "I am trying," he said through his teeth, "to have a really important conversation. But I can't hear myself *think!* So I'd like you guys to shut the hell up and get out of here. *Now.*"

The men hesitated as if deciding whether to challenge his intrusion, but under Ryan's expressionless gaze they folded. There were advantages, he decided, to being a big hulk with a prizefighter's broken nose. Ryan waited as they petulantly picked up their jackets and began to make their way out. Only when the front doors had closed behind them did he set the ashtray down and head back to Karl. Several people nodded appreciatively as he passed their tables.

Ryan threw himself back into his overstuffed chair, half lying, half sitting, and frowned at Karl. "What the hell kind of dive is this place?"

"God, you're so *butch,* Ry!" Karl was smiling again. He'd gotten a new drink while Ryan was across the room. "What'd you say to them?"

"I told them I was going to take blood samples," Ryan said darkly.

Karl hooted, loving it. "What would you have done if they'd called your bluff?"

Ryan sighed, feeling suddenly very tired. "I've got an early flight tomorrow, Karl. If you've got more friendly advice for me, I'd like to hear it now." It came out gruffly, an accusation.

Karl dropped his eyes. "Don't get sanctimonious, Ry," he muttered. "I got into this shit a long time ago. I was a *kid.* You ever do anything stupid when you were a kid?"

Ryan sighed and wished he had another drink and then felt that he'd had enough. He'd had enough of Karl for the time being, too. He stood up and tossed some bills onto the table. Then one final question occurred to him.

"So Karl," he said. "Your childish stupidity—a thing of the past, or something ongoing?" It might be useful to know.

Karl's mouth twitched, a sudden jerk downward, but he rallied quickly. His bad-boy self-possession had returned. "Let me put it this way," he said, his eyes opaque. "No matter how fast you run, you can never outrun your own asshole."

Ryan snorted. "I'll keep it in mind," he said.

Chapter 10

Ryan pounded up the stairs, breathless. He paused at the landing until he heard footsteps scattering down the hall above, then lunged up the second flight and into the hall. But she was already gone, into one of the second-floor doorways. Which? Holding his weapon in front of him, he crept down the hall until he saw a faint change in the light in the big bedroom. He charged in, brandishing his balloon, to see Abebi disappearing into the closet. A muffled squeal came from behind the hanging clothes. He bellowed threateningly, but didn't follow. Instead, he dashed out and around to where he knew she'd emerge, her own room. She was small enough to slip through the narrow, crowded closet that had doors in both bedrooms. Being six years old had its advantages.

When he came in, she leaped off the bed, flailing her weapon, shouting, "En garde! En garde!" He screamed in dismay and backed out of the room, fencing desperately as she advanced, their long balloons buffing and squeaking.

Out in the hall, she gave him one last flurry of blows and disappeared again, into the upstairs office. Ryan waited in the hall, catching his breath, listening intently. He checked his watch. Another five minutes, he decided, then bed.

A nightly ritual: the final explosion of kinetic energy, the last glucose burn Abebi had to accomplish before she could sleep. Some nights it was just general running amok, sometimes it was tag or a wild version of hide-and-seek. Tonight they had been tying balloons and had gotten silly with it and finally slipped over into swordplay, ending up chasing each other up and down the stairs, out onto the decks, into every room of the house. It was Friday, and Ryan had spent the day at home, grateful for some time at Heart Cove after the unpleasant midweek in New York. Jess was at Harvard, not due home for another hour.

He crept down the hall until he heard a panting giggle from the end room. When he burst through the door, she was standing on the bed, a skinny kid still in her pink school dress, stick legs braced, a ferocious expression on her face. They battled until Ryan's balloon popped and he had to surrender. She extracted promises from him to which, disarmed, under duress, he capitulated.

At last he began herding her through the nighttime routine. In the bathroom, wearing just her pajama bottoms, she stood at the sink and brushed her teeth, and Ryan took the moment to inspect her. Bony little body, skin the delicious color of coffee with extra cream, brown hair lit with reddish highlights and lightly kinked, wide face, too-large teeth. Abebi's brown eyes now took on an unfocused look as her attention turned to the sensation of the brush in her mouth and she forgot everything else.

Ryan looked at himself in the mirror, too, looking for resemblances between child and father. What he saw was a large guy with his shirt untucked on one side, red-brown hair that stuck up unevenly, greenish eyes that were not so much penetrating as preoccupied-looking. The nose that encouraged the Irish pub-brawler fantasies. No, he decided, looking back at Abi, beyond the McCloud jaw and the big feet there wasn't a whole lot of resemblance. Which was lucky for Abi—Jess was the one with the good looks.

Abebi: from the Nigerian, meaning *We asked for her and she came to us.* When they'd first brought home the little purplish newborn, they'd thought of her name as *a baby,* generic kid, with the mild cynicism of exhausted new parents trying to adapt to post-delivery disruption of their lives. Later, when she'd grown on them, Abi for short: *Ah, be.*

When Jess had been pregnant with Abi, he had wondered what kind of mind the child of such parents, with combined IQs of over four hundred, would have. So far, she seemed determined to thwart any expectations of brilliance, safely ensconcing herself in the middle of every developmental band except body weight. But whenever he thought about that, he concluded with certainty that, like her looks, Abebi's intellect, her development, her character, were just right. He was vastly pleased with her.

"What?" Abebi asked, through her toothbrush. Her eyes had come back into focus and now met his in the mirror. She meant *Why are you looking at me like that?*

"I'm just thinking what a beautiful girl you are and how happy I am you're my kid." He kissed her on the top of her head, grateful for her.

She shrugged slightly as if to suggest he was a bit daft, and went on brushing.

"I liked swordfighting," she said. "That was fun." Ryan had tucked her in and now sat on the floor next to the bed. With the bedside lamp dimmed, Abi became a living shadow against the white sheets. "Can you tell me a story? About swordfighting?"

"What's with the swordfighting theme tonight?"

She crossed her arms behind her head and thought about it. "I guess the thing on TV," she decided. "Those men who came into that school? They had swords."

Ryan felt a chill, realizing what she was talking about, appalled at how blasé she seemed about it. The TV news, after dinner. *Not really swords: machetes.* The dire event of the week, the Serbian paramilitaries who had launched a new terror campaign against ethnic Albanians in the Kosovo resettlement villages, attacking schools. The video that had escaped a raid, to be played and replayed on every station until the images had been burned into the collective consciousness of the world: the wild-eyed men bursting into the schoolroom. The machetes, the scattering children and overturning desks, all caught by the jerking, gyrating camera. The news anchor reciting the toll in dead and injured children.

What were you supposed to say to your kid about such things? *Yes, my beautiful daughter, there's a lot of that nowadays, get used to it.* No. You were supposed to lie, to pretend everything was fine. And hope that you got lucky and the world never proved otherwise.

"Maybe some, uh, some other subject would be better, Abi," he said, gruff-voiced. "Maybe bedtime's a time for a different—"

"I'm not scared. Please?"

Looking at her now, he had to admit that her reaction just might be the most healthy way to process what she'd seen—externalizing the fearful event, creating a manageable manifestation of it within the safe continuum of family life. Maybe she'd been born with a special talent after all, what the multiple-intelligences theorists called intrapersonal intelligence: Abebi was good at sorting out and expressing her own inner needs.

Still, he began somewhat uneasily: "Swordfighting. Hmm. Well, did I ever tell you about Musashi?"

She shook her head and settled expectantly back.

"Okay. Well, Musashi lived in Japan in the early 1600s, right at the beginning of the Tokugawa Shogunate. Back then, in Japan, the art of *kenjitsu,* what we call fencing, was taken very seriously, and—" He went on, telling her about Musashi's incredible self-taught fighting technique, with which he beat the most famous swordsmen of the era. He explained: *Kenjitsu,* Japanese swordfighting, was the science of positioning the body and the sword and using the geometry of skeletal arcs and the leverage of the sword to defend and to kill. The traditional styles or schools were very effective—but were ultimately *predictable* because through all the postures and maneuvers ran a logic based on *balance.* But when Musashi fought, he'd pivot and nearly fall and lean too far and reach too far, and an opponent never knew where his body would be, or where his sword would come from. For Musashi, balance wasn't static but rather a moving system that pitted motion against mass in surprising ways, an approach that was sometimes referred to as the 'Drunken Buddha' style. He became an *unstable system.* A number of famous athletes had exploited the same ability, like Michael Jordan and Muhammad Ali.

Warming up, Ryan continued: "Nowadays, we could describe his fighting style using the math of chaos theory. See, now we know the world doesn't function like those classical fighting postures, which for the sciences are Newtonian physics and Euclidian geometry, but rather it functions in Drunken Buddha style. In fact—"

"You know," Abi broke in conversationally, "when I spend the night at Jerome's house, or Karen's house? Their fathers or moms tell us bedtime stories, too. But usually it's something like, you know, there was a mother rabbit and her baby rabbits and they went on a picnic or something." She was looking sleepy now, but there was a little smile at the corners of her lips. "Not about like unstable systems and stuff. I thought you'd tell me about like some kitties who were musketeers or something. Stories begin with 'once upon a time,' Da."

Ryan thought back and found he wasn't sure what he'd actually said and what he'd just been thinking. "God, Abi, you're right, I—"

"But it's okay." She took his hand to comfort him, laughing at him sleepily, so much like her mother now. "It was a nice story anyway. Now I should probably go to sleep because Ma will be back soon and you'll get in trouble for keeping me up late."

Ryan laughed out loud. She caught his eye and laughed, too, and suddenly they were both laughing together, one of those priceless moments of absurd communion you got only with your skinny silly pajamaed kid. Laughing at laughing. He gave that a couple of minutes and then kissed her, cut the bedside light.

He was at the door when she called out to him: "Ma's okay, right?"

He turned. "What do you mean?"

She didn't answer right away. "She's not mad at me, is she?"

"No, of course not! What makes you think that?"

"She's been...different? Sometimes she doesn't seem like she's listening to me when I tell her things—"

Oh, that, Ryan thought. *Yes, there is that.* "She's just working very hard right now," he said, feeling increasingly unsettled. "And pregnant moms, it's like they sometimes need to focus inside themselves, see what I mean? Also, she misses her sister, and it's coming up on two years since—you know."

"Da, what's a 'premonition'?"

He wondered momentarily what leap brought her to the subject. "Well, it's when you know a certain thing is going to happen, long before it takes place. Like I had a premonition when I met Jess that I was going to marry her."

He could just see her head nod in the darkened room. "That's kind of what I thought. I think I had a premonition." She tried the word tentatively. "When I saw those men on TV—like I knew it was going to really happen someday. Like I'd really see that." Her voice had a disturbing resignation.

Ryan started back toward her. But then he thought better of probing it, of showing her his concern. Sometimes it was better to just let it go. One of the most basic lessons of being a parent, yet so hard to master.

"Go to sleep now," he commanded. "I'll never, ever, let anyone hurt you."

Chapter 11

He poured himself three fingers of Laphroaig, and took glass and bottle outside to the sea-facing deck. Leaning on the railing, he sipped some whiskey, chewed it and savored the dusty, peat-smoke warmth on his tongue. *Perfect.* Some ancestral connection, the taste of distilled malt gone bone-deep, as if laid into the genes by generations of whiskey-tippling forefathers. The burn spread from his stomach out his limbs and he gratefully accepted its calming effect.

"Premonition?" "Is Ma okay?" What the hell? He'd have to talk to Jess about it. Then suddenly he thought: *Where is Jess?* She should be home by now. He took another swig of whiskey, aware that he was a little spooked after the episode with Abi. Scaries everywhere. Already this god-damned forensic neuropsych job was snowballing, upsetting the equilibrium of the family: interviews with maniacs, Ridder's corporate hit men, Karl's killer torpedoes, they were having their effect. Especially on Jess.

The visit to Allison's grave, earlier today: On one level, Jess had done very well. She hadn't made a big thing of it. Bates had come with them to the graveyard above the Mystic River, just the three of them, Abi at school. The two men had followed behind as Jess walked up the grassy slope carrying a little spray of forget-me-nots.

Allison's gravestone was as unassuming and unpretentious as the woman buried beneath it, as graceful in its simplicity. *Beloved daughter and sister.* There really wasn't much to do once they got there. A mischievous May breeze teased their hair. Jess set her flowers on the grass, dipped her head for a moment. She rubbed the stone affectionately, almost as if it were her kid sister's head. She looked out over the river. She stooped to adjust the flowers. Then she was leading them back the way they came.

She broke down just once, at the gate, and oddly enough it was Bates who was able to comfort her: Bates looking ageless and wise, finding the right touch and word as Ryan hung back, hesitant to break into her self-imposed solitude. She had come out of it quickly, but it occurred to Ryan that maybe she was handling it *too* well, that there was too much kept locked up and hidden.

The mystery of one's wife. The contradictions and conflictions. *Every-body's half something and half something else.* On one hand, Jess was hard-working, practical, ambitious, driven, self-critical. On the other hand: whimsical, sentimental, sensual, intuitive, forgiving. She'd been born the latter, he was sure, but her family household had not been one where such traits were tolerated.

He'd become aware of the contrast the first time he'd visited her house, an impeccable Back Bay brownstone decorated with flawless antiques. For two months Ryan had sat with Jess as she wolfed food at restaurants, joking and laughing easily, he'd walked with her as she swung her arms and skipped and did dance moves down the sidewalk. But here in front of the unsmiling face of Judge Maywood she squared her shoulders and held her hands down passively at her sides. Ryan suddenly saw the whole pattern of it, the conflict inside this girl he had come to love. The origin of her covered smile.

Allison became an instant ally, but the judge didn't soften. The inevitable showdown took place that summer, on a weekend when the Maywoods had reluctantly allowed Ryan to accompany them to their cottage near Provincetown. They had all changed into swimming suits and were about to head down to the beach when the judge saw Ryan glance at the long scar that seamed his left side.

"You're wondering where I got that," the judge said. He had a big, barrel-shaped body with silver chest hair, as imposing half-naked as he was in his three-piece charcoal pinstripe.

"Sorry," Ryan began, "I didn't mean to—"

"Knife. When I was a teenager. From a bigoted, piece-of-white-trash Irish kid."

The three women froze.

Ryan's heart was pounding and he thought of a lot of things to say. "Well," he managed finally, "I may be white-trash Irish, too, but I'm not bigoted. I'm just in love with your daughter."

"We'll see," the judge said. He slapped his towel over his shoulder and started to go down the stairs.

But Jess yanked the old man's arm and spun him half around. "You've already won your fight, Judge! Nobody'll ever accuse you of being the poor *black* trash your parents were. Okay? You're a credit to your race!" Henry Maywood's face showed his rage, but Jess wasn't done. "Just so you know, I've already won, too. I've escaped the tyranny of my parents, too. Ryan and I will be together, or not, on *our* terms. Nothing you can do about it." The judge opened his mouth to respond, but Jess cut him off: "And if you had any *real* class, you'd show some courtesy to my friends! You're embarrassing all of us."

The judge's mouth shut with an audible *clop.* He turned and with regal dignity and scorn descended the long beach stairs, his wife stepping uncertainly behind him. Allison gave Jess a wavering smile before following them.

Yes, that had been a terrific day at the beach.

But he and the judge sorted it out, somewhat, a year later. Ryan had come to pick Jess up for a date, and was waiting for her to come downstairs. The judge moved around the front room, looking for something or pretending he was, a big man with intimidating eyes and that deep gravitas that made small talk impossible.

"You kids ever run into trouble when you go out?" the judge asked. He opened a bureau drawer and rummaged in it.

"Trouble?"

"Interracial couple." Judge Maywood noticed Ryan's surprise. "I dated a white girl in high school. It was tough for us."

"Not really," Ryan told him cautiously. "Odd looks, sometimes, from both sides, that's about it."

The judge nodded, pulled open another drawer. "So maybe things are a little different nowadays." From the way he said it, Ryan realized it was a larger admission: that Jess might be right, each generation faced different challenges within its family, maybe the judge's way of doing things wasn't the only way. "You know, last year, at the beach," the judge went on, still preoccupied with the contents of the drawer, "that was a father's graceless attempt to say, 'You take good care of my precious baby.' Came out badly."

Thanks, Ryan wanted to say, or maybe *I will,* or *Don't worry, that's how I heard it.* But there was Jess, skipping down the stairs, her face alive with pleasure at seeing Ryan, and as always he couldn't think of anything else but her. Still, the oblique apology helped. He and the judge had managed to maintain cordial relations in the years since.

But the truth was that Jess had only incompletely escaped the tyranny of her parents. The judge had come up the hard way, first as a poor kid who raised himself up out of a lousy family, later as a black intellectual in a white-dominated professional world, fighting for every inch of advancement. From an early age, he had held himself to the highest standards of work, deportment, cleanliness, efficiency. He served with distinction in the Marines, he was a literal-minded deacon in the City on a Hill Baptist Church. He married a woman who shared his outlook, and together they imposed the same rigors on their daughters.

But as Jess had pointed out, those uncompromising standards could be as oppressive as the prior generation's poverty and obscurity. Jess, with her brilliance and open-heartedness and physicality and sense of humor—Jess had to shake it off if she were to rise to her own, very different, standards. Which she only partly managed.

Leaning against the deck railing, pouring another shot of Laphroaig, Ryan groaned, feeling his failings as a lover. He was a lousy husband. *Got to give that side of her more room to come out. To trust itself.* They'd been so goddamned busy for twenty years—there was never enough time. Maybe he wasn't taking such good care of her. Maybe the judge was right to be concerned.

Another division in Jess: The family's stern religiosity worked for a conservative jurist and his wife, but Jess's early years of regular church-going were at odds with a high-powered scientific and humanistic education, irreverent friends at Harvard, the exhilarating explosion of scientific knowledge all around, a husband like Ryan. Where do you look for solace or hope *then*—the glorious mercy of God, or the noble aspirations of rational humanism? A recipe for internal strife. You could scoot along ignoring it most of the time, until life gave you a knock that forced you to draw upon your deepest reserves. When Allison was murdered, Jess had found herself divided, without a secure core belief to sustain her. Now that the second anniversary of her death was here, it was clear that Jess didn't know how to mourn.

Not that he himself didn't have a family whose problems he had to renounce, sibling grief stuff. Some of the religious thing, too, raised among "the bells and smells" of Roman Catholicism. But he had never liked the medieval gloom of church and had experienced mystical awe only at moments of scientific insight, like reading Gödel's gorgeous proof or Einstein's sketches on his unified field theory. But where Jess's contradictions were separated in her, each keenly and distinctly felt, Ryan had wadded his all up in the middle. His coping strategy: You put them all in a lump and tried to ignore the impenetrable wad as well as you could, you adopted a generally surly, suspicious attitude about everything but tried to be more or less decent to people despite it.

He heard the screen door slide open behind him, and he turned with relief to see her, stepping out of her shoes, tired but smiling. He put his arms around her and they kissed before she leaned back and looked him over.

"Wow," she said. "I was going to ask if the mosquitoes weren't bothering you out here. But with that much ethyl alcohol on your breath you're probably knocking 'em out of the air all the way to Gloucester."

"Haven't noticed any."

She took the glass from his hand and tasted the whiskey. "And what were your ruminations out here, dare I ask?"

"Drunken Buddha—unstable systems." The parallel cognitive track, always running. "How you can tell which phenomena are Drunken Buddha and which are just background noise, epiphenomenal or coincidental."

"And what did you figure?" She fitted herself back into the shape of his body.

He skipped the middle and gave her the end of the ellipse: "I decided Descartes was off by several degrees. 'I have a purpose, therefore I am' would have been more accurate. Your purpose orders phenomena around you. That's the only through-line. That's what makes a person's life Drunken Buddha and not just drunken."

"Seems to me there's a bit of just drunken going on, too." Jess smiled.

True, Ryan acknowledged. "How was your night?"

"Oh, just the usual end-of-semester stuff. But now I'm starving all the time—drives me a little nuts." She patted her stomach, and they shared the deck air in silence for another moment. Finally she moved against him, turning so she could see his face. "What else have you been thinking about?"

"About my wife. My marriage."

She looked away and then leaned her head onto his shoulder, more a way of avoiding his gaze than a gesture of closeness. "I know," she admitted.

"You want to tell me?"

"I'm having a hard time drawing lines," she said, angry at herself. "Between personal and professional concerns."

"Yeah," he commiserated, glad she could talk about it.

"Our basic premise is that a lot of violent behavior results from impaired brain function, right?" She paused, and Ryan knew this wasn't just shop talk. It connected directly to the ache in her, the hole in her heart. "The worst ones, anyway—rampage killers, serial murderers, disgruntled postal workers, child abusers. Do we put school shooters in this category?"

"Of course. Prime candidates, I'd say."

She nodded. "I agree. But what about terrorist violence?"

"Like the guys who killed Allison."

"Yes."

"Well, I think we need to be cautious about extending our symptomatology to violence that stems from a political cause—reasoned violence—"

"Ry, everybody has a *reason!* The kids who shoot their schoolmates 'reason' that they've been treated badly and it's time for payback, or that they'll get national press and finally stop being ignored. The postal worker 'reasons' he's been dicked around by management, and killing his co-workers will somehow set things straight. How do they differ from the men who killed Allison, or these Serbs in the Albanian school? You can't tell me that chopping up *children* with *machetes* is really part of a sane, reasoned agenda!"

Of course she was right. Instinctive, basic drives would always be the engine of human action. *Reason tags along behind impulse and emotion, like the caboose of a train pretending it's the locomotive,* Ryan thought, *justifying the insanity, making it permissible.* The history of the Holocaust was full of German "scholarship" about "the Jewish question" and "the inferiority of the darker races." American slavery, the Spanish Inquisition, the Chinese Cultural Revolution—all were justified by whole libraries of rationalization. But the root of it all was just fear, greed, hatred, lust for power. The Serbs could reason that Albanians didn't belong in Kosovo, but it still took something *fucked* upstairs to chop little kids up. Some basic instinct was supposed to recoil from hurting the young, from violence, gore, suffering, conflict. If it didn't—yes, something was very wrong.

But accept that premise, and the orderly system of the study became unbalanced, suddenly the borders were gone. How did you decide which behaviors constituted aberrations or pathologies? When did scientific analysis turn into ethical judgment?

"So what do you want to do?" he asked. "Expand the scope of Ridder's study?"

"I don't know," she said sadly. "I don't know anything."

He rocked her slowly from side to side, wishing he could take her upstairs where they could be naked and make love and together fix everything. He wanted the darkness of her body and the intriguing complexity of her secret places and the sweet smoky smell of her, and the respite from dire premonitions and basic drives gone awry and the sense that one man's purpose was an awfully fragile tool by which to shape and order a universe. But her touch was chaste, the distance coming between them again.

At last she disengaged herself from his arms. "God, I am starving," she said, turning back toward the house. "And I'll bet there's nothing in the fridge. Is there any of that pizza left?" When he didn't say anything, she stopped at the door and faced him again. "I'll sort through it," she said, looking very vulnerable now. "I promise."

Chapter 12

No two are alike, Ryan was thinking. *How're we ever going to pin down what's broken in these guys?*

He and Jess and Logan, along with prison psychologist Dr. Wyman and Hector Morales's attorney, were seated at a table in an interview room at New York's Baynard Penitentiary. Another dingy room, with metal signs telling people not to do various things and listing the statutory punishments for doing them. A large institutional clock high on the wall ticked loudly. Dr. Wyman was a used-up looking guy, slump-shouldered, as dreary as his workplace. Not considered an immediate physical danger to others, Hector Morales was sitting in a steel chair a few feet from the end of the table. Again, Jess had insisted on taking the lead, explaining to Morales the procedures they'd like to administer and what they hoped to learn.

Morales listened closely, occasionally asking questions in a well-modulated voice. He was a handsome man in his early fifties, with dark hair beginning to go gray, a small mustache, a trim body that moved with a crisp economy despite the handcuffs. Anne Sorenson, his attorney, was a tall, haughty blond wearing an expensive suit and carrying an ostrich-skin briefcase.

Seeing Morales sitting composedly with legs crossed at the knee, hands folded on his thigh, Ryan would have guessed he was in jail for some white-collar crime—embezzlement, say, or insider trading. His prison uniform was spotless and looked ironed. But he was another multiple murderer, in his own way every bit as vicious as Oakes, who had killed seven people over a period of two weeks. Three of the victims were Catholic churchgoers he'd gunned down as they returned from Mass one Sunday. One was a minister of the Millennialist Church in Buffalo, and the three others were Millennialist Church officers he'd shot when they attended the minister's burial service. In all three cases he'd done it from a distance, using a rifle with a telescopic sight. But you couldn't say he was squeamish: After his victims had fallen, Morales had come up to point-blank range and shot each between the eyes. From the medical examiner's files, Ryan had learned that human heads explode when hit by high-powered bullets fired from that close. Morales's exceptional thoroughness was proof enough of some pathology.

According to the files, Morales was a minor officer in the popular Church of Revelation and Redemption. Led by a charismatic "prophet," the Reverend Jared Constantine, the church had emerged in the 1990s, riding the wave of millennial hysteria with its apocalyptic "last days of Babel" theme. But the turn of the clock had come and gone, and the church was still growing by leaps and bounds. Constantine's television crusades were common on late-night TV, and items about the church's latest celeb converts, and latest scandals, appeared regularly in the news.

Morales had denied he'd killed under instructions from his church, and the police had never been able to prove any connection. But he readily admitted he had killed for religious reasons: His victims were "impediments to our collective salvation," and therefore his killing them constituted "self-defense." *There it is again,* Ryan thought, *reason trying to justify actions that really originate in basic, irrational drives.*

Jess had finished explaining about the functional studies with the MRI, and now asked Morales if he had any questions.

"Yes, I do," Morales said immediately. "You're a believer, aren't you? A religious person. I can see it in you."

The question surprised Jess, but she opted for candor here, wanting to enlist Morales's cooperation. "I was raised a Baptist, if that's what you mean. I have a great affection for church traditions, and I respect the value of faith. But I'm not an active member of any church. Why?"

"As a believer, you shouldn't have to run these tests on me. You should understand."

"Understand—?"

"How true belief motivates, true belief instructs. That true belief is infallible. That true belief is what separates real human beings from failed human beings."

This was going beyond the planned scope of today's interview, but Jess was quick to seize the opportunity. "Were the people you killed 'failed' human beings?"

The manacled hands gripped each other tightly as Morales leaned forward, eyes locked on Jess's. "They were far worse than that! They were obstacles to God's plan, and it was my holy duty to remove them!"

"How did you know that it was your duty?" Jess asked. Her curiosity seemed genuine, and Ryan couldn't help anticipating the reply with

interest, thinking, *If you get your instructions from little green men, we
all agree you're delusional. But what about if you get your instructions
from God?*

But Morales sidestepped the question. "You know as well as I do that
mankind is passing through a narrow and dangerous strait—I see that
knowledge in you. But what you don't yet realize is that we have one
avenue, *one,* to salvation. These people were enemies of the true church,
who did everything in their power—"

Anne Sorenson cleared her throat. "Hector—" she began. Morales
wasn't due to be executed for another three weeks. No doubt there were
still last-minute appeals pending, and she didn't want Morales's comments to throw a wrench into the works. Or maybe she was afraid he'd
say something that would, after all, incriminate the Church of Revelation and Redemption. Ryan wondered briefly who paid her fee.

Morales shook his head, declining his lawyer's suggestion to put a sock
in it. "These are desperate times. I did what was necessary to help save
humanity."

"There must be a lot of 'obstacles' in the world, Mr. Morales," Jess
said. "If you were free, would you try to kill them all?"

"Hector—" his lawyer began.

But Morales was glad to be understood. "Absolutely," he affirmed.
"Absolutely!"

Anne Sorenson had had enough. "I advise you not to continue this
conversation and not to consent to these tests! It's opening the door to
complications, to self-incrimination." She glanced angrily at Jess, as if
she'd deliberately led Hector into this unsafe territory.

But Jess countered immediately. "Hector, look at me," she said softly.
"If you don't take the tests, you will be executed with the world believing
that you are simply insane. That you have a damaged brain, and that
your belief is the product of hallucinations. Taking these tests is your
chance to prove otherwise."

Again the lawyer started to object, but Dr. Wyman decided it was time
to take control: "Hector, do you feel you have been adequately informed
about the test procedures and goals? Would you like to sign the consent
forms?"

Hector thought about it for another moment, and seemed to gain
resolve as he came to a decision. "Perhaps," he said finally. "On one condition."

Jess began: "Mr. Morales, you understand that we have no authority
to—"

"No, no, it's very simple. My condition is that you come to me, right now, here in this room. That you place your hand in my hand and make a simple contract with me." He raised his manacled hands toward Jess. Ryan noticed that they were trembling slightly.

Dr. Wyman raised a hand in protest, but then stopped uncertainly as Jess stood up. Ryan gave her a look, *Don't, Jessie,* but she ignored him. She stepped to the end of the table, approached Morales. Ryan got his feet under him, ready to lunge.

But Morales just took her hands in his, still looking at her intently. "I ask this of you because I can see that you are as dismayed and fearful and wounded as I am by what is happening to the world. To mankind."

Again Jess looked surprised. "Please tell me your condition," she prompted.

"And you are a person of faith," Morales said forcefully. "But you are hiding from yourself. So my condition for taking your tests is that you agree to take *my* test. And my test is that you inspect your soul. That you stop hiding from your soul, from the truth that you fear." For the first time, Morales seemed unbalanced, fanatical in his intensity. "I know I have nothing but your word to assure me. But I believe you are a person of your word. Do you agree?"

Jess hesitated. "I'll do my best, Mr. Morales. Yes."

He looked up at her for another moment, holding her two hands in his. Then, with a last squeeze, he released her and turned to his attorney. "Where are the forms? I'll sign them now."

They flew back to Boston without talking about the episode, but that night, back at Heart Point, Ryan couldn't hold on to it anymore. "Goddamn it, Jess! What is it with you? Are you going to get cozy with every killer we interview?"

"Please keep your voice down, Ry. Abi's asleep. She doesn't need to hear this." They were in the bedroom, Jess jotting some notes in her journal as Ryan sat on the edge of the bed. She was wearing one of his T-shirts, her usual pajamas, and looked infuriatingly beautiful as she bent over the small desk.

He went on in a furious whisper: "You're pregnant, okay, you don't know what a guy like Morales is going to—"

"Physical assault is not in his behavioral repertoire. Anyway, he's a condemned man, it meant a lot to him to feel he was contributing to my spiritual development. Plus, our interaction allowed us a firsthand look at some of his—"

"I think your compassion for killers is misplaced."

"Why? If he really does have an organic brain syndrome—isn't that our basic premise?—he's as much a victim as the people he killed! But that's not the point, Ry. He had a simple condition for giving his consent, and I very much wanted him as a subject. I think we'll learn a lot from discovering the origins of Morales's pathology—more than we can from somebody like Oakes."

"Why's that?"

She put down her pen and explained patiently: "One, because Oakes probably has ten different neural dysfunctions, and we'd never isolate the primary pathology or its etiology. Whereas in someone like Morales, otherwise normal, we can better isolate aberrant brain patterns. Right? Two, because in the long run, more violence stems from motivational profiles like Morales's than from blatantly deviant psychology like Oakes's. Meaning that what we discover will have broader applications to more social problems."

Ryan frowned. Jess was too good a rhetorician for him to score any points in a debate. Anyway, this was supposed to be about their relationship, not about the nuances of the goddamned study. The real issue was that in his evangelical fervor, Morales really had touched a nerve in Jess, had seen something in her. And she was dodging that fact now.

He was trying to decide how to bring it up when Abebi appeared in the doorway, a tottering figure in rumpled pajamas. She rubbed her eyes with one fist, squinting at her parents as if she didn't recognize them.

"Abi!" Jess said. "What, honey?"

"Had a bad dream," she mumbled miserably. She was still mostly asleep.

Jess stood up and went to her. "Oh, baby! What was your dream?"

"Don't remember," Abi said. Jess bent to her, but surprisingly Abi pushed past her, came to Ryan. He gathered her up, and she nuzzled her face against his shoulder. "I want Da to tuck me in," she said.

For an instant Ryan felt a flash of satisfaction, as if Abi's preference was some kind of vindication: *See, Jess, this is where your obsession is leading.* Immediately he disliked himself for the feeling. It was childish. Worse, it was unkind to someone going through what Jess was. He bent to let Jess kiss their daughter, then carried Abi to her bed. He could feel her body already going slack in his arms.

"It was only a dream, 'Beb," Ryan whispered. "You don't have to worry about anything. We're always right here."

Chapter 13

Wednesday morning began under the vague mental overcast always induced by unresolved marital disagreements. But then Jess came to Ryan in the hall and they made up wordlessly, with kisses and caresses. Still she stayed quiet, distant. She'd also had a bout of nausea that kept her munching saltines and feeling funky.

As soon as Abi was off to school, they went down to the Genesis offices. The sea-level story of the old marine research station had been a warren of dark, tunnel-like rooms that served as mechanical workshops and storage space for the assorted tools and technologies of oceanic research. They still called it the Catacombs, but when they remodeled they put in big windows on the sea-side, made it spacious and comfortable for the four head researchers and four support personnel who made up the rest of Genesis's core staff. A pleasant lobby and conference room faced the bay; farther in were several offices, a staff kitchen and lounge, and then Leap's data-processing studio, windowless and set well into the bluff. The morning was devoted to working with the secretarial staff on a preliminary draft of the Four Corners report—dictating, indexing component documents, verifying citations, agreeing on language. The boring phase.

After lunch, they found Leap sitting in the data-processing control room, fiddling with a mouse and looking through the glass wall at the brighter room that housed Genesis's main computer. Installing the lab back here had helped simplify security and atmosphere control, but it also created the kind of semidark environment that made Ryan claustrophobic. Leap, though, seemed to thrive in it—apparently the video monitors, the VR goggles, the banks of glowing LEDs and controls, were windows enough for him.

As they came in, Leap's ferret, Sneaky Pete, slipped through the plastic tunnels that linked its cages, popped out, and leaped onto Leap's shoulder.

"One word, folks," Leap said. *"Petaflops.* And soon."

Leap was already off and running, answering questions that hadn't been asked. He was wearing a hooded sweatshirt with ATF stenciled on the back above a yellow smiley face, cut-off shorts, black high-top sneakers. As always, he was chewing gum rapidly.

Now he tapped in a command and watched as the LEDs began to blink in the computer room. He had named his rig Argus after the watchful herdsman of Greek mythology, who was said to have a thousand eyes. *Flops* were floating-point operations, the number of separate calculations a computer could perform in a second. Lovingly designed and assembled by Leap, Argus was a hundred-gigaflops computer, capable of up to a hundred billion operations a second. The DOE lab at Sandia had built the first teraflops, Janus, in 1997, and now had the country's first petaflops, ten thousand times more powerful than Argus. Though the Janus II supercomputer was mostly committed to military projects, Genesis and the Four Corners consortium had arranged to use it to test and apply RAINDROP. Leap was saying that they'd be ready for the RAINDROP trials at Sandia soon.

It always took a moment to adapt to Leap, to his shorthand communication, the ellipses—yes, the leaps—required when talking to him. Around Leap, Ryan had to overcome the sense of moving in slow motion. Born Philippe Ferrer, Leap had once been a notorious teen hacker in France, wanted for a number of spectacular if ultimately harmless computer crimes. After fleeing to the United States, he had spent ten years constructing a virtual identity as Phillip Rivers, with a life history as an American citizen that was completely intact, completely mundane—and completely bogus. They'd brought him onto the team for his exceptional talents as a mathematician and statistician, but Ryan couldn't deny that his invisibility and hacking skills had served them well on several occasions.

"So Ry," Leap said, "I did a little digging into the possible long-term neurotoxic agents your friend Karl suggested."

"Yeah?" Ryan said uneasily. Leap's "doing a little digging" raised a tingle of concern. Leap was easily tempted, and wasn't concerned about the fine points of legality.

Leap waited until Sneaky Pete had poured down to the pouch of his sweatshirt, and then handed Jess some printouts. "All three look good to me. Borna and related viruses attack central nervous systems. Used to be found only in horses, but they've adapted to human metabolisms. Now there's evidence that Bornaviridae play a role in depression and other human neurological conditions. Can live undetected in the brain for years, then manifest as a variety of symptoms from mild depression to complete meltdown. The rabies virus is so small it can travel through the neurons of the brain, mimicking neurotransmitters and screwing up brain metabolism. It's thought there are many rabieslike viruses, as well as prions like the one that causes that bovine brain-meltdown, that could cause human brain pathologies."

"How about the others?" Jess asked, scanning the pages.

Looking over her shoulder, Ryan could see that Leap had pulled up some good data on the endocrine disruptors, too. The most concentrated sources were man-made, chemicals such as the polychlorinated biphenyls found in pesticides, or bisphenol-A, found in plastics, flame retardants, adhesives. Mercury, lead, tin, cadmium, and other metals screwed up the endocrine system, too. All were capable of causing brain damage in fetuses, infants, and adults. Even at low exposures, they were known to affect the brain and hormonal systems and cause behavioral dysfunctions, including aggressiveness. There were plenty of natural sources, too: groundwater, soil dust, and many fruits and vegetables.

"Anything on electromagnetic fields?" Jess asked.

Leap turned away to his controls. "I was just getting to that. Here—take a look." On the screen a string of digits appeared, resolving almost instantly into letters and words. It appeared to be a summary of a scientific study:

> ...left prefrontal repetitive transcranial magnetic stimulation...changes in relevant phase baseline of Hamilton scale...2.45 Ghz at 1 mW/cm2 of body surface with a specific absorption rate of 1.18 W/kg of body mass...presenting as schizoaffective with somatic manifestations including excitability, irritability, confusion...

Leap's eyes popped wide in guilty surprise. Ryan wondered if Jess had caught the implication of the digits: This had been encrypted data. Meaning that Leap had been rummaging in somebody's forbidden treasure house.

Jess frowned but didn't comment. "You want to summarize?"

"Most studies of EMFs focus on cancer risks from high-tension power lines, radio and TV broadcasting, cell phones, microwaves, workplace exposures. But in recent years there's been a lot of research into behavioral effects. In tests, monkeys have been made to get violent when exposed to strong magnetic fields or microwaves. They're also using magnetic fields to treat depression in humans, and have experimentally *induced* it. Let me print some of this out." He tapped his keyboard, and one of the printers began warming up. "Again, the most powerful sources are man-made, but there are natural sources, too: the Earth's magnetic fields, sunspots, electrical storms—"

"So where'd you get this, Leap?" Jess asked, nodding toward the screen. The sweetness of her voice was terrifying.

"Well, a lot of it's public domain. *Scientific American,* journals like *Psychotechnology*—"

"That was encrypted data—not *Popular Science*!" Jess stabbed a finger at the monitor. "For heaven's sake, Leap, we've been through this! We're willing to stretch the rules a little for the right reasons. We're *not* willing to invite legal problems because you've hacked into—"

"Sure you are," Leap countered. "You just want to be sure it's on behalf of a good cause, and that you've got a good chance of getting away with it! Jess, Ry, believe me when I say the precautions I've taken beat anything anybody anywhere, can do." He went on to tell them about some hacking technique he'd designed, involving a combination of microwave phone taps, handheld computers, cellular relays to Argus's enormous power, hermetic prophylaxis against traces.

Jess waved her hands to cut him off. "Leap! We need to be very clear on this. *No illegal digging.* If and when anything like that is required, we do it under guidelines and by a set of protocols that Ryan and I will design—and that *you will adhere to!*" She shook her head and turned to Ryan. "Ry, you should have known better than to...to wave enticing morsels in front of *Leap,* of all people, without *very* clear ground rules about how we do and do *not* get our information!"

For a strained moment nobody said anything. Then Leap clapped his hands. "Emotions—ain't carbon-based life grand?" But his grin seemed strained.

"What else, Leap?" Ryan asked. "What's bothering you?"

Leap flicked his dark hair off his forehead and turned back to his controls, but he didn't say anything for a moment—an uncharacteristic hesitation. Sneaky Pete oozed out of the sweatshirt pouch, slid like a shadow up Leap's chest to perch again on his shoulder.

"Torpedoes," Leap said finally. In the dim light of his studio, his face looked greenish and sorrowful. Sneaky Pete seemed to be whispering in his ear. "I found one, Ry."

Shit, Ryan thought. He had talked to Leap about it, but had wanted to avoid telling Jess about Karl's warning, at least until he had more information.

"Torpedoes?" Jess echoed, perplexed.

Leap twitched visibly when he realized she didn't know about it: the discomfort of a man who had stumbled into someone else's relationship issues.

Ryan blundered through an explanation: military programs, human killing machines, programmed assassins. Jess listened until she'd gotten the gist of it, then cut him off. "Ryan, will you *please* stop protecting me? I know that human beings can be vicious, nasty creatures. I *got* that, okay? We're professionals, we need to incorporate this...this *torpedo* business into our thinking." She tugged her hair back from her forehead in exasperation. But after a moment she relented, shaking her head, putting a hand on Ryan's forearm. Sweet forgiveness. "Okay. You're being gallant. I can see why you'd keep it from me just now. Okay. So give me the scoop, Leap."

Leap summarized: According to documents released through the Freedom of Information Act, some high-credibility mainstream press sources, some private lab data he'd tapped into, the U.S. government had conducted hundreds of research projects into behavioral modification since the 1950s. Most were classified, but some had leaked over the decades, including the "torpedo" experiments, which got national attention, briefly, when several surviving "guinea pigs" brought lawsuits against the Army in the 1980s. Citing national security concerns, the Army had never admitted anything, and the lawsuits had faded away. But the issue still cropped up periodically. Leap had found recent papers by several prominent psychologists who claimed that the serial killer Arthur Shawcross was a "manufactured personality," an Army Intelligence–created torpedo who had returned from Vietnam after being an MKULTRA guinea pig but had never recovered from his programming. Once back in the U.S., Shawcross had killed ten women and done terrible things to their bodies, including eating parts of them. The doctors who ran the initial brain scans said they found two tiny scars on his frontal lobes, symmetrically positioned as if from a surgical process, Leap said. But the scan prints themselves were now "lost," along with Shawcross's Army records, and neurologists asking for access to the killer for further testing were always turned down by prison officials. It all pointed to a cover-up.

This was getting horrible, Ryan thought. Tinkering with the human brain to make monsters, government cover-ups—the project was taking on some very scary dimensions. Karl was right: They'd have to be careful here, both scientifically and politically. He blew air out through his lips, thinking that a drink would be nice. The invigorating burn of whiskey.

For a moment they digested what Leap had told them, saying nothing. Sneaky Pete retreated down Leap's back, skittered along the counter, and slid back into its cage.

"It's so *shitty,*" Jess said at last. "It's just so *fucked up.* God damn them! God damn us all." Jess was no admirer of the weapons R&D establishment in general, but Ryan couldn't remember ever having seen her like this: seething with anger, but at the same time devastated, injured again. The torpedo thing was yet another indictment against any presumed "goodness" of humanity.

"On the bright side," Jess went on, "this means that somewhere there's a body of research on the neurology of violence, specific and reliable enough to induce violent behaviors on demand. We don't have to reinvent the wheel here, these torpedo initiatives can tell us which parts of the brain are involved, or..." She petered out, not all that enthused by the bright side. But after another moment her face took on a determined frown. "Okay. Thanks, Leap. You're right, we'll need to think through this. Will you print off what you've found?"

"Yup."

They were done for now. Ryan went into the hall, but at the doorway Jess turned back. "You heard me, though, right? Tell me this is clear, Leap: *no hacks.*" A steely voice.

Leap nodded unhappily. "Clear."

In the hall, she stalked ahead of Ryan, chin on her chest, heels loud on the tiles. "Not yet, anyway," she muttered to herself.

Chapter 14

"**Hello, Dr. McCloud,** it's Alex Shipley, returning your call. What can I do for you?"

Though it had been almost six years since he'd last talked to Shipley, Ryan recognized the voice immediately: bland and pleasant and gray, like Shipley, just a little oily. After meeting with Ridder last week, he had stewed over Shipley's lapse of confidentiality about Genesis's Secret Service work, and had finally put in a call to the "black acquisitions" administrator's number in Northern Virginia. The NSA secretary he'd spoken to took a message without actually acknowledging that Shipley existed.

"What you can do for me is explain why Jason Ridder knows about a project we had to sign oaths in blood never to talk about."

"Oh, Jason," Shipley said affectionately. "Tsk. Jason and I go way back."

"Yeah, he told me. *I* go way back with lots of people, too. So it's okay if I tell them—"

Shipley cleared his throat. "Tell you what, Dr. McCloud. By all means, let's talk about this. But not over the phone, if you don't mind."

"I don't have time to come to Washington, so unless you're—"

"I'm in Boston right now. I'd be happy to meet you. Today."

Ryan felt the cold splash of suspicion. "What brings you to Boston?"

"Oh, we maintain a field office here," Shipley assured him pleasantly. "As you can imagine, it helps to have facilities close to contractors."

Of course, Ryan thought. Shipley's title was "Deputy Coordinator, DIRI." The acronym stood for Defense and Intelligence Research Initiatives, and from their meetings six years ago, Ryan deduced that Shipley's job was to oversee certain scientific research contracts made by the NSA. Though the motion-variable analysis and crowd-scanning protocols Genesis had developed for the Service were intended to defend the President and other leaders from attack, Shipley had been interested in possible applications to intelligence work and urban crowd control. Ryan and Jess had only grudgingly shared data with his office. The thing that really pissed Ryan off was that in order to take the Service job, Genesis had submitted to an exhaustive and very intrusive security check. Since Shipley presumably had all that information, he was in a position to tell Ridder just about *everything,* down to the color of Ryan's boxer shorts.

Ryan checked his watch. Eleven-thirty. He had other errands to do in the city later, and could pry free an hour to get this cleared up. Shipley gave him an address and they agreed to meet in two hours.

When Ryan turned in to the street-level entryway, he was startled to come face to face with Shipley, a lighter shade of gray standing motionless in the shadows. Ryan had puzzled over why the NSA would keep an office on Newbury Street, of all places, but finding Shipley waiting for him put it suddenly into perspective. Shipley had simply picked a very public address for their rendezvous. The spook had no intention of letting an outsider, even one with security clearance, know where his local office was.

"Didn't mean to surprise you," Shipley said. He smiled, pale lips making a broad, thin line. He was dressed in a nondescript gray suit, pale blue shirt, wallpaper tie—a career bureaucrat's uniform. In one hand he held a little bag of caramel corn, something he'd obviously picked up from one of the candy stores on Newbury. With his other hand he steered Ryan back into the muted sunshine and down the sidewalk toward the Boston Common. "It's just such a nice day, I thought we could meet outside, have our chat as we walked."

Actually, it wasn't a nice day. The sky was hazed with a thin overcast, and the air was sticky with humidity. A faint smell of burning plastic filled the air, blowing in from some outlying factory.

The lunch rush had passed, but Newbury Street was still bustling with the tourists and suburban professionals who thronged the outdoor cafés. The brightly painted historic wooden buildings, mostly galleries and gift shops and restaurants, were well preserved but too cute by half for Ryan's taste.

"Caramel corn?" Shipley asked. He proffered the yellow-striped bag.

"Listen, I've only got an hour—"

"And you're angry with me. Well, vent if you must."

"It's not a matter of venting. I thought about calling Barringer to talk about your being so close to Ridder. Thought I'd get an explanation from you first." Burt Barringer was the Secret Service officer who had served as chief liaison with Genesis.

Shipley stopped walking, and with his free hand took out a tiny cellular phone. "Please, call him. Here." He flipped it open. "Got the number on memory."

Ryan dismissed the offer and kept walking. Shipley walked right at Ryan's shoulder, leaning his head close, so that although he wasn't whispering it would be hard for any passersby to overhear. He held the little yellow bag stiffly in front of him, the only color on his person, and Ryan saw that it was his passport to the normal world, a little disguise appropriate to the bustle and gaiety of Newbury Street.

"The explanation you're looking for," Shipley went on, pocketing the phone again, "is hardly sinister. Jason Ridder is more than a good friend of mine."

"Meaning what, he's somebody else's friend, too, or he's got other roles beside being a buddy?"

"Both." Shipley seemed pleased with Ryan's astuteness. He paused to admire a shop window full of antique brass, then turned back and continued his leisurely stroll. "You're welcome to call Barringer anytime. In fact, I can give you a summary of what he'll tell you. In a nutshell, Jason Ridder plays a large role in the world. He has his finger in a lot of pies. We can't control him, especially in these, ah, post-public-sector days, but naturally it behooves us to maintain a friendly and reciprocal relationship with him and others of his, ah, station. He has…been of service to his country on several occasions."

"And I suppose his country has been of service to him."

"Naturally." Shipley seemed oblivious to Ryan's sarcasm. "So we're accustomed to fairly candid communications. My comments about your Service work were perfectly well intended, and very general. And Jason understands that certain information is…not for general consumption."

No reply seemed required, so Ryan just walked on. Even with his jacket off, the air felt hot, and sweat began to tickle his forehead and underarms. By contrast, Shipley was completely dry, almost dusty looking.

After another minute, Shipley spoke up again. "Now, if you feel you've scolded me sufficiently, I have two little agenda items myself. Coincidentally. First, I'm very interested in the study you're doing for Jason."

"Why? Cutting too close to one of your pet projects?"

They had come to Arlington Street. On the other side, the green expanse of the Public Gardens opened: wide lawns and winding sidewalks, shadowed by soaring elms.

"Let's go have a seat at the lagoon," Shipley said. "Such a nice day." He raised his nose and sniffed the smoky air as if it were ambrosial.

They cut through stalled traffic to the park. On the benches surrounding the lagoon, well-dressed professionals ate bag lunches, and at the edge of the water tourists tossed chunks of bread to clamoring ducks. Kids ran on the paths, dodging the occasional roller-blader. Shipley found them a bench well separated from the others, and took a seat, carefully hitching his trousers before crossing his legs. Sick of having the Gray Ghost at his ear, Ryan sat at the other end of the bench.

"Certainly a man of your intelligence can imagine the possible relevance of the project to defense-related concerns," Shipley said.

"Why don't you tell me about that? Not my field."

Shipley looked over at him, and Ryan saw a flash of impatience in his eyes, quickly covered. "Are you always so truculent? I thought we had established a good rapport when we worked together before." The wide, thin, humorless smile.

Rapport? That was almost funny. Ryan pointedly checked his watch. "If you want information about our study, you can always get it from Ridder. Since you're such good friends and go so far back."

Again the flash of irritation, quickly suppressed. Beneath Shipley's soft exterior, his guise as the Invisible Bureaucrat, there lurked a hard, determined presence.

"Thank you, Dr. McCloud, I had already considered that fact. But I have to wonder why you are so suspicious of me, of my agency. We are committed, *absolutely* committed, to the safety and well-being of the United States. This project, and your last one, bears directly upon matters of national security. How? It's common knowledge that as a nation we face threats from enemies who are perfectly willing to use terrorism as a political instrument. We are at risk from biological and chemical weapons attacks. A biological outbreak, in, say New York, of weaponized microorganisms, could kill millions before we knew what hit us. Yes, your RAINDROP program could be the one thing that saves us. But—and I can understand your reluctance to accept this irony—RAINDROP could also be used by an enemy to calculate the most effective way to *deploy* a bioweapon, couldn't it? In either case, it's a defense-related technology and is therefore under our purview. And whether you like it or not, your research into the neurology of violence could turn up all kinds of new ideas that hostile nations or terrorists could turn into weapons technologies. Don't think they aren't interested! Don't think they won't be watching!"

Ryan absorbed it, not disagreeing. *Terrific,* he thought. *Terrorists.* Another scary to look out for. But he couldn't resist a jab at Shipley: "New ideas like torpedoes?"

"Torpedoes?"

"Human killing machines. Neurologically programmed assassins. I understand it's a vernacular term in your line of work."

Shipley laughed. "Paranoid fringe! The stuff of dreams! Really, Dr. McCloud, I'm surprised—I mean, a scientist of your stature—"

"Hey, Shipley, since you and I have such rapport and I'm a scientist of such stature, how'd you like to get us access to Arthur Shawcross? Arrange for us to do some tests on him?"

For the first time, Shipley couldn't suppress a momentary expression of discomfort. But he regrouped quickly, not so much changing the subject as switching to the offensive: "Perhaps we should move on to the second item on my agenda. A report crossed my desk, sent to me by one of my contractors, a private lab in Florida. It seems one of their databases was hacked, very skillfully, a few days ago? They were unable to trace the hack, except to place its origin in the Boston area. North of Boston, actually. A flag popped up, you know how it is."

Shit, Ryan thought. So that's where Leap had gotten that encrypted file, something about the neurological effects of electromagnetic exposure. He kept his face immobile, but a glint of satisfaction passed over Shipley's face as he read Ryan's reaction.

"I don't know anything about it," Ryan lied.

"Of course not," Shipley agreed. "But I suppose the lesson is that these can be…dangerous waters. That there are all kinds of people who would like access to the type of information you'll be gathering. That nobody's safe from intrusion. Hmm? Something to keep in mind." The words were soft, but the hard thing surfaced again on Shipley's face.

"Is that what this meeting is about? You warning me to stay away from this stuff?"

Shipley looked aghast. "Warning? My interest here is entirely benevolent! We're on the same side here, aren't we? Aren't we?"

Ryan wondered about that. They sat there for a while, Shipley still holding the bag of caramel corn on one knee and looking rather satisfied with himself. A siren hooted by on Arlington Street, and heads turned to watch the ambulance zig and zag through traffic. Ryan thought to probe Shipley further, but decided that they had each made their points.

When Ryan got up, Shipley stood with him. "I'll walk you back to your car," the Gray Ghost volunteered. "It's so nice to spend time with you again. Always such stimulating conversation. Please stay in touch. And you will say hello to Jessamine for me?"

They left the park. On the way out, without having tasted even one kernel, Shipley dropped his caramel corn into a trash barrel.

Chapter 15

Saturday got off to a good start, promising some much-needed distraction. On Thursday, a nor'easter had come in from the North Atlantic, knocking down an old white birch that had anchored the yard at the edge of the bluff. Ryan had been particularly fond of the tree, but it didn't hurt to have some firewood, and the weather had blown away the smog that had hung over the area since his meeting with Shipley. A few hours of working hard in the wind-scoured air would be a nice antidote for the accumulating complexities of the Ridder job, the boring final details of the Four Corners commission.

He used the chain saw to trim away the smaller branches, which he dragged to a burn pile at the edge of the woods. But then it occurred to him that, in a big tree like this, a deciduous tree with radial brachiation, the mass at any cross-section from roots to buds would be roughly equal. At the lowest extreme, the millions of hairlike rootlets would add up to about the same volume as the thickest part of the trunk, as would the thousands of fine branch tips or any point in between.

He returned to the garage and got a tape measure, a hammer and a nail, and a ball of string. The root mass was unavailable, but the above-ground section shouldn't be too hard to figure. He drove the nail into the main trunk just above the bole, tied the string to it, and let out line so he could scribe an arc through the branches at three representative distances. By measuring the cut ends at each arc, he could calculate their collective cross-sectional area. If his theory was right, it should come out about the same at each line.

At the nail, the old birch was thirty inches in diameter, giving him a cross-sectional area of about 706.86 square inches. At the first major brachiation, ten feet farther up, the trunk divided into three big branches that yielded a cross-sectional area of 709.81 inches.

Less than four-tenths of a percent deviation! Ryan thought excitedly. He resolved to get out and do yard work more often, and was just starting to make cuts along the second arc when Jess came out with the telephone.

She looked over his operation, covered her smile with one hand, gave him the phone. "Dagan," she mouthed.

Ryan killed the chain saw. "Hey," he said into the receiver.

"Hi. I've run into some interesting data that I think you guys should see." Dagan had a warm, melodic telephone voice, even with the lousy transmission of the radio phone. "Can I bother you today? Jess says it's fine, but she wanted me to ask you."

"Of course. C'mon out. We're doing yard work."

Dagan laughed. "Yeah, Jess told me about your idea of yard work," she said.

With Dagan due in an hour, Ryan decided to forgo the rest of his experiment, and got to work bucking the firewood. Big wheels of yellow wood rolled away as the chain saw spewed a steady fountain of chips, and soon the tree lay flat in crooked lines of stove-length segments, turning the lawn into a dinosaur boneyard. Then came the best part, swinging the heavy maul, *pow!,* watching the split chunks cartwheel away across the grass, breathing the library-paste odor of birch sap. Jess was working on the rosebushes, Abi was scooting around the yard with her friend Jerome, an equally skinny neighbor kid. *A typical day at the McClouds' of Heart Cove, Massachusetts,* he thought gratefully, horsing another wheel of tree trunk into position. This was nice.

Dagan came around the house, carrying a fat briefcase. She was wearing jeans, a white blouse, and a seersucker jacket with the sleeves rolled up. Her dark hair tossed crazily in the buffeting breeze as she looked around the yard, squinted out at the bay, grinning. "Hi, fatty," she teased Jess.

"Well, you certainly have got that look, D.," Jess said. She reached over and tucked a strand of Dagan's wild hair behind her ear. "This must be a good one."

Ryan rolled over some unsplit slabs and tipped them onto their flats, and the three of them sat down.

"Have you guys ever heard of 'Syndrome E'?" Dagan asked. When they shook their heads, she rummaged in the briefcase and handed Jess a sheaf of papers. "You can read about it in there, but the skinny is this. The hypothesis was first floated about five years ago by a guy named Itzhak Fried, neurosurgeon out at UCLA Medical Center. He makes a good case that a particular brain disorder is the root cause of violence—

not just the acts of individuals, but widespread social violence. Basically, he blames epidemics of Syndrome E for extreme violence, genocide, atrocities in war—the Holocaust, Pol Pot, Rwanda, East Timor, Bosnia, Kosovo. Symptomatology is repetitive violence, obsessive ideas, diminished affective reactivity—lack of usual emotion about killing. What else? Compartmentalization, the ability to stuff kids into gas chambers from nine to five and return home to a cheery supper with your own family after work. Oh yes, and group contagion—Syndrome E is *catching*." Dagan's mouth drew down. She had kept her tone light, but the topic clearly wasn't easy for her to get distance on.

Ryan leaned close to Jess as she looked over the material. The first pages were photocopies of Dr. Itzhak Fried's original paper in *The Lancet:*

> A pathophysiological model—"cognitive fracture"—is hypothesized, where hyperaroused orbitofrontal and medial prefrontal cortices tonically inhibit the amygdala and are no longer regulated by visceral and somatic homeostatic controls....

Jess frowned. "Looks like a credible paper. Anything to support it?"

Dagan nodded, her excitement returning. "As far as etiology goes, clinical literature suggests several causative agents. The big three we know about already—viral brain pathogens, endocrine-disrupting chemicals, and electromagnetic fields." She took the papers, peeled back several pages, found what she was looking for, handed it back to Jess. "The most interesting angle for me here is the central idea—the concept of neuroepidemics. The first solid studies of widespread neurological impairments were the heavy-metals projects done in the sixties, most of them focusing on lead. Low-level lead poisoning resulted in widespread neurological and behavioral disorders in children born during the fifties and sixties. A good case can be made that the violent-crime wave that peaked in the seventies and eighties resulted largely from high environmental lead levels in the preceding twenty, thirty years. Oh, and there're even a couple of good papers about a previous lead 'epidemic'—the fall of Rome. Apparently the upper classes liked to eat off lead dinnerware and sweeten their wine with lead. Which is why guys like Nero and Caligula and the rest of the ruling class went nuts and let the empire fall apart. Fifteen hundred years later, a couple of generations of Americans were more prone to violent crime because they'd been exposed to lead in car exhaust and house paint! You have to wonder how many other neurotoxins are affecting us. What really amazes me is how little we know about this—I mean, can you believe we split the atom and put men on the moon before we noticed that lead was a neurotoxin?!"

When Dagan was on a roll, her excitement was contagious. Now her eyes flashed, and the wind had brought color to her cheeks. Ryan could share with her the thrill of discovery, but at the same time he felt a wave of anxiety come over him. The lines that had delimited their study of violence were eroding fast. He had a sense, almost a prescient awareness, of the course of things changing.

Jess had changed as she speed-read the papers and listened to Dagan. Her summer-day serenity was gone, replaced by the distant, hard-edged focus that Ryan had been seeing more and more of. When Abi and Jerome came tearing around the corner of the house, screaming like crazies, she turned to them and called out, "Kids! I want you to go in and eat some lunch now. I made sandwiches—on the kitchen counter. Go! And wash your hands first!"

She turned back to Dagan. "I don't want Abi to hear what we're talking about," she explained. "On this job especially, we've got to insulate our family life from our work. It's hard enough to protect her from this kind of stuff, just with the damned TV news." She frowned at the papers again. "So where do you think we should go with this?"

Dagan had seen the change in Jess, and when she spoke again she seemed a little more cautious. "Well, I'm still sorting out the implications. But I guess the most immediate ramification for our research is deciding what forms of violence meet our criteria. Right? For our subject population, are we going to stay with violent criminals and psychiatric patients with violence disorders? Or do we start looking at terrorists, war criminals, um, I don't know, mercenary soldiers.... And for social trends that could result from neurological disorders, forget crime waves—do we include wars, civil conflicts, riots, revolutions? Religious persecution? Yikes!"

As usual, Dagan had hit the nail on the head. One of the most difficult challenges they'd face would be to determine which behaviors and social trends they would decide were indicative of a brain disorder, and would deem appropriate to study.

They talked about it for a while, Dagan getting more and more excited, Jess seeming to withdraw. At last Dagan stood up, brushed off the back of her jeans, and stretched her arms wide. "Well," she said. "I'm going down to the 'Combs to do some online work. I hope this is okay—I mean, I probably shouldn't have barged in—" She was looking at Ryan as if she realized that the topic would get to Jess, asking his forgiveness.

Ryan smiled at her. "No, this is fine. Good work, Dagan. Why don't you plan on giving a presentation to the crew sometime next week? We'll figure out where we should go with it."

Jess just gave Dagan a wan smile and tugged affectionately at her jacket hem, then let her go, down the bluff to the offices.

"Jesus, she's a smart kid," Jess said. He knew what she meant: Dagan was moving up fast, maturing cognitively, becoming more assertive about developing her own research initiatives.

Jess went inside to check on Abi and Jerome. Ryan got started hauling and stacking the firewood, again feeling that nagging itch of prescience, a sense of impending threat that he couldn't define. Wondering where all this was going.

Chapter 16

Ryan had always believed that coincidences could usually be explained through the simple but sometimes startling laws of probability. And if they couldn't, synchronicities were best viewed not as anomalies but simply as features of a pattern that was not yet fully perceived or understood. Still, seeing the TV revival so soon after hearing about the Syndrome E hypothesis put his beliefs to the test.

Late that night, after Abi had gone to bed, he sat at the kitchen counter, sipping whiskey and jotting thoughts on a yellow legal pad. Jess took a bath and then came into the living room, turned on the TV, sat on the couch. She wore only blue jeans and a thick towel wrapped around her head. Unconscious of her effect on Ryan, she leaned against the back of the couch so that her breasts rose at what felt to him like a provocative angle.

"Come take a look, Ry," she called. She held an arm out to him, beckoning him to join her. "It's Constantine. The evangelist—the guy Hector Morales is so devoted to."

Ryan sat next to her as she used the remote to bring up the volume. On the screen, a tall man stood in front of a purple curtain, bracketed by large vases of flowers. The camera zoomed in for a close-up of his face, young but gaunt, with a burning gaze that he bored into the homes of his viewers.

"I know why you have joined us here tonight," Constantine said into his cordless microphone. "You're watching because you are *scared*."

"How about *curious*, Reverend?" Ryan said.

"You're with us tonight because you know something is *wrong*. Because you're worried about what's in store for yourself and your kids. Because in your heart of hearts you're getting desperate. And you don't hear anyone admitting what's happening, you know the politicians aren't doing anything about it and the police aren't doing anything about it, and the scientists sure are not doing anything about it. Because you know it can't go on, you need some *answers*."

The camera cut to a large auditorium, where perhaps five thousand people sat, rapt with attention. It zoomed in on the somber face of a well-dressed elderly man, then a middle-aged Asian woman, then a blond teenage girl who nodded, brows knit. Then back to Constantine, who had ratcheted up his confidence one notch.

"Well, *I'm* here tonight to talk about that fear that's eating at you, *I'm* here to speak to your heart of hearts. I'm here to face the obvious, and I'm here to show you what you can *do* about it!" The prophet's voice had risen until it was almost a shout, and then he stabbed the air with a forefinger and stopped abruptly, leaving the hall reverberating with the intensity of his feeling. When the echoes had died, he said quietly, "But, my friend, be forewarned, it's not going to be easy. It's going to require more honesty and courage than most of us are used to. All I ask is that you hear me out with an open mind and an open heart. Can I ask that of you? Can I?" He looked gratified when the audience murmured its assent.

"Stimulus progression," Ryan said. "Affect rotation." Standard revival-tent techniques for capturing and retaining an audience's attention.

Jess just nodded as she found the remote and thumbed the volume up again.

The camera pulled back to show Constantine, isolated on the stage, where he began to walk, side to side. He was wearing cowboy boots, Ryan noticed, and a hip sportcoat that hung well on his slim frame, and he handled his radio mike with practiced skill. With a different script, he could have been a sophisticated country-and-western singer, an underfed Garth Brooks.

Pacing, Constantine went on. "I know what you've been thinking because I've been thinking it, too. You've been thinking, 'Gee, my neighborhood is falling apart, the streets aren't safe anymore.' Or maybe 'Gosh, America is getting polarized, I wish those Democrats and Republicans would quit fighting and get to work running this country right.' Or maybe 'Gee, the world is going to pieces, look at that nightmare in Kosovo or Congo, what's the matter with these people?' Or 'Gee, I hardly know my wife or my husband anymore, gee, I feel so alone.' One or the other of these has hit you where you live, right? And you know that there's nothing *sadder* than feeling a barrier between you and your loved ones, nothing *scarier* than seeing the society around you get angrier and more divided. Nothing more *terrifying* than the unrest and upheaval we see in so much of the world. You've laid awake wondering just when some weirdo group is gonna bomb your post office, or the airplane you're flying on tomorrow. You've heard the knock at the door, or seen the shadow at the window, and you've felt the fear, you've wondered if it's

somebody gonna rob or hurt you, or come for you because of your religious belief, or the color of your skin, or the way you wear your hair.
You've been waiting for a bus and found yourself surrounded by people
of another race, or another income bracket, and you've wondered, 'Are
they looking at me funny? Is this gonna be okay?' Or you've been doing
the ironing and watching the TV news about another—*another!*—school
shooting and you've thought, 'Oh dear God, is my baby okay?'"

Constantine stopped and addressed the live crowd with arms spread.
"Can you say you haven't felt these things?" Now he faced the camera: "I
ask again, can even *one* of you honestly say you haven't felt these things?!"
He waited as his shout echoed, outrage and mock expectancy on his
sweat-sheened face.

Jess pouted. "Well, he does have a point."

Ryan hit the remote's mute button, starting to feel concerned about
Jess's absorption, wanting to deflect some of the impact of Constantine's
spiel. "There was an article in *The New Yorker* a couple of weeks ago—I
didn't really read it, but it seemed to be saying the guy's more of a con
man than a—"

"I'd really like to hear this," Jess said. She took the remote from his fingers, brought the sound up again.

Constantine had pulled back, gathering his powers again. "And I
know you can't help but look at the TV news, all that ethnic cleansing
and refugees and atrocities, and wonder how soon it's gonna happen here
in America! You look around and you can feel it heading this way! You
can't help but wonder what's it like to live in a place when it's not just one
person here, one person there, but whole groups, whole *armies,* going
wacko like this. Well, I'll tell you what that's all about! It's about
pogroms, and persecution. It's about food not getting to your grocery
store! It's about you turn on the tap and no water comes out because that
reservoir thirty miles out of town?—that reservoir is now in the hands of
somebody that doesn't want you to have water! It's about getting into
your car to escape and finding that there's no gas at the pumps, and the
roads have been cut, and believe me, if you've got engine trouble there's
no breakdown truck gonna come for you. *You are out there alone on the
highway to hell!*"

Constantine pulled into himself again. Gently now, quietly, sadly:
"Can any one of you say you haven't thought about this, seen we were
heading that way, feared it in your heart of hearts?" He appeared to look
into individual faces in the crowd, finding the answer in them: "No.

No. No." Again the camera picked out sober faces, shaking heads, a mother holding her child protectively, a brawny young man wiping his forehead.

Abruptly Constantine reared back and roared: "So I have to ask of you: Is that any way to live?! *Is that any way to live!* And the answer is *no,* it is *not* what God our Father intended for His children when He created Adam, it is *not* any way for a human being to live!" The crowd began to answer with him, *no, no, no sir.*

Ryan and Jess had both startled at his sudden change of intensity, and Ryan felt a moment's discomfort that he'd let Constantine's theatrics get to him.

Again the camera lingered on the audience, which was moving, disturbed. Then back to Constantine: "Now, some of you'll say to me, 'Whoa, wait up, hold on, Reverend! Sure, we're seeing those terrible things, but what do they have to do with each other? I mean, crime, war, separatist movements, political polarization, divorce, alienation, they're different things, right?'" For a moment he looked perplexed, acting the part of a well-meaning skeptic. Then he dropped the act. "Well, I'm about to show you how they're all connected, all part of the same thing. And it's very simple, brothers and sisters. Because we've seen it before, it's right there in the *Bible.*" Again he paused, this time to glare a challenge at his audience. Then he shoved his jacket sleeves up his forearms, a working man about to get to the job. "Okay. Now, when I started talking tonight, I promised you I'd name that fear that eats at you, which I have done. Then I said I'd tell you why all this is happening—so now let's get to that, my friends. Why. Like I said—it's right there in the Bible."

"He's really quite good," Jess said. "This is lecture-hall technique, reiterating the overall structure of his talk and telling us where we are in it. Where'd he learn this stuff?"

"Lecture-hall technique plus bodyguards," Ryan said, pointing to the screen. "Look at this guy. And here." Positioned around the auditorium were a dozen men, standing facing the crowd. An earphone wire was clearly visible behind the closest man's ear. "You want me to get that article? I'd kind of like to see—"

"You'd like to prevent me from hearing this, apparently. For God's sake, Ry!" She gave him an offended look, grabbed the remote, brought the sound up again.

"…Genesis eleven," Constantine intoned. He held up a small black book, a Bible, but barely referred to it with his burning eyes. Instead he scattered his gaze around the hall and into the television cameras, force-fully bringing home the drama of the text. "'Once upon a time all the world spoke a single language and used the same words. As men jour-neyed in the east, they came upon a plain in the land of Shinar and settled there. They said to one another, "Come, let us make bricks and bake them hard"; they used bricks for stone and bitumen for mortar. "Come," they said, "let us build ourselves a city and a tower with its top in the heavens, and make a name for ourselves..." Then the Lord came down to see the city and tower which mortal men had built, and he said, "Here they are, one people with a single language, and now they have started to do this; henceforward nothing they have a mind to do will be beyond their reach. Come let us go down there and confuse their speech, so that they will not understand what they say to one another." So the Lord dispersed them from there all over the earth, and they left off build-ing the city. That is why it is called Babel, because the Lord there made a babble of the language of all the world; from that place the Lord scattered men all over the face of the earth.'"

Constantine slapped the book shut. "Do you see it, my friends? Have we not attempted to build a city and a tower with its top in the heavens? Have we not tried to 'make a name for ourselves'? I'm not just talking about buildings and towers, I'm talking about the whole range of our works—our machines, our medicines, the wonderful technologies we love so much. Our rearing dams, our sweeping highways, our rockets to outer space! At our whim, we fell the forest, we level the mountain, we dam the very sea! Have we not decided that, just as the Bible says, hence-forward nothing we have a mind to do will be beyond our reach?!" Con-stantine looked around to see that everyone saw the outrageous absurdity of it.

"Now, the sins of this are severalfold. First, there is the sin of pride. *Hubris*—we mistakenly think we have the wisdom to take over from God what should only be *His* right, *His* responsibility. And such hubris is *loathsome* in His eyes. But worse? Worse is that we have come to love our own creations too much—so much that we forget to love and revere the God who gave us the power to do any of this, gave us the good earth as our domain. We forget to love and *fear* Him. And without a steadfast love of our God, our acceptance of His guidance, our fear of His displea-sure, we are indeed *lost*."

Speaking quickly, almost matter-of-factly: "So with both the compas-sion and strictness of a wise parent, God our Father now seeks to bring us back from our errors. God says *No more!,* and what does He do? He does as He did in the days of Babel! He causes us each to speak a separate tongue—not just of words, no, but of feelings, of beliefs, of goals and intentions—*He scatters us each away from the other!* You see how this works now? Like an earthquake, it starts small and gets bigger and bigger until all the ground shudders! Starts right here—" he struck himself over the heart with one fist—"and spreads out there"—a gesture that included the auditorium, the TV cameras. "God scatters husband from wife and father from son, then neighbor from neighbor, then nation from nation! He makes us destroy the things we have built. And *that* is what you are experiencing when you go to the marriage counselor and can't reconcile with your wife and go home more lonely than ever. *That* is what you feel when you look at your teenage daughter and see a complete stranger. *That* is what you feel when you flinch at the knock at your door, *that* is what makes it too frightening to read a newspaper anymore because the whole world's going to pieces. It's all the same thing! *We are being driven apart!* And the consequences are far, far worse than in the first Days of Babel. We're not just being scattered. This time, the tower we've built is so big it'll fall on us when it comes down. It'll crush us like the worms we are beneath the weight of our own hubris."

Constantine stood facing the camera and the crowd, arms outspread as if he'd said all that could be said, it was self-explanatory, obvious. The camera pulled back to put him in the context of the hall, the dense crowd, which was totally still now, captivated.

"Fascinating," Ryan said. "Part of his power is that he's tapped into a whole mythological tradition. The consequences of challenging the gods with our works. There's the Babel story, and Prometheus, and later Faust, Frankenstein…And he *is* charismatic, I'll grant him that. For a con artist."

Jess had moved away from him on the couch and was holding the remote in both hands, as if pointedly keeping it away from him. "Why are you so intent on interrupting this? Why does this make you so uneasy, Ry?"

"I was just saying—"

"Shh!" Jess said. She pointed to the screen, where the camera had zoomed in on Constantine again. The prophet dropped his arms to signal that he was about to speak.

"Earlier," he said quietly, "I promised I'd tell you what you can do about all this. Well, first let me say that God's process of punishment and corrective action has only just begun. It doesn't happen all at once, our God has eternity to work with. The bright side for us is, we have time to do better. We can still remedy our errors. We can escape the loneliness of being dispersed into the desert, one by one, alone, and we can escape the agony of hunger and privation and violence of that tower crashing down on us. There is a way! I'm here tonight to offer you that way!

"The simple part is to come to me right now, get up and walk down the aisle and join the Church of Revelation and Redemption. Give up your fears, take the first step toward the mercy of God. That's the easy part. God in His kindness has made the first step easy for you, all you have to do is say, 'Yes, Lord, yes, Reverend Constantine, I am scared and I am lonely and I am sinful, and I want to come home to your comfort. I want a way out of the darkness and chaos of the Days of Babel.'"

The audience was stirring now, a gathering noise of mutterings beneath Constantine's voice. The rhythms of his words battered at them while the promise of what he claimed to offer touched them. Louder now, he went on: "But I said there's a hard part, and now let me tell you what that is. When you join the Church of Revelation and Redemption, you have to give up everything. It's not a free ride. You have to surrender your arrogance and dishonesty, your money and your comfort and your time, you have to carve yourself down, pare yourself away to that clean, strong soul you were born with! We have a great work before us, the saving of mankind in the light of God, and if you aren't ready to take up that work, that great fight, then don't come down this aisle! You go on home huddled in your fear and uncertainty! If you aren't ready, if you aren't strong enough, I don't want you! But if you've had enough, if you are ready to make the righteous sacrifices He asks of you, then come forward! Come to your holy work and your own redemption! Come to me, come to God, come out of the shadow of the Tower of Babel!"

Constantine had begun chanting his words, a rhythmic incantation above the swelling, oceanic noise of the audience. Now the camera played over the crowd as it stood to the prophet's beckoning arms. The weeping faces, the stumbling movements as people stepped laterally to the aisles, the numb, submissive march forward. Still Constantine chanted: *Come.*

At last Jess used the remote to cut the sound. "Well," she said, obviously unsettled. "I didn't mind it until the end. He got remarkably unspecific when it came to his agenda. I mean, what do we do differently so that God doesn't disperse us and bring down the tower on us?"

"Be sure to tune in for our next episode," Ryan quipped uneasily.

Jess just frowned. They watched for another few minutes in silence as the crowd converged on the stage and Constantine was lost in a clot of bodyguards and converts. Ryan shook himself, a little involuntary shiver.

"All right, so let's look at that *New Yorker* article," Jess said. "I wish we'd read it before we interviewed Morales. It might have helped me anticipate his responses better." She unfolded from the couch, unwound her towel turban so that her tangled hair fell dark around her shoulders. For a moment she rooted in a stack of magazines on the telephone desk, then returned and began pacing back and forth, reading out loud. Ryan watched, half concerned about her intensity, half just admiring her. Naked from the waist up, brows knit and breasts swaying, she looked like a Watusi warrior woman.

According to the article, the Church of Revelation and Redemption was growing by leaps and bounds, buying property in a dozen cities, starting its own radio and television networks. In the last month alone, it had picked up as prominent converts a chart-topping rock group, two state governors, and a dozen members of Congress. But the church's popularity was marred by scandal. Some of its officers faced criminal charges for fraud, theft, racketeering, and computer hacking. Most disturbing was the intersectarian violence attributed to church members, of which Hector Morales was only one example. In Illinois, two local church heads were suspected of fire-bombing the headquarters of the Millennial Church, and in Florida, CRR members were involved in the beating deaths of two Methodist churchgoers.

"'Predictably,'" Jess read, "'Constantine claims the charges have been fabricated to persecute his church, but many observers suggest a more cynical explanation: the CRR has overextended itself financially, driving its members to overzealous pursuit of spiritual "market share."'" She waved the magazine as if she wanted to fling it away. "That's ridiculous! You can't meet Morales and pretend that was his motivation. That his faith is anything but sincere. If we're going to understand him, or Constantine, we have to be realistic about their beliefs!"

She shook her head and went on reading: The church's prescription for its believers was unclear. Constantine's published *Prophecies* spoke inspiringly but vaguely of a future global state, united under an unnamed spiritual leader who resembled, big coincidence, Jared Constantine. The church's theology seemed an amalgam of Old Testament history and the prophecies of Constantine, with a gloss of New Age pseudo-science.

Since technological achievements were often offered as proofs of mankind's hubris, the *New Yorker* reporter reasoned, one might expect an anti-technology agenda, but so far nothing like that had emerged. On the contrary, the church maintained state-of-the-art databases, communications, and security at its churches and offices.

Jess concluded: "'Beyond Constantine's uncanny ability to move crowds, the church has shown little to differentiate it from any other confidence scam.'" She slapped the page with the back of her hand. "See, this is what bothers me—maybe this is all true, but I hate the *tone* of these articles whenever the subject is religion. This mannered urban *irony,* the undertone of ridicule...Personally, I *liked* that part about 'paring yourself away to the clean, strong soul you were born with.'"

"Yeah, I agree, sounds good." Ryan looked down at the illegible jottings on his pad and felt the weariness of the day come over him.

"The world *is* in a mess. And his basic thesis about the problem—I mean, give him a scientific vocabulary, and he could be describing a global neuroepidemic, something like this Syndrome E."

Ryan shrugged, not able to disagree but not willing to give in, either. It was getting late for this stuff. He'd been drinking steadily since dinner, and the combination of religion, global epidemics, and whiskey made a poor mix.

"Jessie," he began, "can we, shouldn't we maybe slow down a bit here—?"

"What do you mean?"

There was so much to say: *Baby, I know you're hurting now from Allison's murder, I know how desperately you want answers and solutions. Let me kiss it away, love it away.* But it sounded soupy, and anyway that level of intimacy didn't seem available just now. "I mean this has blown up very big, very fast...We've gone from looking for an overview of neurological conditions precipitating violent behavior to, what, looking for the origins of huge social movements—"

He had held his arms out to her, wanting the warmth of her skin, but Jess stayed away, rocking her head from side to side. "Maybe that's how we *have* to look at it! Ryan, we're systems thinkers. We put perplexing phenomena in the context of larger systems. That's precisely how we solve problems that others don't. This, this... 'Babel effect' could well be the dynamic we need to explore if we want to understand individual violence."

Ryan groaned. The stimulus of the whiskey he'd drunk had vanished, and now he felt too thick-headed to process this with her. "So what's our goal here? Are we trying to help reduce violent crime or, what—end war? Save mankind from itself?"

She didn't answer, but she had a light in her eyes, some spark that had caught and was starting to glow. He had the clear sense that she was moving outward on some conceptual arc or trajectory, well ahead of him, and that he had almost no idea where that trajectory led.

Chapter 17

On Wednesday, Dagan delivered a brilliant oral brief on Syndrome E to the crew, and predictably they voted to include the hypothesis in the research agenda. The big view tempted Ryan, too, but more and more he worried that their focus was fading, energy scattering. In just under three weeks they'd gone from looking for a neurological basis for violent crime to hypothesizing that neurological epidemics caused large-scale social violence to considering whether the whole goddamned world was now in the grip of a brain plague.

It made sense that if an individual's mental health could shape historical events—Hitler and Stalin, for example—so could the general mental health of larger populations. And that if epidemics like the Black Plague or influenza or AIDS had shaped human history, so could neuroepidemics. And that if the symptoms of every other disease occurred in varying degrees of severity, of course the behavioral symptoms of neurological disorders did, too. Which meant that Constantine was right, the epidemic would manifest as a spectrum of symptoms ranging from subtler ones like personal alienation and dysfunctional families, through polarized communities, to outright nightmares like murder, war, genocide, and social collapse.

And yes, the world was in a mess. Constantine had lived up to his promise to give a name to the sickness of the age: *The Babel syndrome. The Babel effect.*

Ryan sprawled on the couch during the staff meeting, just observing, thinking, *If only it didn't make so much sense. And if only Jess weren't so susceptible to such ideas just now.*

Again, Jess insisted that trends did seem to support the global pandemic view, this time supporting her argument with data on twenty years of mental-health trends: alarming increases in schizophrenia, depression, attention-deficit disorder, panic disorders. Skyrocketing hospital psych admissions, consumption of neuroleptic medications increasing tenfold—what some health statisticians called the "secret epidemic."

Then she went on with a grab-bag of other indicators: more crimes against children, refugee populations at record levels. Incidence of genocide or ethnic cleansing: thirty record-breaking years, even measured against the Holocaust. As Ridder had pointed out, violence stemming from defective social integration, like mass or serial murder, was still rising. The number of separatist movements, hate groups, and armed cults investigated by the FBI or ATF each year had tripled in the last decade. On and on. She handed out graphs for each statistic, all disturbingly similar: almost flat on the left, then taking a steep bend up, until the last section was nearly vertical. A nasty line, the graph of pressure rising in a boiler.

Despite the dire implications, Ryan found himself in awe of Jess. So that's what she'd been doing for the last few days, locked in her office, or visiting the libraries at Harvard. Still, he couldn't see where she'd found the time. When she was motivated, she became a rocket.

More gently this time, wary of Jess's reaction, Bates countered by arguing that none of this was a new phenomenon. Violence was a species norm, not an aberration, a genetic program selected by evolution because it conferred certain advantages—on the survivors, anyway. He gave a concise summary of human history, starting with his own experiences in Vietnam, then moving backwards: the Holocaust, the Rape of Nanking, the Turkish Armenian genocide, on and on. He got as far as 1200, Genghis Khan's mountains of skulls, before Jess signaled she'd heard enough. Chagrined at himself, Bates touched her shoulder, a wordless apology.

Dagan articulated the obvious synthesis: that it wasn't really a choice between "new nightmares" or "intrinsic evils." That it was no doubt *both:* the syndrome could be pandemic throughout the world, always present but increasing and subsiding in one region or another throughout history, like influenza or polio or a hundred other diseases. The indicators Jess mentioned were then just a revisitation of an ancient plague, one now gone global in the era of international trade and transportation and overpopulation.

The ramifications fanned before Ryan's mind's eye like the tail of a peacock, broad and colorful and complex. *Ancient plague, new nightmare.* Could they really zero in on something that big? The hopeful voice in his head said, *Maybe.* Maybe the time had come—advances in biochemistry, neurosciences, epidemiology, virology, toxicology, mathematics, data processing, might just allow them to get a handle on it.

Another voice said, *Are you fucking kidding?* The sciences weren't ready. The bioethical ramifications weren't sorted out. Global databases weren't there. And there were serious personal concerns: the scientific reputation of Genesis, which would surely get savaged on this by a skeptical scientific community. Or the dangers that Karl had mentioned, that Shipley had warned against: nasty corporations, governments, terrorists. Maybe more than anything else, the emotional impact on Jess, Abi, their family. For the first time in his life, he wondered if he had the sheer courage, the *chutzpah,* needed for such a study.

The best he could do was to insist they formalize their stance on the issue, have Jess and Bates compile a preliminary brief for review by the joint Brandt/Genesis steering committee. That left it theoretically contained for now, but from the look of the crew he suspected this was one genie that couldn't be stuffed back into the bottle.

———

Later that afternoon he left the house and headed down the shore stairs, carrying a jam jar half-filled with Laphroaig. His second. The sun was dropping toward the rim of the bluff, and the lowering rays had turned a pack of high cumulus clouds into a slow-motion refractive hippo ballet. Ordinarily he would have stopped to admire such a fine light, but there was domestic damage control to be done. He scanned the shore rocks for Jess.

After the staff meeting, she had seemed unusually preoccupied, spontaneously setting up with her laptop computer at the dining-room table. Abi hadn't seen much of her mother for a couple of days, so when she came home from school she tried to seduce Jess into play, first trying to engage her with words and then, giving up, starting a game that involved tossing pillows onto a throw-rug target. Jess kept working, mistakenly trying to concentrate despite the proximity of a quick skinny itchy kid whose voice etched adult eardrums with a high range that'd make a bat wince.

A little later, as she went to the kitchen to get a drink, Jess had nearly tripped over a pillow, and had kicked it away. "Not where people walk, Abi!"

"Okay," Abi agreed cheerfully. Getting any kind of a response struck her as progress.

So two minutes later, the pillows were sailing closer and closer to the dining room table, and then one bounced and hit Jess's leg. "Abi, cut it out. Right now! That's enough roughhousing."

"I'm trying to get you to play, silly."

"And I'm trying to get you to do what your mother says. Now pick these up and go to your room."

Abi had been startled by that, a little stung. "No. I won't. You're the one who's wrong!" She gave Jess a defiant-unto-the-death stare. Not up for it, Jess shut down her computer and left the house for the shore.

Ryan found her sitting on the seawall, hugging her knees. When he came to sit next to her, she just kept staring east, out into the empty water of the bay.

"You're right," she said. "I'm fucking up. Can we skip the lecture?"

"Jesus, Jessie—"

She turned to him abruptly. "But I'm not the only one! Maybe you need to inspect your own actions, Ry. Look at yourself. My God, you're supposed to be instilling confidence and, and esprit de corps, and you sat through our staff meeting this morning with your eyes closed. You didn't say a word except to snipe and sabotage the group's process."

He hadn't anticipated this level of vehemence and didn't have an immediate response. Instead he took a fortifying swallow from the jam jar.

"And you're drinking too damned much. Put that down." She didn't wait for him to put it down, just jerked his forearm so that he spilled the whiskey into the bay.

"So it's true what they say—the best defense is a good offense?" he suggested pointedly. And then immediately regretted it. Her expression caught at a nerve in his heart, and all he felt was the need to connect.

Jess looked out to sea again.

He tried a fresh start: "Jessie, I'm not trying to do some one-upmanship thing here, really, but I do think we've got to talk about how we're adapting to this job, and that means just we should talk about, you know, why this thing with Abi happened, what you're going through and why it's so hard to talk about"—he inhaled, finished the sentence—"it." It was a bit of a drunken ramble, but had the virtue of honesty.

Jess looked at him, obviously angry with herself. Ryan waited for her to find a route into what needed saying.

But then Dagan appeared, walking up the slope from the beach on the north. She wore white pants rolled almost to her knees and a peach cotton T-shirt and her black hair had been blown into a tangle. Her face was knit, thoughtful. Carrying her sandals in one hand, picking her way up the rocky slope, she didn't notice them until she had almost reached the seawall.

"Oh!" she said, startled. "Hi. I didn't expect to see anyone."

"Hi, D.," Jess said. She managed a ragged smile.

Dagan looked quickly from one to the other. "I didn't mean to interrupt—"

"You're not interrupting," Jess lied graciously. "Don't be silly."

Dagan came to sit on a boulder across from them, putting one ankle across her knee and brushing sand off her foot.

"So what's the wrinkled brow about?" Ryan asked.

"It's complex," she stalled, putting on her right sandal and slipping the straps snug.

Jess just pitched a pebble at her, meaning, *Spill it.*

Dagan squinted up at the sky and Ryan followed her gaze. The sun was brilliant above the edge of the bluff, sending the shadows of the tall pines into the water. The pink hippo ballet had drifted ponderously to the south.

"I've been thinking about what it really means to accept the premise that an organic brain syndrome accounts for violence—the Syndrome E perspective, the epidemiological side of it," Dagan said. She paused to draw a deep breath. "It's a huge, *huge* idea, it has so many ramifications! I mean, from Genghis Khan's massacres to babies abandoned in rest-room trash-cans, we've been telling ourselves that this self-inflicted misery is our lot, right? In the old days we might've called it our punishment for 'original sin,' and later we reasoned it away as 'intrinsic evil,' and then Freud gave us a psychiatric perspective and called it a built-in death wish. And now evolutionary psychology tells us it's an aspect of our genetic makeup. I mean, that's the postmodern paradigm, isn't it? To find the serial killer within? To blame the worst atrocities on the soul of all mankind? The vocabulary changes, but every intellectual or philosophical tradition has its own way of telling us we are all 'that way,' we're all locked into a dire fate through our own inner evil."

"More or less," Ryan agreed. Jess was just listening, looking a little undone.

"Jess, Ry—what would happen if you woke up one morning, and you *exonerated* yourself of all that? How would you feel if you could believe that we're *not* all somehow implicated in these horrors, it's *not* built into all of us? What if you could look in the mirror one morning and say with certainty IT IS NOT TRUE? *How would you feel?* Because that's what looking at murder and war as a neuroepidemic means!"

Dagan stopped again, and as Ryan looked over at Jess, a lance of pinkish sunset light reflected off one of the upper windows of the house, *bam!,* blinding him. A chill shimmied up his spine. Looking at the women in the rare light, Ryan felt it rising in him, the terrifying hope that came with Dagan's words. The idea hung like a pool of molten light, the fire of it thrilled his nerves. He realized how absurdly drunk he was.

Dagan said quietly: "God, I can hardly let myself *think* this! It's like a violation of our one unquestioned paradigm, it's a betrayal of the culture of intellectualism, it's..." She made a broad gesture with her sandal, at a loss for words.

Jess squinted up at the house, the ray of pink, and a shiver seemed to shake her, too.

"Look," Dagan went on, "should we say that smallpox or the Black Plague was an aspect of 'basic human nature'? No! We eventually learned that they had specific, identifiable causes, a virus and a bacterium that overcame our immune systems—"

Ryan felt compelled to counter it: "War and genocide are caused by human actions. The Plague wasn't."

"Sure it was! We didn't take *baths,* we didn't dispose of *garbage,* we were superstitious and killed off *cats.* Through our *behavior,* our cultural *habits* and *assumptions,* our lack of *knowledge,* rats proliferated and their fleas gave us the Plague bacterium. How do we know we aren't ignoring obvious causes and preventions for this Babel disease? Maybe this stuff is *not* 'who we are,' but really is a form of *sickness,* literally, that we've lived with so long we've started to *think* it's who we are!"

"You're arguing for the perfectibility of mankind, Dagan," Ryan said gently. "I'm tempted by it, too, but it's an old, old fallacy—"

"No! If we accept the argument that 'it's always been this way,' or 'it's built into us,' isn't that just another way of saying it's 'destiny' or 'fate'? I thought we'd abandoned those ideas!" She slapped the sandal into the palm of her hand. "If we approach our problems that way, *that's* superstition, *that's* regression. That's *our* brand of superstitious fatalism! Sure, it's been accepted as doctrine forever, and now it's reflected in the...the dark ironies of pop culture and couched in hipper terms than the Old Testament used. We've all eaten and breathed the assumption of our 'intrinsic evil' in one form or another since the moment we were born. *That assumption is an old, old fallacy, too.* And I am so, *so* tired of accepting it!" She stamped her sandaled foot.

Wow, Dagan, Ryan was thinking. He pulled back and just admired her fervency, the blaze of her eyes. *Righteous anger and passion. Holy Jesus. Dagan on a roll.* Yes, she was definitely growing, her passion and intellect converging and giving her the divine fire. So much like Jess, when she was that age.

Jess objected halfheartedly: "Of course, we have to be careful about pathologizing typical behaviors—what's 'sick' in one culture may be a norm in another. You invite some very complex questions...Really, it's an ethical quagmire, it's—"

"*Life* is an ethical quagmire!" Dagan responded instantly. "Mine is, anyway. Isn't every thinking person's? It's only from wading through it that I've ever learned anything!"

They were all silent. For a time, Jess just gazed at Dagan as if from a great distance. At last she asked softly, "Why is it always so hard to voice our deepest hopes?"

Nobody had an answer for that. Dagan was right. That humanity's worst excesses, throughout history, were *plagues* was an idea promising beyond measure, an absolution for the worst of humanity's sins. Something everyone, especially a very lapsed Catholic, yearned for. But again Ryan's instincts screamed that this was getting out of hand. Yes, they were supposed to be the Skunk Works here, chase the wilder theories. But between Karl's "torpedoes" and Dagan's ancient plagues, and Jess with her in-turning and her "Babel effect," Genesis was beginning to get fragmented. Where would they find the through-line to guide them?

Dagan seemed emptied of pressure as she slid on her sandal and buckled the strap. Jess stood, walked a few paces down the shore, and paused to prod some cast-up sea thing with her toe. The lance of light had faded, the sun gone too low.

Then Abi came out onto the deck. "Mom! Phone!" she yelled. A strong voice for a skinny kid. She waved hugely, extravagantly, as if they were across the bay.

———

Dagan drove home. The McClouds of Heart Cove began cooking dinner, putting together a big pan of refried beans with tortillas, diced vegetables, salsas of various thermal potentials. Jess asked Abi to help and she readily agreed, capably mashing the beans with a fork as Ryan stood at the bar, chopping cilantro and grating cheese.

Fascinated, he watched them from behind. Abi stood next to Jess on a footstool at the inner counter, their relationship obvious in the proportions of their limbs, the color of their skin, and more than anything else, the rhythms of their movements. If Abi held anything against Jess for their earlier tussle, it didn't show.

"When I was a kid," Jess said, "we used to read *Mad* magazine. Allison and I had to sneak it past my father, who didn't approve. They still publish *Mad,* right?"

"Yeah. It's sort of funny and sort of gross."

"That's the one. Well, back when I used to read it, they'd always have somebody pulling this prank where they'd tape a sign on another person's butt that said 'Kick me hard.' I feel like I've got one of those on my butt right now. So go ahead." She turned her back to Abi, patted her rear. But Abi didn't seem to get it, so Jess clarified: "This is an apology, 'Beb."

Abi just looked over at the back of her mother's jeans. "Nope. No sign," she said, almost deadpan. She went back to mashing the beans.

Jess looked over her shoulder to Ryan, and patted the taut curve of her jeans pocket again. "You?" she asked wryly. She was genuinely contrite, almost shy. Ryan just shook his head and smiled.

Abi gave him a quick glance of fellow-feeling, and they went back to their work. Ryan covertly admired them both, loving them fiercely. How had he gotten so lucky? *The luck of the Polish-Irish.* And looking at Abi now, he had to agree with Dagan: original sin, intrinsic evil, death wish, nature red in tooth and claw? Bullshit. All you needed as a counterargument was a single glance, one casual act of forgiveness from your kid. So why *did* people hurt each other? Maybe it really was time to look for a more scientific answer.

Chapter 18

They had several errands to accomplish in New
York City. One was an interview with a particularly deranged murderer,
Edward Michael Brenner, to try to get his consent to be studied. The
other was to attend the neurological workup of Hector Morales at the
famous Peabody Psychiatric Clinic in Manhattan, the first full diagnostic
to be arranged. Finally, since they'd be in the city anyway, Jess wanted to
meet Karl at Montgomery Labs to bounce the neuroepidemic thesis off
him. They reserved a room at a midtown Manhattan hotel, left Abi and
the house in Dagan's care, and flew to New York for what promised to be
a nasty couple of days. On the other hand, Ryan had seen almost nothing
of Jess during the last week, and having a couple of days with her
sounded like a nice idea.

Brenner was on death row at New Jersey's Tilling State Prison, an
hour's drive from Manhattan. He was a huge, pathetic man in his late
fifties, his face disfigured from a Vietnam War injury. He had stalked and
killed eight women, and earlier diagnostics had confirmed a powerful
misogynistic psychopathology, so Jess didn't plan to take the lead. In any
case it was a moot point: the whole show blew up before they got as far as
the interview.

Jess and Ryan and Tilling's psych director, Dr. Ianelli, waited in an
observation room for Brenner's attorney to arrive, watching Brenner
through a one-way window. Ianelli seemed like a decent guy, tall, long-
faced, a good sense of humor. He confessed that he personally suspected
high androgen levels—the proverbial testosterone poisoning—or maybe
double-Y chromosome, as the physical origin of Brenner's pathologies.

Brenner filled the containment room with his bulk, pacing wearily
and distractedly like an old zoo bear, leg irons clanking, speaking to himself in mumbled monosyllables. As they waited and chatted, Jess watched
the murderer intently, and again Ryan got the uncomfortable feeling she
was heading rapidly outward on some conceptual path, himself plodding
along far behind.

The lawyer who finally joined them was not the bland, court-appointed attorney who had halfheartedly offered Brenner's appeals for several years, and with whom they'd arranged this interview. Instead, a short, hard-mouthed, deeply tanned man with a military buzz-cut came in and introduced himself as J. Robertson Bork, Brenner's new lawyer. After giving them brisk handshakes, he opened his briefcase and pulled out some papers that he waved at them.

"My client declines to be interviewed or to take any tests whatsoever," he said bluntly.

Dr. Ianelli looked puzzled. "But Mr. Brenner personally expressed a willingness to—"

"Mr. Brenner received poor legal advice. This"—Bork shoved a form at Ianelli's face—"is a statement signed by him authorizing me to represent him and declining interviews or medical tests."

Ryan took the form, and Jess scanned it with him. Brusque legalese, a sloppy signature with Brenner's name typed under it. A witness's signature. Bork's, too. All very official.

In the observation room, the murderer had drifted close to the one-way window, a hulking figure shifting his weight uneasily from foot to foot as if somehow sensing the tension on the other side of the glass. Close up, Ryan could see that his face was badly scarred, sucking part of his nose into a crevasse of cheek flesh and baring his teeth on one side. Despite the slanted snarl, he looked more helpless and sad than dangerous. If anybody nearby felt dangerous, it was Bork.

"My client has an appeal pending and is concerned that your tests might constitute self-incrimination," Bork summarized. "End of story."

"But as long as we're all here," Jess said levelly, "and given his earlier verbal consent, mightn't we revisit this decision with him?"

Bork pursed his lips contemptuously, sorted through his papers for a couple of documents, this time shoving them into Jess's face. "Mr. Brenner has appointed me his legal power of attorney on all matters. So the answer is *no,* we 'mightn't.' In any case, Mr. Brenner specifically declines to take the PET or MRI scans due to his concern about the procedures' possible health hazards."

Ryan decided he didn't like the man. Ianelli must have agreed, because he barked a little laugh and said, "That's a joke! The only health hazard this guy has to worry about is the lethal injection he's gonna get in exactly two weeks."

A thump from the window interrupted Bork's retort. Brenner, alone in the beige-painted, over-bright containment room, had tentatively knocked on the glass with his manacled hands. "Anybody there?" he asked, gazing toward them but clearly seeing nothing. "How long? It's been like an hour…Anybody there?"

"It's a done deal," Bork snapped at Ianelli, ignoring his client. "And now I think that's all for today."

"Mr. Bork," Jess said firmly, "two weeks ago we requested Mr. Brenner's service medical records. If you won't let us test him, can you at least let us review the records? His injuries might—"

But Bork had yet another document. This time Ryan moved to intercept him before he could brandish it at Jess, catching his wrist and holding it hard as he removed the paper from his fingers. Bork made one jerk to free his hand, felt Ryan's weight and strength, settled for a furious glare.

Ryan blinked languidly. "I have a medical condition," he explained. "I'm allergic to people being aggressively physical around my pregnant wife."

Ianelli grinned. Ryan tossed away Bork's wrist and read the form with Jess. This one was from the Veterans' Administration, bearing a raised VA seal and formally stating that, regrettably, Brenner's service history and medical records had been lost.

Bork stuffed his papers back into the briefcase, hyper-officious, his mouth a slit. After he slammed out of the room, the three of them just stood there for a moment.

"Just a real sweet guy," Ianelli said. "Well, I'm sorry you came all this way for—"

Brenner thumped the window again, then leaned his ruined face against the glass, shielding his eyes with his manacled hands. He seemed to stare into the air of the observation room, blind, perplexed, pathetic. "Anybody there?" he called softly. "Hey—anybody in there?"

Hector Morales had insisted that two representatives of the Church of Revelation and Redemption attend the diagnostic session at Peabody Clinic as his "advocates." One was an older woman with narrow eyes and startling silver hair, the other a muscular, red-haired man who shook hands with Ryan and Jess only reluctantly, as if afraid he'd catch something from them.

The killer arrived in an armored New York Correctional Department van, along with eight shotgun-armed prison guards, a deputy warden from Baynard, some NYPD cops, and a couple of journalists. When the van pulled up to the ambulance entrance, the city police stopped traffic on the street while prison guards formed up a double line between the truck and the clinic doors. Morales emerged wearing an orange jumpsuit, paper slippers, irons. As he shuffled and clanked past Jess, he acknowledged her with probing dark eyes. Something familiar there, Ryan decided. It took him a moment to connect: Morales's eyes had all of the intensity, if none of the smirk, of Charles Manson's dire gaze.

First came the PET scan. Ryan and Jess sat with the church representatives and a pair of Peabody neuropsychologists in a cramped observation room that was dominated by a bank of video screens and a big one-way window into the procedure room. The monitors would show live scans of Morales's brain as well as morphometric and volumetric models derived from averaged scans of hundreds of "normal" brains, the idea being that visual and computer comparisons between the killer's scans and these "brain atlases" would isolate deviations in Morales's neural equipment. In the week since seeing the TV revival, Jess had been on a tear, doing research on Constantine. Her logic had been that to create the desired evoked potentials in Morales's brain, the clinical tests had to use stimuli relevant to his priorities and passions. Which meant developing protocols that included questions about Constantine, the church's theology, other religions, Morales's beliefs. It had kept her away from home a lot, but Ryan had to admit the day's tests would be far more effective for her contribution.

In the spotless procedure room, three nurses strapped Morales to a stainless steel shelf and inserted the intravenous line that fed fluorine 18 into his bloodstream. The radioisotope would take the place of the oxygen molecules in glucose, the brain's main fuel, and concentrate wherever brain activity was taking place. Morales watched disinterestedly as the plunger sent the milky fluid into his veins, the circular chrome mouth of the PET scanner gaping hungrily behind him. An audio link brought the sounds of equipment adjustments and the technicians' muted conversation into the observation room. Morales kept his eyes fixed on the observation window, an accusing look.

The Peabody staff in the observation room were prattling on about various theories of the origins of violence, showing off for their distinguished visitors, but Morales interrupted them: "Are you there, Dr. McCloud?"

"Mr. Morales—" one of the technicians began.

"If you are watching, then you can see the atrocity you are commit-ting, can't you?"

When Jess didn't respond, the silver-haired woman goaded her: "Aren't you going to answer him?"

Ryan gave the woman a look, but Jess just leaned forward to the microphone on the control panel. "I'm here, Mr. Morales." The flight and the aborted morning session with Brenner had taken something out of her, but she rallied resignedly.

"Is this really the way you hope to find your way to the soul of mankind?" Morales called.

Oh shit, Ryan thought. So that's what this was about: an indictment of scientific materialism, of the biomedical paradigm. A guilt trip to lay on Jess, a woman Morales had correctly perceived to be vulnerable. Still, he had to agree that there was something grotesque, neo-Medieval, about the scene: a man immobilized on a pallet, masked tormentors probing him, spectators watching, armed guards patrolling nearby.

"Does it gratify you to see a human being as no more than a slice of *tis-sue* on a microscope slide? An excised *tumor?*" Morales asked. "Do you hope that perhaps you'll find my *belief,* my *faith,* somewhere in my brain matter? Do you really think that your quest could be this easy?"

"Amen," the silver-haired woman said fervently. She watched for Jess's response with slit eyes. The red-haired guy was looking suddenly very keyed up, and Ryan wondered just what Morales and his "advocates" had in mind today, how far they intended to take their moral lesson. You never knew with these nut cases. The tension in the observation room rose.

Ryan could see by Jess's face that the little shit had pierced her again, and he thought, *No, Jess McCloud had never claimed it was easy.* But to his relief she found her tough side. "Thank you for your concern for my spir-itual development," she said levelly. "I assure you, I'm fulfilling my part of our bargain. Now it's your turn, Hector. No, I doubt I'll find your faith in your brain, but I was truly hoping it would show in your actions—that you would demonstrate the courage of your convictions. So show me, Hector. Put up or shut up."

Ryan looked at her admiringly. Morales's advocates were outraged, but glanced at each other in a way that again suggested they were expecting something.

It went that way for most of the afternoon: Morales acting martyred, Jess navigating him through his resistance, the church advocates emanating distrust and loathing and a curious expectancy. With the Peabody staffers, they watched Morales's brilliantly colored, computer-assembled brain scans on the video screens, eyeballed variations between his brain and the atlases. To the eye, his morphometrics looked to be within normal variation, but computer analysis suggested some frontal-lobe atrophy, a small degree of widening of the interhemispheric fissure, and possible hippocampal hypertrophy. The likely cause, they speculated, was the high level of cortisol that earlier tests had found in Morales's blood. Cortisol was naturally secreted by the body to help cope with stress, anxiety, danger, or injury, but chronically high levels could damage the brain and were often associated with violence disorders.

Suggestive, Ryan thought, but conclusions would have to wait for extensive analysis of all the data. The functional MRI with evoked potentials was their best hope of observing activities in Morales's brain.

By the time they got to the MRI, Morales looked tired, and was no longer baiting or challenging Jess. Ryan wondered if, after all, he was coming to grips with his own mortality, facing the reality of his execution in only twelve days. But the church people in the room were still going the other way, getting more keyed up and alert. Again, as if expecting something.

Another antiseptic procedure room, another observation chamber. Like the PET scanner, the MRI machine was a tube with a doughnut mouth. It blasted the brain with a magnetic field thirty thousand times stronger than the Earth's, and when the magnetic axes of the atoms in the brain were aligned it pulsed a whopping radio signal and read the resulting "echo," the radio signal the brain cells themselves sent out. The electromagnets in the MRI's curved panels had to be cooled by liquid helium, and the massive electrical current amplifiers, cooling fans, and compressors made a deafening roar. The machine's vibration shivered the floor and every surface in the observation room.

Morales was strapped to the sliding gurney, this time wearing earphones that would shield him from the noise and relay verbal stimuli to him, read from a carefully crafted script by a Peabody neuropsych technician. As the body inched into the narrow steel throat, Ryan felt an inadvertent flash of sympathetic claustrophobia.

Like a polygraph test, the evoked-potentials program began with commonplace stimuli, intended to trigger neural responses that could be easily compared to "normals" and would provide Morales's baseline response profile.

"Hector Vincent Morales," the technician read. In the depths of the machine, strings of data bytes aligned and assembled into three-dimensional images, mapping the way Hector's emotional responses activated his brain. On the monitor screens, a patch of red, yellow, and green blossomed in the dull blue image of his brain, near the back: Wernicke's area, Ryan knew, a typical speech-processing response. But smaller, fainter lights came and went, too, mainly in the right prefrontal cortex, thought to activate more often for negative emotions. Hector's EEG tests, earlier, had shown a similar right-side activation bias when he'd been shown photos of personal enemies or the religious rites of other churches.

"Joan Reynolds Morales." Hector's mother.

The technician read the name of Morales's wife and son, and then on through another dozen normatives as Jess followed her copy of the script. Suddenly she gripped Ryan's hand and leaned forward, her attention torn between the script and the viewing window. It was time for the technician to throw Morales the first curve.

"God," the flat voice read.

There was no way to see Morales's face in the narrow tube, but his hands clenched. The video monitors sparkled briefly with a galaxy of color. Too much to assess visually—they'd have to interpret it by computer analysis later.

"Jesus Christ."

More rainbow scatters against the dull blue. Morales appeared to be straining at the clips and straps that held him.

"Remington .308 Model 7400." Morales's murder weapon.

"Wait," Jess said. "What's he doing?"

"Jared Constantine," the implacable voice said.

Jess's alarm grew. "He's—he's got to stop moving."

In the MRI tube, Morales was arching, a distressed movement like an injured animal. And then they could see he'd worked a hand free and was pushing, pounding at the curved walls over him. His legs were shuddering, and now they could see his head shaking, battering from side to side in the shadowed tunnel.

"Stop the procedure!" Jess shouted. "He'll damage himself!" She leaped up, fumbled with the switches on the communications panel, gave up and began pounding on the window. Morales was throwing himself around in a magnetic field strong enough to rip surgical steel plates or pins out of repaired bones.

The Peabody staffers bolted from the room. Within a few seconds the preposterous whine of the machine peaked and began to subside. But Morales's convulsions continued even after the gurney slid out of the tube.

By the time the medical personnel had lifted him off the gurney, Morales was bloodied and stunned. He looked confused, staggering as they moved him to a wheelchair. He placed his feet as if the floor was slanted, lurched, grabbed a nurse to stay upright, his head swiveling.

Jess had pulled into herself, breathing fast and looking ill. Morales's disorientation was genuine, but Ryan couldn't tell whether he'd truly had some kind of seizure, maybe brought on by the MRI's fields, or had staged the whole thing. Or maybe he'd suffered a crisis of faith and had gotten very scared of what the MRI might reveal. From the look on the faces of the church people, he guessed it had been planned, Morales purposely injuring himself to screw up the test. Or to make a point to his persecutors—to Jess. Whichever, it had worked. Back out in the bright corridors of Peabody, she hurried into the women's room, and through the door Ryan could hear her retching and heaving.

He waited in the hall, wanting to comfort her, wishing she wouldn't pull away from him when something hurt her. Feeling a little sick himself. That image of Morales's humping, shuddering, flailing body.

Fucking Morales. *Mother, son, God, gun,* Ryan was thinking. Apparently the cardinal points of Morales's emotional and moral universe.

They left Peabody at four o'clock, just in time to fight Manhattan rush-hour traffic back to the hotel. They were both drained. Later they had dinner at a nice place in Chinatown, but it wasn't a romantic evening on the town by any stretch of the imagination. Just two people with a lot on their minds.

Chapter 19

The Montgomery Genome Laboratory, housed in its own building on the edge of the NYU campus: spacious plaza, fifties-era chrome-and-glass portico, marble-floored lobby centered around a huge, modernistic metal sculpture shaped like a DNA molecule. They registered at the front desk and the attendant called up to Karl's office. A few minutes later, Karl appeared, puffing from his walk, managing to look both harried and imperious.

"Had lunch yet?" he asked. When they shook their heads, he took Jess's arm and led them through a glistening corridor to the cafeteria, complaining about his staff and the demands of his various positions. Karl preceded them through the line, filling his tray with a large cup of black coffee and five plastic cups of fruit yogurt. "I'm big on intestinal livestock nowadays," he explained.

Jess picked out a pasta salad and a bowl of fruit, Ryan settled for a cup of coffee. They made their way to a table near windows that overlooked an interior courtyard, a few shrubs and flower beds surrounded by brick walls. Scattered at the other tables, Montgomery staff ate, drank coffee, talked.

"Almost four months gone, I thought you'd look like a real gunboat by now, Jess," Karl said. He peeled the foil tops off his yogurts. "But you still got a bod like Halle Berry." He put his two hands flat against his own paunch, *thin tummy*, and then cupped the air well in front of his chest, *big tits*.

"Why, thank you Karl. Ever the gentleman," she answered. She selected a grape and put it into her mouth. Jess had always been able to handle Karl, taking only the mildest of offense at his excesses and playfully offering only the driest of reproaches. Ryan saw now that her response was just what Karl was soliciting, a kind of ironic mothering she did so well. He took a sip from his cup and scalded his tongue on the burnt-tasting coffee.

"So Karl," Jess said, "I know you don't have much time today. But I wanted to talk to you about the idea I mentioned to you on the phone."

Karl spooned yogurt mechanically into his mouth for a moment, and then rubbed the milky mustache away with his napkin. "You mean a global pandemic of some neuropathology? A biomedical explanation for why the whole planet is going nuts? 'The Babel effect.' Love it. Totally love it."

"Any thoughts—?"

"Sure. If you're right, I'd have to say the human race is fucked in one of three ways." Karl quickly stuffed a few more spoonfuls of yogurt into his face. "From least to worst: One, there's a widespread stressor or pathogen that *directly* affects us, as adults, that's making us all nuts—in which case we're fucked now, but we can get rid of the problem by getting rid of the stressor." Karl raised his hand and counted off his stubby little finger. "Two," he went on, ticking off his ring finger, "there's been for some time a stressor or pathogen that has affected us *developmentally,* a teratogen affecting gene expression during critical stages of neural development—in utero, or maybe in certain phases of infantile development—which means that everyone now living is fucked for life, but we can still get rid of the problem in future generations by getting rid of the stressor. And finally, three: Some widespread stressor or pathogen has caused a mutation in our germ lines, giving us some inheritable counteradaptive neurological characteristic—in which case the human race is fucked for good!" Karl ticked off the third point on his middle finger, which he brandished triumphantly at them.

Jess stared at him deadpan, too weary to appreciate his humor. "Thank you, Karl. You're a lot of help."

"No, wait! I just thought of a fourth alternative! There *is* no change in us, it's just our species' natural genotype—we've *always* been totally fucked!" Karl sucked at his coffee, scalded himself, and spat it noisily back into the cup. He grimaced and swore viciously. "Personally," he concluded sourly, "I'd favor the last hypothesis."

Ryan blew across the top of his own cup. Jokes aside, Karl's summary was on the money: a factor directly and continuously affecting people; a factor causing crucial developmental impairments; a factor that had already caused germ-line genetic defects; or, as Bates had also argued, simply a species characteristic. Translation: fucked temporarily, fucked for the life span of everyone now living, fucked forever hence, or fucked from the get-go.

"Okay," Jess said. "That's good. That suggests four very different lines of research. But I know you've got something more we need to know.

Some reason this topic makes you so uncomfortable." She was right, as always, seeing the subtext or body language that told more than Karl's words. He wasn't enjoying his own wit as much as he should be.

Karl was frowning, still fingering his burnt lips. "What're you talking about?"

Jess reached across the table and took Karl's hand in both of hers. "Come on, Karl. You know we'll run across it anyway—wouldn't it be better for us to know about it up front?"

For a moment Karl let her rub the back of his hand, watching her brown fingers at work. Then he took his hand away, rejecting the seduction of her touch. "You know, right, that I've always considered your outlook idealistic and naïve? That I think your 'service to the betterment of humanity' thing is bullshit? Our genes program us to be selfish, to look out for our own advancement. Screw the other guy! It isn't natural to sacrifice for others, and you don't improve your survival chances, and you don't get anywhere in life. I think there are people who figure this out, and free themselves to act. We call them 'leaders.' And then there are people who don't figure it out, and who stay imprisoned by their own self-imposed rules and values and philosophies. You know what we call them? 'Losers.' I keep thinking you two will grow the fuck up, but you never do." He glared a challenge at Jess.

"Some people are just slow learners, I guess," she said, with mock resignation. "You know what I think, Karl? I think this is an argument you lost to yourself, long ago. Or there wouldn't be so much heat in it."

Karl sipped at his coffee and made a face at it. "This stuff tastes like *shit!* They take *excrement* and grind it up and brew it, so help me!"

Ryan just watched the two of them work it out. Jess was amazing, the way she could find the way to reach a person's better parts. There was something resigned, almost sad, about her approach. And yet implacable, too—steady, certain.

The combination seemed to undo Karl. After a few more minutes of back-and-forth, he sighed, gave up. He glanced around the cafeteria, then scooted his chair so that his back was to the nearest other diners, a couple of tables away. "I gotta tell you, there's an avenue of research that would seem to support your 'Babel effect' thesis," he admitted. "It involves a weapons technology—sort of."

"Go on."

"Torpedoes—Ry tell you about that?—are just the tactical end. There have also been *strategic* behavioral modification research projects. Designed for controlling large populations."

Jess began, "I know you hear about this stuff on the paranoid fringe—"

"See? You don't even want to hear about it! Because you live on the *Pollyanna* fringe. But for the last thirty years, Cold War and post–Cold War, there's been a shift of emphasis in defense technology research. Nukes are great, but you can't *use* them. Not since globalization has changed the map, changed the goals of conflict. So now most research is geared toward development of *nonlethal* weapons—weapons that disable but don't kill opponents. More politically *permissible,* see? Don't cut into your prospective *markets,* see? Better for your little *civil conflicts,* your *public relations.* Industry vernacular for this—you'll love this—is 'soft kill.'"

Jess didn't say anything, but her face showed a touch of distaste and, oddly, sympathy: If Karl had accepted these realities, it was not without bitterness on his part.

"But how does this bear upon the 'Babel effect' idea?" Ryan asked.

Karl lowered his voice another step. "Some of these new-world-order projects are geared toward behavioral control of large populations. One goal of these is to cut productivity—to produce social problems that would render a population 'unable to sustain a prolonged military conflict' or 'unable to offer significant economic competition in expanding markets.' *Soft kill,* kiddies, sometimes referred to as 'denial of service.' In the large population behavioral-mod area, three primary technologies— neuroleptic chemicals or weaponized viruses or electromagnetic technologies. All can affect the brain and make populations docile, lethargic, violent, disoriented, or 'otherwise unproductive.' The U.S. government has conducted over four thousand behavioral modification experiments since the 1950s. The Russians, the Israelis, the Chinese have been at it just as long."

"These are experimental projects," Jess said. "But what kind of progress have they really made?"

"Projects like CORONA, ARTICHOKE, PANDORA, I can name five others, have made big strides. They can remotely affect behaviors of large populations to a statistically significant degree. How specific a behavior can they produce? Don't know. Disorientation for sure, and on a large scale that would produce social chaos. Also schizophrenic behaviors, and chronic excitability and anxiety. Any of those could accomplish your anarchy trick."

Ryan chewed on it for a moment. "So what are you saying? That the mess the world's in is the result of, what, a secret war of mind control? Or an experiment that got out of hand? I'm sorry, but—"

"No. I'm saying, one, that your basic premise is viable—that large populations can be subject to external neurological influences, large numbers of people can be made to turn dysfunctional and antisocial and ultimately violent. That there's a body of science that proves it's possible, there's been research on how it can occur. And, two, your poking around this stuff is going to be *frowned* upon, so *stay the hell away*. Fuck me, you know? I mean, why do I have to explain the obvious?"

"Karl—" Ryan began.

Karl leaned closer to them, whispering angrily. "You guys're gonna push me, but fuck you, huh? Because you have *no idea*. See, this goes way back, to the *forties*. After the war, the U.S. didn't just grab Wernher von Braun and the other Nazi rocket scientists. We grabbed their behavioral scientists, too. They're mostly dead now, but their legacy lives on, the thrust of the programs is the same. *Remote mind control.* They call it psychotelemetry, or RHIC, radio-hypnotic intracerebral control, or biocybernetics. Not a fringe thing at all, big program, *the* hot item. The 'Star Wars' missile defense program? It's a fucking joke, everybody in the industry knows it's just a cover, a funnel for RHIC black budgets." Karl's voice had become a hiss: "Everybody knows about it, but even the hard cases I know *don't talk about it*. Because people who leave these projects, or outsiders who sniff around? They end up *dead*. Beischer, worked on PANDORA, got pangs of conscience, disappeared mysteriously in 1977. Puharich, worked on MKULTRA, disappeared the next year, and coincidentally his house burned to the ground shortly thereafter. You want to know what happens? You have a heart attack. Or you go nuts and get involuntarily committed, end up having a chemical lobotomy. Or you unexpectedly commit suicide in a gruesome way. Guy I personally *knew*, John Ferry, worked on a General Electric SDI subcontract in England, committed 'suicide' by *chewing* on some live wires. Okay? Is that how you want Abi to find *you* some morning?"

When he was done, Karl took a moment to catch his breath, looking a little alarmed at himself. He checked the other diners around them again, looked relieved that no one had overheard, then pulled himself together with an effort. While Ryan and Jess sat, stunned, he gulped down another yogurt, licked his lips, considered his coffee and rejected it.

When Ryan finally started to speak again, Karl held up a hand. "No. Don't ask me any details, Ry, because I don't know them. Not my specialty, this shit's compartmentalized. And if I did know details, I wouldn't tell you anyway. You'd make a federal case out of it and get us all killed,

I've only told you this much to *maybe* save your asses and my own. And now I gotta get going. This is fun and all, but I'm up to fucking *here* with work. Also I've gotta go can somebody's ass on the cafeteria staff."

They stood up, brought their trays to the kitchen conveyor window. From Jess's subdued expression, Ryan could tell she was thinking, *All the shapes of evil. All the ways we murder what's best in ourselves.*

"Thank you, Karl," Jess said quietly. Karl's foul mood said a lot about how serious this was.

Karl ignored her. He brandished his coffee cup at a startled cafeteria worker. "Would you tell me what this is supposed to be? I mean, what, we're upstairs sequencing billions of nucleotides, but you guys can't make a decent cup of coffee? Give me a break! Who made this shit? You?"

Chapter 20

That night, back at Heart Cove, they had dinner on the deck, and then played board games until Abi's bedtime. Long day. By midnight, Ryan and Jess agreed they were shot and it was time for bed.

But they didn't sleep. It was a warm night, with a brisk offshore wind that raised a chop and drove waves racketing against the shingle beach. Ryan threw wide all the windows so that the bedroom filled with salty air and the floor-length white curtains blossomed, dancing far out into the middle of the room. Arms crossed behind his head, Ryan admired them for a while in the dim light. Unbidden, a phase-space graph took shape in his mind, and he marveled at how the ever-changing, billowing shapes so resembled the strange attractor that would probably be depicted if he represented their chaotic motion in a phase-space portrait. Really, it was almost the Ueda attractor. He conjured the equation from memory. So pretty. So sensual. Jess lay down beside him and watched the white phantoms with him.

"We don't have to do it," Ryan began. "We could back out. Marsh would understand."

"Why should we?"

Because it's gotten too big, he wanted to say. *Because it's putting too much at stake.* But he said only, "For starters, the things Karl mentioned." *Chewing on live wires.*

"You know as well as I do that Karl is prone to exaggeration and self-dramatization," Jess said. "You can't take any of that at face value." But she didn't sound all that confident.

"But that guy Bork, his attitude, the lost records—it stinks, Jess. We're being denied access to Brenner for some reason. And we've already seen how interested Shipley is—"

She just reminded him of the obstruction and bluster and threats they'd gotten from the Pentagon, so concerned that the Gulf War be a public-relations success, when Genesis had first probed the Gulf War syndrome. Genesis's response had been to press forward cautiously but relentlessly, gradually enlisting support. Tact and persistence and integrity had won out. "All I'm saying is," she concluded, "we've worked around these people before. We can do it again."

Maybe, Ryan thought.

They both watched the curtains for a time, and then he tried again, tentatively, hoping she'd take the initiative: "And there's the way it's affecting our personal lives. And our daughter's."

"Oh—I meant to tell you about the notice Abi brought home from school today," Jess said. Ryan waited, knowing that she never digressed without good reason. "Apparently there was an incident at school—"

"An 'incident'?"

Jess propped herself on one elbow to face him, barely visible in the darkness. "Apparently they arrested an intruder yesterday."

"What!"

"A strange man was wandering in the halls and wouldn't leave when asked. The police found a revolver in his car. They're not sure—"

"Jesus Christ! Who is this nut?" Ryan sat up in bed, his protective juices pumping.

"Well, they don't know yet—I mean, what sort of problems he might have. The school superintendent said they were hiring guards in the short term and were probably going to install metal detectors at the doors."

"For God's *sake.* This is a small town. It used to be—"

"Ry, stop bridling and let's keep talking about the subject at hand." She tugged his shoulder, pulling him back onto the pillows. "My point was going to be, it's not just 'somewhere else.' It's not something we can just ignore anymore."

Whatever they were arguing about here, he felt himself losing. The momentary serenity he'd felt in the swell of sea air and the dancing curtains had been destroyed.

"Okay." Ryan scowled into the dark. "So what are we going to do to make sure our family stays close while you and I become even worse workaholics and one or the other or both are off doing research who knows where? Jess, we've got a baby coming, and this 'Babel' thing, you've already been gone half the time, Abi's feeling it, I'm feeling it—"

"I'm aware of that." Her toned stiffened. "And I assure you, I'm very clear what the risks are. But, yes, Ryan, okay, I do have personal issues at stake here, things that mean a great deal to me. You think I don't know who I've been since Allison was killed? *I don't like that person either!* So I can either be a wife and companion and mother who is so caught up in a gloomy existential tangle that she can't be there for anybody, or I can sort some of them out and come back. Which would you prefer?"

He was surprised at how certain she sounded, as if she'd thought this out and decided something. He felt confused and in pain for reasons he couldn't entirely identify.

She sat up. "Well, I know which *I'd* prefer! And it may mean that you and I have to get some distance from each other for a while. I'm sorry. There are a lot of reasons, one of them being that you're a very strong presence, your viewpoints color mine, your rational processes affect mine. But we've always had different approaches to some things, and right now I need to track my own intuitions without your well-intentioned...interference."

That gave him chills, a sudden panic. "You asking me for permission? To—what? Separate or something, just because—"

"No! I'm asking for your understanding. More than anything else, your trust." Her voice snagged, got rough. "I am very fucked up right now. But, yes, I am very determined I'm going to proceed with this. Yes, it probably will mean my having more independence in my research agenda. And probably in my personal life."

She still wasn't being very specific, but suddenly he was afraid to probe it. "You'll still need to see your daughter," he mumbled. Bringing up Abi as if she were his last line of argument, of defense.

Jess heard it in his voice. "Oh, Ry," she said softly. "Of course. And my wonderful husband."

Her words felt good. Yes, that's what it was about. Being with Jess. Being loved by Jess. How badly he needed her, how many ways. He started to answer, but she leaned closer and put a hand over his mouth. "Just make love with me now," she whispered. He couldn't see her face, just her silhouette. "Just be close to me. Please."

Always an easy request to honor, Ryan thought. It had been so long since that wonderful night in the kitchen, since he'd felt he could get so near to her, and his body felt full, aching. She kissed him lightly, so tenderly it was almost tentative. Little gusts of sea air brushed their skin with vagrant caresses, and when at last they came together they moved for a long time in the rhythm of the waves outside. Release came not like thunder but as a long, gentle musical chord swelling to great sweetness. He flowed and filled her, feeling her silent climax midway.

Afterwards he watched the sinuous dance of the curtains. Jess was quiet so long he assumed she was asleep, and then she startled him by speaking.

"The things Dagan said—so much promise there, I've been touching the edge of it myself, afraid to go closer. I mean, it's no secret to anybody where I've been at. But wanting to find a cure just for some deep, altruistic love of humanity—it's not my only reason for wanting to take this project on. I wish it was. But I'm not that virtuous."

"Tell me," he prompted. Her voice was different now, husky, as if their intimacy and the release of sex had released something else as well, some barrier breaking and letting the hurt flow through.

Jess sat up again, barely visible but emanating a heat he could feel on his skin. "I've got this grudge, this bitterness. About what happened to Allison. When she was killed I wanted to go out and find the guys who did it and kill them, I wanted to tear them apart. I'm not, *not* over it." She struggled with the feeling for a moment. "So for two years I've been *hating* somebody invisible out there, somebody I don't know, I can't possibly find, for what they did. For wasting the life of my beautiful sister. For hurting me so badly. And then this project came up, and I've started seeing her murder in clinical terms, and now I'm thinking, *this is my chance to get them.* Only I don't have to find *them,* or hurt *them.* I'm going to go after the fucking, *fucking* godawful sickness in them, and I'm going to kill *that."* A tear splashed on Ryan's forearm from her invisible eyes, and her voice came out choked, the stifled cry of an agonized creature. "So help me, I'm gonna go out and find it and kill it, Ry, I'm gonna stick it with a pin. Because I can't live like this anymore, so full of these horrible feelings." She was crying and rocking on the bed, talking more to herself than to him.

Ryan waited it out. He didn't touch her, didn't dare comfort her, not right away. He'd tried in the past, and she wouldn't take it from him. For some things, taking any comfort was betrayal. You hungered for the blade of grief and anger.

The bed shook with her sobs for a time, and then she lay down again, moved closer to him, put her arms around him.

"Okay, babe," he said. "Okay. It's okay." He felt as if they'd cast off from shore. They really were going to do this. They really had to.

His fingers found her hair and tangled in the stiff resilient coil of it, so different from his own, so fascinating to touch. He synchronized his breathing with hers, felt the gentle drum of her heart as she lay against him. After a time her body became slack as sleep took her.

He watched the curtains billowing into the room: like wraiths, like clouds, like banners, like ships' sails.

Part TWO

I have seen the future, baby:
It is murder.
—LEONARD COHEN

It is the business of the future to be dangerous. . . . The major advances in civilization are processes that all but wreck the societies in which they occur.
—ALFRED NORTH WHITEHEAD

Attempted interview with Edward Michael Brenner, June 13:

Was to be preliminary interview to secure Brenner's consent to be tested.

Crimes: Eight victims, all women. Systematic stalking. Consistent appearance of victims (blond, petite), sexual assault, postmortem dismemberment. Vaginal rape both pre- & postmortem in all eight, ejaculation in abdominal knife wounds in four.

CV: 58, tall, overweight, thinning blond hair, repairman for Maryland Electric, unmarried, no children. Vietnam vet. Insanity defense (post-traumatic stress syndrome) didn't fly. Death row 12 yrs., due to be exec. June 29.

Affect: surly, confused, sad. More than anything else, lonely.

A repulsively ugly man. Disfigurement of face due to war injury & poor reconstructive surgery 30 yrs. ago: deep scarring on right cheek pulls lips up & exposes teeth, nose badly scarred, misshapen. Tilling Pen. prison psych. Ianelli says physical deformities/disfigurements common in heinous violent crimes because they negatively impact social development & integration. Have Dagan dig up stats, look for role of alienation, isolation, sexual (& parental?) rejection in profiles of disfig. (esp. facial) perpetrators. Data needed from Vets Admin. to establish brain trauma assoc. w/ wound.

(Had funny, inappropriate thought about Ry & his broken nose, its role in his asocial mind-set!)

???: Why the sexual dimension to so many serial crimes? Is it as simple as "crossed wires"—proximity of attractive sex objects or prospects trigger instinctive drive to copulate, but some neurological dysfunction causes parallel trigger of aggressive drives or overstim. of domination urges? But then what's the role of the stalking, which is anything but spontaneous. ???: Ianelli suggests double-Y here, maybe high androgen levels? ???: Again, repair work for electric co. suggests exposures to poss. neurotoxic agents—electromagnetic fields? PCBs?

???: Racial element. Brenner tests as xenophobe, has delusions of persecution by blacks. But victims are all white! Question arises, though, why are there almost no African-American serial killers? Ask Karl re: genetic foundations of obsessive/ aggressive traits, Negroid vs. Caucasoid.

Post: Visit to Tilling concluded with his new attorney's refusing interview and tests. Argues Brenner could self-incriminate, shoot down final appeal. Our request for Army service/med records met with denial, too (suspicious). ???: Could Brenner be former guinea pig of Army behavioral mod experiments?

Surprised at my reaction to Brenner despite what he's done. Something sad about him, like a lumbering tired-out farm animal, or a big confused child. Maybe it's his isolation from anything like normal, warm human contact, family, touch, nurture. Also, doesn't really understand what's happening to him, or why.

??? Such diversity of crimes, psych profiles, neurological conditions, etc. Is it realistic to think there might be a single underlying element shared by all these killers? I keep coming back to objectification, the epiphany I had during the Oakes interview: being able to treat people this way because they're just "things."

Ry argues often & well that our pursuit of the 'Babel effect' angle is dangerous, esp. after Brenner & the diagnostic session w/ Morales. He's right—maybe more than he knows. Must get more independent for this one, become the Skunk Works' one-woman Skunk Works. Try to insulate reputation of Genesis, esp. Ry, from some of controversy & peer/press flak we'll take for the radical tacks I need to use. From the more material dangers, too: compartmentalizing at this point will help protect Ry & Abi. Can't stand to put them at risk, but can't ignore this. Can't tell Ry, either, he'd never stand for me taking it on my shoulders. So far I've just put it in terms of my personal needs, which is also completely true—got to protect Ry & Abi from *me* right now. Maybe most of all.

Chapter 21

SEPTEMBER 16, 2002

Ryan braced himself against the fuselage wall as the plane hit a rough spot and the floor heaved. On the bench across from him, the two guards said nothing, but their faces tensed with strain. Both wore boots, camo outfits, and Kevlar vests, and held automatic weapons between their knees. The big one, Becker, had pale, pocked skin, a small mouth, eyes the chemical blue of a copper sulfate solution. The other, Omar, was a black man with delicate features, narrow shoulders. A glob of yellow marred the side of Omar's left eyeball, some scar on the sclera, probably an injury from his long career as a mercenary. Their shoulders bumped easily, as if they'd spent a lot of time together, and Ryan wondered briefly at what affections or loyalties might grow up between soldiers-for-hire.

A night flight, the last leg of his trip to the field site at Kalesi. Below stretched the night landscape of Central Africa, visible only when rare scatterings of light from towns gave dimension to the land. Twice already he'd seen the stuttering flash of artillery fire down there, leaving him with fleeting impressions of tiny trees and buildings, there and gone like fireflies in the summer grass. In the distance, exploding shells lit the night sky intermittently, inaudible, remote as heat lightning.

Mother Africa, in her agony, Ryan found himself thinking. *Like Korea, Algeria, Eastern Europe, Indonesia, Mexico. Like half the world.* Once you glimpsed the Babel effect concept, it was hard not to see it everywhere.

He'd taken commercial flights to Rome and then to Addis Ababa, where he'd met his guards and boarded this cargo plane for the flight to the tiny airfield at Kalesi. The dangers of the flight included passing over various contested borders and terrains, where the lone aircraft could be viewed by one or another side as a threat. Or where, just as likely, some disgruntled soldier with the right kind of weaponry might take a casual potshot at it. Back at Addis Ababa, Omar had offered Ryan both pistol and flak vest; he had accepted the vest, declined the gun.

Brandt Institute and Genesis had agreed to assist the World Health Organization in applying RAINDROP to an outbreak of a viral brain disease, a variant of the Venezuelan equine encephalitis strain, in the eastern Democratic Republic of Congo. It would be the system's first application in an actual epidemic, a little premature: Jess, Bates, and Leap weren't due to run the first tests of RAINDROP at the Sandia lab for another three weeks, and that was to test the system against either well-charted past epidemics or carefully designed hypotheticals. But the likelihood that RAINDROP could save thousands of lives warranted the Kalesi trial. If the system worked, WHO could not only anticipate the VEE outbreak's spread, but also trace it back to the natural reservoir in animal or insect from which it had made the jump to humans.

That alone would be hard enough to do—conducting medical tests on hundreds of people in a rural area without much high-tech, doing the exhaustive epidemiological intelligence work needed to establish a database. To make matters worse, the political situation in Central Africa had deteriorated in the month since they'd agreed to the trial. The whole region had become a war zone of competing tribes, factions, warlords, outlaws. For the victims of VEE, the social upheavals meant shortages of food, shelter, and medicine, and turned what should have been a comparatively minor infection into a lethal epidemic. For the WHO team, it meant they'd have to conduct an already difficult study in a crisis situation, a society in collapse. Dr. Ralph Gedes, WHO's administrator, had decided to go on only because the warlord currently in control of the area claimed to have stabilized the region around the Kalesi Regional Medical Center. For fat bribes, Colonel Banewe had guaranteed them safety on the ground and transport in and out—for whatever Banewe's "guarantee" was worth.

Aside from consulting on the Kalesi trial and the pending tests at the Sandia DOD lab, Genesis's involvement with RAINDROP was finished. The crew had been mostly engaged in Ridder's violence study since the beginning of August. Though the clinical end of it was primarily Brandt's responsibility, Genesis staff had so far sat in on sixteen complete death-row tests. They had looked at brain scans and functional studies and psych evaluations, pondering things like lesser atrophy of the vermis of the cerebellum, dopamine metabolism dysfunction, paroxysmal irritative patterns in bifrontotemporal areas, neurological disorders ad infinitum. Still, the medical database would have to broaden considerably before Genesis could really begin its main job: constructing the theoretical systemic models that would organize the clinical data into a meaningful, predictive pattern.

They'd designed a data-exchange protocol with Ridder Global, and would soon be establishing a dedicated land-line that would allow Genesis to look into Ridder's corporate data. In mid-August, a team of paranoid-looking security staff from Ridder had invaded the house and offices at Heart Point, inspecting the computer networks, the security systems, the windows and doors, the phones, the file safes. Ridder had even sent his black-jobber, Darion Gable, who had glided through the house and offices like a barracuda, sleek and cool, eyes appraising. At Gable's recommendation, Ryan had agreed to install new security systems and encryption technology for the phone lines.

Jess: finally getting fat. So very lovely. And so distant. She had pulled away a little when she was pregnant with Abi, too, a mysterious inward-turning that seemed to accompany baby-building. But this was different. She badly needed space, both personal and professional, and he had no choice but to grant it to her. For the last month she'd been gone four or five days a week, often requiring that they hire babysitters for Abi. Fortunately, Dagan was happy to step into some of Jess's mothering responsibilities, and had started sleeping over at Heart Cove almost every other night.

Though Jess said it wasn't about their relationship, he couldn't help seeing it that way. At the best of times it looked to Ryan like a temporary rough patch in an otherwise good marriage. At other times it felt as though something was slipping away, permanently.

He stared down at the lonely darkness below, missing her acutely and thinking, *Here's genius extraordinaire and Polish-Irish idiot savant Ryan McCloud, playboy of the Western academic world, hunched in his Kevlar vest, too tired to think, pining for some whiskey, missing his daughter, worried about his wife who is seven months pregnant and is spinning away from him. He's airsick, homesick, and he's got to take a piss. He's here to save the world.*

It would almost be funny if it weren't so pathetic.

The bulkhead door opened, and the copilot came back into the cargo hold. He spoke rapidly to Omar, who shook his head, then looked over to Ryan.

"We'll be landing in a few minutes, Dr. McCloud," he said. He was a big man with a high voice surprisingly at odds with his fierce face. "Please make sure your belts are secure. Also, the pistol Omar offered you earlier—I suggest you take it. You will probably find a use for it." When Ryan shook his head, declining, he shrugged and headed back to the cockpit.

A heavy *clunk* shook the floor, and then hydraulics whined as the landing gear descended. The wind noise rose alarmingly. Ryan looked out the window to see a handful of lights in the velvet black below, closer now.

Here we go, he thought. Supposedly his mission was to help the WHO staff troubleshoot the RAINDROP data-gathering protocols, teach the WHO field teams how their work contributed to the systemic analysis that would eventually result. But part of him kept coming back to Ridder's job, to the Babel effect. What better field of research than the tormented land and people of Central Africa? If the Babel hypothesis was accurate, there was another brain sickness at large in Central Africa, far worse than the VEE virus. He could almost feel it down there: like some demon snake, a great, twisting, fanged serpent, its gargantuan convulsions laying waste the land.

How do you protect yourself from such a thing? How do you hunt it and kill it? *Thanks, Omar,* he thought, *but there's no point in accepting your handgun. It will not suffice.*

A noisy, uneven descent to a jarring landing on rough tarmac, pounding heart and adrenaline tingle, smell of aviation exhaust, blurred lights speeding past the windows. The plane slowed enough for him to see that the runway lights were crude oil torches lashed to short poles, then taxied around to the terminal. The headlights from several trucks lit a clot of men, and Omar and Becker peered out the windows, taking a professional interest in what awaited them.

"It's okay," Omar reported. "I see Dr. Fahey there. He's probably paid off Banewe already. We'll be able to move the stuff to the trucks and be outta here."

Becker opened the forward hatch as men outside rolled up a mobile staircase, and Ryan carried his bags out into the African night. Humid air, the tarry smell of torches, the metallic crackle and yammer of a walkie-talkie. Below him stood a half-circle of men, most in camo outfits and carrying automatic rifles. Standing next to a huge man in a military uniform, Marshall wore a smile of welcome heavily slanted toward wry.

"Dr. McCloud!" Marshall called. "Aloha! Welcome to Kalesi!" He came forward and made a show of embracing Ryan and clapping him repeatedly on the shoulders, talking in a low machine-gun monotone the whole while: "This large fellow is nominally the local Rwandan Patriotic Front faction's officer in charge, but mainly he's running his own very profitable enterprise here. We like to keep him happy so he doesn't fuck us badly at some future date. He likes gifts—money first, whiskey if you've got it. I've taken care of the money for tonight."

"Meaning I'm on for the whiskey," Ryan muttered.

"I knew I could count on you!" Marshall smiled broadly as they turned and approached the giant, who waited expectantly with a pair of bodyguards. "Colonel, this is Dr. Ryan McCloud—Ryan, our good friend and protector, Colonel Banewe."

Ryan's hand was engulfed in a hand the size of a baseball glove. He thanked Colonel Banewe for his hospitality, then dug in his bag and reluctantly offered up the bottle of the Macallan he'd looked forward to sharing with Marshall.

"This kind I like," the colonel said.

"I thought you might," Ryan told him.

They transshipped the cargo to two heavy trucks, and by two in the morning set off toward the clinic, a twenty-mile drive. Ryan sat with Marshall, Omar, Becker, and a morose-looking driver in one of four jeeps, miffed about the Macallan and missing Jess and high as a kite on exhaustion and the excitement of being in a strange new place. In the bouncing glow of their headlights, the night landscape struck Ryan as eerie: deep forest on each side, palms and giant bamboos reaching into the night sky, occasional clusters of dark buildings.

"This road is pretty good," Marshall told him. "Whoever's in control keeps it open for access to the airport. We're lucky that way. The main refugee routes are north of here, and those'd be hard to travel. People on the road all night, and there's debris. And you can encounter... incidents."

They started as a solitary goat, tethered near the edge of the road and ghostly in the headlights, glared at them with an eye like an orange laser. Becker made a gun out of his forefinger and silently shot it.

Marshall went on: "I'm new at this myself, but I'm getting the hang of it. See, war is a great opportunity. Especially civil conflict. The moment central authority fails, everybody gets very entrepreneurial. Little fiefdoms spring up as some strongman gets control of one necessity or another, so you're constantly jumping through hoops, greasing palms, trying to secure alliances. Problem is, it's always changing and always escalating—you want your truck fixed this week, it's just outrageously expensive. Next week, who knows? Bribery, what they call *matabeesh,* was always standard here, but now it's a royal pain in the ass."

"But the field site's shaping up okay?"

"Getting close. With the equipment that came in tonight, the WHO people can finish assembling the CT scanner. If everything goes well, they'll begin the study in a couple of days."

A tall shape loomed suddenly in the road ahead. An old man, dressed in rags, walking unsteadily away from them, weaving, oblivious to their headlights. The driver blared the horn but didn't slow down. Instead he accelerated, nearly hitting the man, sending him reeling away.

"Jesus Christ!" Ryan turned to see the dark silhouette briefly outlined in the headlights of the truck behind them, then turned back to berate the driver. "What the hell? You nearly ran that guy over!"

"Doesn't speak English," Omar told him, looking back to check the convoy's progress.

"You don't stop," Becker explained. "That could be an old man, drunk or sick or fucked-up senile. Or just a way for somebody waiting in the bushes to get us to slow down."

"Those are the social niceties that are operant here, Ry," Marshall said, feigning indifference. "You get used to it."

The clinic's main building was a low rectangle of pocked concrete blocks and barred windows beneath a rusted tin roof. Its large compound was surrounded by a head-high mud-brick wall, backed up by crop fields and then the wall of jungle trees. Ryan hadn't seen the nearby Lindi River, but he could smell it, rich and wet in the night air. As the convoy pulled up, he was momentarily confused by the dark forms that littered the fore-court: humped, irregular, tented shapes of different sizes and mottled colors. *Boulders?* he wondered. *Animals?* Then he saw that they were people, lying down or sitting hunched under blankets or tarps. Some solo, some families clumped together.

Refugees, he realized.

He brought his bags to the veranda of the darkened main building, where he turned to look over the compound. The arrival of the trucks required moving the refugees nearest the clinic doors from their dusty beds, and now the whole yard was in motion. As the WHO security people moved among them, the dark forms moved and changed shape, casting strange shadows in the harsh headlight beams. Faces of weariness, anger, fear, resignation. A baby started crying. Ryan felt a chill contract his skin, despite the humid warmth of the night: It was one thing to see this on the TV news, another entirely to *feel* it, to know that these were people like yourself, kids like your kid. To hear that baby crying—the raw, reedy voice of exhaustion and outrage.

Five hours later, 8:00 A.M., Ralph Gedes paced at the front of the room, dressed in khaki pants and shirt, fidgeting with a laser pointer. One of the world's great virus hunters, he was the World Health Organization's administrator for this mission. He was a small, rugged-looking man with a deeply seamed face and short reddish hair, who spoke passionately as he limped back and forth. He had worked on the big Ebola outbreak in Rwanda in the mid-nineties, the peak of the genocidal turmoil there. After that experience, he'd assured Ryan, the current situation in Kalesi looked like a vacation at a luxury resort.

On the wall behind him, Gedes had set up large charts of human cranial anatomy, showing close-up cross-sections of the brain in bright colors. His audience was arranged in several rows of hard chairs: mostly WHO staff, translators, and various assistants, along with Ryan, Marshall, clinic director Dr. Joseph Tsonga, and his nursing staff. Altogether, around two dozen.

Tuesday morning. Through the open windows came the sounds of power saws and hammering as a WHO team built temporary buildings and a small supply warehouse for the project. Badly jet-lagged, Ryan had spent three unsleeping hours on a cot in the common room of the staff dormitory. The rule here was to make use of daylight, given the limited availability of fuel for the generators, so he had gotten up early with the others and spent an hour touring the facility and conferring with Marshall and Gedes. Just after breakfast he'd staggered to the communications center and managed despite bugs in the uplink setup to spend a few precious minutes talking to Jess, back at Heart Cove.

Gedes cleared his throat. "For those of you who haven't met me yet, I'm Ralph Gedes. My staff and I will be in charge of the medical aspects of this mission, but we're grateful for the presence of two of the RAINDROP system's main architects, Dr. Ryan McCloud and Dr. Marshall Fahey. They will be here just temporarily, to help with the first implementation of RAINDROP in the field."

Gedes took a moment to thank Dr. Tsonga and his staff for hosting the WHO team, and acknowledged the monumental job the clinic had done. Ryan had talked with Tsonga earlier, finding him to be a man of exceptional dignity, soft-spoken yet uncompromising. Solemn eyes in a coal-black face, graying temples, an English accent acquired at Oxford Medical School. Having strangers at his clinic was inconvenient, he admitted, but he was glad for their presence. Aside from the possibility that RAINDROP could halt the spread of VEE, there was another advantage: For the two months the study would take, the clinic would have a pipeline to desperately needed antibiotics and other supplies. And the refugees would get some food. Also there was the reassuring presence of the WHO's twenty-four-man security team, who could keep bandits or renegade army units away. Definitely a worthwhile trade.

"You all know the rough outlines of the project here," Gedes went on, "but I know some of the clinic staff are not familiar with RAINDROP, so I'd like to give you a quick overview." Using charts and laser pointer, he went on: So the key element of RAINDROP was *information.* More than a simple relief mission, their goal was to "map" their patients and their environment, gathering information and plugging it into RAINDROP's analytical system. This required three main teams. The medical team would conduct physicals and take tissue and serum samples from three hundred victims of the virus. The tests would culminate in something never before attempted in this region, CT scans of the patients' brains that would pinpoint the degree and type of neurological damage. Meanwhile, the epidemiological intelligence team would interview each patient to get personal and family histories from each one; the epi intelligence people would also go out into the countryside, locating medical records, workplace information, data about livestock and pets and insects, folklore about illnesses, oral traditions about wildlife—anything that could help identify patterns of infection. The third team, the vector-control people, would be out catching bugs and animals, likely sources of contagion—unlike prior VEE outbreaks, this virus didn't seem to be spread by mosquitoes. All data and samples would be flown to the United States, and after lab analysis the information would be run through RAINDROP on the DOD supercomputer at Sandia. With luck, RAINDROP could accomplish in weeks what had required years to do with Ebola, AIDS, and so many other infectious diseases.

Gedes gimped across the front of the room. "Our test subjects will be selected from the distressed population that's camping outside. At the intake stage, we'll do some screening, based on the criteria listed on page two of the handouts. After we select our test population, we'll move on to a thorough medical workup on each individual, and then on to the interview stage, where we'll establish the personal histories of our subjects. We'll save the CT scanning for last so that we build up a basis of trust before we subject anybody to too much high-tech."

Gedes waited while translators completed explaining his remarks to the Kinyarwanda- and French-speaking clinic staff, and then fielded questions on the logistics of processing so many people. The intake and interview work, he said, would be done in the open-air sheds now being built at the back of the clinic; the tissue work and cranial imaging would be done in the main clinic building. Samples would be refrigerated temporarily at the site, then shipped off to labs in the U.S. every five days, accompanied by the interview and personal-history paperwork for that batch and whatever data the vector-control people had turned up.

Outside, a bulldozer rumbled slowly past the windows, and the racket of hammers crescendoed. When the questions stopped and the translators caught up, Gedes went on. With his pointer he outlined the anatomy of the brain on the wall chart and talked about the specific damage that the VEE virus caused. Ryan shut his eyes and listened to the hammers, calculating the polyrhythmic drumbeat made by five or six men, each pounding and pausing and then pounding again on his own cycle. It took force of will to focus on Gedes again.

"One reason the serum samples are so important," Gedes was saying, "is that we'll want a genetic analysis. We'll want to cross-reference all data against genetic profiles, see if the disease moves differently in different families or tribal groups..."

Ryan stretched out his legs, feeling his awareness divide, the familiar stereo of cognitive multitasking: Gedes's voice, the voiceless internal flow of thoughts, the sounds outside: *Only two men hammering now. Five over seven: one of the hammerers striking faster than the other. Each man hammers, then pauses for an interval of about three strokes' duration, then swings five or seven more blows. Now the third man joins in again. Bulldozer hums a bass line.*

"Ryan! Hey, Ry!"

He opened his eyes, startled at the movement all around him. He jerked upright to see Marshall standing over him, the rest of the staff standing, stretching, leaving the classroom.

Marshall grinned and leaned to tap Ryan's temple with his forefinger. "Up, up, and away, huh?"

"Mmmph."

"Feeling a little jet-lagged?"

"Rosebud," Ryan croaked. His lips felt puffy and parched.

"Funny guy. Let's go. We got work to do."

Chapter 22

Wednesday night, Sept. 18

Dear Jess,

So good to talk to you, just to hear your voice, even for the few moments we had. Sorry about calling so early in the morning, your time. I have so much more to tell you than our live-time permits, so I'll send this as a fax later, now that problems with our uplink have been fixed. I am indulging myself, letting myself think about you—oh you my good wife who graciously accepts the overflows of my mind and body, even persuades me these excesses and fulminations are welcome!

I am in a staff dormitory at the back of the clinic, a big room with concrete floors and uncomfortable cots, and am writing this by penlight so I don't disturb the others—they deserve good sleep after the work they've been doing. Nearby I hear gentle snoring, outside I hear the murmur of our guards as they patrol the grounds, the thin cries of refugee babies in the courtyard. Beyond that a vast subtle night symphony of insect noises, and far away in the jungle darkness some cow is lowing, sounding distressed.

This morning Marsh and I (with several bodyguards) took a jeep and ran errands in the countryside. The clinic end of it is pretty standard medical work, but we need to help out the WHO epi intelligence people, who are a bit at a loss with the different data needs of RAINDROP. By day the Kalesi road carries a lot of foot traffic, mostly refugees plodding along, some carrying bundles of possessions or pulling carts. At intervals we saw their encampments, with fire pits, makeshift tents, people drowsing as they sat with heads on their knees, mothers with babies at wizened breasts. Several times we passed swollen corpses in the roadside ditch, the air above them hazed with flies. At first you avert your eyes, but they soon stray back out of sheer horrible fascination. I felt nauseous after the first, soul-sickened, but each one—I hate to admit this—affects me less.

It's a place of contrasts. Most people wear light slacks or shorts, and bright polyester or cotton shirts, but some still wear handmade tunics in traditional designs. On one hilltop an old barn made of bricks of rammed earth and straw, and on the next a red and white microwave relay tower (defunct). A burnt-out roadside general store/gas station had the remains of an air conditioner in one window, while chickens pecked in its doorways, guarded by a barefoot boy wearing a military tunic and carrying an automatic rifle. Even before the upheavals of the last twenty years, this had been a transitional society, caught between centuries-old agricultural traditions and the silicon era. Now an ugly new pattern has been superimposed on both, leaving an alien, disordered land—the Babel effect in action.

This afternoon I took a drive west of here, to the villa of an old Belgian, Gregoire Blyie, who has run a tea plantation in the hills for almost fifty years. I thought his perspective on changing events might offer me something we could use on the Babel project. In the last ten years his farm has become an armed camp, literally: he's set up machine guns in the windows, half his employees are functionally soldiers. I didn't really get anything useful off the old man, who's pissed off at everyone for everything, and talking with him means listening to his wandering diatribe, told in despicable English—he wouldn't let me speak French.

But to his credit, crusty old Gregoire has done a good thing. He has a tiny, private clinic—just eight sickbeds and a little dormitory, originally built for his workers—where he's been taking in people who got into trouble for resisting the various waves of genocide. About fifteen live there more or less permanently now. These are Tutsis who'd been tortured by other Tutsis, Hutus maimed by other Hutus, all because they didn't go along with the exterminations both sides had carried out. One guy's head was covered by long, finger-thick scars from machete wounds, another had no nose or ears, some can't walk. I talked to several of them, and was very moved.

These are sights that change your worldview, Jessie. This is long-term potentiation stuff, memories that won't ever leave me. My neural networks are literally branded with these images.

Like any traveler in a new place, I have had revelation upon revelation for the last three days. I struggle to write them down fast enough, but here's a couple of immediate importance to me:

1. In the clinic classroom there's a beat-to-shit upright piano, and tonight I was plunking on it for a while. Spreading my hand to play middle C and the C an octave higher, I realized that it was exactly the stretch it takes to place my hand on your belly (when you're not pregnant!) with my thumb touching one of your pelvic bones and my little finger touching the other. Your pelvic bones are an octave apart! Then I got into other thoughts of your body. And how beautiful you are now with that big belly, that odd, clumsy grace.

2. The people here—refugees and clinic staff—are mostly Tutsis and Hutus. (Usually I can't see physical differences, and tend to agree with those who say it's more of a socioeconomic distinction than an ethnic one.) Their faces have characteristic features: broad cheekbones, eyes with a slight uptilt as if there's a hint of a smile in them, skins brown and not the bluer black you see elsewhere. Revelation: Jess, they look a lot like you! You've often talked about the mystery of your ancestry—the great curtain that the relocations of slavery drew across the family histories of most African-Americans. Could you have Tutsi ancestors? Despite their exhaustion and demoralization, I find these people especially attractive because of this resemblance to you.

3. This is a land where terrible violence has been happening for decades, perfect for research into the origins of widespread violent behavior. I get all kinds of ideas, but the insights that click for me are vague and not very scientific. Here's one: Aryeh Levi, the guy who commands the WHO security unit here, told me a saying he'd learned from a Somali fighter when he was over there some years ago: "My son and I against my brother. My brother and I against my cousin. My brother, cousin, and I against another sub-clan. My clan against another clan." I get twitchy, thinking about it. You'd tell me that's just the uncharacteristic absence of whiskey in my veins.

In any case, there's a lot that I look forward to talking to you about when I get home. I realize how dependent my thought processes are upon you—the way your cognitive strengths complement mine, counterbalance my glaring weaknesses. I feel incomplete, stupid, without your input and feedback.

Another thing about being so far away is the perspective you get on your own life. Most important to me is our marriage. I feel I've been remiss or negligent in attending to ours. You and I were blessed, right from the start, with a magical sort of love and attraction, but I know it takes more than that to keep a marriage good. I realize now that we've been drifting apart for a time, I'm not sure how long. In the last three-four months, I've been blaming your work on the Babel effect, but now I wonder if that's just the symptom, not the cause. For years I've assumed it's just some temporary thing, the old magic will just automatically "fix" it. I know you have your reasons for getting distance right now, but it can't help matters that I'm a socially inept person, and that I've been such a workaholic. But maybe it's something needing our conscious work and attention. If you're willing. I hope you are.

But that's for when I get back. All I want to do now is tell you how much I love you. Your absence is a kind of torture.

Ry

Thursday, another staff meeting in the clinic's classroom. Today Ralph Gedes was filling them in on some very specific clinical concerns. *A bright guy,* Ryan thought, *top notch.* And yet after only a few minutes his thoughts were picking up speed, preparing for lift-off. Outside, the percussion section of carpenters' hammers and heavy sledges was in full swing, accompanied by the whine and screech of a circular saw and the occasional rumble of the bulldozer.

Gedes paused to pass out sheaves of paper. "What do we expect to see in patients with VEE? Mostly problems of classic encephalitis, as the lining of the brain swells. Fever, muscle pains, headache, prostration, suppression of startle-reflex responses. Please refer to section one on the handouts..." His voice went on. Ryan shut his eyes and hunched lower in his seat. Gedes: *Acute photophobia often demonstrated by covering the head and eyes, or other light-aversive behaviors...* The carpenters: *Ba-DOOM, takka-takka-racketa-takka... Historically, characterized by abrupt onset, but in this variant we're seeing incubation periods of days or weeks, which unfortunately improves the rate of subject-to-subject transmission. In the cranial scans, we'll be looking for progressive degeneration of... Pak-pak-patak, ba-DOOM, tak, tak, tak.*

Graphing the hammer rhythms, Ryan abruptly sat forward. Then he stood up, interrupting Gedes. The hammer music had gone bad.

"Excuse me, Ralph," he said. "That's gunfire."

The moment of shocked silence was immediately punctuated by the unmistakable staccato burst of an automatic weapon. Then the room exploded as two dozen people reacted. Tsonga began barking orders to his staff, people ran to the windows, Marshall and Gedes joined the crush at the door. Outside, several men of the security team charged past the windows. The refugees in the crowded compound began to move uncertainly, directionless.

Ryan ran out onto the front veranda, where he could hear that the gunfire came from the back of the clinic, beyond the construction area where the sheds and warehouse were being built. At the far end of the courtyard, a refugee man dropped suddenly to the ground and began to writhe, screaming, clutching his abdomen. A chorus of shrieks rose from the crowd, and they pulled away from the north end of the yard, massing against the head-high wall that surrounded the compound to the south and east. Three holes appeared in the door of a jeep parked at the end of the veranda, and then its windshield exploded.

Ryan felt his mind accelerate and expand, encompassing the scene. Pattern, interweaving causes and effects. *Priorities,* he thought: *damage control.* The north wall of the compound was little more than a ruin, and the attackers must be shooting over it or already inside it. Which meant that the six hundred refugees crammed into the main courtyard stood to absorb a lot of stray bullets. They had to be spread out. He grabbed a passing member of the security detail, recognized Becker, and shouted at him, "We've got to move these people! Disperse them. Out the south gate." The big, pale-faced mercenary ran across the compound and began herding the crowd by wild gestures and incomprehensible shouting.

Priorities: intelligence. The clinic staff couldn't respond effectively because they didn't know what was going on. Somebody had to find out. Ryan scuttled down the veranda toward the firefight.

He dove behind the shattered jeep and paused to listen. Crazy erratic gunfire. Still all small arms, no grenades or heavy machine guns yet. Part of his mind registered that off to his right the fallen refugee had stopped writhing and now lay motionless in a smear of blood-soaked dust. Farther back, the mass of refugees was pouring toward the south gate.

Peering around the front of the jeep, he could see the construction area: several incomplete sheds, the cinder-block walls of the warehouse, the yellow bulldozer, stacks of lumber and sheet steel. Beyond was the north gate and the tumbledown outer wall. Several security-detail men crouched behind each end of the warehouse wall, and others knelt or lay among the construction materials, firing into the scree of trees and scrub beyond. A worker lay sprawled on the roof of one shed, a runnel of blood spilling from his body and down the slant of corrugated steel.

Ryan spotted Omar among the men behind the warehouse, and darted forward. The mercenary didn't look up as Ryan piled into the dust near him.

"Omar," Ryan panted. "What's going on? Who's out there?"

Omar glanced at him with his yellow-clotted eye. "Not sure. We got scouts out and nobody saw anything, so we're thinking it's not a big force. But we don't know if that means twenty dipshit freelancers or a hundred members of a renegade army unit."

"There's not enough firepower for a hundred. More like a dozen or so, right?"

"Yeah. But that's assuming they're all coming in from this side."

Shit, Ryan thought. So this could be a diversion. Another force could be coming around to the south gate. Right where the refugees were trying to get out.

"What do they want?"

Omar shrugged. "Food, medicine, trucks, women? Who knows? Ask Levi." He jerked his thumb toward the other end of the wall. Ryan looked back to see Aryeh Levi, the security unit commander, hunched with a couple of men, talking into a headset microphone.

The corner of the wall exploded, spraying shards of concrete, and the man at the end fell back swearing. He wiped his eyes and his hand came away with blood. Omar snarled and leaped forward to fire a long burst around the corner, then pulled back as the fire was returned. Shooting picked up all along the line of defense. The injured man kept swearing as he groped his way back toward the center of the wall.

Aryeh Levi put a hand over his right ear and listened intently to his headphone. He shouted orders into the microphone, and then turned impatiently to Ryan.

"Dr. McCloud," he barked. "You should not be here."

"Who are they?"

"What I know right now is that we're facing about fifteen men. They have the advantage of good cover, the brush and the old wall. But their weapons aren't as good as ours."

"What's the danger of another attack on the south end?"

Levi wrinkled his face. "Yes, that's a concern. I have five men in position who will let me know if there's activity there. If there's going to be an attack from that end, it will start at any minute." Meaning, *Go away,* Ryan thought.

"Can you flush these guys out? Finish off this offensive and get more men to the south end?"

"That would be very nice. If we were playing video games. Charge them? We'd lose half our men before we reached their position." Levi winced as an urgent message made static in his ear. He listened, then cocked his head toward the new crackle of gunfire from the other side of the clinic. "There's movement at the southeast wall. If it's in force we're dead."

The attack at the south end was cue for a storm of shooting from the brush in front of them. *Predictable,* Ryan thought: *pin us down here, roll up the weaker defenses at the south gate.* The air hummed with bullets, the ground erupted, stacks of lumber exploded in splinters, metal cans and barrels tumbled and spewed streams of liquid. For the first time Ryan felt a visceral stab of fear, the instant shakiness of an adrenaline rush.

"Bulldozer," he panted. "Clean these guys out, get your men to the other side."

Levi started to snap a retort, but then eyed the bulldozer speculatively. "If it has not been too badly damaged to run," he said. And then he was shouting orders.

Under heavy covering fire, one of Levi's men ran fifty feet to the big yellow machine and, hunching low in the cab, started up its diesel. He yanked the hydraulics to bring up the earthmover's wide blade, and then, protected by the heavy wall of steel, set the tracks in motion. It became a standard armor-supported infantry maneuver. Bullets spat and shrieked off the blade and ripped up the ground, but within half a minute a dozen of Levi's men had massed in the shelter of the machine as it ground toward the enemy position. The bulldozer crashed through the old wall as the enemy, not prepared for a counterattack, broke cover and began to scatter. Levi's men cut them down.

Observing the adrenaline-stoked crouching and rushing, the harsh geometry of limbs and weapons, the sudden stumble and the contortions of wounded men, Ryan had a sickening revelation. He was seeing the fight, the pattern of movement, in clinical terms. *This is the body language of the disorder!* he realized. *A kinetic manifestation of the Babel syndrome.* It was as distinct as the characteristic stoop and shuffle at the Red Cross cholera camps he'd visited, or the wildly disordered gaits and gestures of mental-ward populations he'd studied. Suddenly he could feel the illness all around him, an invisible plague, infecting everyone and everything in this place. Now some of the security detail were stooping to fire their pistols into the heads of wounded men.

The human condition in the plague years. Hoc est corpus meum, he thought incongruously, *This is my body.* He threw up into the dirt.

It took only two minutes to finish the fight at the north end, and immediately Levi sent a group of men racing around the clinic to the south. Ryan heard the firefight there, but did not see it. He was full of revelations, choked with them. *Jess, my Jessie, I need to talk to you. Are you okay. Are we being crazy.* He trotted back into the courtyard to find clinic staff already out and tending to the wounded in the littered square. Beyond the south wall, the firing crescendoed as WHO mercenaries surprised the attackers there. Within moments it subsided to a pattering of individual shots.

One of the fallen bodies turned out to be Becker. He lay facedown in the dirt, and Ryan saw no blood until he turned him over and found a neat red hole below his right eye. The big torso was already inert as a side of beef.

They held a late-night meeting in the clinic classroom, where Levi briefed them on the day's events. They had been attacked by a force of about thirty men, he said. After questioning the three prisoners, he'd determined that most of them were former soldiers in a faction of the Tanzanian Regional Stabilization Army who had begun to forage for themselves. Their band had picked up recruits from the desperate towns and villages in the Kalesi region, and survived by preying on farmers and small merchants. The clinic had looked like easy pickings—food, medicine, salable equipment—but the renegades had scouted it before arrival of the security forces, and they'd been unprepared for a well-armed defense.

"What is the word for such men?" Levi asked with distaste. "If they oppose you, you call them criminals or bandits. If you are a local warlord and they are your friends, you pretend they're a legitimate army unit, you call their stealing 'appropriation of supplies.'" In Central Africa, he reminded them, over a hundred thousand men now roamed in similar armed bands, without homes or loyalties or restraint.

"And now let's do the numbers," Levi said grimly. His men had killed seventeen and captured three; of those who got away, many were no doubt injured, and he didn't expect them to try another attack. Of the security force, Becker and two other men had been killed, six wounded, and two construction workers had died. Four refugees had been killed, eighteen injured, by bullets hitting the packed crowd. Many more would have died if they hadn't dispersed quickly. Levi took personal blame for the clinic's unpreparedness, and vowed to remedy his oversights immediately. He would also requisition another dozen men, additional weapons and communications equipment.

Ryan sat at the back of the room, bone-weary but electrified. His mind was seared with the images of the day: the convulsing movements of the first refugee he'd seen hit, the drip of the carpenter's blood from the shed roof. The awful hole below Becker's eye where a bullet had violated the privy mystery of his head.

A succession of horrors. And yet the most persistent and painful image was that of a living man—Omar, who had returned to the compound to find Becker dead. He'd rushed to Becker and shaken him by the shoulders and slapped his face and yelled at him. Yes, mourned him like a lover. He would have butchered the three prisoners, but Ryan stepped between them, and several mercenaries held back poor Omar as he struggled and spat. The prisoners were exhausted, underfed black men in ragged khaki uniforms, abjectly hopeless as they knelt side by side with hands bound behind them. Again and again Omar lunged at them, face shining with tears, teeth bared, his love reduced to grief, grief boiled down to a poison.

Love in the Days of Babel, Ryan thought. He let himself touch lightly the feelings he had for Jess and Abi, holding them close inside and feeling supremely privileged, lucky beyond measure.

Chapter 24

The jeep bucked in a deep pothole, and Ryan steadied himself against the burning-hot dashboard as he tried to read the fax. One of the communications crew had handed it to him as he and Marsh and three bodyguards had pulled out of the clinic's parking area. They were driving the twenty miles to Colonel Banewe's headquarters because Gedes felt it was important to let him know about the raid. Hopefully, they could also get an update on other military activities in the area.

The fax was from Jess. Parts of it were spotty, garbled, owing to technical problems that had plagued the uplink equipment from the beginning.

> I love you and miss you. Got your fax, found its implications profound. I've been very busy here, doing some research along the lines you suggested, and I do think we're on to something! Which means I'll be traveling again and out of touch for a few days. But I'll be back in time to pick you up at the airport next week.
>
> Dagan has volunteered to stay at the house full-time to look after Abi, who is being a terrific kid, although she misses her parents very badly. So far the impending sibling hasn't awakened too much jealousy, and she claims to be looking forward to November 11....

Reception had faltered, and the rest of the message was mostly illegible: ...*every day another...Bates and I...nice to know our friends are keeping an eye on us!...Abi's new teacher says...* Maybe the missing text would find its way to the clinic later.

I do think we're on to something, she'd written. Ryan thought: *"We"? "Along the lines you suggested"?* Nothing he'd said to Jess was particularly cogent or specific. She gave him too much credit, as always.

"I'm going to tell him we want some goddamned stability around here," Marsh was saying. He sat between the two guards in back, scowling. "I'll remind the son of a bitch that if anything happens to this mission, he loses those nice fat payoffs Gedes has been handing him."

Marshall's complaints expanded, taking in staff problems at Brandt, red tape, lousy suppliers back in the States. Ryan just rode the bucking jeep and watched the countryside: deep forest, black-green beneath the merciless sky, broken by occasional clearings where naked children, their hair orange from malnutrition, played around crumbling mud houses. He pondered Jess's fax and reviewed his own objectives for the day. While in Kalesi, they'd stop in to see Stu Richardson at the WHO vector-control team's headquarters, located in an abandoned bicycle factory. He wanted to talk to Stu about some vector-related issues, but, more important, he'd heard there was a black-market distributor nearby, reputed to have a cache of the region's infamous raffia palm wine. Stu might know where it was. Five days without booze was enough.

The jeep slowed as they approached a crowd of pedestrians, shuffling determinedly westward, carrying their meager possessions: bundles of cloth, wicker baskets, nylon backpacks. One man struggled to walk a bicycle to which had been lashed a preposterous pile of furniture and clothing. Behind him walked a woman in a formal pantsuit, carrying nothing but a portable television. Near a bridge abutment, the river of refugees detoured around a heap of tumbled bodies—a whole family, several children as well as adults. More trucks rocked among the foot traffic, and motor scooters veered crazily between pedestrians.

"There's something different," Marshall observed. "The activity level's different. More traffic. More…anxiety. Don't you think?" When Ryan didn't answer, Marshall pounded his shoulder. "See? I can't even get my *friends* to listen to me."

Ryan looked around at him, feigning surprise. A joke. But Marsh was right: It all felt more urgent. More sense of imminent menace.

————

They came around a bend and saw the farm compound that Colonel Banewe used as his headquarters. The colonel had commandeered the property of a wealthy farmer, set up his officers' residence in the house, and converted the mud-brick storehouse to an armory. The farmyard was full of military equipment: battered troop trucks, light artillery, piles of armaments and supplies. Khaki-uniformed men bustled among the piles, loading trucks, tending weapons.

Ryan was surprised to see a large crowd of men sitting motionless in a barbed-wire enclosure that flanked the drive. Armed guards stood at intervals along the fence, and as they drew closer Ryan could see that the men inside were in bad shape—emaciated bodies, falling-away clothes, a beaten look. Many had oozing wounds, and some were too exhausted to chase away the flies that clustered on their eyelids.

"Who are those guys?" Ryan asked.

"Banewe says they're 'war criminals.' People he says committed atrocities during the last wave of genocide."

"Hard to imagine the colonel suddenly suffering pangs of humanitarian conscience."

Marshall gave him a sour grin. "No. My guess is that the RPF is trying to curry favor with the UN. Or, more important, they'd like to look good to the U.S.—they want to look legit so they'll be allowed to purchase more weapons from American arms suppliers. Probably so they can commit more genocide, more effectively. Ironic, or what? As far as the colonel's personal motivation goes, I suspect it's just another way for him to advance his own situation—win some international recognition, position himself for future leadership roles. The war-crimes trials of '98 and '99 were a fruitful cottage industry, helped make some major careers."

Ryan nodded, looking over the mass of men, and thought ahead to the day's agenda. *Change of plans,* he decided. *Conditions permitting.*

The mood at the colonel's headquarters was uneasy. After passing through several heavily armed perimeter guard posts, the jeep pulled up in front of the villa, where wary soldiers took away the WHO bodyguards' weapons. A line of trucks stood in the forecourt, mechanics working under their hoods, as men hurried to load boxes of munitions and supplies. Officers barked orders and glared suspiciously at Ryan and Marshall as they were ushered into the colonel's presence.

The colonel himself had lost the clownish quality Ryan had seen at the airport. His wide brow was as dark and disturbed as a thunderhead. He sat in a wooden chair on the villa's veranda, talking angrily into a radio phone. An unfinished meal was spread on the table before him, along with piles of papers, a pistol, and Ryan's bottle of the Macallan, half down.

An aide told Ryan and Marshall to sit while the colonel finished talking. "He has very little time to see you," the aide said. "Five minutes only." He frowned and held up a hand with five fingers outspread.

The colonel tossed down the phone and shouted orders to an officer in the yard, and then turned to glower at Ryan and Marshall. He muttered something in Kinyarwanda, and the aide translated: "What brings you here today?"

Marshall told him about the attack on the clinic, the aide translating almost simultaneously. "We, uh, thought you would like to know," Marsh concluded lamely. Ryan was grateful he'd omitted any complaints against the colonel.

Colonel Banewe looked at him wide-eyed and then reared back, opened a cavernous red throat, and laughed uproariously. When he came out of it, he spoke rapidly to the aide.

"He says he is glad you came to amuse him this afternoon, because your little concerns offer humorous relief from other pressing matters. And now, if that is all, you can go."

"What pressing matters?" Ryan asked. "What is all this activity about?"

The colonel took on his dour face again as the aide translated: "Military events are putting pressure on this location. The TRSA has unexpectedly won a victory over our allies to the north, and a force is moving this way. We are mobilizing to retreat or to attack, as the situation demands."

Marshall looked stunned at the news. Colonel Banewe's little domain had been a shelter. The WHO mission had counted on a period of relative stability, at least a steady ambient chaos, in which to complete the RAINDROP study. Outright war could put an end to the project.

"There is more," Ryan said. "More that worries the colonel."

Quick conference, then the translation: "The colonel says you are astute. Yes, our allies in the southern RPF are at odds, a faction has split off. We must choose to go one way or the other."

"Can we help you?"

Again the colonel reared back, opened his throat, and laughed until tears came to his eyes. This time when he was done he spun the top off the Macallan and sloshed some into a metal cup. He spoke with obvious sarcasm, and drank quickly. "Yes," the translator said, "you can give him ten thousand more men and some tactical nuclear weapons."

"If you move, you will have a problem with your prisoners," Ryan countered. "What will you do with them? They are the price of your legitimacy in the eyes of foreign governments, but here and now they slow you down, they drain your resources."

"What're you doing, Ry?" Marshall muttered.

The aide's eyelids tightened in dislike as he looked at Ryan, but he translated again: "He never wanted the prisoners—they were imposed on him by our regional commander. You want them? Take them. Otherwise he will have to shoot them all, or let them loose again." Banewe feigned indifference, but Ryan sensed his interest had been piqued. The big man tasted the whiskey, waiting for Ryan's reply.

"First, give me a sip of that," Ryan said.

Banewe understood without translation, and spoke immediately, holding Ryan's eyes. "He says, 'First tell me why you are called after an animal that stinks,'" the aide said.

Ryan was momentarily at a loss, but Marshall laughed nervously. "When we were waiting for your plane," he explained, "I described you as a very famous man, who solved problems. I used the words 'Skunk Works' to describe your...your expertise. He must have asked his translator to clarify. This man has a good memory, Ry."

Ryan explained it to the colonel's satisfaction, and was rewarded with a dollop of whiskey in a red plastic cup. Then the baleful look returned to the colonel's eyes. "You were going to explain how you could help me, Mr. Skunk."

Ryan was running on automatic pilot. He downed the whiskey quickly and cherished the heat of it. "Who are these men, Colonel? Are they really war criminals, or are they just a collection of your own insubordinate troops and political enemies? So that you can pretend to care about justice and dispose of your opponents all in one gesture?"

Colonel Banewe slapped his hand on the tabletop so hard the plates jumped, and then he picked up the big pistol, eyes blazing. He pointed the gun at Ryan and talked like a jackhammer for a long moment. The aide translated: "He says he is not in a mood to be insulted. These are bad men, who killed and tortured children and women. He has kept them at great expense to bring them to trial so that the UN will know the RPF is a serious political force. He has files on many of them. He says you are so smart that you are stupid, because he is the one holding the gun and you are not. So now you must solve two problems—how to help him and how to help yourself. Because if you have been talking through your ass he will kill you right now."

Ryan kept a relaxed façade by force of will, but sweat began to roll down his forehead and into his eyes. In the square, soldiers had stopped to watch the confrontation, and the WHO guards who had been smoking cigarettes at the jeep were suddenly surrounded by a tense knot of men with weapons raised.

"Tell him that our problems are now identical. I can stave off short-term danger by levering against long-term resources. Just as he can."

The aide translated. "Okay," the colonel prompted in English. His gun didn't waver.

"Marshall," Ryan said, "you're not going to like this, but it's important, and we'll work it out with Gedes. Trust me, okay?" Marshall threw up his hands, baffled, and Ryan turned back to the colonel. "Select the twenty worst criminals, men you are sure have committed the worst atrocities. Turn them over to us. Give us any files you have on them. We will subject the men to some tests, and maybe we will learn why they are such bad men."

The aide translated contemptuously: "And the others? There are over two hundred!"

"When you leave here, let them go. Wait, hear me out! You wish to be disencumbered of them. At the same time, you wish the world to know you are sincerely attempting to remedy the atrocities. So today you compose a message to the secretary general of the UN, saying that due to field exigencies you were forced to release these men, despite your best intentions. We will use our satellite uplink to send the message, tonight. In a few days I will be leaving here, and I will carry your original document and files with me. I'll deliver the materials to the UN myself and tell them how you cooperated with me. You are free of the tactical problem of what to do with them, and you win your side a small long-term advantage."

It took a long time to translate, and then the aide and the colonel exchanged words for a time. The gun drifted down into the colonel's lap.

"What the fuck're we going to do with twenty *war criminals?*" Marshall hissed. "Jesus, Ry, now I remember what a pain in the ass you are—"

"A differential study for the Ridder job. We're going to test them. Compare them to their opposites—to people who've resisted atrocities. The people we saw at Blyie's place."

"And then what? It's a clinic, not a prison camp!"

"Fuck if I know," Ryan said.

"Ry, comparison studies for behavior come with a lot of ethical freight. We're not—"

"A once-in-a-lifetime opportunity, Marsh! For once, all the elements are in place—the high-tech and the staff and a big subject population, Ridder'll reimburse Gedes—"

But the colonel interrupted them. "Okay, Mr. Skunk," he said. He panned his yellow gaze over them, then looked away and tossed the gun to the table. He muttered on in Kinyarwanda as he shoved plates aside and began spreading out a large, badly creased map.

The aide said, "He says he will personally select the men for you. He will send a truck with the prisoners and whatever papers he has on them—tonight. And now you can go because you are giving him indigestion."

Chapter 25

SATURDAY, OCTOBER 5, 2002

The differential study came off with surprisingly *little trouble,* Ryan thought. *Too bad it was all for nothing.* Because fourteen days after the visit to Colonel Banewe, here he was with nothing better to do than count paces. He took another turn around the cramped cell: three short steps, left turn, four steps, left again, three steps, left, four steps back to the little window just above his head.

On the bright side, being a prisoner allows you plenty of time to reflect. Too much time, actually. They'd taken everything, even his watch, his pen, his notebook. It was Sunday, and he'd already stayed in Kalesi two weeks longer than he'd originally intended. Three days in this rustic version of sensory deprivation was beginning to get to him. The moaning of the invisible prisoner in the next cell didn't help.

After the first day they had not given him any extra water to pour into the toilet gutter in the floor, and the stink was beginning to get suffocating. He clung to the windowsill and inhaled the gentle current of fresher air that occasionally wafted in from outside. Getting an actual cell at the Kalesi jail, one of his guards had told him, trying out his English, was the local equivalent of the VIP suite at the Ritz. Most people taken prisoner by the TRSA ended up packed into a steel Quonset hut in the industrial end of town, standing in their own shit as they died of heat and dehydration.

Fame has its uses after all, Ryan thought. It meant he was worth more alive than dead.

The cell had a mattress, two inches of insect-infested stuffing in a canvas shell, which after the second day Ryan had propped upright against the wall. Now whenever the rage threatened to overcome him, he'd take it out on the mattress, brutalizing it with his fists. The skin over his knuckles was raw, and the bones in his hand had started to spread and ache. The pain was a distraction from worse discomforts. Like not knowing whether anyone knew where you were. Whether Jess had gotten back to Boston all right from wherever. Whether your kid was okay. Whether you'd get back in time to be with your wife in the last difficult days of pregnancy, or even for the delivery, only five weeks away. Whether you'd get back at all.

Gedes had valiantly opted to continue the Kalesi study despite the radically changed situation. "We're the goose that lays the golden eggs," he'd explained. "Doesn't matter who's in control—we'll just bribe 'em, persuade 'em it's in their best interests to keep us happy. Why kill us or shut us down?"

Ryan hadn't mentioned that logic wasn't necessarily the TRSA's strongest feature. Or that in outright conflict the clinic could become collateral damage with one misplaced artillery barrage. The deepening lines of worry between Gedes's brows suggested he knew it, too.

Colonel Banewe had retained control of the airport for a few more days, and Marshall was able to fly out on schedule. Ryan had originally intended to fly with him, but he'd opted to stay another five days to oversee the testing of the twenty war criminals and an equal number of volunteers from Gregoire Blyie's mountain sanctuary. Marshall had argued against the study, citing the excesses of the eugenicists in the U.S. and Britain in the 1920s, who had looked for physical and genetic explanations for every human failing from murder to marital infidelity to spitting in public. Ryan had answered that in the face of tortured kids, cut-off limbs, and piles of bloated corpses, such ethical niceties seemed a little too nuanced. Anyway, the clinical tools and medical technologies of the twenty-first century allowed a vastly more detailed assessment. The study might just answer the critical question, *Under the same environmental conditions, what makes one man become a violent sadist, the other a saint?*

Those last days at the clinic had become increasingly tense as artillery battles made a muffled thunder, a storm drawing closer. By Thursday, when Ryan finally got to the airport carrying his two hatbox-sized liquid nitrogen coolers full of samples, it was too late. The soldiers standing on the field weren't Banewe's men. They led him away at gunpoint to be questioned by their commander. He'd looked back to see them already ransacking his luggage—including the precious sample cases, which were opened, shaken, tossed away. The glass tubes of hard-earned evidence spilled and shattered, steaming, on the sizzling pavement. The psych-test records flung and blowing away across the landing strip, paper trash in the hazy sun.

His interrogator was the new warlord who had taken the airport: a small, evil-faced officer who introduced himself as General Wiselle. He had shining blue-black skin seemingly stretched too tight over the bones of his face, as if he had pulled a nylon stocking over his head. He spoke English well and was a fastidious dresser, looking dandyish in an overly ceremonial uniform, drawing sensuously on a cigarette. When Ryan bluffed indignantly at being detained, Wiselle got a greedy look in his eyes. He had issued orders for this important American to be treated well, but as a reminder of who was in charge he had flicked his cigarette butt into Ryan's face.

Whap! Whap whap whap! Ryan savaged the mattress.

The worst part was not knowing anything. But presumably Ryan's having the VIP suite meant General Weasel figured he was somebody worth extorting favors or ransom for. Presumably when he hadn't arrived, Marshall would have figured out what happened and begun efforts to release him, informing the U.S. State Department, the UN, maybe the Red Cross, who would contact the Weaze. By now, presumably, Jess would have gotten safely back from wherever the hell she'd been, Marshall would have kept her informed. She'd know he was okay, that efforts to get him back were under way.

Presumably.

That night he put the mattress back on the floor under the window, where a cooling thermal current descended over him and banished some of the shit smell. From this angle he could see a rectangle of sky that offered some slight relief from the sense of confinement. His arms ached from punching the mattress. He listened to a generator droning outside, muttering voices, an argument. Someone weeping in one of the other cells. The tick and whir of insects.

At Project Alpha they had done a number of experiments on the cognition of subjects in sensory deprivation. The volunteer was placed naked in a covered tank half-filled with a saline solution heated precisely to body temperature. The fluid buoyed the subject's body, reducing the sensations of weight, friction, and temperature, and the tank was kept completely dark and insulated against external sound.

In the absence of any sensory input, without physical tasks to occupy it, the mind did strange things. First, mental imagery became foregrounded—without the usual distractions of real events, mental events such as memory or fantasy took on an unusual vividness and continuity. Second, the subject in the tank soon lost all sense of time, and without external referents would experience hours or days of mental life in minutes or seconds. After a while, as if desperate for stimulus, the subject's brain began improvising mental narratives—hallucinations, fantasies, dreams, memories, all intermingled seamlessly. By normal standards, the subject went temporarily crazy.

Ryan had tried the tank several times and hated it. He was always out there to some degree, always able to distance himself from sensory phenomena, didn't need deprivation. And he needed to *do* things. He needed to be physical, to draw or write or fiddle, to hit, to go jogging, to work with his hands. After two hours in the tank he'd start to experience an acute sensation of irritability and uneasiness.

Now, after three days in this bare six-by-eight cell, nothing to occupy his hands, he was beginning to enter a mental state like those times in the deprivation tank. Trying to ignore the lice on his skin, he forced himself to talk in his head, make some headway, stay above this situation. You had to be disciplined if you wanted to survive.

Without laboratory analysis of the samples and other data that had been destroyed, he couldn't reach firm conclusions about the differential study. But several of the war criminals had shown what looked at a glance to be slight frontal-lobe atrophy—maybe. A definitive determination would require computer-assisted morphometric and volumetric analysis. Like Morales, they'd also had elevated blood levels of cortisol. Of course, that would be expected of any highly stressed population.

In any case, the crucial question was, What did any of these neuroanatomical and neurochemical features actually *do?* What behavioral programs did they skew, inhibit, or upset?

Recent developments in the cognitive neurosciences might help provide an answer. One of Project Alpha's claims to fame was its role in developing the modular/computational theory of mind, which held that within the brain exist numerous separate functions—modules—each doing its job in a quasi-independent way. The job of each was to do computations, and any behavior was dependent on which specific modules were activated and what their collective computations added up to. To survive in the gene stream, these modules evolved to effectively serve survival-enhancing needs or drives or behaviors.

Ryan paced three steps, four steps, three. He punched the mattress, wanting to smash the close walls, get a long view, some air.

Simple example, he lectured himself: You're working in the yard, when you look up to see someone striding rapidly up your driveway. His sudden appearance startles you, and in response, several modules in your brain kick in. The first are a set of modules that collaborate to compute danger. They forward a provisional risk assessment to another module, one that activates heightened alertness and encourages you to seek more information on the potential threat.

So you look the intruder over more carefully. He's still a hundred feet away, but now your eyes report that he's a large guy with a lot of agitated body movement, carrying some kind of a heavy stick. Now your risk-assessment modules are leaning toward a danger scenario, so they report this information to another module that kicks your body into a risk-response mode of accelerated heartbeat and breathing, a readiness to run or fight.

One second later, the guy is closer and more visual data is available. Some of the risk-assessing modules are dedicated to computing social contexts—vital, in a social species, to avoid conflict when possible and to help build useful coalitions. Now you can see that his face is red, he's breathing hard, and the stick he's carrying is a baseball bat. Social clues that signal probable aggression.

At this stage you've got three choices. If he's really scary and your cost-benefit modules calculate he'd beat you in a fight, you should run—retreat, get a weapon, get help. If those same modules figure you might frighten him off, or win in a fight, you should stay put and confront him here. And if your social-context modules say that he's not actually scary at all, you'd do better to hold off, engage in a beneficial transaction. Your cost-benefit modules confer with your social-context modules and certain memory modules. They check up on each other, asking, *Does this jibe with past danger experiences?* or *How extreme is the danger?* or *What's his emotional state?* or *Do I know this guy, and if so, what was my last transaction with him?*

As it turns out, the guy is close enough now to see that it's Ed Jones, your neighbor—a tall, overweight, pleasant guy, a pediatric orthodontist. He's carrying a baseball bat because he's been hitting a few with his seven-year-old son, and the ball has come over the hedge into your yard. He's red and breathing hard because he's out of shape and the walk up the drive has winded him, and he's agitated because he's a little embarrassed, he's afraid maybe the ball broke a window. Using visual and now linguistic cues, your social-context modules calculate all this and send definitive information that calms your risk assessors down. Your cost-benefit modules calculate that a friendly transaction is to your benefit, and it all soothes your fight-or-flight modules, which calculate the state of metabolic readiness appropriate to talking to Ed Jones.

Good thing you didn't take a swing at him with your rake, or run for the gun.

The advantage of the modular/computational model was that it could theoretically allow you to pinpoint what exact behavior had malfunctioned when somebody went violent. The problem was that there were so many modules, and none were lumps of tissue located in any specific site in the brain but rather circuits running through various regions, interconnected in various ways. And no behavior stemmed from a single module, but rather from many acting in concert.

So then you had to look at the genetic imperatives that operated through these modules. Every computational module had been selected by evolution because it worked effectively for the survival of those who possessed it. Obviously, dealing with threats was a basic survival instinct, and a lot of violent behavior clearly had to do with the perpetrator's failure to calculate risk accurately, or with an overactivation of the fight-or-flight response, or with the failure to accurately calculate social contexts.

But survival required innumerable other drives, needs, responses, and behaviors, and the dysfunction of any of them could conceivably result in violence. Status was a big one—as Bates had said, status-seeking instincts became the engine of violence when individuals felt compelled to compete extra hard for position in a social hierarchy, access to mates and resources. Sex, and all the instincts of courtship and competition and copulation, was another genetic imperative. So was food sharing, caring for children. Spousal bonding.

The thought brought him abruptly back to the cell, to the absence of Jess. For a moment he hung from the window bars, gulping air and trying to steady his emotions. Then his discipline failed him, and he thought of her. Holding her, talking, caressing. Her scent. Her weight in his arms. The sense of harmony, almost telepathic, when they worked together.

Before the last few months, anyway.

That brought on a wave of anxiety and despair. He realized that what really moved him, more important than identifying the origins of violence, far more compelling, was the need to understand his wife. What she was thinking, what she was doing, where she was going. Far more important. Far more mysterious.

Somewhere on the outskirts of town, shots were being fired. Not a firefight, but an even, slow tempo: *pom! pom! pom! pom! pom! pom!*, six shots, three seconds apart. The shots stopped for a moment, then started again, stopped and started again. Methodical, like target practice. *Why waste ammunition? Why the middle of the night?*

It took him another moment to comprehend. *Of course.* In his sensory-deprived, hyper-cerebral state, the image came to him with vivid clarity. He had the clear sense that General Weasel was seeing to it personally, a pleasure he reserved to himself. The executions.

Chapter 26

Another day. Another single meal of manioc, a lump of pasty starch on a tin plate shoved through the door slot. Another night of undiluted mental activity. Tonight the rain fell in a rumbling torrent outside his little window, Noah's deluge, and with it came the past. He fought it for a few tortured hours, and then, exhausted, felt it carry him away. Memories. Way back, vivid as a film.

Moving to South Boston from Chicago. Late June. Ryan was eight and Pa's mother had died and they'd inherited her house on Linden Street. Ryan rode with Ma in the Chevy, Tommy with Pa in the U-Haul, and when they pulled up in front of the narrow, clapboard house it all seemed foreign and forbidding. Strange kids had eyed their little caravan as it navigated the narrow streets of South Boston. No yards in front of the houses, not even a little patch of grass like the ones back on Campbell Street in Chicago. Ryan was acutely conscious of being an outsider, and of the McCloud tribe being not much of a shelter from the big world they'd just driven through.

But by the next day his sense of their new home began to change. Linden Street topped off just above them, and the steep hill offered visual perspectives unlike anything he'd seen in Chicago. From various vantage points he could see views of the Hub skyline, the mouth of the Fort Point Channel, and Boston's inner harbor, an intriguing mix of land and water and sky. This had potential, *Ryan saw immediately. Despite its strangeness South Boston very definitely had possibilities.*

They took right to the streets. Tommy made friends with Mike O'Brien, a boy his age next door. Ryan busied himself with drawing a map in his notebook of the nearby streets, filling in the blocks with notes on important landmarks: House with orange cat in window. Tree with baseball glove stuck in top branches. *Already looking for the underlying systems, he borrowed Ma's Baby Ben wind-up alarm clock and lugged it around, writing down the times of arrivals and departures of planes from Logan Airport across the water.*

In the mornings, with the houses so close together, he could hear the sounds of neighbor families as they started their day. Telephones, footsteps on stairs, doors slamming, radios, dishes clinking. Voices: Ginny, I need to use the bathroom! Mom, Larry used up all the sugar. Honey, will you be sure to—*The sounds were so similar to those of the McCloud household that he felt an almost ecstatic sense of inclusion. It was then that he glimpsed the concept of the pattern that is part of another pattern that is part of another, each level self-contained and yet part of a larger design. In his notebook he tried to illustrate the idea: a circle that was Ryan abutting three other circles that were Ma and Pa and Tommy, the four enclosed by a circle denoting the limits of their nuclear family. That circle abutted other circles on all sides, the neighboring families. Collectively, these would make a unit that might be their neighborhood; a number of neighborhood circles became Boston. And so on, out into the world to include, eventually, the whole human race. All connected, interdependent, integral. As a new kid in a strange town, he took great comfort in that awareness.*

The next morning he brought the drawing down to breakfast and tried to explain it to Ma.

"That's called a mandala," *she told him, serving him scrambled eggs.*

"What, Ry's being precocious again?" Tommy rolled his eyes.

Without looking up from his newspaper, Pa said, "He can be precocious all he wants as long as he's got a good work ethic to go with."

Mandala: *He wrote the word in his notebook. In later years he'd learn the term* fractal structure *and the math that went with it. But now the idea gave him the confidence to face the other kids in the neighborhood. By the end of the week, after a few obligatory fistfights, he had made two good friends, Durrie Clancey and Johnny Blaine. Serious connoisseurs of fun. The three of them skillfully foraged for amusement up and down South Boston, out Broadway and Dorchester, sometimes all the way down to the piers at the north end.*

Oh, but Tommy. So much of it was about Tommy. Two years older, handsome where Ryan was homely, outgoing where Ryan was in-turned, quick-witted where Ryan was deliberative. Tommy: fine-boned, lean-limbed, good with his hands, full of nervous energy, spinning basketballs on one finger, card tricks and cigarette gimmicks, all the good moves. Ryan: too big, clumsy, thick-fingered. Tommy with his good looks and his ability to focus his attention so completely if fleetingly on other people. While Tommy accumulated friends, made out with girls, Ryan mustered along with his elaborate journals, odd private projects, incommunicable thoughts. While Ryan got into fights defending himself from other kids who thought he was a weirdo, Tommy sought out fights for the excitement they afforded him, and the badge of a black eye above his insouciant smile the next day.

And then Tommy had learned to drive, *Tommy bought a fucking* motorcycle *and gave girls rides home from school. Yeah, the motorcycle, all that heat-blued chrome, the smell of the damned thing with its leather seat and rubber tires and oiled cables.*

But that brought him too close to the locus of pain, and he pulled back from the memory by force of will. He opened his eyes, panting, listening to the rain, hoping it was done for tonight. But then the neural pathways lit up again, had to finish.

Yes, the motorcycle, see Jess, Tommy's motorcycle. Tommy had mastered this stunt. The bike was a Harley Sportster with a teardrop tank polished so bright you could see your own envious face reflected in the sex-red paint. Tommy could rear the bike up onto its back tire and ride a whole city block with it up between his legs like the world's biggest dick or the neck of a rearing stallion. It was dangerous and outrageous and it drove girls crazy.

A Tuesday night, late July, one day after Ryan heard that he'd been selected for a scholarship at Emerson Institute, a special school for extremely gifted high school kids. He felt stunned as he went about his duties at the ABC Electronics warehouse, seeing it all with a special clarity, knowing it was a world that would soon be passing out of his life forever.

His main job was to move boxes of TVs and stereos and VCRs around the cavernous steel building, locating specific lots and hauling them on a big hand dolly out to the loading dock to be trucked to retailers. Evening work was okay because as one of only four night staff at the warehouse he knew he'd be mostly left to his own thoughts.

He was out on the dock, stacking boxes for pickup when Tommy coasted up on his motorcycle. He grinned at Ryan's surprise, swung a leg high over the bike, hopped up, and tipped a box back to look at the label. "Panasonic twenty-two-inch," he read. "A good choice."

"Nobody's supposed to come up on the dock," Ryan told him.

Tommy peered through the swinging doors and into the warehouse. The others, Ryan knew, were drinking chalky vending-machine coffee in the employees' lounge. "Listen, Ry, I got something I want to talk to you about."

Somehow Ryan knew what was coming. Maybe it was Tommy's unusual curiosity, several nights ago, asking about the warehouse, who worked there when, what Ryan did.

"Oh no, Tommy. Fuck no," Ryan said.

"Look, Ry—you bring the stuff out here, you stack it, you're in and out for three-four loads, right? And pretty soon the truck comes. How is it

your fault if somebody makes off with half a dozen TVs while you're back inside?"

"Somebody'll see you."

"Mike coasts in with his van. You come out and to your shock and dismay some TVs are missing. Or maybe nobody even notices until the retailer says something."

"Tommy, the guys who run this place aren't that stupid—"

"But I am that stupid, right?"

"If you think I'm going to help you with this, yeah, I'd say so."

Tommy's eyes got that flat, serious look. "Ry, your brother has a serious problem and he's asking for your help. No one loses. Insurance covers ABC's losses—"

"What kind of problem?" Even as he said it, Ryan knew it was a mistake, a rhetorical concession that made room for qualifications of principle.

"It concerns Jeannie. You don't want to know. The real question is, What are you, Ry? What comes first—being my fucking brother, or being a fine upstanding minimum-wage stooge who humps boxes in a warehouse?"

Ryan looked down the branching lines of probability that radiated from this decision and saw disaster down every line. "I got to say no, okay? Go away now. I'll give you some money when I get paid, you can owe me."

Tommy stepped toward him, crowded him. "You are feeling high and mighty, aren't you? What, getting into this special school is giving you some kind of an ego trip? You're thinking maybe it's going to make you into something besides the introverted creep you've been all your life?"

Oh yes, those were the buttons to push. Yeah, there were other factors here, too, an impenetrable knot of sibling emotions with no beginning and no end. Recently Ryan had been devouring books on animal behavior, and for weeks he'd been seeing his friends and family with an ethologist's objectivity: the same posturing and displays, the proximity indicators, the lateral or forward approaches, as animals jockeying for status. And what's Ry McCloud doing? *he'd been asking himself, seeing it with that same stark objectivity.* Solitary male, outcast observer at the periphery of the group.

And now Tommy was pushing him in the chest, direct frontal aggression, and out of pain and confusion Ryan struck at him. The heel of his open hand hit Tommy's cheek, shocking him backwards. In an instant Tommy was all over him, all those good reflexes, all the pent-up brother shit.

Tommy had always come out on top before, but it had been several months since their last fight. By this time Ryan was two inches taller than Tommy, twenty pounds heavier, he'd been lifting boxes all summer. So now he punched back and knocked Tommy down. Tommy got up raging, but Ryan socked him again and he went down again. When Ryan hit him the third time, some cruel understanding came over them both.

"Son of a bitch," Tommy said incredulously. "This is almost fucking comic, isn't it?" Some grudging admiration there, but something bad too.

"I'm sorry, Tommy, Jesus—"

"Fuck off, Ry, huh? At least show the balls to admit you feel good, fuck-head." He sat down on the edge of the dock, went to the motorcycle. Before he drove away he said, "You're still a creep, Ry. You haven't got the panache of a can of Spam."

By midnight Ryan was exhausted from self-recriminations and justifications. He stumped homeward in a sulfur-smelling drizzle that spattered down from a dirty overcast. He was on Dorchester Street, hunched against the rain, wrapped around his confusion, when Tommy came by on the bike and saw him. Tommy gallant and electric and free, Ryan trudging along in the shadows. As if to underscore the difference between them, Tommy turned back and did his wheelie. The Harley's engine roared. He was half a block away, still on one wheel, when the semi came through the intersection and hit him.

A flat crump! *of impact, a midair vision of Tommy tumbling, tangled in his bike, the truck's hooting air brakes, the bike crashing through a hardware store window. Ryan ran to the gaping window, the chaos inside. As he leaped through something struck the bridge of his nose and knocked him flat on his back, and with the blinding pain came a wonderful joy, that it was Tommy who had hit him, Tommy was okay and had seized the opportunity to get back at him and everything would be okay. Then seeing the broken metal frame of the window hanging above him, swaying from his collision with it.* Not Tommy.

The motorcycle had bowled a swath through metal shelves and stacked merchandise, and in the shadows at the back of the store Ryan could see the glint of chrome. Then Tommy, half under a shelf of house paint. He dug away the debris, picked him up, and carried him out of the store. Couldn't look fully on the wreck of his body. Not supposed to move an injured person, but they'd get help faster this way than waiting for an ambulance. He got to the street and began to run. The hospital was six blocks away.

Tommy felt surprisingly small in his arms. That was heartbreaking all by itself. Ryan was crying and it was raining and Tommy's body was convulsing, a pitiful hiccup of breath. "Tommy," he cried as he ran. "I know why, man, I know it bothers you I'm going someplace different." Over the curb, diagonally through an intersection. "I mean, half the reason I'm like I am is you! I can't do what you do, I can't catch up with you! So I have to be more like this. Like

I am." He was afraid to look down at Tommy's face. The only comfort was that awful, irregular hiccup against his chest. He was shouting wordlessly into the night air, a prayer, a terror-struck song of revelation as all the mysteries of sibling feelings seemed laid bare. An old man saw them coming and stepped off the curb, afraid. Two blocks ahead, he saw the red and white illuminated sign of the emergency ward. Ryan screamed: "Tommy, I never thought you were stupid, I never said that, okay?"

Halfway up the next block he became aware that the little hiccup in Tommy's body had stopped. Ryan ran, raising his eyes to the night sky, calling out, "Sacred Heart of Jesus, have mercy on my brother!" It felt like an empty plea. "Oh please," he cried, not to anyone, "I don't want to know this stuff. Don't let this be a lesson to me!" He'd called the probabilities all wrong, in trying to avoid trouble for Tommy he'd begotten the worst of all possible outcomes. Far worse was that, yes, knocking Tommy down, feeling his own ascendancy, had felt good, oh yes. Worse still: As Tommy had sailed by on the bike, Ryan had hated him—for forcing the fight upon him, for being scornful and, yes, for being so handsome and free. Hated him until, as if he'd conjured it, the truck had come plunging out of the dark.

And then he was through the door and into the bright, sterile light of the emergency room, glass doors reflecting a big blood-smeared crying boy holding his fallen brother in an agony of revelation, faces looking up alarmed as this creature burst out of the night.

Ryan twisted on the mattress, bathed in sweat. He sat up and gulped deep, gagging breaths. Outside, the rain had slackened. At least there was no shooting tonight. For the moment, apparently, everybody needing killing was already dead.

Tommy had ended up in a cooperative halfway house for paraplegics. While Ryan was exploring dynamic systems theory at Harvard, Tommy was relearning how to go to the bathroom by himself. For the last fifteen years he'd had a job with a company that specialized in hiring the handicapped for telemarketing kitchen gadgets. Ryan's attempts to connect with him were always rebuffed, apparently the last available gesture of pride for Tommy. Tommy had made it clear his visits weren't welcome, wouldn't even connect at Ma's funeral, fifteen years later. A shrunken man, embittered by his life sentence of imprisonment in a wheelchair, blaming Ry as Ry blamed himself. No amount of exculpation from Ma or from Father Connelly or from anybody had let him off the hook.

But it left you with a lot of things you couldn't explain to the Diana Reeses of the world. Your aversion to conflict, not so much a moral choice as a visceral revulsion. The battered nose, broken so badly on that hardware store's window casing. Better to deflect people than allow them into this very private part of your life. *See, Jessie, when you cry and hold your grief close and let no one in, I understand. I do.*

Am I my brother's keeper? No. Just his brother. But what did that mean? The perverse and powerful dynamics of brotherhood: such a rainbow of emotions, such bright and dark. *Something to keep in mind,* he thought, *when dealing with the Babel effect. Or the Cain effect, or whatever the hell it is.*

Then he thought: *Did I try hard enough with Tommy, that night on the loading dock, or the years afterwards? Did I really work through every last possibility for reconciliation?* And that led to, *Have I been trying hard enough, smart enough, long enough, with Jess?* Maybe the problem was not so much about the origins of violence as about the difficulty of loving.

And then he thought: *I've got to get out of here before I eat myself alive.*

Chapter 27

On the sixth day—seventh?—he was jolted out of his thoughts when the cell door burst open to reveal a cluster of soldiers. Without speaking, two of them took his arms, handcuffed him, pushed him into the corridor, hustled him out of the building. They packed him into a waiting Fiat and drove him to the airport, then shoved him out of the car and steered him toward the terminal building. At the far end of the landing strip, a crew of men haphazardly squirted foam onto the smoldering wreckage of a small airplane. The rain had stopped and the clouds had parted to reveal a silvery cobalt-blue sky. Ryan squinted, unaccustomed to the klieg-light sun.

General Wiselle was sitting with his feet up on a large metal desk, wearing a crisp blue uniform shirt and tie. His parade jacket hung neatly on a coatrack nearby. He waited as the soldiers pushed Ryan into a chair, then steepled his fingers and gazed at Ryan with half-lidded eyes, a face as hard as a skull. He didn't say anything for a long moment.

At last he took his feet off the desk and sat forward, still gazing at Ryan with that look, something like *affection,* on his tight face. "Are you a religious man, Dr. McCloud?" he asked in his rhythmic English.

Ryan was taken by surprise. "What the hell kind of question is that?"

The Weasel enjoyed his reaction, spread his hands, palms up, as if the answer were self-explanatory. "Irish, Polish, American, Boston. A Catholic upbringing, no doubt?"

"What's with the background research, General? What do you want here?"

"I simply thought this must be troubling for you—being imprisoned far from home, uncertain circumstances, no news of the outside world, no contact with your wife and child. I wondered what you drew upon for strength—how you sustained yourself. Prayer, perhaps? The Father, the Son, the Holy Ghost? Mother Mary—?"

"I'm a scientist."

"Oh! Then there is no one to plead with, is there? Your world has no mercy—only cause and effect. But wouldn't you be better off if you believed the universe had a moral agent at work in it? Some great presence that *cares* about your fate, intercedes on your behalf, attends to your moral guidance?" Wiselle stood up and came around to sit casually on the front of the desk, looking down at Ryan and enjoying himself immensely. He wore a holster with a large revolver in it, bone-handled, engraved silver. *A dandy's gun,* Ryan thought. *A cowboy's six-shooter.* Thus the clusters of six in the late-night executions.

"I'd probably be better off, yes," Ryan said.

"I myself am a very religious man," the general said, nodding with satisfaction. "I could not live in your mechanistic world. In the absence of a moral absolute."

This was marginally amusing, Ryan thought, but it was hard to draw an exact bead on the general's irony indicators. He was obviously a very smart man. By his accent, probably educated in the United States. Apparently he'd learned more about Ryan and now wanted to show off, to fence with another smart guy in a situation where he was the one with the gun and the Uzi-armed guards.

"I'm having a hard time engaging in this conversation with a lot of enthusiasm," Ryan told him. "Under the circumstances."

The general's thin lips took a disappointed line. "Too bad. I was hoping that as a religious man you could tell me more about one of your countrymen. This fellow. That perhaps you were one of his adherents." He rummaged on the desk and found a copy of *USA Today,* which he tossed onto Ryan's lap.

It was hard to hold the paper with manacled wrists. The headline told about a passenger jet crash in Michigan, believed to have been caused by a bomb, and the second story above the fold concerned the escalating tensions between Greece and Turkey. The other front-page story was about Jared Constantine, the Church of Revelation and Redemption: CONSTANTINE LAUNCHES AFRICAN CRUSADE. Scanning the article, Ryan read that Constantine had raised millions of dollars to begin an aggressive conversion campaign in central Africa. He was starting missions in ten locales to "bring the Word to the land of Babel." In the current political and social chaos, the article went on, Constantine's financial power and tight organization could make the church a major factor in African affairs. The newspaper was dated September 27, two weeks old, and Ryan wondered briefly how the Weasel had gotten hold of it.

"I don't know anything about the guy," Ryan told him.

Wiselle raised his eyebrows skeptically, shrugged, then beckoned him to rise. "Let's go for a walk, Dr. McCloud. It's such a nice day outside, and you and I have a number of topics to discuss." He gave an order to the guards. Ryan shook off their hands and stood under his own power.

Outside, they began a slow promenade along the length of the airfield, with Ryan and the general in front and the two guards several paces behind. The handcuffs rankled, but still it was good to be outside after a week in a six-by-eight room, to breathe air that didn't smell like your own shit. To take some sun after a week of twilight.

On the other side of the runway a platoon of men jogged in formation, high-stepping to an officer's barked commands. Behind the group a naked man ran awkwardly, carrying a railroad tie across his shoulders, followed by two soldiers who prodded him. A pair of armored cars stood guard on the landing strip, but the smoldering wreck at the end of the field was the only airplane in sight.

"You see," the general said pleasantly, "I like to think of myself as a strategist. I value the big picture. I like to know what forces are at play— what opportunities or risks present themselves. If this fellow Constantine and his minions are to visit the region, I want to know how best to make use of his presence. Support him, get his support in return? Play him against my enemies? Oppose him, win the allegiance of others who oppose him? To decide this, I need to know what he really wants. What he really is. Is he, for example, CIA?"

"I don't know. I doubt it."

"How is he regarded in your American press?"

"With cautious skepticism. Skepticism because he looks like a con man, and because nobody's sure what his agenda is, and because he incites end-of-the-world hysteria. Caution because he's increasingly popular—the media don't want to offend their viewers or readers who like him. Even some of his critics think he has a point about the Babel stuff— the social disintegration."

The Weasel pondered this for a moment. "And what do you suppose he intends to accomplish here?"

Ryan thought about it. How sophisticated was Constantine? How ambitious? "I don't know," he answered.

"Mmmm," the general said thoughtfully.

They were approaching a ridge of recently dug earth, back behind several gutted aircraft hangars and overhung by a forest of vine-snarled trees. A battered backhoe stood at one end, idle, its digging arm tucked like the curl of a scorpion's tail. Ryan didn't notice the long, shallow trench until he had walked a little farther. He stopped when he saw the rags of cloth, the other odd shapes so wrong in the reddish dirt, and only then realized that the general had fallen several steps behind him. He turned, his back to the killing ground, to see the general holding his pistol, the guards fanned to either side with their Uzis pointed at him.

"I really would like to know," Wiselle said.

"I don't know anything about the guy! I'd tell you if I did." Ryan caught the smell now, heard the drone of flies, and felt sick, dizzy, bathed in a sudden toxic sweat. The sun, hot but pleasant only seconds before, took on a naked, desolate heat.

"You're reputed to be a highly intelligent man. Favor me with your... best guesses."

The muzzle of Wiselle's gun was a perfect silver circle, and for a moment Ryan felt his sensorium contract to that hovering ring, the black hole. Then the paradoxical shift, the expansion of his awareness to integrate everything, the whole landscape and the mesh of sounds and the stench and the internal voice: *Jessie, Abebi. My beautiful ones!*

"I—I'm surprised," Ryan blurted. "I wouldn't think he'd take on the challenge to proselytize in Africa. If he's only a con man, he'd do better continuing to bilk his fellow Americans. No money to be made here. So maybe his starting a mission in Africa means he's sincerely religious and wants to bring his word here, do his idea of good for a troubled region. Or maybe he isn't thinking of money so much as power, he sees central Africa as a short route to political influence. Or, I don't know, maybe it's a desperation move, deflecting his followers' attention outward to new challenges and not inward to the church's internal problems." He stopped, out of breath.

The general smiled slightly. "You see? You had all kinds of interesting perspectives. I have always found it amazing what the right incentive does for one's thinking."

"I'm just guessing. I don't know anything about Constantine."

"Then tell me about yourself. Are *you* CIA, Dr. McCloud?" The Weasel was still smiling slightly, but now a tic throbbed in one cheek, tugging at his eye. *A symptom?* Ryan wondered. *A clue to a neurological condition?* The general drew back the hammer of his gun.

"I'm not CIA! I think you know this. You've been doing research on me. Jesus, I've been in legal fights with the U.S. government! I—"

"And your wife, Dr. Jessamine McCloud—what are her associations?"

Ryan hated hearing him say Jess's name. "She and I work together. Not for the CIA or anything like it."

"What is the focus of the epidemiological study at Kalesi Medical Center?"

Is, Ryan thought, *is,* present tense. Maybe the goose was still lay-ing golden eggs, the VEE study was being allowed to continue. "It's complex."

"I've got all the time in the world. You, on the other hand, may not. That will depend upon your forthrightness."

Ryan gave him a general overview of the RAINDROP project.

"Hmm. But I am confused by your desire to study war criminals. What does that have to do with, what was it, a Venezuelan horse virus?"

So Wiselle knew about the differential study. He must have found out about it from somebody at the clinic—maybe Gedes himself, or Dr. Tsonga. Ryan told him the rough outlines of their research into the ori-gins of violence.

"Mmmm. And who is funding this study?"

Ryan had no choice but to tell him: "The American Forensic Psychia-try Association, with a grant from Ridder Global Corporation. That's—"

"A giant transnational conglomerate! One of our beloved new colo-nialists!" This information pleased the general. "Tell me, how does Ridder Global stand to gain from such a study?"

This would be impossible to explain to the Weasel, who saw every-thing in terms of competitive advantages. Who got what, who took it up the ass. He'd never understand or even believe larger, more philanthropic goals. On the other hand, Ryan thought dizzily, maybe Ridder *did* have motives that Brandt and Genesis knew nothing about. A plan to use their findings to develop a marketable weapons technology? Facing a calculat-ing psychopath, your back to a mass grave, it was hard to believe in the reality of any higher motives, anywhere.

Wiselle had watched the sudden uncertainty play on his face, enjoying his hesitation. "Well, about that we shall continue to ponder," the gen-eral said. "One more item on our agenda, Dr. McCloud. This one is very much to the point. How much are you worth?"

"Worth?"

"Exactly how famous and important are you? How hard a bargain shall I drive? Various, um, sources are interested in your safe return to the United States. They wish to negotiate for your release. But what shall I ask for? Gold? Antibiotics? Ammunition? Recognition? Or maybe I should just kill you for being a spy, or for being an unwelcome inconve-nience. You can see it is a challenging problem for me."

"I have no idea what I'm worth," Ryan said.

General Wiselle's face glowed with satisfaction. "There you are again! You see what your lack of religious faith does for you?" He laughed at his own wit, the skin on his face stretching hideously. "Well," he said, checking his watch, "it *was* a difficult question. And now I want you to take several steps backwards, Dr. McCloud. Keep facing this way."

Ryan's body sensed the pit behind him, felt the empty sky and the stark sun, and it did feel like an ending. An arc surged in his chest: *Jess. Abi.*

When he didn't move, the general gave a command and one of the guards bolted forward to drive the stock of his gun hard against Ryan's cheek. He staggered backward, felt the soft earth at the edge of the trench give way beneath his feet, then lurched forward and fell to his knees. Involuntarily he glanced behind him. Half covered in dirt, the tangled limbs. Swollen torsos, nubs of bone showing through falling-away flesh. A wave of charnel stench.

"Just so," General Weasel said. He spoke again, and one of the guards took out a small camera, raised it, and took several shots of Ryan. Despite the sun, the flash popped white and left ghostly blotches hovering in Ryan's eyes.

"Perfect. I am sure that these photos will convey the extremity of your circumstances most persuasively to your associates, don't you? Don't look so downcast, Dr. McCloud—whatever you're worth, these images will certainly expedite our bargaining."

The soldiers hoisted him up by the armpits. They marched on either side of him the length of the field, until General Weasel dismissed him with a backhanded wave.

Chapter 28

By day, the boredom and frustration of living within four close walls. Pummeling the mattress with his fists. Doing sit-ups, push-ups, running in place: anything to tire the body, to assure some sleep. By night, the flood of loneliness, of missing Jess, the ordeal of reliving good memories and bad, both painful. The worry about Abi and Jess and the baby and the human race. Thoughts racing around and around in tiresome grooves.

After another couple of days they began bringing three meals each day—the lump of manioc, now swimming in a fiery red pepper sauce, some bruised oranges and bananas, metallic-tasting canned meat—and water to wash in. Ryan interpreted this as an indication that bargaining for his release was progressing. The real giveaway was the second photo session, a week after the first, for which he was posed in the Weasel's office, sitting with a television and a floor lamp positioned prominently behind him. Proof of how well they were treating him. They were careful to shoot from the left side so his swollen cheek wouldn't show.

One night the air throbbed and rumbled for several hours and the little window strobed faintly: a distant artillery battle. *The game of musical chairs continuing,* Ryan decided. *Another warlord moving into the area, or another faction broken off and pressuring the general.* He figured then that if he were going to be released, it would be soon: If the Weasel wanted to get anything for Ryan, he'd better consummate his deal while he still had control of the airport.

Then one afternoon they took him outside, sprayed him down with a utility hose, and handed him a clean pair of pants and a shirt. They even returned his wallet and passport. He spent an hour in a chain-link-fenced storage yard and then was walked to a battered transport plane. Goodbye to Kalesi and the permeating stink of death. The sense of relief was so great it made him giddy, dizzy. He wasn't absolutely sure of the date but had it figured as Thursday, October 24. He'd been in the cell for twenty-three days. It was two weeks until Jess's due date.

As he climbed into the plane, one of the guards handed him a sheaf of faxes and letters they'd neglected to give him earlier. He began looking through them as soon as the plane leveled out at altitude.

From Marshall, dated two weeks ago, not long after the session at the trench grave:

> Ry: I've enlisted the State Department, the UN Human Rights Commission, and Ridder Global to get you back here. Of the three of them, Ridder has the most clout. We're making good progress with Wiselle. He assures me that you are being well treated. He refused to allow any direct communication between us, but after dickering he did agree, as "a humanitarian gesture," to allow you to receive correspondence until your release.
>
> Poor Jess returned from traveling only to have me apprise her of events. Since then she has been working every day with Ridder's people and the State Dept. to expedite matters. She looks fat and healthy, and appears confident that you'll return safely. She claims to have made big strides on the "Babel" project, but we haven't had the time to go into details, given that we are both rather preoccupied with securing your release.
>
> Today I bought a bottle of the Glenfarclas, 21 yrs. old, to share with you when you get back stateside. So stick it out, my friend.

Ah, Marshall, Ryan thought fondly. Then: *Ah, Weasel, you little sadist. It would have been nice to get these two weeks ago.*

From Jess, dated the same day as Marshall's first fax:

> Ry—I love you intolerably. I am of course very worried about you, but Marsh assures me General Wiselle will value his own claims to legitimacy (also the fat ransom he'll get!) enough to keep you from harm.
>
> Abi is doing well. She has a loose tooth! Since my return we've been spending lots of time together, so please don't worry about her. And don't worry about me, either. My body's timer is ticking steadily away toward delivery day, the baby is moving around like a little acrobat, and so far I feel great.

Ry, I know I've been distant and difficult, and I know how patient you have been with me. I haven't talked about the synthesis I've been working toward because it often seemed more personal than scientific. But I've moved well beyond that now. This last trip was very productive, and I've begun some other promising research initiatives. I can't wait to talk with you about it. (For obvious reasons I won't go into details here—hello, General Wiselle, I'm Ryan's wife!)

Ryan felt the longing swell in his heart, sweet and painful. For six weeks he'd ached for her, yearned for her, uncertain that he'd ever see her again. Now it was only a matter of hours until he'd be alone with her. Making love would be awkward, she'd be too pregnant and he'd be too full and too needy. But she'd rightly accept his urgency as a measure of his love, and they'd manage and it would be splendid. One of the wonders of being with someone long enough. Contrary to the myths of popular culture, desire could be enriched by context. Oh yes. And Abi, he'd squeeze her until she shrieked and laughed and kicked at him.

The envelopes contained letters from the Red Cross, apprising him of their efforts on his behalf. Then another fax from Marshall, dated twelve days ago:

By now, presumably, Wiselle has informed you that we've got the deal. Ridder's paying. Wiselle wanted munitions, but he settled for gold bars and antibiotics enough for, well, an army. We're still working on the details of transport, but expect to see you in four days. Now I'm thinking Glenfarclas with a Dom Perignon chaser.

See you in four days? Wouldn't that have been nice. Ryan scratched his armpits and realized that of course the tepid hosing he'd gotten hadn't gotten rid of the lice—he'd have to delouse and burn these clothes before getting too affectionate with Jess or Abi.

There were several more notes from Jess, the kind of thing you write to a prisoner or hostage or whatever he had been: reassuring, wryly cheerful, focusing on pleasant domestic details. The last was dated eight days ago:

My beloved one—Now that you are "in the pipeline," as the State Dept. assures us, I am feeling greatly reassured.

They've shown me photos of you in some hotel room in which you look very much your regular self: feeling put-upon having to pose for the camera but not too much the worse for wear. I love you!

Since the matter is now in hands more experienced than mine, and there's nothing more I can do to hurry you home, I am leaving today to follow up on several projects that can't wait. I'll check in daily to get reports on your whereabouts so that I can be at the airport when you arrive. You will be very interested in what I've developed in your absence.

I am feeling very burdened by my tummy, and am counting down to D-day. And to your return. Oh Lord, how I am going to hold you!

None the worse for wear? Ryan mused. He did an inventory. Cheek still aching; probable sepsis, and he'd have to have an X-ray to see if there'd been a fracture, but he guessed the prognosis was okay. Lice still hyperactive, but that was easily remedied. He had not eaten well and had picked up some intestinal parasite and thus had lost maybe ten pounds, but the gut bug could be dealt with, and he'd had the weight to spare.

But that was the surface stuff. Harder to assess were the internal effects of the whole experience. The scene at Weasel's private target range had been deeply disturbing, but not in the way the sadistic little mummy probably thought. It had underscored the hidden effect of meeting the wrecked human beings at Blyie's sanctuary, smelling mass graves, seeing Omar's twisted grief, the refugees, the corpses in the ditches, the oozing eyes of Colonel Banewe's prisoners. Erosive images that undercut your sense of human nature, of what the human experience really was, or really meant. It left you changed. How, exactly? *Jessie,* he thought, *I know I should figure a way to face into this stuff and still find a way to believe in the goodness of mankind. But I don't think I'm that strong.*

For an instant the thought occurred to him: The Babel effect—what if he had he caught some virus or absorbed some toxin that was even now starting to wreak invisible but monstrous changes in his brain? The idea shook him, and he dismissed it only by an effort of will.

Then there was the loss of the precious samples and records the soldiers had tossed out onto the runway that first day. A priceless differential study wasted, one that would be hard to duplicate. The Babel effect had a way of covering its own tracks. That brought him around to: What was Jess on to? Her deliberate avoidance of details in her letters was understandable, given that the Weasel no doubt read every word with great interest. And yet she had let her composure slip with that one line: *You will be very interested…* Something of great importance. What were the pressing errands she had to run? Where was she going with this? The hard part was admitting that he'd lost track of her, some months before he'd had the excuse of being imprisoned and out of touch.

This we will fix, he vowed. *Immediately.*

A pair of U.S. embassy staffers met him at the Rome airport, offering their help or company on the return flight, but he assured them he was fine. They gave him skeptical looks, but saw him to his connecting flight and said good-bye.

In Paris he had four hours between flights, so he used a credit card to buy a change of clothes and various supplies at airport stores. Then he rented an airport hotel room, where he shaved, deloused, took a scalding shower, dressed in new jeans, a white shirt, a jacket that almost fit. He dumped the clothes he'd been given. The face that gazed back from the bathroom mirror was only vaguely familiar. Somehow *hollow* looking, and not only from the loss of weight.

But back at the Air France gate, his spirits rebounded. *Six more hours,* he reminded himself, *and I'll see her again. We'll take some time off until after the baby comes, we'll all take the time to get to know each other again.* Wanting to check in with Jess, to hear her voice, he put in a transatlantic call to Heart Cove only to get a bunch of bleeps and boops and static. A call to the Genesis front office, down in the Catacombs: more noises of dysfunctional silicon and copper. He'd try again from the jet's seat phone.

He bought some perfume for Jess and some souvenirs for Abi, and, thinking he should catch up with world events, bought a European-edition *New York Times* full of disturbing headlines. Greek Cypriots rioting when Turkey conducted another nuclear test. The Turkish ambassador to the UN warning that a new vaccination program in Greece was proof of Greece's imminent intention to use biological weapons. The EC and NATO divided on how to cope with the crisis. For an instant the thought tempted him: *Wouldn't it be nice if we got lucky. If we isolated the Babel effect and could head off World War III.*

After a half hour in the air, he put aside the newspaper and used the seatback phone to call again. This time he got a recorded message at both numbers: *The number you have dialed is not in service at this time.* Please stick your head up your butt and give up. Another wave of anxiety, and his hands shook as he replaced the receiver.

"Can I get you something to drink?" The stewardess's lightly French-accented voice startled him, and he looked up to see her bending toward him, an expression of concern on her pretty face. "Wine, cocktails, soft drinks? Coffee?"

"Whiskey," he said reflexively, fumbling for his wallet. "Double." And yet when she served him, he looked at the amber fluid in its plastic cup only to find he was too sick and scared to touch the damned stuff.

Chapter 29

Five more hours of hell, strapped into the confining seat of the jet and full of the darkest fears. He tried to tell himself he was overreacting, irrational, post-traumatic and exhausted and culture-shocked. It didn't work. He called Brandt headquarters to ask for Marshall and was told that Dr. Fahey had flown to Boston to meet him. They gave him Marshall's hotel number, but all he got when he called was the voice-mail system. He didn't leave a message. He called Dagan's home number only to get her answering machine.

It was raining when the plane touched down at Logan Airport. Ryan strode into the arrival gate to see Marshall waiting with Dagan and Leap, *no Jess, no Abi,* and immediately he felt a blow, like a big gong or bell struck hard, a column of pain that resonated in his body from heels to head. Their faces—the mixture of worry and apology, the look of brave fronts badly maintained.

"Ryan—" Marshall began. He leaned forward to embrace Ryan.

"Tell me."

"There's been an incident," Dagan said. She was the only one of them who could meet his eyes, and the expression in her look was one of, horribly, utmost sympathy.

From the county road there was no indication of anything amiss. The neighbor's houses looked serene and untroubled. The driveway was the same pleasant lane, meandering through a semi-wild meadow and a copse of trees that had become a calico of mottled autumn hues, dulled by the rain. For a moment Ryan felt irrational hope: *Surely it's all some sort of mistake.* But then they came to the circular drive and upper parking area, now filled with unfamiliar vehicles: a crime-scene box van, two marked police cars, a fire department van, several dark sedans. As they pulled up, a pair of men in dark suits emerged onto the deck from the kitchen door and lifted a yellow crime-scene tape strung across the stairs. They stepped into the driveway, eyeing Ryan with suspicion.

Marshall got quickly out of the car. "Agent Burke, this is Dr. Ryan McCloud. He needs medical attention, but he insisted on coming here immediately."

"I need to know what happened," Ryan croaked.

Dagan and Leap and Marsh had run interference against a handful of reporters at the airport, and had told him what they could during the drive. Dagan said she'd come Friday morning at around eight. "Jess and I were going to have coffee together at the house. I knew Bates had been there pretty late the night before, and his car was still in the lot. But no one answered when I knocked, so I went down to the 'Combs. I could see there'd been a fire. I tried the phones and they didn't work, so I ran back up and tried the house phone. Didn't work. I had to drive down to the Mobil station."

"Abi?" No air.

"The police found her when they came," Dagan said. "Upstairs in your bedroom. No one hurt her. The police wanted to talk to her, but she didn't have much to say and your father-in-law and I thought—well, we—we wanted to give her some time. She's at the Maywoods'. She'll be fine, Ry."

Burke stepped forward as Ryan got out of the car, shook his hand. "Bob Burke. Assistant special agent in charge at the FBI Boston field office. With the kidnapping, we're claiming presumptive jurisdiction, and will be in charge of the investigation. I'm a big fan of yours, Dr. McCloud. Sorry we have to meet under such lousy circumstances." Burke was a head shorter than Ryan, a lightly built man in his early fifties with a small mustache, short graying hair, a fan of vertical wrinkles between his brows that gave him a look of weary concern. His charcoal suit looked rumpled, and there was a blush of dust on the knees of his pants. "This is Special Agent Fred Hlavacek, also from the Boston office."

Hlavacek just nodded and stared at him with chilly gray eyes, saying nothing. He looked more the part of the federal agent than Burke did: tall, dark suit smooth across bulky shoulders, impassive face. When Ryan moved to go past him into the house, Hlavacek turned subtly but decisively to block his way.

Burke made a short, flat gesture with one hand, and Hlavacek took a step back. "We're still processing the house," Burke said, "so we can't allow too much traffic. But I think we can have a chat in the dining alcove, don't you, Freddy? We've gone over that area pretty well?

Dr. Fahey, if you and the others could wait for us out here, I'd greatly appreciate it."

Marshall nodded. Hlavacek shrugged, stood aside, let them enter. Ryan sensed that Hlavacek deliberately took up the rear so that the big man could keep an eye on him.

Inside the main room, several more people were at work. Two men looked up briefly, then back down at their tasks, apparently lifting fingerprints. One woman panned an electronic device along the front wall, and another black-suited man took notes on a clipboard. Otherwise the room looked almost normal. The only exception was the telephone desk, where the drawers had been pulled out and their contents scattered, the cluttered papers from the top swept onto the floor. The telephone itself lay on the desk, partially disassembled. Lanes had been defined by strips of tape on the floor, and they followed one through the big room to the little addition he and Jess had set up as a dining room.

"As you can see, this room wasn't badly damaged," Burke explained. "It's worse upstairs, and the offices down the bluff have been torn up pretty badly. Let's have a seat, Dr. McCloud, and we'll compare notes. I'm sure you're anxious to find out what we know, and we are very interested to hear from you anything that might give us a lead."

Despite his worry-creased brow, Burke projected an aura of competence that Ryan found slightly reassuring. His soft-spoken courtesy, his informal approach and rumpled suit, suggested a man whose authority allowed him such niceties.

They sat at the dining table as rain teared on the solarium windows. Except for faint smudges of gray here and there, traces of fingerprinting dust, the room was just as he'd last seen it. The oak table had four bamboo place mats on it, a wire basket of fruit still hung from the ceiling beam. Potted cycads and ficus trees lined the window wall. A drawing of Abi's, a house with imaginary parents and kids in it, hung on the wall in the frame Ryan had made for it, only slightly askew.

"I understand you've just been a prisoner of sorts yourself," Burke began. "It's been in the press for several weeks. I'm sorry you had to come home to this. There are a lot of questions I'd like to ask you, but I'd like to start with the projects you've been working on recently. Dr. Fahey has given me a rough idea, but would you mind telling me more?"

Ryan started to complain: *Screw the projects—tell me what happened here. Tell me where my wife is.* But then he caught himself. Beneath Burke's seemingly casual questions he sensed the systematic inquiry of a mind not unlike his own, casting the wide net, taking nothing for granted. He looked at the agent with new respect, and gave him a general overview of RAINDROP and of Ridder's project, mentioning briefly Genesis's emphasis on the idea of neuroepidemics. Hlavacek's fingers played with one of the place mats, his mind obviously wandering. Burke nodded minutely, his unwavering hazel eyes on Ryan's face.

"Whew," Burke said, his eyebrows lifting. "So, in the simplest terms, you could say you've been out looking for the root of evil. From a medical perspective."

"I suppose."

"And then you come home to find evil's been looking for you, too." He shook his head sadly.

Hlavacek stirred his big frame and cleared his throat. "Let's talk about that. How evil starts at home. Let's talk about your relationship with your wife, Dr. McCloud."

"What—"

"And then let's talk about why this guy Bates was at your home, *very* late on a Thursday night, while you're—"

"Freddy," Ryan said, understanding Hlavacek's attitude better now, "I'm into nonviolence. But push this angle and I'll stuff your balls down your ugly throat." Ryan shoved back his chair slightly and got his legs under him.

Hlavacek stared at him hard, but then Burke waved a hand between them like a fight referee. "Special Agent Hlavacek has correctly pointed out that when we see something like this, it's often a domestic situation," he said. "He's also concerned that your daughter isn't willing to talk, which can be an indication of, uh, divided loyalties on the part of a child witness."

"So, what, you guys are thinking that *I* hired somebody to—"

"Nobody's thinking *anything* at this stage. But I assure you both, no possibility is being excluded. Okay? Now let's get back on track." Burke's tone had stiffened, and Hlavacek put his big hands in his lap. "Dr. McCloud, the reason I ask about your work is simply to find out if you or your wife or Dr. Bates have made any enemies. People who might have a reason to do any of you harm."

Ryan thought of all he'd seen, the madness of the world. *"Reason?"* he said, suddenly overwhelmed. "People can invent 'reasons' for anything."

Burke nodded, sympathetic. "You're tired. You've been through a lot. This is a lousy way to come home. *Motivation* to do you harm, then."

"We've done a lot of work over the years that has made various people mad at us. I'd have to think about it."

"Looks like there was another one here, Bob," one of the technicians called. Ryan glanced over to see her kneeling to inspect a wall socket.

"Get photos," Burke called back. "Freddy, will you go find Taylor, ask him to shoot that outlet? Thanks. When you're done, bring me the one we found."

Hlavacek got up and disappeared into the house.

Burke turned back to Ryan. "Let's keep going here. Can you think of anyone who would do this to get information you might have?"

Information somebody wanted? Ryan wondered. *Or information somebody didn't want somebody else to have?* "Again, it could be a lot of people. I'd have to think about it, get you a list tomorrow." He rubbed his face, avoiding the damaged cheek. "Now it's your turn. I need to know what you've learned here."

Burke looked at him with the penetrating, weary, patient gaze. "What we know so far is that somebody came here late Thursday night. How many people we don't know, but probably three at a minimum. They cut the phone wires, came into the house—"

"What about the security system? How'd they get past it?"

"It wasn't armed when we got here, and there's no sign it was tampered with. Apparently your wife hadn't turned it on for the night."

Oh, Jess, Ryan thought. *So unaware of how deep these waters are!*

"From signs of struggle down here and in your upstairs office, they roughed up Dr. Bates and your wife. Apparently they didn't know your daughter was here, and how much she observed we have yet to find out. We know they went through the office upstairs, because the file cabinets are opened and papers are spread around, the computers have had their hard drives removed. My guess is that they subdued Dr. Bates and forced your wife to go down to the office complex and unlock the door. Then they ransacked the place. They took every hard drive, opened your locked file cabinets, and broke into your data lab. On the way out, they set your papers on fire—it may be hard to determine just what was taken. Fortunately, your sprinkler system limited the fire damage. When they left, they took your wife and Dr. Bates. Exactly why, we're not sure."

Burke's steady, sympathetic gaze had never left Ryan's face as he talked. Ryan felt as if somebody had pulled a plug at the bottom of his being, all the energy sucking out a dark hole, leaving emptiness. He struggled to stay clear-headed.

"It was a well-planned operation," Ryan said. "With specific objectives."

"Yes."

"The goal was information. My wife and Bates were taken either because they had information, or because they were needed to interpret the material that was stolen." A terrible thought occurred to Ryan: "Or because somebody didn't want—"

"Anybody left to identify them," Burke finished for him. "That I doubt. Why not just kill Dr. Bates and your wife on the spot?"

The idea gave Ryan a bit of hope. If they needed Jess, they'd keep her alive. But for how long? *Time,* he was thinking. About thirty-six hours had already elapsed. What did they say about solve rates? If it didn't get solved within sixty hours, it was probably never going to be solved.

Hlavacek had come back into the main room with a pair of technicians, and they'd been fussing over the outlet for a few minutes. Now the big agent came into the dining alcove holding a clear Ziploc bag. "Got it."

Burke took the bag and handed it to Ryan. The object inside looked like an electronic sperm, a small plastic cylinder trailing wires from one end.

"It's a bug. Your phones and your living area were wired. Somebody's been listening to you. There apparently had been others, removed now. Once we found this one, though, we could see from marks on your wiring where the others had been."

"What about the offices downstairs?"

"Same," Burke said. He glanced at Ryan's shaking hand as he set the bag on the table. "You're exhausted, Dr. McCloud. You've come out of one nightmare into another. And Dr. Fahey is right, you need medical attention. One more question, and then I urge you to get some rest. We can have a more productive talk after we've finished processing this scene and you've had time to think about the things we've discussed."

"Yeah," Ryan said.

"Your wife—what was she working on? Recently, I mean? I don't know much about your research methods—please don't take this the wrong way—like how closely you two collaborate or how independently you work. Are you aware of anything specific *she* might have done to arouse someone's interest?"

Ryan started to snap back at him: *She's the other half of my goddamned soul, of course I know!* But then he came abruptly up against the awareness that he didn't, not really. Not recently.

Burke's bland, steady gaze had watched the realization change his face.

"It…varies," Ryan said. "I'd say we…we work closely, but we don't work in lockstep. Also, being gone, I—I've…" *Lost touch. Lost everything.* "Again, I'd have to think about it."

Burke stood, offered his hand across the table. "Please do. Now go see a doctor, and get some rest. We'll do what we can here. Let's talk again tomorrow."

Ryan nodded numbly, and stood up to go. But Burke turned back to him. "Oh—one more thing. Given the nature of this crime, this is obviously not a typical kidnapping, and there's nothing to be gained from press exposure. The last thing either of us needs is a media circus on top of everything else. I've given my staff strict orders to keep this quiet, and request that you do the same. Do you agree?"

Ryan nodded again.

Hlavacek had turned slightly and was waiting, his way of inviting Ryan to leave.

Chapter 30

"I know where you're going," Dagan said as Ryan gunned the engine. "Marshall will be pissed, but I don't blame you. My only question is whether you want her to see you when you're like this? Maybe the doctor should come first."

Ryan drove toward the Boston skyline in the fading light. Streetlights had come on, reflecting off the wet pavement and giving the landscape an eerie, plastic feel. Dagan sat next to him, his chaperone, while Marshall drove his rented car back to the hotel, expecting them to meet him there.

Maybe Dagan was right. At the same time, he couldn't wait any longer to see Abi, to hold her and comfort her and calm his body's fear for her. To feel Jess in her.

"You wear makeup, don't you?" he asked.

The question surprised her. "Sure. A little." She waited for his explanation, leaning against the passenger door, watching him, her face serious but lovely in the changing light. He was grateful for her presence.

"Do you carry any with you? Can you do my face? The bruise, maybe under the eyes."

Dagan hoisted her purse. "Different skin tone, but probably we can get close."

Half a block from the Maywoods' Back Bay house, he pulled over and let Dagan minister to his face.

"First thing, let's put some drops in your eyes, get rid of the red. God, you look like a—" She decided not to elaborate. Instead, she switched on the dome light, opened her purse, gently pushed his head back against the headrest. The drops stung, and Ryan's eyes teared. Dagan dabbed his face dry with a tissue, then spent several minutes on his ruined cheek, the skin under his eyes. When she was done she combed his hair, inspected him critically, and put away her equipment.

Ryan shut his eyes, summoning his energy. "How is she, Dagan? What do I need to do here?"

"She's cooperative, but she isn't verbalizing. I can't tell whether it's just the trauma, or whether she's deliberately holding back, not trusting anybody. Ry, given your current condition, I'd recommend a limited agenda here. Show her that you're all right and spend some low-key time with her. You can work with her on what she saw another day. Tonight, just be her father."

"Okay." He opened his eyes, took a deep breath. "How do I look?"

"Not great. But not Jack Nicholson, either."

Henry Maywood let them in, opening the door and then standing aside with the kind of disapproving look that Ryan hadn't seen in years. It would be like the judge to blame him. *Another of the many mechanisms of fragmentation.*

"Clarissa has gone out for groceries," the judge said. "Abebi's in the living room." He led them out of the entryway, through the formal parlor, and into the big, lavender-scented living room. And there was Abi, sitting on the couch in pajamas, surrounded by small stuffed animals. She gave Ryan a look of wary recognition, dubious, too alert.

He picked her up, wrapped her close in his arms. "Oh, my little critter kid," he said. "Oh, baby. I've missed you so much." She accepted his hug in a perfunctory way. He stroked her bony back, rocked her, inhaled the sweet girl-kid smell of her. He wanted to enfold her entirely, to incorporate her safely inside him until this had passed. "Did you miss me?"

He felt her head nod slightly, hair tickling his face. Her body seemed to vibrate, a little tremor, and sensing it he felt a terrible stab of fear for her.

"I brought some presents for you. From Paris. Do you want to see?"

Again the little nod.

Judge Maywood stood in the middle of the room, arms folded across his chest as if demanding that Ryan prove something. Ryan sat Abi back down, took out of his jacket pockets a little Eiffel Tower coin bank, a tiny metal box of bonbons, a French comic book. Abi looked at each one politely but without real interest, as if she were waiting, waiting it out. Dagan looked from one to the other. Finally she caught Ryan's eye meaningfully and turned to the judge.

"Judge Maywood, may I have a drink of water?" She didn't wait for his answer, but took his sleeve and turned him toward the kitchen. *Thank you, Dagan,* Ryan thought.

When they were gone, he said quietly, "This is terrible, isn't it? But it's going to be okay. I promise you that."

Abi looked over his shoulder at the kitchen door. At last she whispered, "I didn't say anything to anybody because I know it's secret."

"Good girl," Ryan said, not sure what she meant.

"Because Ma wasn't going to tell them anything, that's why they were mad." Another raspy whisper.

"Okay. Good kid. She's very brave, isn't she?"

Abi nodded.

She didn't speak again for a few breaths. Outside, a siren rose and howled past the house, signaling somebody in pain or danger, and Ryan felt the world and its disorders intrude. Abi's body registered the sound too, stiffening slightly.

"We're going to get her back, you know," he said. He couldn't have said it with any fraction of this determination without Abi there.

"Tomorrow?" she asked.

"Maybe not that fast, but soon." That disappointed her, and he felt her credulity wane. "Abi, did Ma tell you where I was all this time?"

"Africa."

"Yeah, but did she say why I was in Africa so long?"

She shook her head. From the kitchen came the sound of Dagan and the judge talking, his measured questions and her equally sober answers.

"Well, some bad guys caught me. Just like they did Ma. They put me in jail."

"The same guys?"

"No. But my point is, look, here I am—they let me go and I'm back and I'm just fine. And Ma will be too."

She seemed to brighten a little. "Can I come back home now?"

"It's probably better if you stay here for a while." *Home is busted up and full of cops and empty of Jess. There isn't really a home just now.*

"But I don't like staying here," Abi said.

"Why not?"

She made a finicky gesture with her hands. "Grandpa's so stodgy."

Stodgy was what Jess called him. "Well—"

"And he prays all the time, and makes me pray. For Ma and our baby."

Ryan thought about that, trying to find the right handle on the complaint. "What's the matter with praying?"

"There's no one *listening!* It's just talking to yourself, it's stupid. I want to come home."

Ryan felt his eyebrows go up involuntarily. This was getting beyond him. *No one's listening.* An age-old quandary.

"Abi, here's the deal," he said finally. "You can't come home right now because I'm going to be very busy finding Ma. I may not be there all the time. And the house is kind of a mess. So I need you to be strong and brave like your mother."

She seemed to be drawing away, into some protective shell, and again he felt the pain in his chest. He tried to pull her back: "And I need you to believe, for sure, that I will bring her back safe and sound. Okay?"

She just looked at him dubiously. Dagan was right. In his current condition, mental and physical, he was in no shape to persuade anybody to believe anything. And he thought, *Poor Abi. Here's another grown-up, asking for unreasoning faith.*

Chapter 31

He awoke with vague memories of Dagan herding him out of the Maywoods' house and to the hotel, of Marshall guiding him to his room and the bed. The clock radio informed him that he'd slept for thirteen hours. When he lurched upright, he found Dagan and Leap waiting. They shepherded him through an itinerary they'd prepared: Dr. Ackerman's office for X-rays and a general checkup, a visit to Heart Cove to check up on progress with Burke, an interview with the state police. Outpatient surgery to remove a bone chip from his cheek muscle. Back to the hotel. A short phone call to Abi. Then he collapsed on the bed for another twelve hours.

Monday: another meeting with Burke and the Beverly police, a debriefing by some State Department types who wanted to pick his brain about political developments in central Africa, a short interview downtown with a handful of reporters who wanted the scoop on his African imprisonment but who were, thankfully, unaware of Jess's abduction. *Thank you, Burke.* Time with Abi in the afternoon, playing lovingly but warily, saying almost nothing—she was still not ready to talk about that night. Dinner with Marshall before his flight back to Stanford: Yes, Jess had called him in mid-September and alluded to a breakthrough that she hadn't described in detail.

By bedtime, Ryan felt like a walking pharmaceutical experiment: in his bloodstream swam antibiotics, painkillers, and anti-inflammatories, while his gut bubbled with antibacterials, the megavitamins Dagan had forced him to take, and the steak and oysters Marsh had made him eat.

After everybody left the hotel room, there was just the sudden quiet and the big strange battered haunted guy in the hotel-room mirror.

Burke and he had spent another hour together at Heart Cove. The FBI ASAC had again impressed Ryan with the strange authority of his courteous, mild way of talking, his worried yet determined eyes. Today they had concentrated on General Wiselle, exploring the possibility that

Ryan's imprisonment and Jess's abduction were connected. After review-ing a State Department intelligence workup on the general, Burke con-sidered the likelihood of the Weasel's having either the motivation or the capacity for the operation to be nil.

As for the crime scene, there was good news and bad news.

"The good news is more general than specific," Burke told him. "In the overall pattern of what was done here, we see a professional opera-tion—a high level of planning, coordinated execution, sophisticated technology. What's good about this is that it limits who we might look for—we're not going out chasing after rank-and-file hoods, known offenders. No one has contacted anybody to bargain for your wife's or Dr. Bates's release, meaning it's not a ransom situation. Nobody has pub-licly claimed responsibility, so it's not the kind of terrorist statement thing we're seeing so much nowadays. It means we know something about their motive—it's obviously about information. The bright side is that if the perpetrators value them for what they know or what they're capable of, they're unlikely to harm them."

At least not right away, Ryan thought miserably.

"The other good news is the bug. You were apparently under some level of surveillance for some time—how long we don't yet know. But their leaving the bug was a big mistake. It gives us the best physical evi-dence we have. We can look for its manufacturer, or where its compo-nents came from—"

"Did you check the homes of my staff? If somebody wanted informa-tion, maybe—"

"Yes, we did. Including Dr. Bates's apartment. No bugs or signs of intrusion, implying what we suspected—that your wife was the primary target."

Ryan stood up, went to the sea windows, leaned against the sill, looked out over the water. The tide was out, revealing barnacled rocks and float-ing mats of black seaweed that undulated slowly in a gentle swell. It had stopped raining, but he wished the overcast would break, let some sun down.

"Okay," he said, turning back to Burke. "That's the good news."

Burke picked at some lint on his pants leg and smiled sadly. "Not much, is it? I'm sorry. The list of bad news is longer. We've canvassed the area, and none of your neighbors recall seeing any unusual vehicles or suspicious activity. From the house and offices we've compiled a large collection of fingerprints, hairs, and fibers. But it won't help us find anyone—the best it'll do is help convict someone when we catch that person. Unfortunately, I doubt it'll accomplish even that."

"Why?"

"Talc residue. Unless you people have a habit of wearing disposable latex gloves, the residue was left by the perpetrators' gloves. For all I know, they wore hair nets and sanitary jumpsuits, too."

"Professional."

"Very." For the first time, Burke's eyes wandered nervously, as if he wished he didn't have to continue. "Dr. McCloud, I respect you too much not to be frank. This is going to be hard. The kidnapping is within the Bureau's purview, but we have limited resources for anything this complex that isn't perceived as a national security threat. I've already pulled every string I have to get the level of technical forensic work we've done here. I'm disappointed we haven't turned up more that's useful."

Ryan looked out at the water. Burke stood up, put his hands in the pockets of his pants, and came to stand at the window at his shoulder. An intentional gesture of comradeship. Ryan felt a sudden affection for the man.

"So," the agent said after a time.

Ryan turned to look at him, and Burke waited out his perusal as if expecting what he was going to say. "So you've got next to nothing."

"So we're not done yet. I'll wait on getting pessimistic until all our lab work is done. Until you get your staff back in gear to give us a better idea of what was taken, and until your computer guy checks out your data system. I'd also like to hear what your daughter can tell us."

"How about me?" Ryan asked. "Still your number-one suspect?"

"Hlavacek's been reassigned to another case. He's a good man, but he's...young."

Ryan grunted.

Burke hesitated. "Dr. Fahey says your wife's pregnant. Due soon. This must be very tough for you."

"Tough. Yes." Ryan felt as if he'd been hit. "Thanks," he added.

Burke had blown air out through his mustache, a gesture of both resignation and determination. "Well. In the absence of physical evidence, our strongest leads concern *motive*. And there we should be able to make some progress. I'll be especially interested in what your wife has been doing for the last month." Burke had looked penetratingly at him with his sad eyes, and Ryan had wondered where it came from, that sorrow. "Frankly, as you can see, a lot of this is going to be up to you."

———

The large stranger in the hotel-room mirror caught his own eyes, then went to the little refrigerator and took out four minis of different whiskeys. He cracked the tops off all four and downed them without tasting them. The strangest thing was that despite the holy fucking terror of Jess being in danger, the shriek of anxiety in every nerve, a still stronger feeling dominated his emotions: He missed her. He longed for her. He wanted to touch her and share something funny with her and exchange a glance that said a lot without a word being spoken. That gentle drumbeat of syncopated talk and activity—washing dishes together and talking in the shorthand, elliptical language only lovers knew: *"Still—" "Exactly!" "Unless—" "You really think so?"* Good luck surveilling *that,* assholes.

I'll be especially interested in what your wife has been doing for the last month, Burke had said. That was clearly the crux of it. Ryan had been taking a mental inventory of people who might want to know something they knew. If the break-in and abduction was fallout from the Four Corners job or an earlier commission, why wouldn't whoever had done it acted before now? Given that Genesis had already handed off results of all their earlier jobs, and any cats were already out of their various bags, it had to be the current job. Meaning that Jess was taken because of something connected with their work on the forensic neuropathology study, the Babel effect.

Or, rather, *her* work. Rotting in General Weasel's cell, having lost the materials from his differential study on war criminals and altruists, Ryan had hardly learned anything worth knowing.

You will be very interested in what I've developed in your absence, she'd written. He balled his fists and berated himself. Why hadn't he stayed closer to her for the last several months? He went to the minibar and, finding no more whiskey, took out a couple of vodkas and a gin. He thumbed off their caps and fueled himself, and then, beginning to feel the alcohol, looked at the bottles in his hands. They looked like spent shell casings.

But the pressure-wave of increasing drunkenness pushed in front of it a froth of accelerated mental activity, a rich foam of idea, concept, association, correlation. Enhanced cognition resulting from transitional neuro-chemical states. Opposition-process, two metabolic tropisms in conflict.

Until the alcohol peaked in his bloodstream and sedation overpowered stimulus, he often found his best thinking here, surfing fast on the leading slope of the wave. *You and me, Dylan Thomas.*

Burke was a smart guy: He'd seen where this was heading. *It's going to be mostly up to you, Dr. McCloud.* Who else could track Jess? The way they'd find her would be to figure out who needed what she knew, or who feared what she knew. And the only way to do that would be to retrace her steps. To walk in her mental footsteps. To do that, you'd need to know where she'd gone, whom she'd talked to. But most of all, you'd need to figure what she'd been thinking, what hidden design she'd glimpsed, what conclusions she'd drawn. What inner idea or motivation or principles guided her from place to place and person to person. In most crimes you sought the criminal's motive. In this one, it was the victim's motive that mattered.

Ryan thought: *To answer the question "Where is Jess McCloud?" I must start with "Who is Jess McCloud?"*

Only one person in the world could begin to answer that question.

Suddenly weak, he sat clumsily on the bed, facing the big window overlooking Boston. He'd forgotten to draw the curtains. Eleven o'clock, and the lights in the whatever building across the Common were still on, top to bottom. A criminal waste of electricity. Car headlights and taillights flowing below. Big lonely urban night sky above.

Seeing the task in front of him as if it were a visible equation or mandala, Ryan felt overcome with humility and another emotion, inexplicable and nameless until he probed it and decided it was *gratitude*. It brought tears onto his cheeks. *How many men had ever received such a royal gift? The opportunity, the necessity, to come to know your wife so very well. The need to think about her so closely, to inspect and test your own understanding of her so absolutely. To devote yourself so entirely to stepping into her mind and her heart.*

He cut the bedside lamp and fell back, too exhausted to undress, still staring at the night sky. *Oh, the elegance of it,* he thought. *The economy and grace: Who is Jessamine McCloud?*

And then he went over the precipice and into sleep.

Chapter 32

Tuesday morning, the police and FBI finally relin-
quished the buildings. Ryan called a staff meeting, letting them know
their banishment had ended and it was time to get to work. Dagan was
the first to arrive, of course, kissing him at the door and heading into the
kitchen with a bag of groceries. She prepared coffee for the staff and then
set out a mixed bouquet of cut flowers. "Got to keep our priorities," she
said firmly.

Dagan, Leap, Logan: minus Bates and Jess, the core research staff.
Sharon, Wesley, Peter, Dolores: the core support staff. They sat in the living room with tentative, sympathetic expressions, not saying much, as if
hesitant to intrude on Ryan's anguish.

He gave them a status report on Burke's investigation, and then told
them his conclusions of the night before: "I believe Jess and Bates were
taken because of something related to their work on the Babel effect. Our
house was bugged and Bates's wasn't, so I'm going to assume Jess was
their main target. Given the lack of forensic evidence here, the only way
we're going to find out who took Jess is to find out who she came to the
attention of—who needed what she knew, or who felt exposed. We'll
need to look at everything we've done on the project to determine who
we might have interested or offended. We'll need to retrace Jess's steps to
see who she was in contact with."

But he was appalled to discover how little anyone knew. Jess had been
working almost exclusively with Bates—reasonably, since the two of
them had taken the lead on the Babel effect brief for the review committee. Usually responsible for travel arrangements, Dolores had been on
vacation for three weeks, and said Jess had scheduled her own flights.
Dagan had spent a week at Brandt headquarters in Stanford. Jess had
been very preoccupied, everybody agreed, working mainly out of the
house or traveling. When word had come that Ryan had been imprisoned, she had worked in the offices for ten days, tasking the whole staff
to assist efforts to free him. Once they were sure he was going to be

released, she'd gone back to her research. Logan felt that she'd been deliberately keeping her agenda to herself.

They agreed to jointly assemble a calendar of Jess's known itinerary and communications for the last two months, and scheduled another meeting for that evening.

"One more point," Ryan said. "This is the shits. Somebody violated this place, took people dear to us. Information was the obvious motivation—either to procure information or to prevent us from having it. Which means that if we resume operations, or somebody thinks we still know something, we're in danger. All of us. The FBI being here has been a deterrent, but from here on in there's no guarantee somebody won't be back. We'll get some guards, but you all know from our Secret Service work there's no defense against a determined adversary. What I'm trying to say is, I'll understand if anyone wants to become scarce until this is over."

He looked at them, and they looked at each other.

Peter just stood up. "I'm going to work," he said blandly. "Hey, let 'em come back. I'll rip their fucking jugulars out with my teeth." He disappeared into the hall.

Dolores Nguyen stood up, too, a small chunky woman, conservatively dressed even for the dirty work this day would require. "I think we all feel the same way, Ryan. We've got a job to do." When she was ten years old, after living her whole life in a country at war, Dolores and her parents had escaped from Vietnam in a ten-foot sailboat. Not easily intimidated.

"Maybe I'll break out the big coffee urn," Sharon said, heading back toward the kitchen.

And so they went off to begin. Leap started the painstaking job of assessing and restoring the computers; the support staff went at putting the partially burned, water-soaked hard-copy files into order, determining what was destroyed or stolen, and rebuilding the offices. Logan took charge of coordinating recovery operations, scheduling repair contractors, researching security services, dealing with insurers.

Which left the house to Ryan. He asked for Dagan's help because if anybody on the crew thought like Jess, it was Dagan. Also because this would be an emotionally loaded job—it would help to have the company.

———

In the upstairs study, the file cabinets had been opened and their contents strewn around, and holes gaped in the two computers' hard-drive bays. The floor-to-ceiling bookshelf had been ransacked, a chair was knocked over, a lamp broken, paintings torn from the walls. Being this close to where they'd had their hands on Jess, Ryan felt the heat in his temples, the ache for violence in his hands.

Dagan made a sound of dismay in her throat. "Where do we start?"

"We look for the pattern," Ryan growled. "What should be here that's not? We look for what they wouldn't have known was important. We piece together Jess's thinking."

Dagan stooped to recover a painting from the floor, inspected it briefly, and hung it back on the wall. "You did well with the crew, Ry. Struck the right balance."

"Aah," he muttered in self-disgust. "I can never figure out how to talk to people. All my life I've felt that I was missing something. Some piece of information, some specific insight about human beings that everyone else knew and that I alone was in the dark about."

She looked at him with her brows lowered. "I can't believe you're saying that."

"It's true. I'm solitary in my head. Human beings are the one thing I've never figured out. I get along by more or less just faking a semblance of being human. Except with Jess."

"Well, you're faking it pretty well. There isn't one of us who wouldn't follow you to the ends of the earth!" Dagan looked at him, incredulous, and then continued scanning the floor. But the heavy sheaf of her dark hair fell across her face and she swore quietly. She tilted her head back and shook her hair free of her face, then gathered the wild mass behind her head and worked an elastic around it.

"Anyway," she went on, "I think everybody feels that way. As if we're just outside it, not quite speaking the common language. If you're missing some detail about the human race, it's that you're not alone in feeling alone." She chuckled without humor.

Ryan found the cork bulletin board that had hung near Jess's desk. He hung it on the wall again and inspected it. Jess was in the habit of jotting ideas, things she really wanted to remind herself of, on yellow sticky notes. When she was on a streak, the notes could be thick at eye level on every surface near her desk. After a while she incorporated the stickies into formal research notes and removed them.

Now the board was almost empty. A list of office supplies: *staples, highlighters, diskettes, coffee creamer.* One of Abi's drawings: sailing boats, blithe and graceful as swans. A Post-it: *ZOO!* The capital letters and exclamation mark were indications of its significance, and Ryan asked Dagan about it.

"Oh. She and Abi went to the zoo, in Stoneham. Just after you left to Africa. I don't know why she'd write it down, though."

"How about this?" He showed her another scrap that read *VNO???*

Dagan shook her head. "No clue."

A scrap that quoted the Somali saying Ryan had faxed her from Kalesi: *My son and I against my brother. My brother and I against my cousin...*So that had struck her, too.

Finally, a hastily scrawled Post-it, barely recognizable as Jess's handwriting: *Ry—Doughnuts.* It bothered him. Why not write it on the other shopping list? The handwriting was anomalous, too: so messy. The doughnut principle? Too vague to have any value, except possibly as a private mnemonic for Jess.

He realized he was in too much of a hurry. He deliberately down-shifted, shut his eyes, conjured a vision of Jess. *How does she work? How does she think?* She'd talk on the phone, use the computer to do basic research on the Web or to send e-mail; she'd read books. She'd jot systematic notes on legal pads, important spontaneous thoughts on Post-its. After hunching intently over her work for a time, she'd need to stretch and would throw her shoulders back and her arms out, rolling her wrists to work the kinks out. A beautiful gesture that thrust her breasts out and could yank Ryan back to earth from anywhere at all—

Back to her working habits. He tried to freeze the image of her at work, mentally inspect every detail. She'd have her big calfskin briefcase nearby, and her main appointment calendar, and the electronic scheduler she kept in her purse—all missing now. Computer on, books open on the desk, several pads going at once. At intervals of a few days, she'd get sick of the chaos of handwritten notes and she'd type them into her computer research journal as dated, outline-form notes. Then she'd rip out the used pages of the pads and throw them away—

Wastebaskets! he thought, and rushed to look into the overturned wicker baskets. But they were empty.

After an hour or so, they both ground to a halt. They had put the room more or less back together, and something of a pattern had emerged.

"So what're you seeing?" he asked.

"Mainly the negative space," Dagan answered. She sat in Jess's big reading chair, looking drained. "The reverse image of what she was working on, created by the gap of what's been taken."

"Yes." Another doughnut hole.

"There aren't any Babel files in her drawers, and I know she kept a bunch of them. No yellow pads, no backup disks—"

"And there's an even bigger hole," Ryan said. "The way she kept everybody else out of her process. Any idea why?"

Dagan tapped her chin with her fist. "Well, she was working primarily with Bates. Anyway, she's done it before, Ry—when she's incubating something important, she likes to consolidate it before talking about it. You two are so close, you're probably not as aware of how independently she works at times. You were gone, so you were out of the loop, too, this time."

It was true. Jess could get so wrapped up in her work, her nose to the trail, that she got distant. She worked so fast, a human rocket, even delegating took too much time. But his being gone wasn't the only reason.

Ryan shook his head, feeling a painful twist of guilt. "I was out of the loop even before I left."

"What do you mean?"

"Aaah. I, we...we weren't connecting real well. She was going through that stuff—sorting out Allison's murder. Figuring out what she believed in. I just thought...I mean, she needed to be left alone."

Dagan just nodded and watched him, her eyes warm with sympathy.

His morale faltered again, and he had to consciously rally himself. "What about a positive pattern?" he asked.

"Well, the books on the floor—the ones on animal behavior and the neuroscience texts make sense in terms of our general theory for the Babel effect, but don't let us get very specific. The e. e. cummings collection I don't know—I didn't know she was a fan of his poetry."

Ryan made a note about it on his clipboard. Scratch her telephone redial: The FBI had already checked it, and found only the number of Henry and Clarissa Maywood. Maybe some aspect of her scrap notes would make sense later. Maybe they'd find something in her e-mail records, once they got a computer up and running. But it wasn't much. The room hadn't revealed as much as he'd hoped.

Chapter 33

Logan led off the evening staff meeting. The eight of them were standing or sitting in the sea-facing meeting room in the Cat-acombs. With nothing in it but chairs, table, and basic conferencing paraphernalia, the room hadn't been ransacked, although a humid, smoky smell from the paper fires hung in the air. They'd opened the windows wide to the chilly but fresh sea air. It was five o'clock and the late-October sun had slipped behind the bluff, drawing a curtain of shadow over the near shore.

Everyone had a gray look, Ryan decided. He didn't blame them. He slouched in his chair, waiting.

"As far as we can see from the hard-copy files," Logan began, "it looks like you were right, Ry. There's fire and water damage, but most older files are here. What's missing is almost everything associated with the Babel job."

"Almost everything?"

Logan allowed herself a small smile. "There are all sorts of operations files that give us indirect information—phone bills, for example, or expense account receipts that might show Jess's travel history. Most are fire-damaged, but once we put them in order we should be able to glean some clues from them."

"Fabulous," Ryan said blackly.

Logan was barely five feet tall, a fine-boned woman with frizzy blond hair and a face as gentle as Botticelli's Venus. She looked light as a butterfly, but had the energy of five people, an intellectual power like a howitzer. Now she inspected Ryan's face with unsettling intensity.

"Ryan, let me say one thing before I go on. The people in this room constitute probably the most adaptable and resourceful research organization in the world. We're gonna get Jess and Bates back here safe and sound. We're gonna get the motherfuckers who did this, and we're gonna do it fast, and we're gonna give them a lot, a *lot,* of regret."

When he didn't respond sufficiently, she glared at him. "Ryan. Get it through your head: *We are no longer the hunted here. We are now the hunters.* You got that?"

This from a woman of extraordinary gentleness who spoke with, ordinarily, impeccable diction. Educated at Oxford, but born and raised in Brooklyn. Logan shot sparks when she was in this mode. Ryan sat up straighter. *The hunters.* God, that felt good. Dagan saw it in him and grinned.

Logan went on, "We've made a good start on piecing together Jess's itinerary. I've got a big calendar out, and we've all been filling in dates as we remember something or find something in the mess. We've got her August whereabouts pretty well pinned down, and so far about a third of September and October."

"Good work," Ryan said.

"Progress report on the offices: We've boxed up the damaged hard-copy files for drying and sorting. Some that are irretrievably damaged we hope to replace from backup CD when we get the computers back, or from replaceable billing records of vendor accounts. We've got crews coming in tomorrow to replace carpeting and ceiling tiles, and painters scheduled for Thursday. I've ordered new furniture and office equipment, everything expedited. Also, starting tomorrow, we'll have three security guards from Peterson's here, twenty-four hours a day. I ordered the extra-large, extra-suspicious variety. And that's it for me. Your turn, Leap."

Logan sat down, folding her slim arms across her chest. It had been a good act, Ryan knew, a convincing portrayal of determined optimism, and it worked. You could feel it in the room. Jesus, you had to love Logan.

But Leap couldn't project a comparable aura of confidence. He stood up, purple splotches under his eyes, holding Sneaky Pete and stroking him as if taking reassurance from the ferret's silky fur. "At my end the news ranges from shitty to okayish. The best I've got to offer is that I've requested September and October billing records for the house and office phones, and as soon as we're on line again, I'll get Jess's e-mail history. So, hopefully, we'll be able to reconstruct her communications. On the shitty side: hard drives removed from every computer, backup disks taken from all desk stations. Okayish: I've ordered replacement drives, which should be here tomorrow, so we'll have your units up and running by Thursday or Friday. More shitty and okayish news: As you know, every day's work on our local area network is saved to storage CD. They took the CD that was in the drive, they broke into the safe and took the recent CDs I keep on site. That's shitty. What's okayish is that I replace those CDs fairly often, and archive the old ones in a safe-deposit box at First Marine Bank. I took the last batch to the box in mid-July, so we'll be able to reconstruct any files saved before that date."

"How about Argus?" Ryan asked.

"They pulled all the hard drives. We're talking many terabytes of data lost," Leap said gloomily. "Somebody also took a crowbar to my racks, looks like kind of an afterthought. Nothing systematic, but I've got rebuilding to do. Need a few days just to inventory damage. Longer to reassemble."

"Any indication they played on Argus that night? Or that anyone has hacked in?"

Leap shook his head. "I'm assuming we were hacked. But as for Argus, too soon to tell. Sorry." He seemed to look for the ferret for commiseration.

The damage to Argus would've hit Leap hard, but still his mood was too bleak. An undertone of apology or shame, Ryan decided with alarm. Had Leap been working on something he shouldn't have? Something to ask about in private.

The crew began talking among themselves, but Leap's mood had dampened the resurgence of enthusiasm. For a moment Ryan felt the fear come over him again, the sense of hopelessness.

Then he shrugged it off. *You never give up. You take it and you come back fighting: Thanks, Pa. We are the hunters: Thanks, Lo.* To his surprise, he felt himself coming back, just a bit. A tiny spark, determination if not yet real hope, had truly kindled.

He tested it, found it stronger. Maybe strong enough to talk to Abi at last. She'd need to see it in him if they were going to open the subject of that night.

"Good work, people," he said, standing, unable to express the gratitude he felt, hoping it was somehow evident. "It's six o'clock. I've got a date with a young lady. Let's meet again tomorrow morning."

Dagan saw it in him, that little voltage change. Of course she did. She gave him a thumbs-up as he left.

———

As usual, Boston was ten degrees warmer than Heart Cove. Ryan took Abi out to the front steps of the Maywoods' house and sat her on his lap. He leaned against the railing with his arms around her, and they breathed the evening air together. Back Bay felt aloof and insulated, houses locked down and blinds drawn, no one on foot, no kids playing on the streets. So unlike South Boston of thirty years ago. He wished Abi could experience the feeling of a warm night on the bustling neighborhood streets back then. Probably in her lifetime she never would. The world had changed: An all-permeating fear of the urban dark, of the streets, of your fellow man, had crept up on everybody in the last few decades and was now taken for granted.

"Tomorrow's Halloween," he said. "We didn't get you a costume, but—"

"Grandpa says Halloween is un-Christian." Her lack of inflection conveyed her feelings better than any overt complaint could have.

"He doesn't give a kid a lot of slack, does he?" Ryan said.

"Oh, it's all right. I don't want to go trick'r treating anyway."

"Why's that?"

"I don't like people to be pretending scary things."

"Yeah. Seems like there's enough scary stuff without it."

Abi squirmed around so that she sat sidesaddle across his thighs. "Your face looks better," she told him. "Before, you looked like a chipmunk."

"Well, I feel better, too. I just needed a couple of days. The house is better, too—I've got it all straightened up." He paused. "Listen, Abi—do you want to talk to me about what happened that night? Only if you feel all right about it."

Her face hovered in the shadows, dark on dark. After a moment she said, "Okay."

She began shakily, tentatively: Ma had read her a story, and then as she'd drifted off to sleep she heard Ma in the upstairs office, talking to Bates and then typing at the computer. She woke up to the sound of a fight—loud noises, some man swearing.

"Ma said, like, 'Get your hands off me!' And she said, 'What do you want?'" Abi's body quivered at the memory, and it was all Ryan could do to keep himself calm. Jess had to be getting huge by now—the thought of someone attacking her when she was in that state filled him with rage.

"Oh, baby! What did you do? You must have been very scared."

"First I was going to go tell them not to touch Ma. I was going to *punch* them! But then I got scared and hid in the closet. After a while men came into your and Ma's bedroom and opened drawers and things, and then they went into my room. I heard them coming to look into my closet, so I crawled through into your side and they didn't find me. After a while they went downstairs."

She was crying now, little ragged panting breaths. All he could do was stroke her, give her time. Against his will, he felt a lethal hatred growing in him, for whoever had inflicted this on his child.

As if sensing it, Abi calmed a little. "Are you going to kill them?"

He deliberately dodged that one. "Did you see any of them? How many were there?"

"Sounded like…um, maybe four. But I didn't see them."

"So what did you do then?"

"After they went outside, I knew they were going down to the 'Combs, I tried to call 911. But the phone didn't work. Then I remembered Ma's cell phone, but her purse wasn't there. Then I got scared again and I went into the closet and covered myself up with clothes."

"You were very smart. You did just the right thing."

A van moved slowly up the street, windows black and glistening in the streetlight glare, and Ryan tensed involuntarily. But three houses down a couple of teenagers spilled out, saying noisy good nights to friends. A breeze moved the dry leaves of the little oak tree near the stoop, and Abi nestled in closer to him.

Abi was an amazing kid. Deeply traumatized, but also resilient as hell. That she'd managed to talk about it at all testified to her resilience.

The thought reminded him of another question: "'Beb, when I first came back, you told me you didn't talk to anybody because you knew it was secret. What did you mean?"

"Oh. Because of what the men said. When I was hiding in the closet, I heard them asking Ma about that thing, the Babel thing, that you guys always talk about? They said they would hurt her if she didn't tell them. And she said swears at them and wouldn't tell them anyway, even though I could hear them hitting her. And that's how I knew it was secret."

Again the rage threatened to master him, but he took a moment to breathe and pack it with difficulty back into its compartment, the pressured place that it had to be kept.

She finished her story: lying there afraid to move for a long long time, falling asleep, waking up to find it was morning. She'd listened and found the house quiet, so she got up and went into the big bedroom and got into Jess and Ryan's bed and cried. After a while she heard men in the house again and for a second she thought maybe the bad men had come back, but it was the police. Dagan was with them and she was nice.

Ryan waited for a long minute when she finished, trying to suppress his disappointment at how little he'd learned, giving Abi time to discover any other memories. She didn't say any more.

"Are you cold?" he asked finally.

"A little bit."

He pulled her closer so that he could wrap the sides of his jacket around her. The little bellows of her breathing felt good against his chest, and they made a pleasant cocoon of heat together. "Can I ask you some more questions about Ma, or do you want to stop now?"

"You can ask more."

"Earlier this fall, like when school just started, did Ma ever talk to you about anything she was thinking about?" It was unlikely, he knew. The Babel idea was too disturbing, the concepts too complex, for Jess to have tried explaining it to a six-year-old. And the whole question was absurd—asking Abi to recall two months of conversation. On the other hand, you never knew what Abi might pick up.

Ma was sad sometimes, Abi said, and kind of far away. One time Ma said it was because of Allison. Beyond that, she couldn't think of anything important.

Disappointment seemed to descend on them both, but Ryan was determined not to let it gather momentum. "One more question, kid, and then we should get you inside and to bed. You and Ma went to the zoo, right? Just after I went to Africa?"

"Yeah. It was fun."

"Did Ma do or say anything funny, or...different...when you went?"

Abi responded immediately, perking up now that she had something solid to offer. "Yeah! I made her laugh. When we were looking at the gorillas."

"What'd you say?"

"We were looking at the gorillas and there was a big man-gorilla and I said he looked like *Grandpa!* She thought that was funny. She asked me why I thought he looked like Grandpa, and I told her, just the way his face was. A little bit mad, kind of sad, his eyes watching us?"

Ryan could envision it: the big black face of the gorilla, the alert, deep-set eyes, the solemn, regal, forbidding bearing. Obvious, and yet only a kid, a grandchild, would have the innocence and the insolence to make such a comparison.

Abi seemed relieved to recall a happier memory of Jess. "Right away she started asking me stuff. She did that thing where she pretends she's calm and everything's the same as usual, but I know she's secretly excited? She asked me about it again when we got home. She even wrote on her yellow pad."

Wow, Ryan thought. *Some kind of a jackpot for Jess there.* Thus the yellow sticky note on her board, *ZOO!,* a reminder of the catalyst for some important line of thinking.

"Did you see what she wrote?" he asked, doing the same fake-casual thing Jess did, knowing Abi could sense it and didn't mind.

"Yeah. It was one of her octopuses."

Better and better. Jess was in the habit of diagramming her thought processes when she was brainstorming. Usually she drew and wrote fast, a core idea in a circle at the center of a page, with lines emerging from it, the related ideas or avenues of inquiry it suggested. It was a way to get simultaneous associations down on paper quickly. Language was linear, word following word slow as elephants on parade, but thought was 3-D, radiant, instantaneous. One of Jess's "octopuses" could have three arms or twenty, and the arms could later converge again to make the bodies of other octopi. *So much like the neurons and dendrites in the brain,* Jess had once said about her diagrams. *How like the physical architecture of the brain is the invisible organization of thought.*

He put the thought aside. *Gorilla looks like Grandpa* was the center of something. A beginning place—for what?

"You are a fabulous kid," he told her. He squeezed her and rocked her little ball of a body inside his jacket. "God, you're a great kid!"

She pushed his nuzzling face away. "Too tickly!" she said.

Ryan released an arm to check his watch in the streetlight glow. "We'd better go inside, Abi. And see your gorilla—I mean your grandpa."

She thought that was funny. They went in to find the judge standing, waiting impatiently, his face dour as if disapproving of the little smiles they brought in from the stoop. But Abi ran to him, plowing into him and wrapping her arms around his big middle in a gesture of such genuine affection that the old man's face softened despite his best efforts.

Chapter 34

That night, alone in the house, Ryan sat at Jess's desk and sketched his own octopus on a fresh pad. He drew a circle and wrote in it *Gorilla looks like Grandpa.* What had Jess found in that? Evolution might be part of it: the spurious but persistent misinterpretation of Darwin, the cliché of humans descending from monkeys. So he drew a line out from the center and labeled it *evolution.* Probably it was too obvious, looking for origins of human behavior in evolutionary precedents, but he'd assemble some other arms and see what they added up to. He drew another arm and labeled it *primate studies,* on the chance that Abi's statement had triggered a recollection of relevant lab work on monkeys somewhere.

Then he drew an arm labeled *aggression displays.* Gorillas, not unlike Judge Maywood, were famous for their territorial displays: charging forward, bellowing, beating chest, throwing dirt and branches around. While in fact—again, like the judge—gorillas were quite gentle, and the displays seldom resulted in real attack. But what made gorillas or humans stop, fail to follow through on their threats? Some behavioral program built into their brains, of course; maybe Jess was thinking that was a likely Babel candidate, a neurological malfunction that caused the display to spill over into true aggression.

Another possibility occurred to him. Abi had made a connection between two faces, had recognized features in common. How? Whole-face recognition appeared to be a distinct, self-contained action of the brain, accomplished by dedicated modules in the left visual association cortex and maybe the pulvinar region of the thalamus. The neurological condition known as *face agnosia* resulted in people being utterly unable to recognize familiar faces, even a spouse's or their own in a mirror, despite being able to clearly see and identify each individual feature of the face. Was that the catalyst for Jess? He drew an arm and labeled it *face agnosia.*

He drew a few more arms, but it was getting late and he was running out of steam. Nothing he had come up with looked like a reason to kidnap somebody, wreck up a house and a company's files and computers.

Of course, then there was the note that read *Ry: Doughnuts.* It bothered him, but he couldn't do a damned thing with it.

He put the work aside, and then, thinking to distract himself from the emptiness of the house, made the mistake of turning on the television. The screen popped on to the eleven-o'clock news, and Ryan listened with numb fascination to the night's recitation of world events. Turkey and Greece seemed to be squaring off for war after Turkish scientists analyzed a sample of the vaccine used in Greece's mass immunization program. It wasn't for flu, as the Greeks had insisted, but for a modified pulmonary virus—a bioweapon. A group of Republicans in Congress wanted to ban children of legal immigrants from public schools or food-stamp programs, calling their U.S. citizenship "a technicality, not a reality." The Church of Revelation and Redemption had expanded its overseas operations, but was reported to be in financial trouble despite legions of new converts; Jared Constantine vehemently denied charges that Revelation and Redemption members had killed a New Jersey rabbi and several synagogue leaders who had been critical of his church. Another school shooting in Indiana, this time by an eleven-year-old girl: four kids dead, nine wounded. Beggar's Night trick-or-treating had already resulted in a number of candy poisonings. In Cincinnati, a group of parents were upset over a new, highly popular video game in which the player *tortured* game characters by various virtual means. Highest pain scores won, but you lost if you went too far and killed the character before he or she "confessed." The item featured some vivid graphics from the game.

Cheerful stuff.

He clicked off the set, tossed down a glass of whiskey, and began preparing for sleep. *How long do I have?* he wondered. The hopefulness that had propelled him for the last few hours had evaporated. Twelve days until her due date, the clock was ticking. There'd never be enough time for him to recapitulate every line of her research. At some point Jess would either give her kidnappers the information they wanted, or they'd realize that she never would. In either case, her usefulness to them would be at an end. *What will they do with her then?* Images of the sick video game came back to him.

For a few minutes he worried about Abi, trying to assess the damage. She was only six. This would have to be a huge trauma for her, literally shaping her future, scarring her. Back at the Maywoods', the judge had taken him aside and told him that she'd been having nightmares, wrenching convulsive nighttime screaming and crying. Every night now, getting worse, not better. The thought tied Ryan's gut in a painful knot. *Nothing worse than something hurting your kid.* He labored to think of a way to begin something like a healing process with her. But he couldn't. Not until her mother was back, safe.

He got a blanket and went to sleep on the couch, unable to endure the empty bed upstairs.

Whatever Jess had been thinking, it was easy enough to pin down the date she'd gone to the zoo. At midmorning Ryan met with the full staff, and checked over the big wall calendars on which Logan had been filling in dates with Jess's known whereabouts and activities. Dagan readily remembered that Jess and Abi had gone to the zoo on September 15, the Sunday after Ryan left to Africa.

The other sticky note had been Ryan's Somali saying, which she would have received on September 19. The notes had been put up within three days of each other, side by side. Was there a common element between them?

"Okay," Ryan said. "Wesley, Peter, how are we doing on reconstructing operations files? I'm specifically interested in phone bills for September."

Peter checked one of the temporary file boxes they were using. "We have some of it, anyway."

"Good. Have the staff review the long-distance calls, check off the ones they made. What's left I'll assume Jess made. For right now, prioritize the week of September sixteenth through the twenty-second." Jess worked at warp speed. If either the zoo incident or the Somali saying had meant anything to her, she'd have followed up immediately. The calls she made, the people she talked to in that period, would give a good clue to the direction of her thinking.

The next issue was trickier. As the staff dispersed to get back to their tasks, Ryan signaled to Leap. "You got a few minutes?"

Leap nodded, expecting it, and they wended their way back to the computer lab between carpet contractors who were stripping the ruined hall floors.

In the computer room, the front panels had been removed from Argus's six main cabinets, exposing gaping racks and banks of wires and circuit boards. In the control room, every horizontal surface was covered with electronic components, tools, diagnostic devices, circuit maps.

Despite the dismantling, one monitor glowed, and by the empty card-board box under the counter, Ryan deduced that Leap had bought a new PC to run chores associated with his rebuilding process.

"Sorry about the smell," Leap said, chewing his nicotine gum rapidly. "Haven't had time to change Pete's bedding." The ferret lay happily curled in a wastebasket full of shredded printouts.

Ryan just waited. Leap would know what this was about.

"You want to know where did we show?" Leap said. "What'd we do to draw somebody's attention? Three possibilities. One, that first time, looking for data on your friend Karl's suggestions. I hit a couple of private labs doing defense-related contracts that seemed relevant. I was very, very careful, but if you're starting a list I'd have to say, yeah, mark that down. Army Intelligence, NSA, DIA, FBI."

Shipley, Ryan thought immediately. Could the Gray Ghost have had anything to do with this? "But that was six months ago. Something more recent?"

"Some university and private labs. Sometimes with their knowledge, sometimes—" Leap saw Ryan's face move and went on quickly: "But always with Jess's permission, Ry! At Jess's *suggestion!*"

"Christ, Leap—"

"She had me do some work on nonlethal weapons tech, and on the large-population behavioral mod."

"Give me specifics. Who'd you touch?"

"On the viruses, a lab in Seattle, fat government contract, doing research on weaponized viral vectors for controlled neurological effects. In the EMF area, I looked at tests of electromagnetic frequencies on animal behaviors. One target was Advanced Applications, a Florida outfit run by two guys who used to work at the Naval Aerospace Medical Research Laboratory. Which was the headquarters of some very secret work on EMFs on human tissues."

"Radio weapons. What's the focus?"

"Changing human brain function by bombarding it with radio waves. Upper-gigahertz microwaves, but *pulsed* into lower frequencies that match human brain-wave frequencies, reinforcing or canceling certain normal brain functions. The one that Jess got most excited about was a series of monkey experiments—where they exposed mother monkeys with babies to various types of radio waves. They induced avoidance behaviors—the mothers would push away their babies or even attack them."

Definitely a Babel-relevant subject. *Avoidance behaviors*—maybe the whole human race was exhibiting marginal avoidance behaviors, some stressor overcoming the most basic of instincts. Maybe Abi's *gorilla* comment at the zoo came back to Jess when she heard about the avoidance behaviors. Ryan jotted some notes and tried to rub the knots out of his forehead.

Leap was fiddling with a wire clipper. "Ry," he said finally, "there's one more."

"Oh great. Really fucking great—"

"Not long after you left, Jess and Bates and I went to Sandia to do the tests on RAINDROP. Right on schedule. We ran RAINDROP through four 'outbreaks'—two were the real Sin Nombre outbreaks of '93 and '99. Using only data available *before* the spread, RAINDROP modeled them perfectly!" Despite his bleak mood, Leap's eyes lit up as he remembered. "Ry, if we'd had RAINDROP in '93, we could have anticipated the course of the outbreaks and saved two-thirds of the lives lost—I'm telling you, we just about peed ourselves! Major urinary incontinence."

"And you ran two more," Ryan said, guessing where this was going.

"Yeah." Leap flicked his hair back. "One was a hypothetical outbreak of an insect-transmitted virus, based on population and geographic data from the L.A. area. And then there was a fourth. Jess and Bates had the data, they'd done a lot of homework on their own. They sprang it on all of us, told the Sandia engineers it was another hypothetical. Again, RAINDROP performed perfectly."

Ryan was thinking: *Portrait of a woman in a hurry.* Why take such a risk? She must have believed she was close to something.

"So on the flight back, Jess and Bates are high as kites. I say, 'What the hell was that?' And they tell me that the symptoms were a spectrum of Babel-related behaviors, data from police and hospital and family health services in New England. Domestic violence, school shootings, hate crimes, violent psychiatric admissions, child neglect, juvenile crime, divorce filings—"

"So what happened?"

Leap shook his head. "RAINDROP showed that this shit models perfectly as an epidemic. Same phase-space 'signature' as the known disease epidemics."

They both stared for a time at Sneaky Pete, sleeping with a contented grin on his pointy face.

Okay, Ryan was thinking. So they proved that Babel symptoms, social ills, did in fact behave in a population like a disease. Not conclusive at this stage, but between this and the lab data Leap had uncovered, the Babel idea was rapidly leaving the domain of the theoretical. No wonder Jess and Bates had gotten so excited.

But the more important immediate concern was that running RAIN-DROP for this "hypothetical" could have exposed Genesis, exposed Jess. If someone at Sandia had known enough to see its implications, they'd know it could bear upon military behavioral modification science. And that the RAINDROP system could be used to expose nasty secrets. Reverse-mapping Babel indicators could conceivably reveal the location of leaky labs, or *in vivo* population experiments, or covered-up industrial accidents. And somebody would feel very exposed. Who? Corporate security. Government spooks. *Shipley,* Ryan thought again.

"Anyway," Leap said. He blew out a breath, turned aside to tap on a keyboard, and the big laser printer hummed as it came out of power-save mode. "I compiled a list from my wetware memory of anything we did that might have gotten somebody's interest or offended anybody. Names, dates, summary of subject matter. Let me know how you want me to follow through. And now, if we're going to catch the bastards, I should get back to work on...this." He waved a weak hand at the chaotic room.

Leap looked so forlorn that Ryan felt a pang of pity. He stood up and clapped him on the shoulder in a gesture of sympathy that felt to him clumsy and inadequate. Then he began gathering up the pages that churned from the printer. Leap's list of possible enemies went on and on.

Chapter 35

Jason Ridder pounded his fist on the desk, then stood up and shoved a stapler and pens skittering. Marshall had informed him of the break-in immediately, but this was obviously his first chance to vent. Ryan just waited it out, sitting across from him with Dagan. Darion Gable stood to one side, dressed in a black collarless shirt and black silk jacket, his angular face expressionless and hands clasped behind him.

Ridder turned his red face to Gable. "Darion, what the *hell* did we talk about security for? What was that tour you took of the McClouds' house and offices all about if somebody can just waltz in and—"

"My team assisted Security in assessing risks to the Genesis offices and to the Brandt Institute home offices. Our concern was primarily security for Ridder Global, and only secondarily for the contracting organizations. We made various recommendations, which they implemented." Gable spoke without moving any part of his body, a preternatural stillness.

"What about this access business Dr. McCloud was so fucking macho-boy insistent upon when he signed on? Access to Ridder Global databases? Have we been compromised?" Ridder had shoved an unlit cigar into his mouth, and now it jutted up aggressively, bobbing as he spoke.

Ryan cleared his throat. "We never got that far. I understand the access protocols were still being developed—"

"You 'understand'? Did we or did we not drop our pants and let you stick a flashlight up our butts? Did or did not someone else run off with my corporate data when they knocked you over? You 'understand'? What the hell kind of outfit do you run?" Ridder turned away disdainfully to stalk the window wall of his office.

"There was no compromise of our data," Gable said. "We've only just completed the access protocols for Brandt or Genesis personnel. We haven't yet set up the dedicated land line that'll carry data. Nobody's given or received information. The only information that has been put in...hostile...hands is whatever data the McClouds may have turned

225

up." He turned his reptilian eyes on Ryan, then cased Dagan up and down, assessing her. Dagan drew her legs up uncomfortably, but her alert eyes took him in, too.

"And what *have* the McClouds turned up?" Ridder asked, facing them again. The flush was receding from his face.

"It's too early to claim any definitive—" Dagan began.

"Bullshit!" Ridder barked. "Somebody thought you guys had something! What were they after?"

"I'd also be curious," Gable said, "as to why you don't know more about what your wife was doing. Your six weeks in Africa aside, it sounds like maybe your communication was more than a little spotty." He said it with a tone of insinuation, Ryan felt, an unusual light in his eyes—a look almost of amusement. He'd readily spotted the gap in Ryan's explanations. *A good eye for another person's weaknesses.*

"Tell you what," Ryan said, standing up. Gable was a lizard, beneath contempt. But why did he always let Ridder awaken this stuff in him? He walked to the corner of the desk nearest Ridder, too close, and half sat on the edge, arms crossed. "You talk to Dagan and me with more respect, with more understanding of what this means to us, what we've lost. Then I'll explain where we're at and what we know. Sound good?"

Ridder gaped for only a split second, then turned to Gable with a grin. "What am I gonna do with this guy, Darion? You ever see anything like this son of a bitch?"

Gable smiled minutely along with his boss, but his eyes stared at Ryan without humor. Ryan returned the flat look.

"Okay," Ridder said. He sat back down, found his cigar cutter in the desk drawer, clipped the end of his Hoyo de Monterrey, lit it. "Hell, if I were in your shoes I'd feel the same way—you're missing your wife and you want her back. I'm truly sorry about Jessamine, Ryan. Sorry, Ms. Rabinovitch, for the way I spoke. Got a gutter mouth. Takes getting used to."

Dagan just smiled. "Don't worry. I work with Ryan. Hear it all the time."

Ryan explained that in finishing off the last job, in their preoccupation with helping launch the main Brandt studies, in Ryan's absence, he and Jess had been a little out of touch, but Jess had apparently made some breakthroughs. She was working primarily with Bates, he said, and she'd made unexpectedly rapid progress. They were now retracing her steps, her contacts, but it was hard with so many of their records taken or destroyed. He avoided details. He was tempted to ask Ridder about Alex Shipley, but decided to keep his suspicion quiet for now.

"I have some questions for you, too," Ryan said. "Since Jess was giving you your updates in my absence, you may be able to tell us something that could help us find her. A detail that we're missing."

"Anything I can do to help, sure," Ridder said.

"Did she ever talk about our interest in looking at violence from an epidemiological perspective?"

"Sure did. She was calling it 'the Babel effect.' Global epidemic of a brain disorder that causes the failure of social cooperation. She said if research bore her out, it would change our view of history."

"What was your response to the idea?"

"Are you kidding? Loved it."

"Why's that?"

"Hey, don't get me started. Why? A, because you can't look around at what's happening and not think that something's screwed up. B, because in my position you spend a lot of time worrying about the stability of global markets. Been a pet project for years. I'll tell you what I told Jess. See, our problem is that if we want to stay ahead of our competitors, we've got to jump into emerging markets before they do. At the same time, the world's in flux, we don't want to invest billions in corporate infrastructure in a region that's going to blow to hell three years down the road, right? So a few years ago I hired Rand Corporation, asked them to give me projections on how sociopolitical trends are gonna impact markets, resources, production."

"So what'd they conclude?"

Ridder made a disgusted noise. "All that happened was, these top political scientists and social psychologists and economists and cultural anthropologists and futurologists and the Rand whiz kids, they had conferences and symposia and wrote monographs up the ass. And got nowhere. Half their theories contradicted the other half. 'Postcolonial political consolidation,' 'resource attrition,' 'linguistic diffusion,' 'ethnogenesis'—all those goddamned bigdomes, and they couldn't agree on shit!" Ridder grinned at his own anti-intellectualism. "Talking to your wife, I realized the problem is we've been asking the wrong questions. She's right, you can't put social history in perspective without the biomedical angle. So I told her go ahead, I like this tack, see where it goes."

"Did she ever give you any details about medical specifics? About her research plans?"

"No medical details. Said she had some promising leads, but that it would take a lot of supporting research to back them up."

"Anything else?"

Ridder shook his head. "You sat in on a couple of our meetings, Darion—she say anything I might have missed?"

Gable shook his head.

"I guess that's it." Ridder paused to stare thoughtfully at the ash on his cigar, then frowned as a light began blinking on his phone. "So Ryan. I'll assume you'll be working with the FBI to get Jessamine and Dr. Bates back, and your research activities are on hold until their situation is resolved." He corrected himself quickly: "Until they're safely back. Darion, I'd like you to work with Dr. McCloud and his staff. If they need something in the way of your special talents to resolve this, discuss it with me first, but let's try to give it to them. Everybody understanding me?"

"Perfectly," Gable said.

Ryan nodded.

Ridder grabbed his nagging phone: "What now?" he barked. "Oh, hello, Governor. Yeah, I got about a minute—what can I do for you? Or rather, what can you do for me?" He grinned at Ryan and Dagan, enjoying his role. Gable slipped out his side door, and Ryan led Dagan out to the front office.

––––––

"So what'd you think?" Ryan asked. They sat in the car, stuck in Wednesday-afternoon rush-hour traffic on an access ramp to Route 1. Above them a billboard read, "THE FUTURE BELONGS TO THOSE WHO BELIEVE IN THE BEAUTY OF THEIR DREAMS."—ELEANOR ROOSEVELT. THIS MESSAGE BROUGHT TO YOU BY BANNERMAN OUTDOOR ADVERTISING. As good a way as any to fill up untenanted billboards, Ryan thought.

"God, I wish I had it on film," she said. "See, here's the thing about you, Ry. You can do that macho act as well as anyone alive, but you *choose* not to make a career out of it. You've chosen to become something other, better, than a Ridder."

"What makes you think it's an act?"

She ignored him. "How nice to think of having that snake Gable helping us out, huh?"

"What did you make of him?" Ryan edged the car forward and took it out of gear.

"'With friends like that…'" Dagan shivered. "He likes to be intimidating—that black-on-black look. He's got a real antipathy to *you*—I think because Ridder likes you a lot, sees you as a kindred spirit of sorts, and Gable resents that. He's jealous of his own closeness to his boss, his secret role, which for him is a kind of intimacy."

"That's pretty subtle. Woman's intuition?"

She laughed. "No. Close observation and lack of preconceptions. As you taught me."

Ryan nosed the car onto the highway and they managed another mile before the next slowdown. Dagan's window was open an inch or so, and a slender rope of her hair was drawn up and into the car's slipstream. She felt the tug and pulled the strand back with a graceful, unself-conscious gesture.

They stopped again not far from another billboard, vacant but for its inspirational homily: "KINDNESS IS THE GOLDEN CHAIN BY WHICH SOCIETY IS BOUND TOGETHER."—WOLFGANG VON GOETHE.

It caught Ryan upside the head, and the whole Babel thing slid abruptly down on him and with it a suddenly heightened sense of Jess's absence, the intolerable fact that she was in danger, and that it was only twelve days before she was due to give birth.

Dagan saw it in him and put her hand on his arm, her face instantly full of sympathy. "We're going to get her back, Ry!" she said. "We'll get her back, okay? We will!"

Chapter 36

The Peterson's guard at the entrance to the driveway let them pass, then spoke on his radio to alert the other guards to their arrival. He was a big-shouldered, unsmiling black man, who seemed to take his job seriously. Some reassurance there—these weren't rent-a-cops. In the parking area, Ryan shook hands with the other two men on evening duty, kissed Dagan good-bye. Once she'd driven away, he stood alone on the bluff for a time, watching the darkness come over the bay, a translucent veil drawn across the sky. Then he went inside to find two messages on the answering machine.

The first was unexpected, that unmistakable voice, melodious even through the little speaker: "Hello, Ryan, this is Diana Reese. I left messages with your staff while you were in Africa, but maybe they didn't get them to you? Listen, I don't know if you've seen my new show, but I'm doing a more journalistic interview series now, and I'd like to interview you again. We can talk more serious science, and I'd love to grab the first broadcast feature on your recent hostage experience. I think you'll like the new format—candid, absolutely chock-full of content and integrity. If it's not beneath you—heavy irony here—please give me or my producer a call." She left various numbers.

Before going off to Kalesi, Ryan had seen ads for her new series, and yes, it sounded much better, substantive and respectful. *Sure, Diana, maybe some year,* he thought. He wondered if she'd have called if she had known about Jess's abduction.

He deleted the message and listened to the next.

Which was even more unexpected: "This is Herman Weismann calling for Jessamine. Jess, what'd I do, what'd I say? Seriously, I thought we'd have connected again by now. I'll be in your town for a couple of days, so if you'd like to reschedule the lunch we missed, I'm yours. Don't know my phone number up there, but you've got my home number—give me a buzz."

Ryan knew Weismann only slightly, mainly through reading his work on genetics and evolutionary psychology. Jess knew him better, having consulted him some years ago on another project. Taught at Georgetown.

Without any address books, it took him a few minutes to track down
Weismann, who was temporarily at Harvard as a guest lecturer. Ryan
dialed his number at the visiting professors' residence.

"Weismann." Ryan pictured him at the phone: a tall man with a contagious smile and a frizz of graying hair sticking out almost clownishly
from his temples. He was a famous lecturer, Ryan remembered, filling his
talks with ribald jokes and humorous asides.

"Dr. Weismann, this Ryan McCloud. Have you got a few minutes?"

"Have I got time for the infamous Ryan McCloud? I am due shortly
at the dean's home for a tedious but obligatory departmental dinner,
but for you I certainly have a few minutes. I'd hoped I might hear from
a Dr. McCloud tonight, but frankly I expected the other one. The one
with legs like Tina Turner's."

"Yeah. That's what I'm calling about."

"I'm innocent! Hey, ask my wife. I'm fifty-eight and she'll tell you,
even with Viagra I ain't exactly—" Weismann caught himself as if Ryan's
somber tone had finally registered. "Sorry. This is serious, isn't it?"

Ryan explained briefly the urgent need to locate Jess, to determine
what she'd been working on.

"God, Ryan, I'm—I'm sorry! I hadn't heard."

"So far we've kept it out of the press."

"And she must be due any day now, right? Oh, man. Anything I can
do. Anything."

"She contacted you. She wanted to get together for lunch, but it never
came off, right? What happened?"

"Exactly that. She telephoned, oh, maybe a month ago, said she
wanted to pick my brains. We were going to have lunch, but then she
shows up early, sits in on my eleven o'clock class."

"She came to Washington."

"Yeah. Said she had a couple of errands in town. She comes into the
lecture hall, waves to me from the back seat, but when I finish up my
spiel, she's gone. We played telephone tag for a couple of weeks, but then
it just petered out."

"She didn't give you any details about what she wanted?"

"Hmmm. Not clinical stuff. General theory of evolutionary psychology. But we didn't go into details over the phone."

Ryan thought about it, picturing her in the hard seat of a Georgetown
lecture hall: tall, well-dressed, poised, a little out of place amid the motley
group of students. She waits, then walks out. Why leave prematurely,

without the courtesy of speaking to Weismann? *Not like Jess.* Did she change her mind about the need to see him? Or, it occurred to Ryan suddenly, did she get what she came for from the lecture?

"Herman—what was your lecture about?"

"Tuesday-morning course on ev psych, October first. For the bright kids, but just my standard spiel on the selfish-gene theory, evolutionarily stable strategies, animal behavior—the basics, really. I can't imagine it was anything new to Jessamine."

Ryan tensed as a shadowed silhouette passed in front of the deck windows. Instantly his hands tingled with adrenaline, and he realized just how keyed-up he really was. The indistinct shape paced the length of the deck, then turned back. One of the Peterson's guards, he saw, patrolling silently in the dark.

"Can you send me a transcript of the lecture?" Ryan asked.

"No transcript, but I can send you a recording. By courier, tomorrow morning. Ryan—is Jessamine at risk? Physically? Just how serious is this?"

"Very serious," Ryan told him. He thanked Weismann and hung up, feeling the fear rising again. He jotted notes on his pad, *October 1, Georgetown.* The relevance of the visit was hard to figure. He'd listen to the lecture, but he had little hope it would reveal anything.

The house was mostly dark now, so Ryan switched on some lights in the kitchen. The liquor cabinet tempted him, but he opted instead to open the freezer and take out a couple of pot pies. He stabbed them with a fork, put them in the oven, and threw away the waxed cartons in the trash can under the sink. Then something struck him, and instead of closing the cabinet door he pulled the can out into the light.

The can was lined with a black plastic garbage bag. Aside from his pot-pie boxes, the glistening bag was empty. Of course—Jess would have removed the full bag that Thursday evening, putting in a fresh bag and readying the trash for pickup on Friday. She'd have sent Abi around the house for the wastebaskets, filling the old bag completely before tying it off and taking it to the garage. Then on Friday morning, if the green plastic can was full, she'd wheel it out to the driveway for pickup. Given that they recycled and composted, they sometimes went two weeks between trash pickups.

Jess had been taken that night, hadn't set the trash out that morning. Which meant that unless the kidnappers had been very subtle indeed, the trash was still out in the garage. Containing the contents of Jess's wastebasket, maybe as much as two weeks' worth of transcribed pages from her yellow pads, sticky notes, and other scraps from her desk. Burke's team had worked over the garage and found no evidence of intrusion, nothing useful for their investigation. But they couldn't have known what to look for.

Ryan ran to the inner garage door, opened it, hit the lights. The double roll-up doors were closed, and the garage looked untouched. Just the ordinary domestic mess that had accumulated through the summer, when they didn't bother to park the cars in here: Abi's plastic lawn toys, the bicycles, the lawn mower. A broken chair he hadn't gotten around to repairing, several aluminum-tube recliners taken in when the weather turned. Jess's gardening stuff: terra-cotta pots, sacks of vermiculite, shears and clippers and spades.

And the trash, the big green canister overflowing with bulging bags.

The knob of the outside door rattled, making Ryan jump, and then a cautious voice called out: "Everything okay, Dr. McCloud?" One of the damned Peterson's guys again.

"Fine," Ryan said, heart hammering. "Everything's great."

Going without sleep was a bad plan for your serotonin and norepine-phrine metabolisms, Ryan knew. The quick, uniform cycles of REM sleep were neural-circuit refreshers, the body at rest but the brain anything but idle. During REM sleep, the brain sent tiny voltages down neural pathways, organizing its memory files and maintaining the cellular chemistry required to preserve memories that would otherwise atrophy. Even the most obscure circuits were refreshed, activating to a tiny degree stored ideas, thoughts, recollections, images. Thus the *Eureka!* moment so many scientists experienced at the edge of sleep: In the paradoxical alpha-theta state of REM, the obscure datum was sometimes resurrected and associated with ongoing mental projects. Sleeplessness played hell with your associative-correlative processes.

But by the time the sun came up, Ryan felt shaky but hopeful. He massaged his sandpapery face and stared out the windows at the burgeoning red glow on the horizon.

He had opened the leaves of the dining table and spread out the contents of two large bags of trash, winnowing out anything that might be relevant to Jess. The absence of legal-pad notes at first crushed him, but in the end he'd found two possibly useful items. One was a jotted quote from e. e. cummings: *all good kumrads you can tell / by their altruistic smell.* So the poetry book on her table had been more than just recreational reading. The other was a crumpled cash receipt, for a bratwurst, labeled *Flughafen Berlin-Tegel.* The main Berlin airport. Dated September 22: Jess had gone to Germany while he was in Kalesi.

Suddenly ravenous, he made himself eggs and bacon and English muffins which he toasted and ate with blackberry jam that Jess had somehow found time to make. He brewed coffee and drank a mug of it, black, as the sun cracked the horizon and sent a horizontal shaft of light into the house. It filled the big room and cast his moving shadow on the kitchen wall, *Man fixing breakfast.*

This was one of her favorite times of day: the long pale light gathering strength in the room, full of promise, the house quiet because Abi was still asleep. Once he'd come down to find her sitting on one of the stools here, legs emerging smooth beneath the big blue work shirt she used as a robe. Staring as if hypnotized out over the water. He'd joined her at the counter and she'd said, without preamble, as if he'd been there with her all along, "I'm very happy." She'd hugged him to her side, still staring out almost directly into the sun. The light penetrating, *inhabiting,* her brown eyes, turning them golden. A sun-drowsing cat. "Thank you for this," she'd told him, finally looking right at him. As if he were personally responsible for the beauty of sunrise and sea and of the newness of mornings and the pleasure of quiet houses. How good that felt.

Of course, that was before Allison was murdered.

He roused himself, tossed his dishes into the sink, and went down to the 'Combs to find the half-burnt phone bill for September. By eight o'clock he had pieced together enough to know what the next step should be. At ten after eight, when Dagan came through the front door, she took one look at his face and broke into a smile.

Chapter 37

Ryan looked down at the flexed arm of Cape Cod receding into the haze. He sat in a first class seat, an indulgence he could justify by the size of his frame, and looked over at Dagan, across the aisle. She had fallen quiet as soon as they'd lifted off, and now her chest rose and fell with the slow breathing of sleep. Face rounded, soft, utterly surrendered. She'd worked like a demon to get them this far, a twenty-five-year-old Jewish-WASP human tornado with smarts to burn, on a crusade to rid the world of evil. Her last drowsy words were, "You're manic, Ryan. I can see the symptoms. You'll burn out. Please try to get some sleep." Mothering him with her last energy. Then she was gone, from mother to round-faced child in a matter of seconds.

He had pondered the implications of Leap's hacks, running RAIN-DROP on behavioral data at Sandia, the professionalism of the break-in, Karl's tales of behavioral-mod research. Which brought things back to Alex Shipley and the interest he'd shown in the Babel job last spring. But was the Gray Ghost a suspect or a possible ally? On one hand, Ryan didn't trust him, there'd been the sense of warning about his comments. And Jess had certainly been nosing into some of his turf. Maybe the killer Brenner was a human torpedo, and that's why Shipley was interested, why the powers that be had never granted permission to test him or released service records. On the other hand, Shipley was a friend of Ridder's, and would be unlikely to sabotage his buddy's project. If he felt he had to, there were probably formal, legal ways to obstruct inconvenient inquiries.

Whom do you call when you don't trust the authorities? At last, just before leaving, Ryan had put in a call to Karl, in the hopes that he could prevail upon their friendship for some advice, maybe a favor. No answer, but he'd left a message on Karl's machine.

It hadn't been that hard, once he'd known to look at the overseas calls, to attach names to the numbers on the September phone bill. The

Geneva calls were easy. One number was for the Geneva Institute of
Mathematical Research, the office of Xavier Hoague, whom Ryan
remembered vaguely as a mathematician—some mover and shaker back
in the 1980s. The other was Hoague's home phone in Geneva. After
Ryan had tried Hoague at both numbers, getting no answer or even a
machine at either one, he'd gone on to Jess's calls to Germany.

These were the most revealing, although it took a lot of work to
figure it out: calls to the federal prison in Siemenstadt, outside Berlin,
and to a number of private residences, clinics, hotels, government
agencies. But at last the pieces came together. He should have
guessed—Jess had made these calls not long after he'd faxed her from
Kalesi with his idea about a differential study of war criminals and
altruists.

She had pulled an enormous number of strings to get it to happen, contacting colleagues in German universities, prevailing upon contacts in the
German government, throwing money around freely, using Ridder's name
and Genesis's prestige to get things done fast. Then she'd gone to Germany for a little differential study of her own.

Ultimately she had interviewed and tested two old men, Ruprecht
Freunde and Karl-Heinz Richter. By the time Ryan got off the phone,
Dagan had run a Web search and printed off articles on both men.
They were half-brothers. Both had been covered, at one time or
another, in the German and American press. *People* magazine had
recently profiled them both, in the kind of where-are-they-now piece
that sometimes follows up stories of popular interest. Richter was a
truly nasty son of a bitch, convicted of war crimes and imprisoned for
life at Siemenstadt; Freunde was a famous altruist who had risked his
life saving Jews at Dachau while his half-brother was helping put
them in the gas chambers at Buchenwald. Ryan suspected Jess had
scanned the article casually and had later come back to the idea of
testing them.

That the two men were half-brothers—same father, but Freunde had
taken his mother's maiden name when Richter became well known—
would help eliminate genetic variables in a differential study. Comparing
two men of the same generation, raised in the same culture and political
climate, same father, yet possessing two very different social dispositions,
could be a way to isolate the Babel syndrome: What made one an altruist
and the other a killer?

Freunde had readily agreed to meet with him, but, like Jess, Ryan had

had to pull a lot of strings to set up the interview with Richter at Siemenstadt, scheduled for tomorrow morning.

Dagan was right about getting some sleep, but still the manic buzz persisted. Or maybe it was more like panic. It was now exactly a week since Jess had been taken, eleven days until her due date.

As they'd headed out the door for the drive to the airport, Leap had come running, waving some papers. He had gotten the surviving backup CDs from their safe-deposit vault and had retrieved and printed off the old files. The most recent were from late June, when they'd still been almost exclusively involved in the Four Corners project. But there were a few of Jess's files related to Ridder's commission, transcriptions of her informal journal notes on the death-row interviews. Definitely worth reviewing to see where her thoughts were heading. Ryan read them all, torn between the pleasure of hearing Jess's voice in the writing and the darkness of the topic she wrote about.

The notes from their preliminary interview with Morales on May 21 showed that she was heading toward the Babel hypothesis even then:

????: Unlike Oakes, Morales comes across as average, normal, likable. Due to lack of obvious pathologies, my guess is PET & fMRI unlikely to have much diagnostic value. But paradoxically Morales could provide us the "missing link" between having a particular brain syndrome & actually committing murders. I.e., Oakes's brain, if we could get at it, would probably show a number of obvious anatomical & functional deviations, making it hard to determine which were responsible for his violent acts. Whereas in Morales, a subtle deviation in neural chemistry or function can more easily be labeled as THE causative or predictive factor.

????: Like Oakes, clearly objectified victims: called them "obstacles" or "impediments." Must look into objectification issue from neuro. perspective!

I was the appropriate lead for Morales. My own religious background, respect for relig. trad., helped establish sympathy, cooperation. But his attempts to provoke me worked better than (I hope) he knew. Another reminder that my own uncertainties of worldview make me vulnerable from every quarter. Am esp. troubled by thin dividing line between legit. fervor/commitment & excess, between positive power of faith & sheer delusion. ????: If Morales has brain syndrome, however subtle, what about others who kill for "purpose"—mercenary soldiers, etc. Or, for that matter, political leaders like Milosevic or Suharto who are clearly "intentional" & "rational" but who encourage & thrive upon slaughter?

Am puzzled by my own responses to both Oakes & Morales. Part of me loathing them, repelled by them, as if they were the killers of Allison. Part of me hurting for them, seeing them as victims also— which, if we are correct in the neuropathological view of extreme violence, they literally are. (Neither view good for objectivity!) Must suggest Marsh set up ethical & legal panels at Brandt to sort out these issues as they arise.

Yes, Morales had gotten to her. Partly it would have been the ethical resonances implicit in his "service" to his beliefs. Partly, too, that his apparent sanity gave credence to the idea of a "subtle" effect as an important indicator of the Babel syndrome. Importantly, too, Morales was a stepping-stone toward her broadening of symptomatology to include other forms of social behaviors that added up to the Babel effect. And the objectification issue had to be significant—so obvious, and yet so seldom looked at neurologically.

Preliminary interview with Gerald Rudolph Gibson, June 20

Crimes: Fire-bombing African-American churches, 22 dead in 6 incidents. Our first perpetrator clearly motivated by racial hatreds. Set incendiaries in advance, detonated during Sunday services. Also implicated but not convicted in 3 lynchings w/ classic features: emasculation, genitals stuffed in victims' mouths, slogans carved in victims' chests.

CV: 28 yrs. old, mixed blue-collar work history, mostly agricultural. Ed.: Graduated high school & two semest. community college (engineering, may have helped him to build bombs?). Member Georgia-based racist separatist group with neo-Nazi, pseudo-Germanic culture based on hatred primarily of Af.-Amer., Jews distant second. Death row 3 yrs., chose not to appeal: unrepentant, "martyr for cause," used trial as public podium to espouse views. Due to be exec. July 15.

Affect: Smug, cocky, aggressive, sneering, weak claim of "higher motivation" in crimes, i.e., Aryan Knights agenda (all-white, "pure" nation).

Appearance: Medium height, fitness fanatic, very muscular. Shaved head, tattoos of weapons, swastikas, cryptic runes, Gothic lettering, etc.

Ryan, Dagan, & I viewed from observation room. Bates led interview: seemed approp. with his white-blond hair, strong jaw & flawless German—"more Aryan than thou." Did good job of pretending to some degree of sympathy with Gibson's views, (got consent for testing) but couldn't resist jab at end: "Ever hear of the other Hesse—not Rudolph, Hermann, e at the end? Or Goethe?" Gibson: "Fuck're they?" Bates: "Just some other German guys you might also think about." Dear Bates!

???: Emasculation of lynching victims, though typical & maybe just imitative, suggests sexual pathologies. Is it really any diff. from other ritualized mutilations & arrangements common in serial killers?

???: Gibson's agricultural work history? Exposure to pesticides, herbicides, fungicides, fertilizers, all powerful endocrine disruptors. Check specific working enviros. for neurotoxins.

Like Morales, Gibson's crimes show planning & intentionality, are "justified" by "higher agenda." Am excited by prospect of isolating subtle neural decrements, not cloaked by overt & ultimately irrelevant other pathologies. Objectification again: victims are not "real" but are abstracted artifacts of neo-Nazi culture. ???: Look into Gibson's contact with Af.-Amer. populations, esp. in childhood. Real, physical exposure, or only through racist literature, etc.? Begetting another ???: Look into role of racist family/local culture in childhood brain development per plasticity of brain—if brain can be physically shaped by abusive family enviro., can it be shaped by broader culture of hatred, fear? What an idea—culture as neurotoxin! Which neural loci most subject to such influences? What basic drives affected?

After Gibson, am certain that link can be estab. between those we readily label "sick," "criminals," & those who commit identical deeds under guise of nationalistic, religious, political-philosophy, etc. agendas. Point of statistical fact: we're scared of small-time crimes, but at much greater real risk from larger social violence that we hesitate to label pathological manifestation. Last 20 yrs., thousands dead from violent crime, but millions & millions dead from terrorist actions, genocidal wars, political executions, etc. ???: Could make case that blatantly inhumane public policies (slavery, kleptocracy, ecocide, etc.) are also indicators of widespread subtle neural impairments. Have started seeing political history as record of large-scale mass & serial murders. Very upsetting perspective.

Physically ill & shaken after observing Gibson. Ry similarly affected but very solicitous of me, tender. Construes himself a graceless person, but in evening brought in a single purple iris from garden & presented it to me, talking about its beauty, the math of its architecture, the flowering plants' role in ecosystem—Ry stuff, intended with so much love. Abi caught the drift, gave me little gifts all evening—drawings, a buttercup, etc. Helped a great deal! Me very grateful, then considering: If cultural enviro. can developmentally shape brains to detriment, can't it also heal?

So she had been putting together the Babel thesis, in earnest, as early as June. Yes, the interview with Gibson had shaken them all, the sheer monstrosity of what he was, what he'd done. Looking at her notes, he couldn't disagree with her thesis: You couldn't see Gibson as anything but sick, but his actions were no different from those of politically motivated killers. By only the tiniest of steps, Jess had moved from criminal violence to sociopolitical violence. And yes, she was right, the latter was by far the more dangerous.

For a moment he savored the part about the iris, feeling a swell of longing for her. But then among the papers he encountered her notes from the Brenner interview, the last Leap had been able to retrieve: *Must become more independent...the Skunk Works' one-woman Skunk Works. Try to insulate reputation of Genesis, esp. Ry, from some of controversy & peer/press flak...From the more material dangers, too: compartmentalizing at this point will help protect Ry & Abi. Can't stand to put them at risk, but can't ignore this. Can't tell Ry, either, he'd never stand for me taking it on my shoulders... Got to protect Ry & Abi from me right now. Maybe most of all.*

Oh Jesus, Jess. His eyes filled with tears. So there was another reason for her distancing: protecting her family. And by then she'd obviously made progress, had seen where her work would take her. *More material dangers,* she'd written. What kind of dangers? It suggested she'd known there were real physical risks here. Yet she'd gone on anyway. Another wave of worry, loss, anger overwhelmed him, and to escape he put the journal material away.

The in-flight movie began on the screen just above his seat: the current box-office mega-hit about a serial killer who did ghastly things to women. Ryan watched it briefly with an anthropologist's distance. The film's veneer of intentional *noir* failed to conceal that the director was indulging his own, and his audience's, lust for bloodshed.

Great, he thought, looking away. *Film violence—how has the whole world acquired this insatiable hunger for violent fantasy? Obsessive morbid ideation—another indicator? A predictive early symptom?*

Needing to escape the images, he took out his disc player and headphones, slipped in the recording that Herman Weismann had sent over: the lecture on evolutionary psychology. Jess went all the way to Washington and listened to the talk, but bailed out on her meeting with Weismann. Why? Long odds, but maybe the answer lay hidden in the content of the lecture.

The recording began with a few minutes of auditorium noise, the rustle of bodies and murmuring voices, the clunk of collapsible writing desktops pulled down. Jess was among that audience, Ryan thought. He could almost feel the ambience of that room at Georgetown, the way her presence would for him alter any space. At last there came the *thump-thump* of Weismann tapping the microphone, and the room noises subsided.

"You'll notice that today I'm not speaking from the center of the stage," Weismann's cheery New Jersey voice said. "I've put the lectern over here to the side, because I wish to impress upon you, if I convey nothing else, one single idea: *We as individuals are not at the center of the evolutionary stage.* I even asked my assistant to dress up in balloons and do a dance at center stage, to act the role of a gene. He refused, for which I'll dock his pay, but I want you to imagine it: The star of the evolutionary show is not me, the individual organism, but that colorful little collection of molecules we call the *gene.*"

Weismann's students responded with grateful laughter.

"This idea is like a big hook, coming out from the wings of mankind's egotistical little vaudeville show and giving us the old yank. Of course, Darwin began the process, by saying we weren't created as the darling of God's eye, in his image, but merely evolved through survival of the fittest, like all the other animals. Ouch, right? I have to say this idea bugged the hell out of me at first. I'm not religious, but I've got a big romantic streak, and I'd prefer to think we are who we are not because of some blind mechanical laws of probability and opportunity, but because of something more *destined,* more *chosen, meaningful.* But, alas, like it or not, Darwin's basic theory of evolution answers so many questions that it has become the primary paradigm of the natural sciences."

Weismann paused. The television screen above Ryan showed the serial killer strapping a beautiful woman onto a homemade operating table and preparing his surgical tools. Mercifully, the scene changed just as he bent to his work.

"So the story of life isn't even about *us*," Weismann went on, "it's about our *genes*. A gene is a molecular structure that has a tendency to replicate itself. Over billions of years this structure has chanced upon a wide range of workable strategies to get the better of this or that environmental obstacle to its replication. The individual organism, be it you, me, a sea slug, or Richard M. Nixon, has endured only because and to the degree that it's an *effective vehicle for genes to replicate*. That's why I asked Mr. Glasser to dress up in balloons and dance around in the middle of the stage, and why I, the lowly vehicle, am over here with my ass practically in the men's room urinal."

The students laughed, and Weismann harangued them: "What dance would Mr. Glasser do? Anybody answer? Come on, think! Okay, you all flunk! The *Twist*, of course, so he'd look like that familiar double helix, DNA. The names Watson and Crick ring a bell? Right? Right?"

This was entertaining, Ryan thought, but wasn't giving him any clues to Jess's thought processes. He thought of switching off the disc player, but decided to give it another few minutes.

"Now, the primary characteristic of the gene is that it only 'wants' to make duplicates of itself. It has an absolutely ruthless concern for *numero uno*. All the complicated vehicles, Dick Nixons or liver flukes, exist because they have proven to work well enough to allow their genes to replicate. And if they don't have characteristics or behaviors that help the replication of its genes, that kind of individual just doesn't get made any-more! Now, for me, this idea stinks, it de-romanticizes everything. But, again, it explains a great deal, it *works*. It's a *tool* for solving scientific problems. To understand the behavior of living things, we need to look for *how that behavior benefits some selfish gene.*"

Weismann was quiet for a moment, and Ryan heard the tap and scrape of chalk on a blackboard. On the jet's TV screen the detective was argu-ing with his wife, looking unshaven and troubled. At this point the plot formula would require him to realize that the only way to catch the killer was to step into his mind, to find the same urges in himself, to *become* him.

More chalkboard noises. "So. The selfish-gene theory has spawned whole new disciplines, like sociobiology and evolutionary psychology. What are those? Let me give you an example of a sociobiological solution to a difficult animal behavior riddle: Why do male lions sometimes kill and eat lion cubs? On the surface, it *can't* be 'good' for lions as a species to kill each other. Right? So why would lions have evolved cub-killing behaviors? Well, remember: *Look for how this behavior benefits the selfish gene—not for how it benefits 'all lions.'* The sociobiological answer is that male lions, newly coming into a pride, are programmed to want *their* genes to be replicated. They don't give a hoot about the genes of some other lion! Nursing cubs sired by some other lion keep the lionesses from going into heat. So if the *arriviste* male lion kills off the nursing cubs, the females will go into estrus soon and therefore be available for mating— for the cub-killing lion's genes to replicate."

The jet hit a pocket of turbulence and the seat belt signs came on with a chime. Ryan complied obediently, hating the rumble and bounce of the plane. His eyes were drawn to the TV, where the serial killer now stood in a dark stairwell, waiting as his next victim entered the building and began climbing the stairs, round and round the flights and landings. *The killer like a lethal gene, lurking unobserved in the coils of the DNA helix. A Babel gene?*

Weismann: "So what about us humans? Well, there's another new dis-cipline devoted to the study of the selfish gene's role in our behavior, called evolutionary psychology. Forget Freud—you can explain human behaviors in terms of their evolutionary logic, calculations of benefit to the selfish gene. Most questions are better solved not on the analyst's couch but by the math of Mendel's classical genetics, statistical probabil-ity, and the logic of games theory."

Weismann was silent for a moment, and the disc just played the shift-ings and coughings of the auditorium. Ryan waited for a moment, then slapped the off button and yanked out the earphones. The talk was full of possible resonances—the cannibal lions had a genetic program that could be analogous to the Babel effect in humans—but this was familiar territory nowadays, and there was no way to tell what, if anything, might have served as a catalyst for Jess.

The serial killer caught his victim, a tall black woman, hustled her into her apartment. He dragged her to the kitchen, where without his own tools he was prepared to improvise with cooking utensils. It struck too close to home, and Ryan looked away, sickened by the darkness that seemed to besiege him from all sides. Between Jess's journals on serial killers and Weismann's talk and the film, it was Contemporary World Civ 101. About summed it up. Christ. Enough to make you homesick for the Kalesi jail.

He lowered his seat, mainly as a way to get the TV screen out of his direct line of sight. Rivers of blood. Oceans of misery.

Chapter 38

The Siemenstadt prison administrator, or *Leiter der Justizvolzuganstalt,* was named Schmidt. He had initially balked at allowing another intrusion, only six weeks after Jess and Bates had interviewed Karl-Heinz Richter and disrupted routine by bringing a truck-mounted cranial imaging lab into the prison's inner parking lot. It had taken all of Ryan's own prestige, plus some help from Ridder, Burke, and the FBI's legal attaché for Germany, to overcome Schmidt's objections and set up this interview.

The prison stood alone in broad fields five miles outside Siemenstadt, a western suburb of Berlin. Ryan had unconsciously expected something like Spandau prison, where Rudolph Hess had lived out his life as the solitary occupant of a great, dark, empty edifice. But as he turned their rented VW into the access road, he saw that the prison was in fact fairly modern: a cluster of low concrete buildings, set in acres of pavement ringed by electric fencing. In the dreary light of a leaden overcast, the place was depressing but hardly Gothic.

They showed their identification at a perimeter guard post, then another, then parked the car and were escorted into the administration building, where they were searched thoroughly. Schmidt watched this process with considerable satisfaction, and then left on some pretext and made them wait in his lobby for an extra half hour. The guy had a bug up his butt, Ryan decided, from being countermanded by his superiors.

"How're you doing?" he asked Dagan when they were alone. "You look more apprehensive than usual—"

"I'm feeling more *Jewish* than usual," she said, looking around with a shiver. "Something about dropping by to visit old Nazis. Or maybe it's just that *je ne sais quoi* ambience of German prisons."

They had already decided that she would wait outside and that Ryan would interview Richter alone. Richter was unlikely to appreciate the Semitic features of Dagan's face.

The wait gave Ryan time to review the file Dagan had prepared on Karl-Heinz Richter. Born in Munich in 1916, joined Hitler's SA early on, promoted in rank primarily for his useful sadistic tendencies. When rounding up journalists and intellectuals in Munich, he liked to beat them and shove them down the steps of their homes. If they didn't live through it, Richter would claim in his reports that they died resisting arrest. These contrivances were necessary in the early phase, before murder was officially condoned.

During the war, he was transferred to Buchenwald concentration camp, where he apparently tortured and terrorized the inmates at his leisure. His habit of urinating on his victims earned him the nickname *Feldwebel Gelb*—Sergeant Yellow. His career as an officer was cut short when he was caught stealing and selling camp office equipment, which got him banished to the Eastern Front.

He survived a Russian prison camp and after the war fled to Argentina. He remained incognito in Buenos Aires for twenty-five years, until he was arrested for beating his Argentine wife nearly to death and so caught the attention of war crimes investigators. At trial after extradition to Germany, he never denied his hatred of Jews and continued to assert the superiority of Aryan Germans. Though he was convicted of numerous heinous acts of torture, newspaper photos of Richter standing to receive his sentence of four life terms in prison showed him with an unrepentant smile on his hatchet face.

Ryan skimmed through several more pages and then slid the file away, wishing he could wash his hands. *Feldwebel Gelb.*

Leiter der JVA Schmidt took it upon himself to escort Ryan to Richter's corridor. "You made the correct decision," Schmidt said, "regarding the young lady. There is no need to subject her to…" His hand made a tossing-away gesture.

"When my wife came here, how—"

"She waited, just as your assistant waits. The gentleman with her—?"

"Dr. Bates."

"Yes, Dr. Bates. He conducted the interview by himself. Good Aryan features, Dr. Bates," Schmidt said, without apparent irony.

Inside the blocks, Siemenstadt proved even more depressing than outside: concrete walls that seemed to radiate a chill, rust pricking through the beige paint on the barred gates they passed through. At first Ryan could hear the distant sounds of many voices, the dull thunder of activity, but as they proceeded the sounds grew more remote. He felt claustrophobia rise in him, dark fingers around his throat.

"This is the old block, built just after the war," Schmidt explained. "We had a corridor devoted to a number of war criminals. But every one year or two years one died off, or was sent to our hospital facility. Richter is therefore alone in his corridor."

They came to a final security gate, manned by a single portly guard who let Ryan in and slid the gate shut behind him.

"Here I bid you the best of luck, Dr. McCloud," Schmidt said through the bars. He smiled without amusement and marched back the way they'd come.

The guard motioned for Ryan to proceed, then turned up the volume of the tiny television he'd been watching and sat back on his stool, arms folded.

Halfway down the corridor, the guard's soccer game barely audible, Ryan found himself at an occupied cell, a concrete box ten feet square with a bed frame bolted to the floor, a metal toilet and sink. It was cluttered with the miscellany of life: books in metal shelves, a desk, postcards taped to the walls among posters of rural German landscapes, a crisply made bed, clothes hung on a row of hooks. And a man, seated at the desk with his back to Ryan. Wide, bony shoulders covered with the green fabric of the prison uniform.

"Guten Tag, Herr Richter."

The green back didn't move. "Stop!" an old man's voice grated, in English. "Not another word of idle courtesies. Tell me what your eyes saw today. Tell me what your ears heard." When Ryan hesitated, confused, the back shook with emotion. "Tell!"

The travel posters offered a clue to what was desired. Needing the old man's cooperation, Ryan decided to give it a shot: "When my airplane came over Germany," he hazarded, "the sun was just rising. Below us was a mat of low-lying clouds the texture of, of cotton batting, as if the stuffing inside a furniture cushion had been spread on the ground...But halfway to Berlin the clouds began to open and I could see the green of fields and forests. The rooftops of towns were cupped in folds of the land, bright orange in the sunrise..."

Richter's back swayed slightly. "Continue!" he ordered.

Ryan gripped the bars and extemporized more impressions: The forest of tall construction cranes, innumerable latticed towers in orange and yellow, that filled the sky above reunited Berlin. How pale the women's cheeks in the crisp air, and how red their lips, keen their eyes.

When he stopped, the prisoner's back was motionless for a moment. Then Richter turned to face him. His face had retained the sharp cheekbones and strong chin that Ryan remembered from photographs, but the skin was gray and covered with a short white stubble of beard. The eyes were bloodshot yellow, still full of cunning.

Richter's tongue touched his lips as if he'd just eaten something to be relished. "You see," he explained, "I must…harvest…your impressions while they are still fresh in you. My few visitors are thus my…windows. In my otherwise windowless world." He gestured at the close walls around him, and abruptly stood and strode to the bars, where he clasped one hard talon over Ryan's hand. "I much enjoyed seeing my country from your eyes, Dr. McCloud. Do you know how long it has been since I last saw it as you have?" His eyes blazed, a yellow pulse.

Ryan had to restrain the urge to yank his hand free of Richter's. "You have come a long way to see me. Tell me what you need. And why I should help you."

"I am a colleague of Dr. Bates," Ryan began. "There is a problem, and I need to establish what you and he talked about. What sort of tests he administered."

Richter scrutinized him shrewdly for a time before releasing his hand and standing back from the bars. He sat on the end of his bed, lit a cigarette, blew smoke into the air. "If you are indeed such good colleagues, why do you not already know everything about our conversation, his tests?"

"I was imprisoned myself. In Africa. Only for a month, but it was long enough to lose contact."

Richter seemed to take pleasure in Ryan's having shared the delights of living in a cage. "And where is Dr. Bates now, that you cannot simply ask him?"

This was the hard part. How had Bates explained his mission? He would have detested Richter, would have had a hard time concealing the fact of his hatred. How would he have persuaded the old Nazi to submit to the clinical tests? Not by appealing to his philanthropic principles—quite the opposite. Bates would have exploited his own white-blond hair, his blue eyes, his muscular build and martial carriage. Just as he had while interviewing Gibson, the neo-Nazi church-bomber. *Maybe.*

"Bates has been taken," Ryan whispered. "By our common enemies."

Through a veil of cigarette smoke, Richter looked startled.

"Herr Richter, I know he conducted cranial imaging tests, took blood. I assume he conducted psychological tests. But I need to know the exact content of his questions. And I need you to try to recall if he said what he was planning to do next."

Richter was staring at him appraisingly, the pupils of his eyes shockingly blue in their yellow orbs, alert in his desiccated face. "He said that, as I am the last of my…generation…it was urgent to understand me better. That there will come a time when the world will be grateful for this knowledge of me. That the medical tests, the blood and spinal fluid, the machines—for looking at my brain. And for genetic testing."

Ryan continued to whisper: "Proof of what makes you a German and not a Jew. Proof that we can use for…common ends."

"Aha. Our common ends." Richter stood up, ground out his cigarette in an ashtray. He took a turn in his cell, as if what Ryan said had at last excited him. "He spoke to me for perhaps an hour here. Then the guards put irons on my ankles and I was escorted with grand pomp to the laboratory in the truck. Oh, Schmidt clucked and squawked like an angry old hen!" Richter chuckled at the thought.

From the phone records, Ryan knew that Jess had borrowed the semi-mounted imaging lab from a German hospital association that helped bring the expensive cranial imaging apparatus to rural clinics. The technology aboard the truck told him the rough outline of the tests they'd administered: EEG, MRI, the same basic protocol as the death row tests.

"When I was in the machine, Dr. Bates showed me photographs. Old photographs of my mother. He explained that I would have an emotional reaction to seeing her, that the machine would make a picture of what my brain did when I felt that emotion. Then a picture of my brother."

"Of Ruprecht?"

Richter's skin tightened on the bones of his face. "No. Of Gunther, my youngest brother. Dead from the Communists in 1944."

"What else?"

Frowning, Richter tried to recall. "There were many. A family I did not know, hugging, kissing, smiling. Some men fighting. Reich soldiers dead in the snow. Piles of the dead *Juden,* stacked like cordwood. Then, one after the other, many faces of people. Each time, Dr. Bates asked me, 'Is this a member of your family? Do you know this man?' I did not know any of them. Some were Jews! I asked him, 'Do I look like I am kin to *this?* Why not also show me pictures of apes!'" Richter bristled at the memory, but then regained his amused detachment.

Showing him the faces of strangers was no doubt intended to provide a comparison between Richter's neural responses to Germanic features and his reactions to racial types he hated. The rest was fairly standard stuff, with the advantage of having photos specific to the test subject's life— and a half-brother to compare him with. *Jess, you clever girl.*

Richter talked briefly about the imaging machines, and then went on to tell about the EEG test, again the pictures and questions. Despite his overriding concern for Jess, Ryan felt the itch of scientific curiosity: This would be fabulous data. Correlated with larger studies, invaluable. Where were the results? Who had them?

"Herr Richter, did Dr. Bates say anything about his plans? Where he would travel next?"

Richter tossed his head, a flick of disdain. "Munich. My older half-brother, the much-beloved, practically sanctified, Jew-loving *traitor.*"

"That I knew. Anything else?"

"No. But I know he left here very much upset." Richter smiled at the memory.

"Upset? Why?"

Richter came to push his face between the bars, close enough that Ryan could smell the rotting-meat stink of his breath. "Because," Richter said, beaming with satisfaction, "I told him that he was a terrible actor. As you are. But I suppose I should be grateful for any distraction from routine."

"Actor—?" Ryan tried to look confused.

"Your transparent ploy. Your little ruse for the aged, senile, stupid Nazi. 'Our common purpose.' Neither you nor Dr. Bates came to discover what makes me German, or what gives me my 'exceptional insight' into racial destiny. You came to identify what makes me a monster. To find the gene in my body, or the part of my brain, that makes me what you so fear."

The change in Richter stunned Ryan, and it took him a moment to find his voice. "Yes," he said at last, feeling the relief of pretense dropped. "You're right. A monster. We look at you just as we'd inspect a poisonous insect in a swamp."

"Do you think," Richter jeered, "that I cannot recognize my own species, Dr. McCloud? That I could not tell what sort of creature Bates really was? What you are? You haven't the steel in you. Neither of you. You haven't the fire."

"Good, Adolf. So why did you go along with the tests?"

Richter laughed, truly delighted now. "Because what you are doing is precisely what we would have done had we the technology you have now!

Because in looking to my body, my genes, my brain, for what makes me what I am, you are endorsing the very philosophy you claim to abhor. You have *joined* me, Dr. McCloud! I have every confidence that you will build a fine case for what has been our argument all along! You and your friend Bates and your Negress whore!"

Ryan reacted before he could think, lunging toward the bars and grabbing through them at Richter's sneering face. But the old man stepped quickly back out of reach. "Do you think I am *illiterate?* We have a prison *library,* Doctor. I did my own research before you imbeciles began arriving! Did you really imagine that I am entirely without resources? That I do not know quite well who my friends are? Perhaps being married to a subhuman animal, you have lost a measure of your human intelligence!"

Richter took a quick step forward and kicked the cage door with surprising force, a crash of steel that echoed down the corridor. To the distant guard he called in German: "Hey, pig-shit! Take this idiot out! He no longer amuses me." He looked back at Ryan and spat.

After a moment, sickened, Ryan turned away and began walking back. The sound of Richter's laughter accompanied him for the whole length of the corridor.

The sun was gone behind a heavy overcast by the time they emerged and walked to the car. The gray industrial sky seemed clotted with steel wool, lights were coming on across the darkening landscape. Ryan felt soiled, used, unclean.

Richter had been smart enough to find the core ethical problem that underlay any effort to determine genetic or neurological roots of human behaviors. *If we prove our every action and feeling and way of thinking and familial instinct has a biological origin,* Ryan thought furiously, *do we not then assign ourselves biological destinies? If we show that selfishness is the ultimate natural law, the foundation of all behavior, don't we justify the unrestrained striving of one against the other? Don't we give ourselves hard-science tools to prove the superiority of one individual or family or group— and the inferiority of another? Don't we play into the hands of neo-Nazis and eugenicists, racists and bigots of every stripe? Despite the hope our discoveries might offer, aren't we just going to help* perpetuate *the Babel effect?* This was the ethical mess unavoidably begotten by the ideas Dagan had expressed during her brave, hopeful soliloquy on the beach. The deadly shadow of the brightest aspiration.

It was one thing pondering these questions from the serenity of Heart Cove, but it was another thing entirely having them rubbed in your face by an old piece-of-shit Nazi. As Dagan waited on the other side of the car, Ryan stood at the driver's-side door, feeling frustration build. When the key didn't immediately turn in the lock, he drew back a fist and drove it through the window. It exploded inwards, spraying the interior with jagged pellets of glass. He reached inside and levered the handle, and then used his briefcase to sweep the worst of it off the seat.

That's what insurance is for, he told himself. Dagan watched him, too shocked to speak.

It was a cold day. *Terrific,* he thought as he started the car. He'd freeze his dumb Irish-Polish ass on the drive back to Berlin.

The hotel was just off the Kurfurstendamm, near the railway terminal and the stylish shopping district so popular with tourists. Upstairs, they opened the door between rooms and conferred as Ryan fumbled a beer and some whiskey minis out of the refrigerator, threw himself on his bed, gulped off some beer, and began pouring whiskey into the top of the bottle.

Dagan sat primly in the bedside chair, sipping orange juice. Though still upset, she brought them immediately back to business.

"While you were in with Richter," she said, "I spoke to Schmidt for a time."

Ryan drained half the bottle of boilermaker, disliking himself immensely and trying to figure out a way to ease the impact of his foul mood on Dagan. "You are one hell of an amazing young woman," he told her. "You hang out all day in a goddamned German prison, you have to travel with a violent lunatic, and yet you keep it all together. Dagan, I apologize for being such a fuck-up. You deserve better."

"You're under a lot of stress. Why won't you tell me what Richter said to upset you so much?"

He still didn't want to tell her. Spare the kid's idealism. "Only that I learned nothing that I didn't know already, and that another day has gone by."

"But I think *I* learned something of value. Schmidt told me some interesting things about Richter's contacts in the outside world."

"Oh?"

Dagan nodded. "Richter is allowed to receive some visitors—his lawyers, occasionally members of the press, some relatives. Schmidt says through them he maintains contact with neo-Nazi groups, for whom he is a bit of an icon. Richter corresponds a lot, and although his mail is monitored, coded information could still pass. He can also browse the Web through the library computers, and probably receive embedded messages, if not send them."

"What—they know this and *allow* it?"

"Of course. Tracking Richter's contacts is a way for German authorities, the *Staatsschutz,* to monitor these hate groups. Apparently most neo-Nazi activity originates in the U.S.—skinhead groups, white supremacists, Christian Identity types."

Ryan thought about it as the boilermaker ram-charged alcohol into his bloodstream. "Meaning, here's a candidate for our enemies list. The scenario would be that Jess and Bates came here, and Richter alerted his buddies in the U.S. that some uppity nigger scientist was on to something they should know about. Five weeks later some…friend…of Richter's did the break-in and kidnapping."

"It's a possibility. I even wondered if there could be a connection to Gibson, the Aryan Knights. So I called Burke from Schmidt's office. Asked him to talk to the *Staatsschutz* people, to get specifics on Richter's contacts in the United States." Dagan stood up, grabbed his stockinged foot, squeezed his toe painfully. "Buck up. Please? We're making progress."

She disappeared into her room. Ryan just lay there thinking, *Eight days. Eight days since they took her, and we're no closer than we were the first day.*

Chapter 39

Sat. Nov. 2

Dear Jess,

One-thirty A.M. and I can't sleep. So I'm writing you this letter, which I swear I will put into your hands, personally, soon. I love you and miss you more than I can tell you.

You know what these older Berlin hotel rooms are like: high-ceilinged and elegant in a hard, Bismarckian way, floor-to-ceiling drapes over tall windows, the space dominated by an antique commode the size of a Volkswagen. Decor that goes better with loving company.

This hotel is just down the street from the one you and I stayed in when we were here three years ago. Only a few blocks from the Breitscheidplatz, remember, and the bombed-out Kaiser Wilhelm Memorial Church. I went to bed at ten but couldn't sleep, so I got dressed again and walked around the flame-blackened spire in the raw night air. Here and there along the Kurfurstendamm are food stands, not as many as when we were here that December, but enough for tourists or merrymaking Berliners to buy hot wine and alte bieren and eat hot chestnuts and all those unpronounceable kinds of sausages. I bought a bratwurst in a crusty baguette and heaped it with good German mustard and munched it as I walked.

Of course this brought back memories of meandering the streets with you every night, enjoying the red-cheeked crowds, stopping at the rustic Christmas stalls to buy food and scalding Guhlwein and trinkets for Abi. You were so amused by me—mildly drunk and clumsy, feeling expansive, my bad German getting us into hilarious discussions with strangers. How we loved Berlin and Berliners! And I courted you and pulled you into every dark doorway for kisses and gropes, and you slapped my hands and we laughed, both of us excited by the unfamiliar air here. I'd give anything to have done it again with you tonight.

Maybe I'm just exhausted or paranoid, but the thought comes to me, forgive me Jessie, maybe your activities and state of mind and whereabouts during the last few months are hard to trace because you were having an affair. One of the FBI agents and Ridder's hit man Gable both suggested as much. Usually I can't really see it, but then I think maybe that's just my own inattention, or the false sense of security the marital status quo sometimes encourages. So at moments I get afraid it's true. This is childish crap, forgive me, you're pregnant and a person of integrity. But Jessie, even at the moments when that paranoia is strongest, please know how irrelevant it is to me. I think, Fine, just let her be okay now. Maybe it's Bates, you and he always hit it off, and I think, Fine, let her take pleasure from Bates, just let her be alive now.

It was after midnight when I walked back to the hotel, again past the ruined church. The street stalls were boarded up now, and the few pedestrians walked quickly in the raw weather. But of course the church was still lit by streetlights. Its cratered walls struck me as unbearably sad, the gaping hollow of its bombed-out rose window like a mouth frozen in an expression of shock and remorse. I recalled you, craning your lovely neck to examine what should have been a proud spire, now broken and flame-blackened, and what you said about a church steeple being symbolic of mankind's aspiration toward God. You asked me, What does it mean that we've blasted this spire half off, left it gaping? You answered yourself: The conflicts we contrive between us cost us no less than our divine aspiration.

Tonight your comment struck me as prescient, relevant to our current quest for the Babel effect. I am not religious, but aspiration I understand as well as anyone, you know this about me. And yes, I can't help but conclude we're killing ours, be it religious or humanistic, spiritual or scientific.

So all these thoughts got me gloomy and I headed back toward the hotel in some sleety rain. Half a block from Breitscheidplatz, an ambulance hee-hawed up the street, startling a flock of crows from some rooftop. At first I thought that they were huge bats, these black flop-winged nightflyers, but then they broke into harsh cawing and I realized what they were. The flock filled the width of the street for a whole city block, wheeling and swooping just above the buildings, and somehow there in the shadow of the ruined church they seemed an ill omen to me. I got so scared, Jess.

Then I got to the hotel room and stood tottering in the doorway, looking at the empty bed as if it was a thousand miles of desert. And all I knew was: I. Miss. My. Wife. This is killing me, Jessie. Where are you?

Chapter 40

Munich. The gray sky was beginning to brighten as they left their hotel near the Karolinenplatz and caught a taxi. They sped west along Nymphenburger Strasse, where ranks of huge office buildings had been constructed and now closed out the broader views Ryan remembered from his last visit. Acres of blank glass façades, almost no sidewalks: *Too goddamned utilitarian by half,* he decided. So at odds with the charming, human-scaled streets of the old parts of town. *The decline of public architecture—another Babel indicator?*

According to his file, Freunde was now eighty-seven. His father—and Richter's father—had left his mother when he was a baby, and Freunde had been raised among his mother's family. Before the war, the family had run a grocery store and produce distributorship in the town of Dachau. Helping with the business, Freunde developed good contacts among the farmers and other working people in the area, and in 1933, when the Dachau concentration camp was built, he early on learned the truth of the horrors that took place inside. Its first occupants were intellectuals, priests, and people of conscience who had spoken out against the Nazis; although only nineteen, Freunde began working to smuggle likely targets out of the country through an "underground railroad" he helped create. By 1937 he learned that Dachau would soon be receiving Jewish prisoners. Accordingly, he warned local Jewish leaders, and several dozen escaped using Freunde's apparatus, until a group of them was caught and the scheme unraveled. But Freunde himself managed to avoid being implicated, and when his uncle died he took over the family business and continued selling vegetables, meat, and cheese. The concentration camp itself bought food from him—a fact he soon used to resume his activities.

A man who would not be diverted, Ryan thought. *No matter what.*

By bribing camp guards, Freunde soon arranged schemes to liberate prisoners, finding tiny cracks in security and exploiting them until each scheme was discovered. The last he conceived toward the end of the war, when Dachau KZ often lacked sufficient coal to fire the crematoria, and as a result the growing number of bodies had to be carted to mass graves in the countryside. He arranged to place living Jews among the corpses on the piled trucks, and to free them once they got outside the camp. This saved another seventeen people, but it lasted only a few weeks, until one of his paid-off guards turned on him. Freunde went into hiding, barely surviving the remaining months of the war. After the war he moved to Munich, where he continued to run a grocery distributorship.

In Munich he became involved in other altruistic activities. In 1967 there was a fire in a neighboring apartment building; Freunde rescued a pair of children by running up to the third floor through raging flames and carrying them back alive. He was badly burned and lost vision in one eye. The newspapers made a big thing of this hero, and one reporter revealed that he was a regular donor to charitable causes and a volunteer for community organizations. But Freunde made it clear he did not want to be adulated. Likewise, he always declined the honors periodically offered by Holocaust remembrance organizations.

Ryan looked up as the taxi stopped in front of an older four-story stucco building. They were on a cobbled street closely parked with cars, cigarette-vending machines stuck like barnacles on the walls.

"Where'd this irrepressible urge to help others come from?" he asked, slapping the file.

"Maybe we're about to find out," Dagan said.

Freunde sat in a large armchair near the window as they took chairs across from him. The third-floor apartment was small and although perfectly clean smelled slightly of urine. The decor was half modern, half antique: contemporary throw rugs on polished wood floors, a large television, chrome gadgets in the kitchen, bright halogen lamps. But the carved wooden buffet was ancient, and a collection of antique clocks hung on the walls, pendulums swinging in evolving polyrhythms that Ryan had to force himself not to calculate.

Freunde himself belonged to the antique category. He was a small man, hunched as if his skeleton could no longer endure even the scant weight of his dwindling flesh. His face was deeply etched, folded as if it had collapsed inward, and yet the resemblance to Richter was clear. One eye was covered by a bluish white film of scar tissue, but the other was as sharp as the eyes of the ravens in Munich's parks. He sat clutching a cigarette, which, he confided, his doctor had forbidden him to light.

"We are very grateful for your time today, Herr Freunde," Ryan began.

Freunde waved the gratitude away, locked both the bright eye and the empty eye on him. "As little time as I have left, it is not cluttered with social demands. And I am concerned about your wife—a fine woman. I would like to help you." His English was formal, accented, his voice a gathering of rasps and rumbles.

Without being prompted, Freunde reviewed his time with Jess and Bates: They had conversed for an hour or two, and then they'd gone in a rental car to a private clinic for the medical tests. They had returned, talked again briefly, and then said good-bye.

"They wanted to know what 'makes me tick,'" Freunde said disapprovingly. He waved at the wall behind him, the crazy synch of swinging pendulums. "I told them, a man is not a clock. This part of their request, the four clinical tests, the blood samples—I was doubtful about this."

"How did they respond when you expressed your doubts?" Dagan asked.

"Jessamine said she agreed, a man is not a clock. But, she said, in the last ten years our knowledge of the brain has improved greatly. She said she doubted they would find a difference in the way my brain is constructed, but only, with luck, in how I use it." Freunde coughed, placed his cigarette in his mouth, took it out again, scowled at it. "I told them, 'Yes, how we make use of ourselves—that is the crux of the question.'"

———

They talked for an hour. Freunde proved to be a complex man, alternately gruff and charming, stern and humorous, courteous yet not hesitant to disagree vehemently. Ryan found it easy to like him—his candor, his mix of humility and pride.

"Herr Freunde," Dagan said, "You worked to rescue Jews at a time when anti-Jewish sentiment was very strong among your countrymen. Were you particularly identified with Jewish culture? Did you have Jewish friends?"

"Yes, this is a question the other Dr. McCloud asked. I told her no, I knew Jews only in the markets, before they were forbidden to work. No—I had no close friends who were Jews."

"And yet you put yourself at risk of torture and death on their behalf," Ryan said. "Perhaps you had a religious background—?"

Freunde rasped a laugh. "I have never been religious. My mother's family were Lutherans who did not attend, and they did not particularly care for Jews. If anything, my uncle—well, it is good he never had to face a choice in which his attitudes would be tested! He died in 1937. And you know about my half-brother."

"Then why, Herr Freunde?"

Freunde shrugged. "Since the war, sometimes they are looking for models of good Germans, they make me out to be another Schindler. They are always surprised to find what an unsentimental man I really am." The narrow chest convulsed, another laugh or a cough, and then the wiry brows lowered. "Your American philosopher, Thoreau—I have admired him greatly—what did he once say? 'Save a drowning man and tie your shoes.' Do you see? Saving the drowning man is not an act deserving of special recognition! It is by simple virtue of your common humanity, not some special effort or belief, that you do such things. Only a person who has lost some…some portion of his original nature would do otherwise."

Something clicked in Ryan then, but the next question was already on his tongue: "Is that why you haven't wanted to be honored by the Holocaust groups?"

"The Jewish leaders are very flattering to me, very kind. But what I would say would be of no use to anyone."

"What would you say? I mean, you saved dozens and dozens of Jews—"

Freunde waved his feeble hands. "I didn't save 'Jews'! I saved *human beings!*" He panted for a moment, picking with agitated fingers at the arms of the chair. For the first time his face showed unmistakable anger.

Ryan nodded, wondering what he could say to redeem himself. But the exchange appeared to have tired Freunde. He shut his eyes and leaned his head against the chair back. In the silence, the ticking clocks seemed deafening. Ryan used the time to find the thought that had skipped past a moment ago. He circled it warily, unwilling to tamper with whatever conceptual impulse had sparked it.

At last Freunde opened his eyes again. "I tire so easily," he complained. He turned to a side table and fumbled among several crystal decanters and glasses. "A little schnapps, Dr. McCloud? Miss Rabinovitch? This my doctor also forbids, but here I must ignore him."

Ryan accepted gratefully, Dagan went along. They all touched glasses. Down the hatch, and it felt good and seemed to help the old man feel at ease.

"So refreshing," Freunde said. "Continue."

"One more question," Ryan said. "Earlier you said that only a person who has lost some portion of his original nature would fail to save a drowning man. Herr Freunde—what portion of his original nature has such person lost?"

For a long time, Freunde stared out the window, both eyes sightless now. "When I was young, I could not have told you. Now, I might answer, 'He has lost his love of himself, so he cannot love another.' And so he cannot recognize his own struggles, his own hopes, in the struggles and hopes of another. This is not 'philosophy.' As I told your wife, it is more...more a physical sensation, a visceral certainty. Does this make sense to you?"

There it was again, the subliminal tug, the deep line quivering as some fish tested the hook. But how could the words of an old German grocer possibly bear upon modern cognitive neuroscience? And yet something Freunde said had revealed a dim outline, some part of the puzzle. Yes.

Ryan startled out of his thoughts, wondering how long he'd kept the old man waiting for a reply. Freunde had watched Ryan's momentary absorption with interest, his good eye expressionless and analytical.

Dagan had been listening to their exchange with a slightly puzzled expression on her face. "Herr Freunde, I would also like to come back to something you said earlier. You mentioned *four* medical tests that Ryan's wife and Dr. Bates conducted. There were the PET scan, and the fMRI, correct? The third was the EEG, where they put the electrodes on your scalp. What was the fourth?"

"Oh, that. Yes. They wanted to test my nose. This part I did not understand very well."

"Your *nose!*"

"Yes. It was uncomfortable. A little light tube—fiber optics, yes?—the chemical scents, the brain wires again. But I am too old—I have no sense of smell at all. I am sure they were disappointed."

All at once the connection clicked. *VNO,* the sticky note on Jess's bulletin board. *Vomeronasal organ,* a scent-detecting organ in mammal noses. The VNO was believed to be important in perceiving the chemical signals that clued animals to each other's readiness to mate, and also to the degree of relatedness, a way of avoiding inbreeding.

Oh, Jess. You amazing woman, Ryan thought. His hands were shaking as he reached for his schnapps glass. "Herr Freunde—please, may I have another?"

The old man obliged him with his own palsied hands.

They asked him a few more questions: Did Jess mention anything about where she would travel to next, whom she might see? Yes: She was going to see a mathematician in Geneva. *So Jess did see Hoague.* Did she talk about any of her future research plans? No, Freunde said, nothing. Nothing he could remember.

"But," Freunde said decisively, "there is one detail that in retrospect is very important. While they were here, there was a man in a car." He gestured with his cigarette out the window, to the cobbled street three stories below. "Stupidly, I assumed he was an associate of your wife and colleague, waiting, not wishing to bother this tired old man. But when they left they did not acknowledge each other. I regret to tell you this. The man was watching, following, but your wife did not know him."

Dagan's eyes widened involuntarily, and she glanced at Ryan.

That would have been September 25, Ryan calculated quickly, only one day after she'd visited Richter. Could the Nazi have alerted his friends that fast? Possible, but unlikely. So who else would have had her under observation so early on? The timing had to be an invaluable clue.

Dagan cleared her throat apologetically. "Herr Freunde—are you absolutely sure about this? It is very important."

Freunde's fallen lips smiled sadly on one side of his face. "In my early years...well, let us say I became very, very adept at knowing when I was being observed. It was a skill I relied upon to stay alive. Under such circumstances, the habits and reflexes one acquires do not readily abandon one." He gazed out the window as if looking down the length of his life, his affect muted and bitter now. "Even if one wishes they would."

Chapter 41

While Dagan listened to the recording of Weismann's lecture in the next room, Ryan worked the hotel phone. Saturday afternoon, November 2, nobody in the office, home calls. Below the windows, the traffic of Barer Strasse spun past.

First: Karl. Not home, but Ryan left a message: "Karl, I need your help. Your proctology expertise. I'm in Munich. Call me." Karl would know what he meant. *No matter how fast you run, you can never outrun your own asshole.* Favor time: I need you to use your CIA or DIA connections, and get me some information. Have you heard about an operation, a raid on a private research outfit that came too close to a secret behavioral-modification project? Can you find out if Brenner was an MKULTRA guinea pig? Can you tell me anything about Alex Shipley?

That is, if Karl himself wasn't responsible for the break-in and abduction, maybe by opening his yap about the project in the wrong places. A nice thought. The product of solid inference, or just more paranoia? *Generalized distrust, an early symptom of the Babel syndrome?* Maybe he'd caught the goddamned thing in Kalesi after all.

Next, Burke: Not home, but he left a message. Burke, what've we got on the bug, anything from the labs? What about Richter's neo-Nazi contacts? Burke, please tell me something good. Then Xavier Hoague, the mathematician Jess and Bates had visited in Geneva. No answer, no answering machine, no nothing.

Then, with Pavlovian trepidation, the Genesis offices. Late afternoon in Munich, but only ten in the morning at Heart Cove. This was one Saturday they'd be working.

Logan sounded tired, but she brightened on recognizing Ryan's voice. "How're you doing? Has it been a productive trip?"

Ryan had to think about it. "Yes and no. I'm getting an idea of Jess's thinking, but we're not learning much about who might've...done it. Tell me some good news, Logan."

Logan rallied to the task: "The offices are pretty much back in order. Leap has set up the computers again. We've filled in a few more dates on the calendar of Jess's whereabouts. Oh, that security fellow from Ridder's organization—what's his name—?"

"Gable?"

"—Gable stopped by. Said he had instructions from Ridder to help us out. Wanted to know what progress we've made, wanted to see you."

"What'd you tell him?"

"What's there to tell? I said we didn't know much yet. He's kind of… creepy. Perfectly cordial, but he gave us all the chills. What else? Leap is working on Argus. He's grieving, and it's not just the computer. I think Jess is a mother figure for him."

"Is he there?"

"We're all here, Ry. Half of us slept at your house last night. For all of four hours."

For the hundredth time, Ryan felt a wave of gratefulness for this strange group of people—partly colleagues, partly employees, partly friends.

When Leap came on, he sounded far away—the data lab's speaker-phone: "Hey, Ry."

"Leap, I need some immediate help with this mathematician Hoague in Geneva. Doesn't answer his phone, so if I can't raise him in the next few hours, we'll have to drop in on him in person. Can you get me a physical address for his phone number? With your equipment in its current condition?"

"I could do it with an alligator clip and some chewing gum, Ry."

"Do you know anything about him? The name rings a bell for me, but I can't recall anything specific."

"Brilliant but eccentric. Toweringly both. A legend in the field of games theory. The Godzilla of games theory."

"Okay." *Of course.* "Any news, Leap?"

"Bad news. Our access provider can't reassemble Jess's e-mail history. They *say*—sounds suspicious to me—too much time elapsed, her account's drive quadrant has been overwritten. But the real disaster is Jess's phone calls. Phone company had some kind of meltdown on a big server, they've lost their records for this whole sector. It's no accident. Somebody got in there to destroy our phone records."

The words hit Ryan like a blow to the chest. "You're not just being paranoid?"

"No. Because there's a similar situation with records at the Beverly cellular switching station. Phone companies keep redundant records all over the place, so eventually we'll probably be able to get a list of calls. But for the time being, we can't trace Jess's communications, Ry. Somebody made sure we couldn't."

Somebody very thorough, Ryan thought. *Somebody with formidable resources, or with an ally inside the phone company.* Who'd have such resources? Elite private data security protecting nasty corporate secrets. Or, more likely, government spooks protecting military secrets. Like Shipley.

"Any more thoughts on who our enemy might be?"

"Yeah," Leap's distant voice said resignedly. "Everybody."

He hung up just as Dagan came in from her room. She had put on a black raw-linen blazer over blue jeans and looked very European, Ryan thought.

"How far into this did you get?" she asked, holding up the disc of Weismann's selfish-gene lecture.

"Cannibal lions," Ryan said blackly.

"Well, that's where it gets good. You should listen—I can think of about five ways Jess might have been stimulated by this, especially given what we've learned."

"I've got a lot of return calls pending, I can listen while I'm waiting. Listen, D., I think we'll probably have to go to Geneva and find this Hoague guy in person."

"Fine with me," she said. She handed him the CD player and disc. "Well—if you don't need me for a while, I'd really like to stretch my legs. I'm going to see if I can get a snack in the dining room, and then I thought I'd check out the gift shop. I don't have to worry about...anything...here in the hotel, do I?"

Ryan thought about it: Freunde's revelation that Jess had been followed had intensified his sense of foreboding. The feeling of being watched, that absolutely anything could happen. But after a moment he grudgingly shook his head: *Probably not here in the hotel, no.*

Dagan smiled to reassure him, hesitated at the door. "Do I look okay?" She turned once for his inspection.

"You look great," Ryan told her sincerely.

She patted her pockets for her room key, slipped out.

Actually, she looked terrific, Ryan thought. For some time he'd been registering some disturbance on his sexual radar around Dagan, the faint discomfort that the proximity of a beautiful woman always brought on. Since Dagan's arrival at Genesis, he'd felt toward her rather the way he imagined you'd feel toward an adult daughter—aware of her beauty, proud of her in a rather paternal fashion. But in the last week, all the time spent alone with her, relying on her presence, the ragged lonesome hole torn in his psyche by Jess's absence, there'd been a subtle shift. Dagan seemed to sense it in him. Of course she did.

Should've brought Wesley on this goddamned trip, he thought. Feeling a little guilty and tangled, he put on the headphones and forwarded the disc of Weismann's lecture to where he'd left off.

Weismann cleared his throat and went on: "So I've crafted a dismal view of living things. Everything is centered on the gene, and all behavior is explicable as selfishness. *But wait!* your moral sensibilities argue. We constantly observe animals, especially human beings, doing all kinds of unselfish things. In fact, the whole reason we humans viscerally dislike this selfish-gene theory is that we're so habituated to cooperative, unselfish acts, or what we call 'altruism.' We regard altruism and cooperation very highly. And we should—the greatest survival advantage the human animal enjoys is its penchant for social cooperation! The foundation of human societies is our *biologically based ability to cooperate.*"

Ryan's ears perked up. This was familiar territory, but yes, definitely a Babel-relevant topic.

"So, Dr. Weismann, you say, how do you explain the proverbial circle of monkeys, picking lice out of each other's fur? And humans—even the most cynical of us tend to believe in taking care of our offspring, right? What gives? I thought selfishness was the ruling paradigm!"

Weismann chuckled. "Well, though it *seems* that we love our kids with a deep, abiding affection, the selfish-gene theory holds that our so-called 'love' is actually just a habit, built into us vehicles, for protecting and nurturing copies of our genes in the bodies of others. Since our kids have our genes in them, loving our kids is really just another expression of our genes' narcissism! The selfish gene benefits from altruism because it helps the gene protect itself *in the bodies of other individuals.* Depressing, right? Debasing to our most deeply held beliefs, right?

"But is this really true? Well, a simple thought experiment will show it. If a hephalump, say, were sharing food with other hephalumps, you'd expect it to give food mainly to close genetic relatives—its kids or parents or siblings. Its selfish genes would program it to give food less often to its grandchildren or grandparents, half-brothers and -sisters, even less often to cousins, and so on, because they have fewer genes in common. Theoretically, then, you could predict altruism by degrees of relatedness according to classical Mendelian genetics."

More chalkboard noises. "So now you ask, 'Good theory, Dr. Weismann, but do we in fact see such behavior?' And the answer is *yes!* Computer- and video-assisted observation of animal communities has shown that animals dispense altruism *precisely* in proportion to their degree of relatedness! *Wow!* The social behavior of the animal kingdom, including us naked apes, is completely based on gene nepotism! Hey, that's no news to you political-science majors—does the mayor's brother get the city's highway-repair contract? So the old selfish-gene theory has now given us an explanation of social organization in animals, including us long pigs!"

Ryan heard the faux-baroque hotel telephone ringing, and he pulled out his earphones. It was Leap, who had found Hoague's street address in Geneva. Ryan jotted it down and thanked him, and went back to the lecture. Ryan heard a voice muttering in the distance: A student had interrupted Weismann's talk.

"Excellent question!" Weismann crowed. "If you didn't hear that, the question was, 'Okay, Dr. Wise-ass, social cooperation is based on the selfish gene recognizing itself in other bodies and being selfishly nice to itself. But *can* animals recognize their kin? And *can* an animal somehow calculate precisely how related it is to another?' Super question! And believe it or not, the answer is *yes,* both field and lab studies show that animals distinguish degrees of kin and show altruistic behavior in direct proportion to kinship. Thanks to recent discoveries in the neurosciences, we even know *how*—they do it using sight and hearing and smell, and compute the ratios in dedicated circuitry, dedicated modules, in their brains. This calculation is an autonomic function, just the way our visual circuitry calculates how much to dilate the eye's pupil in response to light. In most animals, highly developed sensors in the nose and in the brain detect and analyze histochemical similarities—the animal literally smells its own genes in other animals. The more social the animal, the more developed the kin-recognition and calculation circuitry in the brain. We humans use a wide range of sensory inputs and computational modules to get very elaborate about it—to build complex societies."

A wave of laughter rang in the auditorium. Weismann: "What am I doing? I'm patting myself on the back. Because who's the most social animal? Who's got the biggest brain, the most social computing modules? Us long pigs!"

Bingo, Ryan thought. *Jess is going after kinship recognition. Gorilla looks like Grandpa. VNO,* the smell tests they ran on Freunde and Richter, the quote from e. e. cummings: *all good kumrads you can tell/by their altruistic smell.*

He took off the headphones and stood up quickly, feeling suddenly hot, too excited to sit still. The course of it came clear to her here, where she had to go next. And the idea of altruism in exact proportion to degree of relatedness—she'd seen it in the Somali saying he'd faxed her from Kalesi, expressed in the inverse: *My son and I against my brother. My brother and my son and I against my cousin . . .*

When the telephone rang and he nearly jumped out of his skin.

"Yeah," he barked.

"Ryan—it's Bob Burke. Calling from Boston—" There was something tentative in the FBI man's voice.

"Have you got something for me?" Ryan asked, suddenly worried.

"This is tough, Ryan—"

"Oh, God—" The world caving in. The sun exploding. The sky dying.

"Wait. I've been out all night because I was called to New York. We've found Dr. Bates. He's dead. Body was found in a Dumpster in Brooklyn."

Ryan tried to talk, but his lips were without feeling. He tried again: "Jess?"

"No sign of her. Nothing. We're working over Dr. Bates's body, maybe there'll be something, I've routed the forensic workup top priority. I know it doesn't look good, okay? But it doesn't mean that your wife, that—" Burke couldn't say it.

"What happened to Bates?" Ryan croaked.

"Cause of death we don't know yet. But he'd obviously been tortured. It was . . . ugly. Somebody's playing real serious here."

Serious, Ryan thought, otherwise empty-headed. The satellite lines whispered unintelligible conversations into his ear.

Burke waited for a long time and finally spoke again: "Still there?"

"Yeah."

"I have to go now. I wanted you to know. I didn't tell your staff—I thought you should decide what to do."

"Yeah. Yeah, right, that's right. Thanks," Ryan said.

After a little while he called Genesis again.

"Lo, Bates is dead. They killed him. They tortured him."

"Oh Ryan, no! What about Jess?"

"No news. Logan, everybody goes home, right now. It's too dangerous there. We're way out of our league. I'll be back tomorrow afternoon, we'll figure out what to do then. In the meantime, all work is suspended. You all get out of there, and you take security precautions at home. This is an order from your employer, not a suggestion from your friend. I'll call back in fifteen minutes. If anyone is still there, I'll call the police and have them arrest you for trespassing."

Stunned, Logan didn't argue.

When he hung up, he sat on the bed with his face in his hands. Just sat, trying to outlive the fear and despair. To find some kind of starting place.

After a time the door rattled and Dagan came in, smiling. But her face changed as she saw him. "Ryan, what? What, Ry? What?"

Chapter 42

What you do is, you get up and start again. *You never give up, Ry. You take it and you come back fighting.* You use whatever it takes. Hope wasn't what did it this time. Bates had been a good friend, a brilliant man, a fucking *contributor* who deserved a goddamned medal, not torture and murder. Somebody owed for Bates.

And if anything had happened to Jess, somebody was going to pay.

It wasn't a good feeling, but he felt it through every cell in his body, and he'd use it if it got him on his feet again.

They ended up taking the train to Geneva because, as the hotel desk clerk informed them, the Munich airport had been temporarily shut down. A bomb had exploded in the main concourse, killing a leader of the Turkish immigrant community, along with his wife and two children and three passersby. At the Munich train station, dozens of body-armored police stalked the lobby and corridors, automatic weapons ready. Kiosk newspaper headlines decried the increasing violence of the German far right, but some suggested the explosion might be the work of Greek terrorists, bent on pushing the crisis there over the brink.

The train was sleek, as smooth as if it ran on ice skates, and fast: Munich to Geneva in only six hours. Before long the mountains of Switzerland emerged from the gathering evening darkness like great, mysterious animals hunching along the horizon.

With what they'd learned from Richter and Freunde, and the tape of Weismann's lecture, Ryan was sure he could put together Jess's thought processes. If only he could concentrate. But the news of Bates's death had shattered his ability to focus. *Jessie!* Suddenly it all seemed too urgent and frightening. The long way around seemed just too slow.

After hearing about Bates, Dagan had seemed to shrink, become more childlike. Her resilient hopefulness had taken a bad knock. Now she held Ryan's hand as they sat side by side. Human touch, some small comfort. Ryan was grateful.

"So we really could be in danger? Someone could be following *us?*" Dagan asked. It was the first time they'd spoken since leaving Munich.

Though they were alone in their compartment, she spoke quietly, as if afraid she'd be overheard.

Ryan had been keeping his eyes moving, scanning sidewalks and lobbies and hallways, checking rearview mirrors. He'd always had good pattern-recognition abilities, and doing the Secret Service job had greatly improved his ability to scan for potential threats. So far, he didn't think anyone was tailing him. But you could never be certain.

"You don't have to be involved, Dagan. You should go home, get out of Boston, maybe take a vacation, or—"

"While the people I love most are going through this. Yeah, Ryan."

He didn't bother arguing.

They listened to the thrum of the rails for a few more minutes. At last Dagan whispered: "Did Burke say what they'd done to Bates?"

"No details. I assume they tortured him during interrogation."

She winced, shifted uncomfortably in her seat, moved again, as if unable to dispel unwanted images. Ryan felt a surge of sympathy for her. When Ryan was twenty-five, his shoulders had certainly not been strong enough to bear the weight of all the world's problems. But Dagan's generation had been born into the avalanche. Everything coming down, every form of shit hitting the fan. Most people her age survived by burying their heads in the sand, taking refuge in shallow self-interest and the distractions of rampant materialism. And then there were the few with brains and conscience—Dagan had too much of both—who tried to do something about it. Ryan didn't envy any of them.

Dagan startled him when she spoke again—he thought she'd fallen asleep. "You and Jess. Tell me about you and Jess." She said it much the way Abi asked for a bedtime story.

"You know us."

"I don't know how it feels to be with someone that way. Are you two really so...so complete? So perfect?"

"Neither of us has ever thought of ourselves as perfect."

"No, but you know what I mean. You're both people who, I don't know, who *yearn,* or hunger, you're both such passionate people. And people change, you two must have changed a lot since high school. Can one person really be the right person for another—forever?"

"Are you asking if we ever wanted to be with someone else?"

"Well, not exactly...But did you?"

"Hmm." It felt good to think about these things, made Jess seem somehow nearer. "I can't speak for Jess. But for me, I've always loved women, the way they move and talk and think. The geometry of a woman's body gets to me. I lose my heart, a little bit, on a daily basis, and I'm by nature a, uh, well—" He felt suddenly embarrassed. Dagan surely had not asked for this. "—a sexually, uh, active guy."

She laughed quietly, enjoying his embarrassment. "You're a *stud,* Ry. Jess says you're a stud. Anytime we get temp help at Genesis, you should hear the women talk about you!"

He went on quickly: "My point is, you'd think I was the world's least likely candidate for monogamy. But Jess and I just…connected…and there's never been a good reason to jeopardize that."

Dagan had gotten serious again, melancholy or resigned. "Is that all a marriage is—good enough until something better comes along?"

"You know that's not what I meant. But there is a lot that's mundane in any marriage. Dishes to wash, diapers to change, his angst, her period—"

"Sounds heavenly," she said darkly. He saw that there was some big sadness here, and wondered at its source.

"I'm just trying not to overly romanticize it. No, Jess and I, we're an anomaly, you can't take us as an example. We fit together a lot of ways. Like the way I rely on her way of thinking, her cognitive style, to complement mine. She's more 'intelligent' than I am—has more conscious access to her own smarts. I'm stupider, but I'm, I guess, more 'talented.' By that I mean I rely on some inborn, naïve, subconscious processes to get results. But put the two together and *pow,* see? And we've generally preserved the magic, the part that makes it mysterious, surprising. If you're not lucky, the mundane stuff drags it all down and turns it ordinary and predictable. And your souls go starving, and the marriage falls apart. But if you *are* lucky, the magic elevates the other. And Jess and I, we've been very lucky that way. I mean we have our rough spots, but—"

She had turned her face to the dark window, and he knew he'd gotten off the track of whatever it was she wanted. When she didn't speak he tried to draw her out: "How about you? You're a beautiful woman. You must know something about this topic."

She pouted, a bitter mouth. "Haven't been so lucky."

"You were seeing that guy…that lawyer, the public defender—"

"Our obituary is old news." She turned back from the window with unexpected heat, almost accusing. She was lovely and wounded and her eyes blazed. "I think I know what the love part feels like, okay? I just don't know what it's like to build on it and let it fill my life. And I spend too much time feeling frustrated by that fact, and lonely, and I'm very tired of feeling that way!" As if it were somehow his fault.

Then she was looking out the window again. Reflected in the glass, he could see her chin dimple and contract. A person trying not to cry.

All the loneliness, Ryan thought. He wanted to comfort her, but suddenly lights were sliding past the window, and then the clamor of the Zurich station enveloped them. The train rocked softly to a halt and the electrical smell of its engines wafted in from open doors.

They changed trains. An elderly couple entered their new compartment, clumsily stashed their luggage overhead, took seats. Just before the train left the station, a younger man came in and threw himself down opposite Dagan. He was dressed in black sweatpants and sweatshirt, and for an instant he seemed to study Ryan and Dagan. Ryan felt a slight nervous tingle.

It was full dark as the train slipped back into the countryside. Once the lights of Zurich had faded, the windows went depthless black again, and there were long periods when the only clue to their motion was the gentle rocking of the car. The elderly couple nodded off to sleep. The young man drummed his fingers, fidgeted with his zippered tummy-pack. A big guy, Ryan thought, hard and fit beneath his baggy clothes. If it came to a rumble, it would be a close thing. Unless the guy had a weapon. Which of course he would.

As if on cue, the younger man unzipped his pack and groped inside, and Ryan felt Dagan tense in the seat beside him. But what he pulled out of the pack was a waxed-paper bag containing a hard-boiled egg. He ate it, refolded the bag fastidiously, and tucked it into the ashtray, then slumped down in his seat with arms crossed and legs splayed. After a few minutes his mouth went slack as he surrendered to sleep.

Of course, Ryan realized. Nobody would need to follow them anyway. Whoever it was would know where they were going. Just following Jess's footsteps. If somebody was interested in what he and Dagan were learning, they'd be waiting at Hoague's place in Geneva.

Chapter 43

"This can't be right," Dagan said.

Ryan rechecked the city map, and they both looked out the windows of the rented Opel at the building that was supposed to be Hoague's home. It was almost midnight. The warehouse looked abandoned: dust-fogged windows, a boarded-up office door set in rusted metal siding. No sign of a light. At the far end of the huge building, a series of empty loading bays cut cavernous shadows. Across the street, a row of collision-damaged Mercedes vans stood in front of another warehouse, empty windshields gaping. The street was one of a maze of industrial avenues and alleys that bordered the huge freight railyards at La Praille, on Geneva's south side. Maybe Leap had gotten the address wrong.

"He's supposed to be eccentric. Maybe—"

"This isn't eccentric, it's scary," Dagan said.

"This? Hey, you should visit my old neighborhood." Trying to cheer her up, falling flat. She was right: If their enemy wanted to hit them, this would be a good spot to do it.

Leaving the car running, Ryan got out and walked to the battered office door. Plywood had been screwed over the window, so he could see nothing inside, and the intercom box was dusty and looked defunct. But he pressed the button anyway, held it for several seconds.

Nothing. He pressed it again, waited. The silence of the street was broken by the thunder of coupling freight cars in the railyards two blocks away. Frustrated, he whacked the intercom and went back to the car.

Dagan peered at the gloomy façade. "Now what?"

Before Ryan could answer, a shadow slipped down off the loading docks and began coming toward them. Startled, he flicked the headlight lever, throwing light onto a gaunt, gimp-gaited man, a pale face surrounded by tufts of wild hair. The scarecrow threw up an arm to keep the light out of his face, but kept approaching them.

He came to the side of the car, bent to the window. *"Que'est-ce que tu veux?"* he demanded gruffly.

"Si'l vous plais, je cherche Dr. Hoague—habit-il ici?" Ryan asked. In the dark, he couldn't make out the man's features, but he could smell his breath, a sharp chemical scent.

"Oué?" A little laugh. "Didn't you know it's rude to blind someone with your high beams? What d'you want Hoague for?" The scarecrow spoke English with a distinctly American accent.

"I want to consult with him on a mathematical question."

"Wrong place. A common mistake. An error on the city maps."

Dagan leaned across Ryan to look up into the obscure face. "We've come a long way, Dr. Hoague. It's urgent. We don't have time for this kind of bullshit."

He led them into the warehouse through a normal-sized door cut into one of the rolling steel bay doors. Inside, their footsteps echoed in a cavernous space. At the far end, an island of light stood amid complex dark shapes that radiated long shadows, and when they got closer, Ryan was able to see that the warehouse was full of carousels and other carnival equipment, layered with grime, in various states of disrepair. The air smelled of dust and machine oil.

A row of battered, restaurant-sized refrigerators partitioned Hoague's living space from the rest of the warehouse. Inside were a makeshift table with three computer monitors on it, a rumpled bed, several glowing space heaters, wooden crates stacked to serve as bookshelves. Judging from the towels and soaps on one side, the electric hot plate and condiments on the other, the huge industrial sink against the wall served as kitchen sink, laundry, and bathtub. Beneath it all lay an unusual rug that turned out to be a gigantic flag, the colors of Switzerland.

Howard Hughes, Ryan was thinking. *Bobby Fischer, Glenn Gould.* Hoague belonged to that tribe of brilliant but reclusive antisocial neurotics. Dagan looked marginally terrified, and for her sake he did his best to project a calm and confidence he didn't feel.

"Sit," Hoague commanded. In the light, Ryan could see he was wearing black leather pants, tight on his pipestem legs, a monogrammed shirt that was grease-spotted and torn. Beneath the dry, frizzy hair, he had a young face, unlined, eyes clear.

They found metal folding chairs and sat at a wooden table. Hoague brought out a bottle and some glasses. "What's yours, McCloud? Ouzo, I hope, because that's all I've got."

"How do you know who I am?"

Hoague poured, then licked the drop from the lip of the bottle before capping it. "I recognize your face from the journals. Anyway, after your wife's visit, I assumed I'd be seeing you soon. Or somebody."

"Somebody like who?"

"Long story. Let me start by showing you something." He stood up again, went to the computers, pecked around. One of the monitors lit up with the image of their rented car, glistening faintly in the dark street. "A habit. Saves me some trouble—I see people before they see me. People have a bad habit of dropping in unannounced."

"If you'd answer your phone—"

Hoague pecked again, and there were the three of them, real time, sitting in the circle of light, surrounded by the dim shapes of carousel creatures and hulking refrigerators. The figures of Ryan and Dagan craned their necks, looking for the camera.

"I also record my conversations with my visitors," Hoague went on pointedly.

And suddenly there was Jess on the screen, and Bates, looking around at Hoague's surreal domain. *Bates, dead now.* Ryan was struck breathless at the sight of Jess, the familiar way of moving, the fine cheekbones and smooth tawny skin. Her wonderful square shoulders, proud bosom. Her swollen belly, much bigger than when he'd last seen her. A pain wrenched his chest, loss or longing.

She stood in the center of the flag rug, turning slowly. Ryan realized he had expected her to appear desperate, driven, haunted by Allison's death, by the uncertainties her new child would face in a Babel-crazed world, by her impossible quest to face the worst and still find something good in human beings. But she was smiling, candidly appreciating Hoague's home and appearing at ease, confident. In the background, Bates seemed to patrol the periphery, looking suspicious.

"Oh, audio," Hoague said. He fidgeted and pecked.

Jess was talking: "...you like carousels."

Hoague: "Circularity. A little comment."

Jess cocked her head, adapting to her strange host, empathizing with him and enjoying him. "A comment on—?" she probed.

"Civilization," Hoague said, off screen now.

Jess, jumping right to it: "Cycles of history, yes. And you're the meta-barbarian, outside, observing."

Hoague, pleased, coy: "And symbol systems—always leading us around, self-referential."

Jess: "Or, at best, depicting not the real world but only our neural pro-grams for interpreting the world. My husband and I often talk about the same thing!"

The real Hoague spoke, watching the screen admiringly. "Your wife is one hot ticket!"

Dagan stirred impatiently. "Dr. Hoague, we are glad to watch this, especially if it shows us something that leads us to Jessamine. But I expect this is a long segment, and we need to ask you some specific questions."

Ryan was grateful for her ability to get to business. He could not have pulled himself away from his mesmerized focus on Jess. He felt starved for the sight of her, the sound of her voice.

Hoague frowned, shrugged, pecked, paused the scene. Jess stood frozen, suddenly a graceful statue. "I can't figure if you're some kind of goddamned J-A-P, or a goddamned W-A-S-P," he said to Dagan resent-fully, spelling out the acronyms.

"A little of both," Dagan retorted. "But for our purposes here, a god-damned Ph.D."

Hoague gave her an appreciative smile, grateful for the repartee.

"Jessamine has been kidnapped," Ryan said. "Bates has been mur-dered. We need to find out who did it, where to look for her. But we have almost no clues. We need to find what they were working toward, why they came to see you. If they told you anything that would lead us to them, or allow us to deduce who was threatened by what they learned."

Hoague opened his mouth to reply, but he was interrupted by a pene-trating chime from the speakers: *dink!* Instantly the image of Jess van-ished, replaced by the street outside. A tiny Fiat 500 trundled past the parked Opel, vanished without slowing down. Ryan felt abruptly hot, his muscles tensing as adrenaline flooded his system. The darkness of the warehouse beyond their circle of light seemed suddenly vast and threatening.

"Motion-sensor activated," Hoague explained. "The *Cinque-cento*, that's a regular. Elderly postal clerk, on his way to work." But he looked suddenly ill at ease himself.

The screen flipped and showed Jess again, statuesque as a pregnant, black Venus.

Hoague still looked discomfited as he started rummaging in the tangle of dirty laundry and papers near his bed. "I'm slowing down. Diurnal metabolism, I'm going cholinergic. Let me fortify myself. Your problem deserves some alertness on my part."

He found a shoebox, opened it, and pulled out a glass laboratory flask the size and shape of a lightbulb. He fumbled in a tiny paper envelope and crumbled some white powder into the bulb, then held a lighter under it and sucked slowly. The air filled with the chemical scent Ryan had noticed earlier. *Crank,* Ryan decided. A methedrine compound, vaporized by heat, instantly accessible to the central nervous system. High gear.

Hoague's eyelids blew back. He puffed his cheeks out. "Now," he said. *"Chug-chug.* Up to speed!" He looked at Ryan and Dagan expectantly, his face radiant with energy, bright and artificial as a mercury-vapor street-lamp. "Hah. Wow."

"What did they consult with you on?" Ryan asked.

"Fairly standard stuff. Non-zero sum, iterative, multiplayer games. I sent her some material on disc." Hoague talked clipped and fast now.

Dagan broke in: "Can you help me here? I—I'm not very conversant with games-theory math."

Ryan debated for an instant. Dagan was a superb adaptive learner. Giving her the basics now might help her spot the connection they'd need at some point. He nodded to Hoague.

"Basic theory is very simple," Hoague told her. "Games theory is a branch of logic that creates mathematical models of transactions between competing forces—self-interested players who want absolutely to win. The whole idea is to model observed survival strategies in nature. Animals or humans, everybody's out to win, right, everybody's selfish. But what's the most effective strategy by which to win?"

Hoague paced now, too much hurry-hurry in his bloodstream to sit still. "Picture two lions, competing for food or mates. There are only three scenarios, three choices. If one attacks and the other runs away, the attacker gets all the available game on that turf, mates with all the girls, all the babies carry his genes, and the retreater gets nothing. If both fight hard, one may ultimately win, but both risk getting killed, and they'll both likely get wounded, be weaker than the next lion to come along or less able to catch food. If *neither* fights, and they cooperate by divvying up available food and mates, they're each guaranteed at least half the resources, and neither suffers the losses that injuries would beget. In the long run, over many generations of lions, which genes would win consistently, to shape lion behavior—fight, retreat, share? That's what games-theory math can calculate."

Hoague laughed suddenly, *hee hee hee,* giddy with it. He had stopped at one of the carousels, where two gaudy wooden lions stood side by side, poles through their backs. He caressed them as if they were housecats.

"Of course every animal has always wanted to win big, take it all. But the genes that program for that selfish or aggressive drive don't survive as well as those that program for some level of cooperation, in part because if the aggressive lion does all the breeding, the next generation won't have many retreaters in it. Playing selfishly wins big only as long as one party plays that way and the other retreats. If both play that hard, the conflict costs them both. If both play cooperatively, they both win, more reliably over the long term."

Ryan could see that Dagan was absorbing this, as if a shutter were clicking behind her eyes, catching each idea and storing it, filing it away. He was glad he'd let Hoague indulge his drug-fueled exposition.

"So we can model competitive transactions to see what kind of strategies win. Play 'nasty'—aggressively selfish—all the time? Play 'nice'— cooperative—all the time? Play selfish sometimes, cooperative sometimes? Respond to the other guy's moves in certain ways? The strategies that work best we call *evolutionarily stable strategies*—they tend to keep winning against various other strategies. So what I do is, I figure winning strategies for corporations and governments and political parties—I show them how to *win!* But mostly I work with geneticists and zoologists and biologists, who want to understand animal communities and other biological systems." Hoague was practically dancing, making expansive gestures, out of control.

Dagan was going *click-click-click* in her head. She interrupted: "Define 'nasty' and 'nice.'"

"Technical terms. 'Nasty' means preferring 'defecting' or selfish strategies, retaliating or holding grudges, fighting for the big win even if it risks both players taking losses. 'Nice' means just the opposite—preferring cooperative transactions, tending to forgive and forget if the other guy gets selfish, seeking long-term stability and overall gain rather than short-term, high-risk wins. There are degrees of both, all mathematically expressed, and their outcomes are modeled by computer programs I design."

Hoague paused dramatically. "And guess who wins, Miss Rabinovitch? Nasty or nice?" He practically skipped to another carousel figure, a baroque swan boat with two seats. He caressed the gracefully arched neck, the benign head of the swan. *"The nice strategies win!* This is what the inestimable Jessamine McCloud just loved! The top fifteen of the sixteen best strategies are *nice! Cooperation* is the winning strategy! Contexts change, but in general strategies that succeed end up playing *nice* five times out of six!"

His voice echoed in the dark room, but then the warning chime went off on his surveillance system. Motion outside. Abruptly he raced back to the computer monitor, which showed a Volvo delivery truck rolling slowly by in the dark street. It was impossible to see anything inside the cab.

"ARJ-423, that's, uh, I think that's a regular," Hoague said. "Got my log book here somewhere—" He flung himself at the bookshelves, yanked at a stack of manila folders and spiral notebooks, spilling them. "I'm pretty sure that's a regular, a regular. Where is that thing? Time is it? Okay. Yeah. A regular." He collapsed into a chair, breathing hard, little muscle spasms twitching his arms and legs. "Okay," he said to himself. "It's okay."

Ryan watched him, trying to control his sense of alarm. Nobody said anything for a moment. Jess returned to the video screen, and Ryan couldn't help stroking the glass in front of her image.

Dagan was struggling, keeping on track only with great effort. "If nice strategies tend to win," she said at last, "how come there's so much nastiness going on in the world?"

Hoague took a deep breath, beginning to come down. "Because people are all sick fucks," he said, tapping the side of his head. "Crazy as shithouse rats. Every one of them."

Chapter 44

Hoague poured another glass of ouzo and used it to wash down a vitamin B complex pill the size of his thumb. His metabolism began to pass through normal band on its way down.

"Seriously," Hoague said, "people might play nasty for several reasons. I'll give you two examples. One is that nasty can win big in short-term games, or at the end phase of finite games—if you really want to get ahead of the other guy, you play nasty on the last move of an otherwise cooperative game."

"But, theoretically, life on Earth should be an infinite game," Dagan pointed out. "So why are people all over the world acting as if we're near the end of the game?"

Hoague looked at her with new respect. "Like I say—crazy as shithouse rats." He said it gloomily this time.

Ryan asked, "Is there any reason someone would want to kidnap my wife and kill Bates, because of the program you sent her?"

Hoague shook his head. "What I gave her is not so different from what I've given dozens of clients in different fields. But..." He looked suddenly abashed, guilty, hanging his head and picking at the buttons on his ratty shirt.

"But?" Ryan prompted. His eyes strayed to Jess, standing in this same space, arrayed in her strange authority and enthusiasm.

"But I know something that would trigger someone's interest. If something happened to your wife, it's my fault, in fact. She told me about your project, the Babel effect shit. We should be cooperating, it's in our genes, it's probably the best survival strategy—but we don't seem to be doing it very well nowadays, right? Begetting the question 'Why not?' So I immediately thought of a friend of mine, someone I thought she should meet. And I introduced them."

"Who's the friend?" Ryan asked.

The chemical light was mostly gone from Hoague's eyes. "I'll give her a buzz." He went to his computer station, tapped in various commands, accessed an audio channel. "Nina, *ma cherie,* it's me, it's about one-fifteen, I got some guests you absolutely must meet. Call or come by. B.B., baby."

"She'll be awake now?" Dagan asked.

"I don't know that Nina actually 'sleeps,'" Hoague said.

"What's 'B.B.'?"

Hoague laughed self-deprecatingly. "Our little code. Means everything's okay, I'm not coerced to call her, the screens don't show any surveillance. We both consider B.B. King very cool, so it means 'everything's cool.'"

Ryan felt compelled to ask: "Why should you be so concerned about surveillance?"

Hoague looked surprised at the question. "Because I'm a raving paranoid schizophrenic!"

He went to the sink, rummaged among the toiletries and dishes there, found some dental floss, tore off an arm's length of it. "Also because I'm acquainted with Nina," he said quietly. "Which entails certain risks." He began flossing his teeth, a painstaking process involving grimaces and blood and close examinations of the floss.

Dagan asked, "So who is Nina?"

Hoague spat blood, rinsed, spat again. "Nina, Nina, Nina," he chanted. "I'm in love with Nina. That's why I'm here in Geneva. So I can be near my Nina." The rhyme pleased him. He went to his bedside table and came back with a framed photo of a petite, unsmiling young woman with short dark hair, small earrings, a little crucifix on a golden chain around her neck. "Nina Renée Lafontaine. She's a physicist specializing in non-ionizing radiation. She worked for the World Health Organization."

"Worked, but no longer works?"

"Correct. She was fired. She had been working for the last four years on the WHO study on the health effects of exposure to electromagnetic fields."

Dink! The motion-sensor alarm again. Hoague froze, blanched, scuttled to the monitor. "Too soon to be Nina," he whispered. Ryan joined him at the monitor, adrenaline-buzzed again and beginning to feel worn by the tension, the sense of siege.

The screen showed a pair of shadows moving on the other side of the street. People on foot. They didn't seem to look at Hoague's building. When they got to the row of wrecked vans, one of them stopped and did something to one of the trucks.

"The fuck's he doing?" Hoague peered closer. "Ah, good. Yes. Scavenging."

They watched as the figure wrestled with the side mirror, broke it loose. Then the two headed quickly down the street, disappeared from view.

"I don't know how much more of this I can stand tonight," Dagan said pleadingly. "I'm not used to this—"

"Why was Nina fired?" Ryan asked. "Why did you think Jess should meet her?"

"Nina helped design the WHO study on EMFs. Whole issue started out forty years ago as concern for fields around power lines, remember? Kids in houses or schools near power corridors were getting leukemia, brain cancers. Then came four decades of exponential growth of EMF sources in the environment—commercial radio broadcasting, satellite relays, cell phones, microwave transmitters, radar, household appliances, video games, long-wave military submarine tracking. Personal computers—these things are irradiating us right this instant. The electromagnetic environment changed. Nina made a map. Look at this."

Hoague tapped in some commands, and a big monitor sprang to light. "Ms. Rabinovitch, Ph.D., come take a look," he said. "She made a 'portrait' or map, depicting changes in the electromagnetic environment. Compared to just eighty years ago, the world of today is *unrecognizable.* From the primordial soup to 1920, we evolved to survive in just the earth's mild magnetic field and as much of the sun's electromagnetic aura our atmosphere let through. But in the last eighty years we've altered this environment profoundly with our technologies. *Billions* of new sources, *thousands* of new frequencies and amplitudes, pulses, harmonics."

On the monitor floated the planet Earth, colored with pale, diffuse blue-green patterns that Ryan assumed to be local geomagnetic fields, overlaid by a fluctuating aura of yellow representing radio fields from the sun. Then a date-meter appeared beneath the placid globe of antiquity. As years began to tick off, 1920, 1921, 1922, the sphere began to blossom with orange and red and purple spots, pinpoints, auras sprouting and spreading. By the time the date meter stopped at 2002, the very shape of the planet was obscured by angry, harsh colors. The shapeless, blurry blob reminded Ryan of an excised tumor or a deformed, poisonous fungus.

They looked at it in silence for a moment. Then Dagan asked, "But why fire her? Isn't that what the WHO study is concerned about?"

"Yes. But they are, A, strongly predisposed to dismiss the idea that there are health effects—half their work is on how to promote a benign public view of EMFs. B, they look at cancer. Cancer, cancer, cancer—does EMF exposure give you cancer? But Nina was concerned with the effects of EMFs on the *brain*. On mental health and behavior! She wouldn't shut up about it, kept trying to steer the study back to it. So they canned her."

"Why?" Dagan broke in. "If there's a scientific basis for—"

"Oh, please! Let me think, Miss Rabinovitch Ph.D., why. Um, are there any industries heavily reliant on EMF-producing technologies? Why yes—*all* of them! TV? Radio? Weapons? Computers? Consumer appliances? Manufacturing? Communications tech? Who's going to be happy to hear that these things are making us crazy? Hey, forget about evil corporations worried about their profits—Joe Consumer doesn't want to hear it, either. Not when his lifestyle depends absolutely on industry, communications, entertainment, medical technology, everything, that produces powerful EMFs! Do you blow-dry your hair? Hey, at user distance, your hair dryer is blasting you with a whopping electromagnetic field. You going to give it up on the off-chance it's doing something to your head besides drying your hair?"

No, Ryan was thinking, *you're not. Especially if by itself it doesn't seem to do anything to you. If the negative effects are caused by the aggregate of all the exposures you get throughout every day of your life. Especially if what it causes is as subtle as the Babel effect.* Hoague had just pointed out a gaping hole in the science of neurotoxicology. Was this what Jess was trying to say in that anomalous sticky note about doughnuts?

"Where is Nina?" Hoague said. His monologue had gotten him cranked up again, and now he began dithering around on his desk, muttering, "Nina, Nina, where are you?" A jagged singsong. "Shouldn't take this long," he said to Ryan. Into the computer's microphone he said, voice rising, "Nina, I'm getting an A for anxiety here, give me a buzz, answer this, okay?" He looked to Ryan with alarm, an appeal for sympathy.

"I'm sure she'll be here soon," Ryan assured him. "Tell us more. Nina's got what sounds like a reasonable thesis, but it's one that'd make her lots of enemies. So you introduced her to my wife. Then what?"

Hoague glanced longingly at his crank paraphernalia. "Nina watches her step, she's had her house broken into, her databases pillaged, she's been very nearly run down in a couple of hit-and-run attempts. So she's gone underground, made herself hard to find. With my help. Doesn't want to become the next Mannie Skovanick."

"That's a familiar name," Dagan said, "but I can't recall where—"

"Mannie Skovanick? Ah, maybe you're too young. Emanuelle Skovanick, murdered by a big electric utility company in the U.S. In all the papers in the early nineties."

Dagan looked skeptical but played along: "Why?"

"She was an electrical engineer for GME, did research and plant design. Became a whistle-blower. She came across company health records that showed definitive correlations between EMF exposure and brain damage or psychological problems in GME employees. Did a covert investigation, discovered a huge, industry-wide conspiracy to shut down the facts. Tried to bring the issue to court. Got herself killed by GME. Her files were never found."

"*We're* not paranoid schizophrenics, Dr. Hoague," Ryan said.

"Nina, Nina, Nina," Hoague sang quaveringly, scanning his screens. His legs were twitching again. "Fuck you, McCloud, it's in the newspapers. Matter of public record. The police caught the killer, who worked for GME's corporate security division. He was convicted, went to jail. Her family sued GME for wrongful death. GME got off the hook because the family couldn't prove the security guy had acted under orders."

"What happened to the killer? Couldn't he have exposed GME?"

"Guy hung himself after a couple days in jail. A convenient death, wouldn't you say? Here's the thing you need to know, McCloud. Your wife and Nina talked about this. Nina gave her some of her own materials, and also talked about Mannie Skovanick. Nina's been digging into the Mannie Skovanick case, see, she wants the data. Mannie's family has always maintained that she kept duplicate files, of course she did, somewhere safe. Only no one knows where. Nina's been quietly looking for the lost files for three years. Maybe your wife decided to look for them, too, I don't know."

The alarm chimed again and they all jumped. Dagan looked ill with tension. The monitor screen showed the street again, this time the Volvo delivery truck heading the other way.

Relieved, then immediately disappointed, Hoague put his face in his hands, stretched his mouth wide open, emerged looking panicked. "Something's wrong. I gotta go. That's it. That's what I know. I'm leaving."

"Can you give me the math you gave my wife?"

Hoague had jumped up and was rummaging again in the mess around his bed. He threw on a black suit coat, then fished a pistol out of the detritus and stuck it in the jacket pocket.

Ryan spoke louder: "I said, can you give me a copy of the program you gave Jess?"

Hoague looked at him as if he'd never seen him before. "Yeah. But not this instant, okay? I'm in a bit of a rush, you see." He went to his computers, rattled the keys. Beautiful Jess vanished into the darkness of a dead screen, Ryan feeling her absence suck the wind out of him. An LED console lit up, obviously a security system Hoague had armed.

They went out through the gloom of the warehouse and into the dim blue night. The freightyard was silent now, the street empty. Hoague pulled a bicycle out of the shadows in one of the loading bays, lowered it to the street, and got awkwardly astride it.

"We'll be in touch, right?" Ryan said. "You'll call us? Send us a disc?" He had to restrain himself from shouting.

The gaunt mathematician waved his hand in vague acknowledgment, and began pedaling away. He reached the end of the block, a gliding shadow, turned left, disappeared.

Dagan was crying softly. "I can't take this, Ryan. I can't stay here anymore."

He opened the car door for her, then went around to the driver's side. He understood how she felt. He just wanted to get out of here, too. Back toward the parts of Geneva where there were bright lights and other people and some vestige of sanity.

He spotted the watcher as he sat down in the driver's seat. He almost paused to double-check, but then just tucked his legs into the car and swung the door shut. As if everything were normal.

The street was dark and without movement, lit only by the residual glow of the freightyards. But a block away, the front end of a car emerged from between two warehouses. The positioning of the driver's-side window was too neatly just in view of Hoague's place while the rest of the car was hidden. And the light reflecting from the windshield and chrome trim was too sharp on a street where everything else was dusted with railyard grit. Meaning it wasn't usually parked there. Whoever it was had stayed far enough away to avoid triggering Hoague's motion sensors.

"Dagan," he said, "check under the seat—is the jack kept there on this model? Should be a little compartment."

"We have a flat tire?" She sounded scared of the flat tire.

"No. Just open the thing up. Should be a folded jack handle in a, sort of a leatherette case." He started the car, turned on the headlights as she groped beneath the seat and came up with the tool, a folded steel rod the diameter of a fountain pen, eighteen inches long, crook handle at one end. "Good," he said, taking it from her.

"What's going on?"

Ryan made a slow U-turn, began the short drive to the half-hidden car. "Maybe nothing. Maybe some motherfucker gonna get his ass caught in a chain saw." God, it felt good to say. He felt a rush of intense pleasure and anticipation. Maybe he couldn't find them, but now that they'd found him, he could gently persuade them to lead him to Jess.

Dagan followed his gaze. "Oh shit, Ryan—!"

"Put your belt on and brace yourself against the dashboard."

He accelerated to what he figured was optimum speed, not completely sure until he saw the dark silhouette in the driver's seat, almost invisible in the shadows. When they were nearly abreast of the car, he cranked the wheel suddenly to the right. The Opel ploughed into the car's left front wheel, driving it sideways, jamming it up against the brick wall of the warehouse. Ryan resisted the forward momentum with his arms and Dagan flung forward, stopped by her belt. Through the resounding crash, he heard her grunt as the breath was forced out of her.

The silhouette in the driver's seat was gone, but a spiderweb of shattered glass now marked the car's side window. *A little conk on the head to slow the son of a bitch down.*

He leaped out, stepped quickly around the Opel's rear with the jack handle ready. Something humped and stirred in the dark car, formless in the shadows cut by the Opel's remaining headlight. A man fallen sideways across the passenger seat, moving his arms erratically, trying to rise.

Ryan pulled the door open, then dragged the guy sideways, out onto the pavement. He put one knee on his chest and leaned to inspect him. Clean-cut, late twenties, leather jacket, white shirt but no tie. Bloody contusion above his left eyebrow. For an instant he felt a stab of fear, that he'd made a mistake: some hapless warehouse manager arriving for a predawn shift—

But then he saw the little pistol in the guy's hand. The gun came around fast toward Ryan's face. Reflexively, he swung the jack handle at it, hit the wrist with a crack and sent the gun away into the street.

"Motherfucker!" Ryan heard himself saying. He put the jack handle across the guy's throat with both hands and leaned his weight onto it, saw the flesh of the neck bulge along the rod. All the anxiety and rage and fear for Jess came flooding into him then, and for a moment he pushed with all his strength, oblivious to the punches that flurried around his face.

"Ryan!" Dagan shouted. "Stop!" She had come out of the Opel and stood just behind him. "You'll kill him! Ryan—"

He had forgotten her completely. She was right. Had to keep the guy conscious, to question him: Who hired him? Where'd his instructions come from? He reduced pressure on the rod.

Jesus I'm cranked, he realized. His heart was pounding so hard his whole body shook. Metallic taste in his mouth, some arousal hormone. *All the primate rage shit, right there,* he was thinking. All these kinetic reflexes. Everything so fast. Everything pounding like the heartbeat, whole street jarring with its bumps. A funny perspective, sideways, of the tires of the cars, broken glass glittering in the harsh chiaroscuro of head-light and shadow. And *bang bang,* big loud noises. *Bang bang bang* again.

He rolled on the ground, wondering where the jack handle had gone, feeling sharp grit on his face and realizing it was all wrong, something had gone wrong. He sat up suddenly, the world spinning, and then he gripped the open car door and hoisted himself upright.

Dagan, standing behind the Opel, holding the gun in two hands. Facing down the empty street. She turned when she heard his groan.

"Happened?"

"I, he—" She was panting. "He hit you with something, a brick, a cobblestone, you fell over. It was so fast! But I got his gun! He came after me and I shot at him. God, I kept shooting at him even when he was running away! I just kept shooting!" She gestured shakily down the street, then looked at the gun in her hands, appalled. Her eyes were huge and wild in the odd light.

Ryan took the gun from her. Then he went back to the other car, quickly looked under the seats, in the glove compartment, the ashtray. Nothing. Not even a bottle cap. He popped the trunk, and groped in the shadows: empty. Nothing to learn. He rubbed the gun thoroughly with his shirt tail, tossed it into the trunk, and slammed the lid. He could feel the pain in his temple now, from the blow that had come the instant he'd let pressure off the rod.

"You did good, Dagan," he panted, brushing gravel and glass off his clothes. "You were great. Now we've got to get out of here. Somebody will have heard the shots."

She just stood there, looking at him, shocked numb but astonishingly vivid, alive, *there.* Heart-shaped face floating pale and beautiful in the darkness. He went to her and stroked her back, kissed her cheek, tugged her crazy hair, trying to bring her around. "Okay," he kept saying, still jarred, almost without thoughts. "Okay. We gotta go."

The Opel disengaged from the other car without too much difficulty. Lucky. One headlight, a bad pull to the right, but drivable. They headed back toward the center of Geneva, Ryan's head throbbing as he wrestled with the steering.

"Fuck, I *had* him!" He pounded the wheel with his fist. "Our first concrete link to Jess. I had him! I blew it! God damn it. God fucking *damn* it!"

Dagan: "I was so scared you were hurt. When he—"

"I'm fine, my *body* is fine, I just—we finally *had* something! Damn it!" She hugged herself in the darkness.

Finally, ashamed at how long it had taken, he asked, "How about you? Are you okay?"

"Hit my head a little when we crashed." A quavering voice. "Not bad."

He cranked the shimmying car with difficulty around a turn, then straightened it out, hoping they'd make it to a hotel before some Swiss cop noticed the condition of the car.

"At first when I shot at him I was afraid that I would, I really would hit him," Dagan said, "I'd shoot a man and have him dying on the street right in front of me. And then like two seconds later when he was running away, I was afraid I'd *miss* the bastard!"

Not easy to find this stuff in yourself, Ryan thought. He put one hand on her shoulder, and she covered it with her hand, not looking at him. His fingertips brushed the skin on the side of her throat, felt the pulse beating there. The speed and heat of it startled him and he brought his hand back to the wheel.

"I'm really sorry about you having to…about all this," he said. But sorry wasn't enough, or really right, wasn't quite all of it.

She just shrugged and reached out to trace the long crack that had started from her corner of the windshield. She said tonelessly, "Jesus, we sure wreck up these rental cars."

Chapter 45

They found a small hotel, the only one with its outside lights still on. A sleepy-looking old man in a striped bathrobe shuffled down the stairs, unlocked the door, dubiously agreed to take a mix of dollars and euros for pay, showed them to a narrow, third-floor room. Two beds, a bathroom with bidet. No mini-bar, Ryan was sorry to see.

Still shaky, Dagan went to the bathroom and began taking a shower. Ryan hit the phone, arranging seats on the first flight back to Boston, leaving Geneva at 11:00 A.M. It was two o'clock now, only 5:00 P.M. in California, so he dialed Marshall's home number in Palo Alto.

"Jesus, Ry, where are you? I call Genesis and there's no answer—"

"Geneva. We'll be back tomorrow. I think I've got it figured, Marsh. I think we've got what Jess was doing, at least the outline of it. It's good. I can't talk about it on the phone. Can you fly east tomorrow?"

"Oh fuck, Ry—"

"It'll be worth your while. Just come."

The tone of his voice was adequate emphasis. "I take it you've had a productive trip," Marshall said resignedly. Good old Marsh. They agreed to meet at Heart Cove Sunday afternoon, eighteen hours from now, and said good-bye.

Yes, in more ways than one, a productive trip. The arc of Jess's thinking was becoming clear at last, a breathtaking vista opening up. Now he knew enough to guess where she'd gone next, as she put the final pieces of the puzzle in place.

But was there any assurance she was even still alive? Were they closer to finding her? The list of possible enemies was just getting longer.

Still, he felt a paradoxical optimism. Strangely, despite getting knocked unconscious and losing the watcher, the source of this new optimism was the altercation in the street. He knew why: He'd reacted opportunistically, without hesitation or fear, when he saw that they were being observed. A sign of a changing internal posture in this whole thing, Bates's death notwithstanding. *The hunters, not the hunted.*

And the way to hunt had come clear, too. A snare. *If we can't find them, we can arrange for them to find us.* As they'd driven the dark streets looking for shelter, a plan had taken shape in his mind. He tested its components, found them workable. Provided it wasn't already too late. But that wasn't to be considered.

———

Dagan emerged from the bathroom through a cloud of steam. Wearing a white terrycloth robe, she sat on her bed with her back to Ryan and began combing the snarls out of her wet hair. "Your turn," she said quietly.

He took a shower, scrubbing carefully around the bruises on his face, then shaved even more cautiously and brushed his teeth. The heat from the shower and the steamy air in the bathroom began to release the tension in his shoulders and neck. With the release came deep exhaustion. And perseveration, his mind involuntarily replaying the fight, over and over again. And now it took on a more sinister light: He'd been full of violence, the desire to inflict pain, so out of control that if Dagan hadn't shouted to him he might have done fatal damage to the guy, crushed his trachea. Abruptly his stomach felt hollow and sick: Maybe he *had* caught the Babel disease, maybe he had received some critical exposure to whatever it was—he was certainly more paranoid now, more prone to violence, even taking pleasure in it. More prone to thinking of others as enemies. Oh, God.

In the bedroom, Dagan appeared to be asleep on her bed, still in her robe. Broad hips and narrow waist, so full and womanly, and yet the way she lay on her side with one hand close to her face on the pillow, it almost appeared that she was sucking her thumb, taking infantile comfort amid the danger and disillusionment. He felt a pang of sympathy. This had to be hard on her. A protected girl, privileged background, and yet she'd shown herself to be tough and adaptable. And unlike most women of great physical beauty, unspoiled, without vanity or pretense. You had to admire Dagan.

The room was chilly, and after he'd turned off the bedside light it occurred to him that she had fallen asleep with the duvet still folded at the foot of her bed. In the near darkness he stood up again and went to her side, unfolded the down quilt and spread it gently over her. She stirred and put out a hand to his face.

It startled him, and now he recognized the charge of feeling that had been between them, on the street after the fight, the inadequacy of his apologies.

"Could you hold me for a minute?" she said in a small voice.

Such a reasonable request, Ryan thought dizzily, and so impossible. He was aware of wearing only boxer shorts, of the soapy-sweet smell of Dagan, of the privacy of their room.

"Please," Dagan whispered. "I'm scared, I'm kind of in shock—I'm not keeping it very together." Completely true, but her hand, moving softly on his face, said so much more.

"Oh kid, it's—I can't get anywhere near you right now—" he said. And yet he sat down on the side of her bed. How deeply they both needed comfort. Just to feel another living being close and caring and without barriers. All the lines seemed arbitrary and indistinct.

She tugged at his shoulders. "Jess would understand," she pleaded quietly. "She would understand what we're going through. She knows how I feel about you, I've told her. My whole life, she knows. She would say it's okay."

How I feel about you. My whole life. The thought stabbed him: Dagan, her unaccountable inability to put up for long with the young men who threw themselves at her. Her presence in their family, the many nights she'd stay over in the guest bedroom after work, the easy way she moved in their house. Her concern for them both, and for Abi, the countless times they'd relied on her. Dagan moving in frictionless concert with them, an attentive dancer closely following their lead. And her loneliness: *I haven't been lucky that way.* The tint of accusation that tinged their occasional talks about love.

"Please just be close to me," she was saying. "I can't stand to be alone tonight. Don't make me feel I'm just…some kind of *mascot* for you and Jess, some—"

"Dagan, you're not—"

"Then what am I?" The bitterness in her voice sharpened. "Foster daughter? Jess's surrogate sister? Number-two wife? Free household help? Tell me what I am!"

Oh heartbreak. He bent to her face, kissed her nose, felt her breath on his cheek. She smelled like spring, and for an instant he thought, *Maybe under the circumstances Jess would forgive, accept.* But he said, "You're our…" But there wasn't a word for her. "You're gorgeous, you're so sexy and fine I have to keep my distance. Especially right now."

She groaned miserably and pushed at him. Rolled away, face in the pillow.

After a moment he got up and went to his own bed, wondering how to fix this. How they could possibly work together after this, how he could continue this heartbreaking search without her.

Her voice came out of the darkness, small, lost: "Then what am I going to do? What happens to somebody who...somebody like me?"

He didn't have any idea. He'd been too lucky in love, given too much right from the start. He didn't know what that empty longing was or where it went or how you lived with it. He'd always had Jess.

"Dagan—" he began.

"Oh, go to sleep, Ryan! Forget it!"

"Dagan—"

"Go to *sleep.*"

Eventually he did.

The travel alarm wheedled. Ryan's senses lurched to awareness to find Dagan lying with her back to him, fitting neatly against him from heels to head. He felt a moment of guilty shock, then realized that she still had on her thick terry robe, he still wore his boxer shorts, the pressure of desire was unrelieved in him. He hadn't betrayed Jess. For a moment he tried to recall how they'd ended up together, but all he could remember was drifting to sleep in his own bed in a torment of sympathy and desire and confusion.

She roused, groped blindly to shut off the alarm. He rose on one elbow to look around the room, disoriented. They were in *her* bed. The fact made him glad: some small token of how much she meant to him, some little thing to even them up, or reassure her or something—

Dagan turned her almond eyes to him, startled to see him so close. Then she turned away, breathed deeply, and for just an instant stretched her whole body sensuously against him, luxuriating in their contact. Turned to him again with a small, rueful smile until the awkwardness flooded in again and she dutifully, chastely, got out of bed.

"Okay," she said. A morning-hoarse voice. "Okay, okay, okay, okay." Pulled her robe tighter around herself and snugged the belt. "All right," she said flatly, "okay." Rummaged in her suitcase, found toothpaste, underclothes, comb. Went to the bathroom, saying, "Okay, okay, all right. Okay."

Chapter 46

They turned into the driveway at Heart Cove, showed identification to one of the Peterson's guards, and drove on up to the house. Though it was a bright day, autumn had taken its toll: the meadow and trees had passed through the colorful stage and now seemed forlorn, threadbare, faded. The pervasive melancholy of fall. Ryan's heart felt twisted, wrung in his chest. November 3: eight days until Jess gave birth. If she was still alive. If she didn't go into labor early.

Dagan: hard to tell what she was feeling.

They came into the circular driveway and Ryan got a shock. The parking area was full of cars: Logan's minivan, Leap's battered BMW, Dolores's big Ford, Wesley's spiffy Saab, three others. Even in daylight, there were lights on in the house windows. After telling Logan to leave, he had expected to come home to an empty place, locked down and dark.

"Son of a bitch," he said. "Those insubordinate—"

"What did you think, Einstein?" Dagan said acidly. "Everybody was going to pack up and run because you told them to? You didn't hear them tell you they weren't going to quit?"

They hadn't said much at the hotel, just packed up for the flight back to Boston. Dagan had looked both angry and wounded. Or something—uncomfortably exposed, maybe. Just as they were leaving the room, she stood in front of him, blocking the door.

"So. Do I have to feel ashamed? That I in effect attempted to, to betray Jess? That you know a secret thing about me—unequal affections and all that rot?" Mustering this directness wasn't easy for her. "Is this something you're going to hold over me?"

"Of course not! Jesus, Dagan—"

"I was scared. I was in shock and very tired—"

"I know that."

"Don't I get anything in return? A secret, anything at all?"

"Listen, Dagan, I don't deserve your feelings," he said, meaning it. "Look at me—I'm fifteen years older than you and I drink too much and I'm a difficult guy to live with. I'm surly and undisciplined and—"

But she was going brusquely out the hotel-room door. "Can it, Ryan. Just *stuff* it," she called back.

To her credit, though, she had rallied with a gritty determination. On the plane, they had talked, if stiffly, they'd taken notes on what they'd learned and made a half-assed pretense that nothing had changed. But their shoulders hadn't made contact, their hands never touched. Yes, an awkwardness and reserve had come between them.

They got out of the Subaru and trotted down the steps to the Genesis offices. A pair of guards stood on the deck—Logan must have increased their security. All the lights were on down there, too. The place was bustling. Inside, the carpet was new, walls painted, ceiling replaced.

Logan was standing at the front desk, talking to Wesley and Peter, and when she saw him come in she turned to face him squarely, face defiant.

"I told everybody what you told me," she said quickly, "about Bates, that we were all supposed to go home and hide in our closets. Everybody felt the same way I did. Call it a mutiny. We had work to do."

He just embraced her. "You did just the right thing," he said. "I was intending to come in here and ask everyone to come back. Change of plans."

Logan tipped her head back to look up at him. Her eyebrows went up. "You've got another bruise. But other than that you look good. Doesn't he, guys?" she asked grimly. "Say yes," she ordered.

Peter and Wesley nodded.

————————

At three o'clock, Wesley returned from the airport with Marshall. Though he wore a crisp business suit, Marsh looked beat, harried, his hair matted unevenly, a shaving cut on his jaw. When they came out to the parking area to meet him, he kissed Dagan warmly but shook Ryan's hand without enthusiasm.

"I'm here for four hours," Marshall said. "That's what I can afford. Then I'm flying back to Stanford. This better be worth my while."

"Let's go for a walk on the shore," Ryan suggested, taking his arm.

"I'm shot. We can't just sit inside?"

"I think Ryan's wish is that this stays a private conversation," Dagan explained. She helped steer him toward the long wooden steps. "Given that we've been bugged before."

Marshall stumped down the stairs, looking out of place in his suit. With the tide just past high, the rugged beach was a narrow strip of gravel between glistening boulders and the water. A light surf broke over submerged rocks, seethed through the seaweed mat, and rattled the shingle, making a white noise that Ryan figured would cloak their conversation on the off-chance someone was listening. Though it was a Sunday the breeze was raw, and as far up the coast as he could see no one else was on the shore.

"Let me start by going over what Jess was doing," Ryan said.

He gave Marshall a summary of what they'd learned from her scattered notes, the meetings with Richter and Freunde and Hoague, Weismann's lecture.

"She was focusing on kinship recognition, Marsh. One catalyst was Abi's comment at the zoo, about how the gorilla looked like old Judge Maywood—"

"Which triggered her thinking about how we recognize people, or generalize similarities in facial features," Dagan cut in. "Ryan says we have a...like a pattern scanner built into our brains, a neural module, specific to the features of the human face."

Marshall nodded, crunching along awkwardly in his brown oxfords, interested despite himself. "Yes. Ry, remember the tests we ran on newborns at Project Alpha?" To Dagan he explained: "Six-minute-old babies. We'd show them head shapes with various rearrangements of nose, eyes, brows, mouth—randomly distributed, no features, symmetrical distribution, and real facial distribution. The babies would track the real face, ignore the others. Shows that we're born with the faculty to recognize that specific pattern, encoded in our neural circuitry. Okay. Then what?"

"Then there were her notes about the sense of smell," Ryan said, "the tests on Richter's and Freunde's noses. Because histochemical similarity is an important clue to relatedness, to kinship. I'm not up on recent literature on the vomeronasal organ, but I know we use it more than we're consciously aware of. Not just sniffing for pheromones, but for basic social relationships. It's well documented that mothers can distinguish their own babies from other babies by scent alone."

Dagan: "Remember what Freunde said about why you should save a drowning man? He said because you recognized yourself in others, which he said was not a 'philosophy,' but a, how'd he say it—?"

"'A physical sensation.' 'A visceral certainty.'" As he said it, Ryan remembered something Richter had said: *There were even some faces of Jews... 'Do I look like I am kin to this?'*

"So then we add in the role of altruism and cooperation in forming societies, the link between kinship and incidence of altruism. The Somali saying I faxed her got her thinking about degrees of relatedness as the basis for degrees of social alliances."

"'My son and I against my brother,' et cetera," Marshall remembered.

"Right. Okay, so Jess is thinking that human societies are based on biologically derived imperatives of cooperation and reciprocal altruism—on being 'nice.' And that being 'nice' starts with our ability to recognize and be 'nice' to kin. She'd have been looking at the olfactory as well as the visual association centers. And that therefore an impairment to the parts of the brain that recognize or respond appropriately to kinship signals—"

"—would result in the Babel disorder," Marshall said.

They stopped at the remains of a concrete wall, some old shore construction mostly eaten by the waves. Marshall had his arms crossed against the breeze, and it occurred to Ryan that he should have known a Californian would find this weather uncomfortably cold. But Marsh was taking this in, getting it, God love him. The irritation was gone from his face, replaced by his look of concentration, the animated look of discovery.

Dagan kicked at the flaking wall, a wrinkle of concern appearing between her brows. "Is this thesis testable?"

"Absolutely," Ryan told her. "Parts of it have been tested already. The localization in the brain of the recognition of others has been well demonstrated in studies of brain-damaged people. Strokes, tumors, head injury, you'll find people who appear normal and alert in every other way, but are unable to recognize their spouse or child, or even themselves in a mirror. Almost always it's damage to the visual association cortex, or the anterior temporal lobe. Which should ring a bell for you, Marsh—the Project Alpha autism studies?"

Suddenly Marshall looked a little stunned. *"Theory of mind.* Same general areas of the brain are responsible for theory of mind."

"Theory of mind is—?" Dagan prompted.

"Theory of mind is our ability to differentiate between thought and reality," Ryan explained. "It's the basis of our ability to impute a consciousness like our own to another person. Another built-in faculty that's localized in modules in the visual association cortex and the anterior temporal lobe. It's how we differentiate between a person and, say, a piece of furniture. A person *experiences* things, *believes* things, a refrigerator doesn't. Normal kids start differentiating between ideas and reality, and between their own mind and the mind of others, between the ages of three and four. Autistic kids don't, which is why they're so isolated, socially dysfunctional. In effect, 'theory of mind' is what allows you to see yourself in other people. Jess first touched on it way back when we were doing the death-row preliminaries. She was looking for a common element, and she found it—objectification of victims. Other people weren't 'real.'"

They thought about that. Marshall winged a rock out over the water.

At last Dagan spoke again: "But that would make a pretty obvious pathology! Wouldn't we have heard of an epidemic of people not being able to...to recognize their own *family?*"

"Not necessarily!" Ryan said. "Functional recognition can still occur. 'This kid is coming in the door at three o'clock, my kid comes home at three o'clock, therefore this is my kid.' But that's just a *logical* process—it lacks the emotional, *visceral* sense of connection, of relatedness. Also, in most cases we're not talking about a fully emergent condition—but rather a sub-threshold condition, not complete dysfunction."

"Anyway, we'd only know it's an epidemic if we recognize the symptoms," Marshall said grimly. "Which, obviously, nobody's done until Jess came along."

The wind, or the excitement of the chase, had brought bright color to Dagan's cheeks. "God, she's brilliant!" she said. "It answers so much!"

Like the question of the spectrum of symptoms, Ryan was thinking. *Start with a feeling of isolation and the inability to really care about others—can't see yourself in them, can't feel kinship! The web of connectedness weakens at myriad points. Soon you'd get social effects like failing families, infanticide, crime, epidemic levels of depression and other alienation-induced disorders. Failure to use the cooperate strategies that are provably successful. 'Not kin,' your brain tells you, 'Not like me.' So others become abstractions. For anyone with anger or impulse-control problems, the last impediment to violence is gone. Subtle effects would spiral back into socioeconomic systems: the easy commodification of human beings, increasingly uncaring social policy, the rise of government by kleptocracy, the delamination of social and economic classes. All creating the feedback spiral toward conflict. You still have your social habits, and you live among the artifacts of culture that suggest others are real—but you just don't* feel *it, intuitively, emotionally. You can't see yourself in others, or feel your kinship with others, so you can't care enough. Because your organ for doing so is failing. Due to the Babel effect.*

"This is good, this is really good," Marshall said, a little taken aback.

Ryan walked on ahead of them. He felt the truth of Jess's basic premise as if it were a material thing, heavy and solid in his head, his belly. The profound bell of truth. His mind dizzied with the implications.

"But where does that leave us?" Marshall asked. "I mean, I instinctively feel she's on a productive track, and the neurological implications mean that we've got to change the focus of our field studies. But why would someone kidnap Jess and kill Bates for that?"

"Because she identified the Babel agent? Or somebody *thought* she did. And they got scared of what she knew. Or wanted the information for themselves." Ryan told him about Shipley's interest and his concern about terrorists, Richter's connection to neo-Nazis, the test of RAIN-DROP at Sandia using Babel symptoms, Hoague's friend Nina and her connection to Mannie Skovanick.

Marshall was shaking his head, dubious. "Come on, Ryan! The Mannie Skovanick files are the Holy Grail of every far-fringe conspiracy theorist. As for the others—this is sounding a tad cloak-and-dagger for my taste, Ry."

"Except that Jess is gone and Bates is dead."

"Okay. We shift our research emphasis, both in symptoms and social indicators, and we boost our focus on EMFs. You've just undesigned our studies, six months' of planning work. Fine. Thanks very much." The sour look returned to Marshall's face. "I'm freezing my ass out here. I don't know how you people live in a climate like this. And I'm ruining my fucking shoes. You know, all I need is to get sick on top of—"

"One more thing," Ryan said. "I need your help, Marsh. As a friend, I need your help, and I need Brandt's cooperation."

Marshall sighed. He looked levelly at Ryan, let his shoulders slump, puffed out his cheeks. The same wind that had brought vividness to Dagan's face turned his nose bright red, face blotchy pale, a Dickensian portrait of cold. "Let's hear it."

"These people will kill her when they feel she's outlived her usefulness, when she's told them what she knows. Or maybe when she has the baby and...But we can't seem to get to them. So I need to lure *them* to *us*—get them to come after us again. That means we send the signals of a breakthrough, we advertise that we now have what they need. Dagan and I have been followed, which tells us they're still interested. And we really have recapitulated a lot of Jess's work, it's not a stretch for them to assume we've found something, too." *We are the hunters, not the hunted.*

"So what's my role—Brandt's role?"

"Just play along. Listen to my tales of breakthroughs. I'm not sure of the specifics yet, still got some errands to run, angles to figure. But if I send you an e-mail crowing about what we've found, affirm that it's crucial and viable."

"Not hard to do. This is brilliant work so far."

"You don't tell your staff, or anyone, about the trap. We keep any communications face-to-face—no phone, no e-mail or fax. I'll get you details later."

"Okay. I got the message. I'll help. This is getting extortionate, Ry, keeping me out here. I'm going in now."

Marshall turned and crunched back down the beach. *Twenty years of friendship,* Ryan thought. And then, seeing Marsh with his shoulders hunched against the chill wind, stepping awkwardly in his smooth-soled street shoes, he thought suddenly, *Jesus, when did Marsh become a middle-aged man?*

Dagan caught up with Marsh and took his arm, and she looked suddenly unfamiliar, too: *When did Dagan become a grown-up woman?* But seeing them together Ryan felt a surge of deep affection: good friends. The best friends you could ever ask for.

They'd have to be good friends, he thought, if they were going to stick with him through what was coming.

Part THREE

What if I told you your home
is this planet of warworn children
women and children standing in line or milling
endlessly calling each others' names
What if I tell you, you are not different
it's the family albums that lie—
will any of this comfort you
and how should it comfort you?
—ADRIENNE RICH

It was six o'clock, already dark. Marshall had gone back to the airport, Dagan had crashed in the guest bedroom, Leap and Peter sat at the kitchen counter, drinking coffee and looking dazed. They planned to work a few more hours, then spend the night in Abi's room. Dolores had gone home, Logan was still at work in the Catacombs; outside, replacements came for three of the six Peterson's guards—Logan had doubled their protection. Ryan felt fatigue in every muscle, but a savage energy drove him on.

Still no answer at any of Karl's numbers, no call back. But he did manage to reach Burke. Burke expected a lab report on the bug by tomorrow morning, as well as the forensic reports on Bates. He promised to call as soon as he heard anything.

Next: Leap.

Ryan waited until Leap had drained his coffee cup, then wordlessly handed him a jacket from the coat hooks in the hall. Leap slid into it, Ryan put on a windbreaker, and they went out to the deck. They took seats in the big Adirondack chairs, faces to the unruly night of the bay. Jess had found the chairs at a garage sale and had lovingly scraped them and repainted them a Mediterranean blue, and just knowing her hands had been there gave Ryan a ghost of comfort. He had turned on the floodlights all around, and now the deck was bathed in light. They nodded to the guard who prowled the side deck, then waited until he was out of view.

"Any ideas on what I suggested earlier?" Ryan asked Leap quietly. He was happy to see Leap's face move: a special smile. When he smiled like that it was because he was feeling particularly clever.

"Homing pigeon," Leap said in a raspy whisper.

"Translate, please."

The grin grew. "Your idea is that we trail our important findings out there for someone to see. The lure, the bait on the hook, right?"

"Right."

"We look like we're trying to keep secrets—a good security perimeter here, encrypt every communication to Brandt. Can't let them know we're inviting them in."

Ryan nodded. "Imperative."

"They'd start by hacking our computers. Find out if we really do have anything worth more strenuous efforts to get from us."

"And you trace the hack."

"No—I'm betting they're too good to trace." Leap leaned back and dug in his jeans pockets until he found a packet of nicotine gum. He blew pocket lint off it, and began stripping foil from a piece. "Nope."

"So how do we catch them?"

Leap popped the gum in his mouth and chewed it vigorously for a moment before continuing: "A homing pigeon. E.T. call home, Ry! Embedded in the information we let them steal is a little packet, think of it as a virus, that does two simple, unobtrusive things. One, it calls us up whenever the files are opened on a networked computer— basically, as soon as anyone looks at the data. Calls us up and says 'Yo! Here I am!'"

"If they're stupid enough to do it from a networked computer," Ryan said. The thought depressed him and suddenly he wanted a drink. It occurred to him he hadn't been drinking lately, one reason or another, hadn't had time or access to booze. Just as well. Given the state he was in, it would shut him down, put him to sleep. Sleep was a luxury he couldn't afford anymore.

Leap: "I'm betting they'll think they're safe, having done the hack from a remote computer. They'll probably, literally, take our information on a disc out of one computer and put it into another, and they'll think that's adequate prophylaxis. Plus, it'll be a ton of data, and they'll almost certainly want to relay the info to other points. But if it's opened on any subnet connected to the Internet—E.T. calls home."

Ryan had to grin. Leap was a devious son of a bitch. "So what's the other thing your package does?"

"We've got a lot of graphics in these files, graphs and molecular diagrams and so on. So embedded in the graphics data, I put an invisible watermark that ends up in a .gif or .jpeg file in any computer that handles it. Undetectable—unless you know to look for a minuscule quirk in the wallpaper or screensaver! It basically says, 'Kilroy was here!' Meaning, when we get our hands on someone's computer, even if our files have been forwarded and deleted, we can prove it's the computer that received the stolen information."

Ryan smiled admiringly. "It's a good thing I saved you from a life of crime, Leap."

Leap spread his hands self-depreciatingly, *ce n'est rien,* one of his rare surviving Gaulish gestures.

One of the security men cleared his throat from the edge of the deck and at Ryan's nod took a turn past the house doors, looked over the far edge, headed back toward the stairs.

"What's the status of our hookup to Ridder Global?" Ryan asked.

"We're close. If we want to look like we've got something worth knocking us over for, getting corporate data from Ridder will be very important. One of the juiciest worms we could put on our hook. I've got my super-user status over there, and I've arranged with Zelinsky, Ridder's IT manager, to start trial data exchanges Wednesday."

"So how soon can you build this homing pigeon? It'll need to be installed in every file, right?"

"I've started work on it," Leap said. He was chewing gum faster as the nicotine hit. "Maybe by tomorrow night. It helps that Argus is up to speed again."

A distant spark lit the sky, a jetliner putting on its landing lights, too far away to be heard. They watched it disappear and then both stood up. It got cold out here when the sun was gone.

Leap had started out optimistic, but now looked suddenly pensive.

"Something the matter?" Ryan asked him.

Leap scuffed his sneaker on the deck. "Only that it may not work. They may smell a trap and not come to us. Or maybe they've already got everything they need. From Jess."

The thought had occurred to Ryan, too. But now it seemed wise to keep Leap up, in high gear. "We're not going to rely on this alone, Leap. We'll keep after other initiatives, too."

Leap nodded equivocally, looking lousy. He had blue stripes under his eyes. Ryan paused at the door to the house as Leap started down the stairs to the Catacombs.

"Hey, Leap," Ryan called. Leap stopped and looked back. "It's going to work. And you're going to be a hero."

It sounded a little condescending, child psychology, but he was pleased to see Leap's smile flicker again briefly.

———

One more thing. Abi. More precisely, Abi and the judge and Mrs. Maywood.

Ryan called, then drove the Subaru into Boston. This being Sunday night, the Maywoods would have spent the day between church, the judge's Sunday school teaching, and an early dinner with the minister. They'd probably be more prickly than usual: The crisis of Jess's abduction notwithstanding, Ryan's disruption of Sunday-night routine would be unwelcome, another proof of his unsuitability. Especially with what he was going to ask of them.

Clarissa Maywood let him in. She was probably sixty-five now, her hair silver and so perfectly coifed it looked artificial. Like her husband, she had a rigidly upright bearing, a faintly disapproving expression etched into her face, but she had kept a trim figure, and her face still revealed the excellent bone structure that ran in the family.

Ryan let her lead him inside, where Abi and the judge sat on the couch. Abi was so beautiful, the sight of her brought tears to his eyes. He grabbed her and lifted her up and rocked her. *No feeling on this earth as gratifying as your bony stringy kid hugging you hard, safe in your arms.* Only after he had set her down and looked her over did he realize that she didn't look good. She was thinner, and her skin had a gray, washed-out appearance. With a pang, he realized how different her aura was—she appeared tentative, closed in. This thing was taking a toll on her that would last a lifetime. *Abi!* He knelt and stroked and petted her, feeling helpless.

After a time he got the three of them to sit down and listen to what he had to say: "I've begun some initiatives that might get Jess back to us. But I have a favor to ask of you, all three of you. I want you to go away for a while—until this blows over. Until Jess is safe back here and we've caught her kidnappers."

The judge growled in his chest. "Go away! Why would we—"

"Because I don't want you, especially Abi, to become a pawn in this game. It's probably unlikely, but I can't take any chances. I don't want them to try to, to...do anything to you as a way of influencing *me.*" He had decided earlier that Abi should hear all of this, but now he began having second thoughts.

"Like they would kill us?" she said in a tiny voice. She hunched further and held her stomach, as though protecting some internal injury.

"Nobody! Never!" the judge rumbled. Clarissa said nothing, just stared at Ryan with wide eyes.

"No. But they might threaten you, 'Beb, or kidnap you so that I'd quit bothering them, or so I'd give them information."

"Couldn't we go to Provincetown, Henry?" Clarissa offered.

"No," Ryan said firmly. "They'd find you there, they'd know about the beach house. If they've got Jess, they could make her tell them. It's got to be somewhere completely new. And you can't leave a trail to it, either. No credit-card purchases, no calls from this phone or to our house, no forwarding instructions at the court."

"This is obscene," the judge said. He got up, fuming, rounded suddenly on Ryan, came up speechless.

"Does it mean I won't get to see you, Da?" Abi asked.

That was the painful part. "Just for a little while."

"I am a *federal judge,*" Henry said. "You don't just vanish, without a word to the court, when you're a federal judge, Ryan! I can't do this. We'll hire a security guard."

Ryan took his arm and led him into the entry hall, then shut the glass door and spoke in a hushed voice. "They killed Bates. The FBI found him—somebody had tortured him to death. They don't care if you're a federal judge. Which means you and I are going to have to work together here, for once—for Abi's sake and for Jess's."

The old man was still breathing hard, too outraged to speak. As if he still blamed Ryan.

"Goddamn it, Henry, I didn't make Jess who she is! I didn't make her become a scientist, stop trying to hang that on me. And I sure didn't urge her to take on this goddamned project!"

Henry was still battling conflicting feelings, his hard stare telling Ryan he wasn't buying it.

Ryan gave it one more shot. He moved so that his back was to the living room, his body blocking Abi's view of the two of them. "Judge," he hissed, "I'm trying to find her. I'm trying to figure out *where* she is, and it means I'm trying to learn *who* she is. It doesn't make me proud to admit, Jesus, we've been married twenty years and maybe I'm trying hard enough for the first time. But you've struggled with this, too, you know you have! You sure *you* tried hard enough? I'm not accusing you. I'm saying we can let this drive us apart, or we can let it pull us together. As a family. You decide."

The judge looked pierced, breathless. And then, something Ryan would never have expected, his eyes suddenly rimmed with tears and spilled. "Yeah," he panted. "Yeah." He drew a ragged breath. "See, I was always so hard on Jessamine!" he whispered. "I thought that was what we needed, she needed, see. Oh, Lord Jesus. When she was little...the

problem with her heart. I thought I had to make sure she was *stronger!*
And she was so smart, so pretty, so shining, I thought there was no place
she couldn't go if she had the discipline, so I…" He seemed to lose his
balance, and Ryan reached out for his arm. They held each other's forearms, a Roman handshake, and Ryan felt the old man stabilizing himself.
"Oh, sweet Jesus, I was so *hard* on her!"

They just stood in the hall, Ryan holding the judge's arm and through
the grip feeling his whole body shaking.

"You did good, Henry," Ryan told him, barely able to talk. "She
turned out great. The best. You did fine. You just tell her this when she
comes home, huh? You did just fine."

The old man bit his lips hard, wincing away the tears. Then he put his
other hand around Ryan's neck and pulled their foreheads together. Ryan
felt the heat of his weeping, the bristle of his hair. It was a little while
before they could go back inside.

Ryan made sure to spend some time alone with Abi. He asked her what
she'd been reading, and they sat with the books as the Maywoods conferred in the kitchen. In addition to the usual kids' stories, he saw, there
were several illustrated Bible tales. On the cover of one, Jesus, a handsome white guy with long chestnut hair and a toga, sat under a tree with
a multiracial group of kids.

"So," he asked, "how're you doing?"

"Okay, I guess." She shrugged. "You know."

"Yeah. Do I ever know."

They leafed through the books, just sharing the space, being near.
Abi's legs stuck straight out in front of her, feet pigeon-toed in white
socks and glistening black patent-leather shoes. Church shoes, Ryan
knew, recognizing them from his own youth. Still Sunday, although it
seemed like days since he gotten knocked out in the street in Geneva.

"It's dangerous, right? What you're going to do?" she said.

"Well, I'll try not to let it be. I'll be very smart and careful."

"You miss Ma a lot. You're so lonely for her."

"A lot, yeah," he told her. "Same as you."

Abi's voice was different, too, Ryan decided, reedy and tired. Everything about her seemed hungry, uprooted, and abruptly she reminded
him of the refugee kids he'd seen in Africa. And why not? Abi was a
refugee of the Babel effect, too.

He recoiled from the thought, looking for something he could say that would make it any better. "I have to tell you something," he blurted. "All my life, I've been…too complicated. You know? Nobody understood me—I don't blame them—except your mother. And you." This was crazy, this kind of confession to a six-year-old. "I mean, you have to know how much I love you both," he clarified. And that sounded wrong, too, almost like some kind of good-bye.

Abi shut the book carelessly and looked up at him. "Is she dead?" she asked.

"No! Absolutely not! She's alive and I'm going to bring her back home."

She looked away, took his hand, ruminated for a minute, then looked back at him. "Don't worry. If Ma's dead, I'll take care of you." She squeezed his fingers.

Ryan couldn't breathe for several heartbeats. He should reject the idea absolutely, condemn it, forbid it. And yet she seemed to have found some strength in her resolve. He couldn't deny her any source of strength.

Finally he tried his voice. "I know you will, kid," he told her.

Chapter 48

"**Let me start** with Dr. Bates," Burke said. "I've gotten the pathology report and the results from our trace evidence labs."

He looked tired, the serious, sad tilt of his eyes more pronounced. Ryan offered him a seat, but he shook his head, preferring to stand looking through the glass wall at the rags of autumn. The strange authority Burke had carried with him earlier seemed to have evaporated: His flat, splay-footed stance gave him the aspect of a broken-down beat cop.

It was eleven o'clock, and Ryan had been up since five. He had offered to come to the FBI field office at Center Plaza, but Burke wanted to meet with him at Heart Cove. Ryan led him into the sunny dining room, poured himself a cup of coffee, set out an extra cup.

"The pathologist says Dr. Bates died of heart failure," Burke said.

"Heart failure? Bates was an athlete!"

Burke held up a hand. "Heart failure precipitated by torture-induced stress. Dr. Bates had electrode burns in his genital area—they were shocking him, something like a Taser, two contact points. In addition, there were ligature marks around his neck. Judging by the incisiveness of the marks, a thin wire, probably music wire. A very hard, flexible steel. Apparently they tortured him with oxygen deprivation, cutting off the carotid flow until he began to black out, then releasing pressure long enough to revive him again. It's painful and scary and it's known as an effective technique for coercive interrogation. Probably the lack of oxygen caused his heart to give out."

Ryan couldn't say anything for a full minute. Bates, the steady, sardonic, integrated being, Bates surviving hell in Vietnam only to die like that. He could hardly breathe himself. Burke's overly clinical, detached telling of the horror seemed inexplicable. And then suddenly Ryan saw it: The outrage of such things had long since percolated through his psyche, leaving only his odd, resigned sadness, a big aching despair for the human condition.

Burke just waited, standing flat-footed with his hands in his pockets. At last Ryan recovered somewhat, again finding the starting place in rage. "What about serology or trace evidence?"

Burke shrugged. "We took hairs and fibers from his skin, but again nothing that helps us identify where he was or who was with him."

Ryan shoved himself back from the table and stood up. There had to be something to do with the outrage he felt, the urge to physical action, but he couldn't imagine anything that would be sufficient. He leaned both hands against the solarium window and looked out at the leaf-strewn lawn.

Burke sat down and poured himself half a cup of coffee. "How have you been doing on reconstructing Jessamine's contacts?"

"My staff and I have made good progress in recapitulating her thinking, some of the science involved."

"Is it important? Enough to justify what happened?"

"It's very important. It could be a crucial synthesis. She made amazing progress in a very short time. The problem is figuring out who was so worried about what she found out. I don't have anything substantial to offer you on that score."

Burke nodded sympathetically. "I spoke at length with the German prison administrator, what's his name, Schmidt, and some people in the *Staatsschutz* over there. They gave us some leads on Richter's contacts with neo-Nazis here, and I'm liaising with our Militia and Civil Rights units. But personally I think it's a dead end."

"Why's that?" Ryan asked. Burke was still uneasy, and Ryan got the sense he was stalling, avoiding something.

"Again, the sophistication of the operation. The neo-Nazi crowd likes more drama and less substance. This was beyond anything those bums are capable of—the type of information they were after, the planning, the technology..." Burke's face moved, a wince of discomfort, and Ryan knew he'd stumbled into the real problem here.

"So: the bug."

Burke's face twitched again. "Sit down, let's talk about the bug."

Ryan remained standing.

"I'm going to be frank, Ryan. I've got two choices here. One's to be me, an individual, a person, the other is to be a good FBI agent. I've been a big fan of yours for years, I respect you too much to give you the straight company line, but I also need to preserve the...the priorities of our agency. See what I'm saying?"

"No."

Burke rocked his head. "We've taken the bug apart," he said unenthusiastically. "We know where it came from, who made it. And that'll help a great deal. In the long run."

Ryan caught the emphasis: "The long run?"

"There are a lot of layers here. A lot of…considerations. It adds up to I can't tell you who made the bug because I can't go charging in and interrogate them, and I can't risk that you'll do it, either. Which I know you'd do. The only reason I'm even telling you we've made progress on the bug is that I want you to know we're doing something. That there are avenues that might lead us to your wife's abductors. Some hope."

Ryan stepped to Burke's side, leaned over him, beginning to lose control. Burke just stared up at him with mild, sad eyes, unimpressed. "Sit down, Ryan. Please," he said.

Ryan held himself back with difficulty. "Are you protecting somebody? Some other federal agency?"

Burke just stared at him, confused and then, as he understood, disappointed and offended.

"Why won't you pursue the bug?"

"I didn't say we won't pursue it. Only that we have to do it with delicacy. Which means it'll take a while."

"Jesus Christ, *delicacy*, we don't have *time* for—"

"Wheels within wheels, okay?" Burke looked into his coffee cup, seemed to reject the idea of drinking any. "I shouldn't have told you anything. But I didn't want to come here empty-handed. Now I'm out on a limb. Help me on this."

Ryan sat down, composed himself, held one hand hard with the other. "I'm *helping*," he said flatly.

"The electronics shop is a freelance high-tech outfit that we've known about for some time. Top of the line. The FBI and other government agencies get a great deal of information from keeping tabs on its clients. I'm talking bomb timers and triggers, illegal surveillance equipment, other weapons technologies that are used by terrorist groups, drug cartels, organized crime syndicates. We need to keep this shop unaware of our knowledge of it. Your wife is very, very important. But the shop figures in other important investigations, that we—this is hard to say, Ryan—that we think take precedence. I'm talking the potential of many lives lost—explosives technology, missile guidance, communications interception. We'll find out who bought this bug. But we have to do it carefully."

Ryan absorbed it, his optimism and momentum sliding away and replaced by a flare of suspicion. *How deep does this go? What is Burke, really?* "You said other agencies were also watching this shop. Which ones?"

"I'm not at liberty to reveal," Burke said.

Ryan looked at him. From Burke's face he knew this was difficult for him to accept—the games within games, the gray zones of justice—but he also knew that whatever his discomfort right now, Burke was unflappable. "Anything else?" he asked finally.

Burke ducked his head, shrugged, *no.* Ryan pushed back his chair again, stood up. Burke wandered behind him to the front door. "I'm sorry," he said. "I'm really very sorry."

Which for the time being left very little. Leap was locked in his lab, working on the innocuous-looking little string of ones and zeros that he'd plant in all Genesis computer files, all online communications, on the off chance the bad guys would come back to visit. Logan and the others were building the data files they'd begin to feed to Brandt headquarters when Leap's homing pigeon was ready. All that remained for Ryan to do was to revisit the last few of Jess's contacts, piece together the remainder of her thesis, maybe isolate some definitive enemy. It wasn't nothing, but it wasn't anything he held out a lot of hope for, either.

The crew had put names to all the numbers on the half-burnt September bill. One of the calls that no one else had claimed struck Ryan as very strange: the rectory at Mary Queen of Peace in South Boston, the church Ryan had attended when he was a kid. What would Jess have wanted there? Ryan dialed the number, wondering if old Father Connelly was still the priest there. He got a secretary who said yes, Father Connelly was around, but not there at the moment. He left a message asking for a call-back. He had just put the receiver down when the phone rang, startling him.

"Ry—Karl."

"Karl! Jesus, I've been trying to reach you for a week!"

"I was in London—a conference. Sorry. So how's it hanging? Your messages sound kind of urgent."

Ryan told him the story of Jess's abduction, the murder of Bates.

"Jesus—they took Jess? You must be going through five kinds of hell. Right after the African thing, too. Huh. I'm sorry, Ry. Huh. Thus your need for proctological expertise." Despite his condolences, Karl's voice sounded unusually cool. "So, exactly how do you want to prevail upon our association?"

Association: a bad omen, Ryan thought. He'd have preferred *friendship*. Was Karl still nursing some petty hurt from Ryan's unflattering comments back in May? Or was there some other reason why he wanted to distance himself?

"I need to meet with you. In person," Ryan told him.

"Oh my! Security issues. Whee, now you're talking my language!" Karl was goading him.

"Karl, you've been acting the part of the complete shit so long you yourself don't know if it's real or not. So I can't pretend to know who you really are. But I need your help now."

"Ry—"

"You can enjoy the ironies of my appeal all you want. When you're done, take a minute to decide whether there's one decent bone somewhere in your body. It might be good for you to sort that out once in a while. If you decide there is, help me. Just tell me if you'll meet me, yes or no, I don't have time to fuck around."

Karl was silent for so long Ryan thought he'd hung up.

Finally: "Ry, Ry, Ry—God, have I ever told you how your paternalistic shit gives me the fucking *hives?*" Karl chuckled deep in his throat, gloating. "Oh well. Why not? Tell you what—I'm supposed to show up at a meeting at Whitehead tomorrow. I could fly up tomorrow early. I'll take a shuttle tonight and call you when I get there. Other than that, no promises."

Good old Karl, Ryan thought sourly. Again he wondered briefly whether Karl might be the source of their troubles, whether the bad boy might have a double agenda in agreeing to meet. Well. It would be only fair—at this point, good old Ryan had a double agenda, too.

Chapter 49

He ate some lunch substance out of a can, then spent several hours charting what he knew about Jess's processes, consulting with Logan, visiting Leap, reviewing files. But by three o'clock he had to move, to act. Something. Father Connelly still hadn't called back to explain Jess's mysterious calls to him, but waiting around was out of the question. He went down to the Catacombs, nodded to the security men, found Dagan in her office.

"You busy?"

"Do I look at all busy?" She gestured at her desk, which was piled with papers, calendars, pads, clipboards, CD program discs.

He bobbed his head apologetically. "I'm going to take a drive. I was hoping you could come with me. Follow up on one of Jess's conversations." Dagan still looked at him suspiciously, so he went on, "You've, your eye has been really good on these things..."

She gave him a look that said it sounded lame. But she had heard the pleading note in his voice, and after another pause she started shutting down her computer.

———

"So Father Connelly was your priest when you were a kid?" she asked. "Why would Jess go see him? And why do you want me along? Ryan, if you're expecting me to be some kind of religious scholar, forget it. Yes, my parents were religious. But with a Jewish father and an Episcopal mother, the two religious traditions kind of canceled each other out." She was still brittle, her hurt badly concealed.

There had to be some way to approach the issue of their relationship, but he couldn't think what it was. So he just kept driving, saying nothing.

But going to see a priest seemed to have put her in a reflective mood. "I was never sure whether my parents broke up because of their religious and cultural differences, or just sort of exploited those differences. To avoid coping with more personal problems."

"Was that hard—growing up torn between two traditions?"

She shook her head equivocally, *yes and no.* "Funny thing is, I don't think the beliefs themselves got in the way. It's more the cultural habits that went with each tradition. My grandparents on both sides were pretty bigoted. To my father's family, being Jewish is a genetic issue, not a matter of belief. And my mother's family, they liked my father personally but could never forgive him his ancestry." She moved around as if the confinement of the car gave her discomfort. "I suppose the end result for me is that I can't *stomach* that stuff. It's more than ideology—my analyst, if I had one, would say I indirectly blame racism for my parents' separation, the pain and insecurity it created. Whatever."

All the lines of fracture, Ryan thought. He took the car over the Beverly bridge, through the heavier traffic in Salem, then onto 107.

Dagan went on: "I guess that's why I tend to see religion as just this... this weird, accidental amalgam of cultural habit and real spirituality. The connection of ritual and observance to underlying principles is so arbitrary. *'Do this, don't do that,' 'eat this, don't eat that'*—I keep thinking if people, like if my mother and father, if they could focus on the core beliefs and not the cultural habits that happen to accompany them, maybe they'd find how much they have in common. Maybe we wouldn't have so damned much conflict and misery." She faded out, drifted into private thoughts.

They hadn't discussed the emotional wall between them, but still she had opened up a bit. Some little progress, maybe. Dodging Monday-afternoon traffic, Ryan drove across the channel and into the streets of South Boston. It took only moments to reach the church, a weather-darkened edifice that looked sad in the wan November light.

Standing on the rectory steps, waiting for someone to answer the bell, he breathed the South Boston air, tinged here with the humid scent of moist masonry from the church's massive walls. The smell of age and solemnity. It brought back a wave of memory: the uniquely bland taste and dry texture of the little round white host. The mysteriousness of the heavy maroon curtains of the confessional, and inside the smell of Connelly's cigarette-breath, the sense of Connelly's compassionate weariness, there behind the screen. The feelings of being forced to attend mass as a too-smart eleven-year-old: resentment, anxiety, guilt, boredom, a sense of unworthiness. And a rational impatience with the stately, ornate illogic of Catholicism, rolling down the centuries glorious and absurd as an antique circus calliope—

The wooden door rattled and wedged open, and Father Connelly stood there, his head tilted to look at them over half-lens reading glasses. Connelly had seemed old back in 1970, but seeing him now Ryan realized that he'd probably been a young priest, old only to the biased eyes of a child: He was probably only around sixty now, white-haired but still fit-looking.

"You're McCloud," Connelly pronounced.

"You...you *remember* me?"

"Yes—from the television," the priest said dryly. "Also because your wife was here not so long ago. And I assume you're Dagan—Jessamine spoke of you. Come in."

The old man led them down a dark hallway to a kitchen that was cluttered with curios and full of the smell of toast and coffee. The room appeared unchanged from the times Ryan had been here, thirty years before, as he'd brought Connelly muffins his mother had baked or helped him with odd jobs. A small room, long inhabited by the same personality, an oasis of domesticity in the gloomy shadow of the church wall visible through the kitchen's rear window. Another mullioned window opened to the street, where occasional cars slid past.

"I was just having my lunch," the priest said. He began buttering two pieces of toast, meticulously covering every millimeter of bread. "I was joking about remembering you only from TV, Ryan. I have followed your career with interest. You were a...most unusual boy. So what's on your mind today? Loss of confidence in rational humanism? Scientific mechanism wearing a bit thin?"

Connelly was gently teasing him, Ryan saw to his amazement. It had never occurred to him that a priest could have a sense of humor.

"I need help, Father Connelly."

"They always do," Connelly said, feigning resignation. He took a deliberate bite of toast, with teeth too white and perfect to be his own.

"Jess has been kidnapped. We've kept it out of the press, but the FBI is working on it. We're trying to retrace her contacts. Who she saw, and why."

An expression of shock registered on the priest's face, followed quickly by one of sympathy. "Oh you poor boy. Poor, poor boy."

"When did she come to see you?" Dagan asked.

"Hmm." Connelly turned to a calendar tacked to his wall, illustrated with a vivid photo of the Las Vegas strip at night. "Humm," he said again, tracing the days with his finger. Each square was filled with penciled-in notes. "Here we are. Yes. October eighth. Almost a month ago."

"It's urgent that we reconstruct her thoughts, her frame of mind," Ryan said. "Why did she come here? Can you remember anything she told you that might lead us to her or her kidnappers?"

Connelly pointed a thumb at the front window. Outside, a red Dodge revved by, the bone-shaking bass of its sound system penetrating even the heavy masonry of the rectory walls.

"That's the first thing that comes to my mind. She and Dr. Bates thought they were being followed. Dr. Bates was at the window, looking out at the street, while we talked. At one point he said something to Jessamine, like 'Our friends are back.' They seemed more irritated, almost amused, than frightened. They didn't tell me about it, so I didn't ask them."

Dagan caught Ryan's eye as they took a moment to digest this. Followed in Munich in late September, followed in the United States on October 8. Knew somebody was interested, but weren't threatened enough to take security precautions or to get their information to some safe place. It didn't compute.

"What did she come here to talk about?"

The old priest raised his eyes to Ryan's. "She wanted to discuss the Bible, oddly enough. Sorry, my sarcasm is inappropriate. I do apologize, Ryan."

Ryan could easily imagine Jess, hurting, trying to piece together a center line for herself, seeking spiritual counsel. "But she was raised as a Baptist! Why—"

"She said you had spoken well of me," Connelly said. "I was deeply flattered. Apparently you had told her that I was a scholar of history. And that I had been of assistance when your brother...you know. The difficulties."

It was true. Father Connelly had been thought of as a "liberal" priest back then, embracing mass in English and the other reforms sweeping the Church, but he'd never succumbed to bogus fads like drippy folk masses and touchy-feely confessions. He'd stayed accessible to his congregation, yet had preserved the dignity of his position. When Tommy's spine had been crushed, Connelly had spent many attentive hours with all the McClouds, providing something to hang on to when everything was falling apart. Something like hope.

"Given your recommendation," the priest went on, "she thought that perhaps I had something of value to offer." A touch of admonishment for Ryan's lack of confidence in him. "You had apparently told her that I could look at biblical events through a historical and humanistic lens. She asked me about the Tower of Babel story."

"And—?"

"Oh, we talked a bit about archaeological sites, the ziggurats at Etemanka and at Birs Namrud. Fascinating stuff. But what most excited her was that there are so many similar folk histories. That legends of people losing their speech and their ability to cooperate show up all over the world, throughout history."

Dagan looked suddenly riveted. "Really!"

"Oh, most definitely." Father Connelly went on to name dozens of examples: The Gherko Karnes, a tribe from Burma, also had a legend about building a tall pagoda and being punished by God, who confounded their tongues and so dispersed them. The same story—the association of the loss of communication ability with the building of towers—was found also among such far-flung cultures as the Mikirs of Assam, the Toltecs of Mexico, the Tuamotu people of Polynesia. Then there were the Wa-Sania of British East Africa, who told of a famine that was followed by people going mad, jabbering strange words, battling each other, and wandering in all directions. The Raminjerar people of South Australia, who traced their different languages to a funeral that included an act of ceremonial cannibalism, after which the people began speaking unintelligibly, fighting, and finally fleeing each other. The Maidu Indians of California, who told of a feast they held, after which everybody spoke differently and dispersed. One African tribal legend blamed the confusion of tongues on eating a rat, and the Kachna Nagas on the killing and eating of a large snake.

Dagan had listened, spellbound. "This is fabulous! You can see where she went with it, Ry! These stories make perfect sense from a modern epidemiological perspective. Oh my God! It's no coincidence that the disease broke out during building projects or feasts—both concentrated people in one place, living closer together than usual, drinking the same water, eating the same food. Bad hygiene, more sexual encounters. All circumstances that would facilitate catching and transmitting disease! It's our ancient plague, Ry!" The thrill of the mystery had erased her diffidence, the spark had returned.

Connelly nodded. "Exactly. Jessamine told me something I didn't know, that researching oral traditions and folk histories is standard procedure in epidemiological intelligence work. She mentioned something about a breakthrough in that Four Corners epidemic—?"

Dagan enthusiastically gave him the background: In 1993, it was the Navajo oral histories that allowed the Centers for Disease Control to identify the mysterious killer virus. Their elders told the CDC epidemiologists that the illness had struck before, always associated with a high crop of piñon nuts and the resulting increased population of deermice. Which turned out to be the natural reservoir for the virus. Tribal history and legend had it exactly right, gave modern science the one clue it needed to identify and combat the previously unknown hantavirus.

Ryan's mind was racing: The consistency of these Babel-syndrome stories, all over the world and throughout history, and the parallels to known epidemics—animals and food, both common vectors for bacteria and viruses, and unusual concentrations of people—gave credibility to a disease origin. Jess would be putting this together with whatever she could garner of the military behavioral-mod work, which suggested specific factors that could influence the brains and social behaviors of large populations. And she had used RAINDROP to demonstrate that contemporary trends in violent crime and other antisocial behaviors had the same "signature" as epidemics.

It added up to a persuasive case that a disorder of communication and social cooperation had been observed throughout the world, throughout human history.

Abruptly he felt the vertigo of standing at the edge of deep time, the sheer length of human experience on earth, the sheer mystery of such clues scattered among the histories of the planet's people. For one thing, the idea suggested an archaeological angle of research: Could they find evidence of Babel-disease organisms in, for example, ancient Mayan ruins? Was this the answer to the riddle of the fall of the Mayan empire? *New nightmare, ancient plague.*

But then he came back. He shook his head to clear the fatigue away. Connelly had given them useful information, but the important questions remained unanswered: Who had taken her? Where was she?

"Can you think of anything else, Father? Anything at all?"

Connelly pondered for a moment, then shook his head sadly. "You poor, poor boy," he said. "I am so sorry. My prayers are with you and Jessamine."

Ryan stepped to the hall doorway and then paused, anxious to get out of the claustrophobic darkness of the kitchen but suddenly reluctant to leave the odd reassurance of Connelly's presence, feeling he owed the old man something. *Bless me, Father, for I have sinned. It has been 1,563 weeks since my last confession.* "See, she's still upset about her sister getting murdered," he blurted. "She needs explanations so badly. And this research, it...opens up all kinds of conflicts for her. She gets desperate, she gets *empty,* I'm sure you could see that when she came—" Ryan stopped, aware that now it was his own desperation making him babble.

Father Connelly looked startled, his red-rimmed eyes widening. "Desperate? Not at all!"

"What do you mean? She—"

"Ryan, in forty years, I have seen countless crises of belief. This woman was anything but 'empty.' People are only empty when they lose something. I would have described Jessamine as a woman who had very much *found* what was lost."

Ryan had no response, couldn't even think of a question. Connelly's portrayal of Jess's mood didn't make sense. But, yes, it jibed with the image he had seen in Hoague's video—her paradoxical confidence and authority.

The cell phone vibrated in Ryan's pocket, reminding him there was other work to be done. He apologized for the interruption and answered. It was Karl: "Hey. Early flight. I'm at the Park Plaza. Meet me in the hotel restaurant at six? Don't forget the special handshakes and passwords." His tone of voice was hard to read.

Ryan agreed, snapped the phone shut. "Dagan, we really should go. Thank you, Father."

Connelly followed them to the door. Dagan shook the old man's hand and went to the car, giving them a moment together. Standing on the front stoop, the old priest shook a cigarette out of its pack and put it to his lips. He looked up and down the street, squinting at the afternoon light bouncing down from the apartment building across the intersection.

"Let me ask you something, Ryan. Before you go and I don't see you again for thirty more years." Connelly looked at him with eyes turned palest blue and very shrewd in the daylight. "Why do you think Jess is still alive?"

The sudden toughening of his tone caught Ryan by surprise. "I don't have a choice," he answered.

Connelly nodded. He lit his cigarette, dragged, tossed the match, exhaled, looked down the street. "A pretty hard article, your belief she's still alive, is it? Even though you have no evidence at all to support it?"

"Right now it's the only thing that keeps me going."

"There you go, then," Father Connelly said. "Maybe you're beginning to understand."

Chapter 50

He dropped Dagan off at her apartment in Cambridge, then battled rush-hour traffic back through the maze of Boston streets. He arrived in the area of the Park Plaza with half an hour to kill, so he bought a newspaper and walked over to the Common. For a time he paced on the paths that divided the broad lawns, swatting his thigh with the folded paper and trying to work the tension kinks out of his shoulders, then found a bench and sat.

His agenda with Karl had changed since he'd called him from Munich. Realistically, the trap they were setting in the Genesis computers might never be sprung. Leaving the bug as the only connection back to the kidnappers. *Sorry, Burke. But we all gotta do what we gotta do.* So now there was also the shadow agenda, the need to broadcast their recapitulation of Jess's findings. If Karl had played any role in bringing Jess to the attention of the wrong person, he could do it a second time. Bring them back to Genesis.

The newspaper was full of the usual. The situation in Greece and Turkey hung frozen at the brink of war, as the Secretary General of the UN tried desperately to broker a deal whereby Greece would give the vaccine for their bioweapons to Turkey in return for a reduction in Turkish nuclear capacity. One more incident on Cyprus, one more murder of Turks or Greeks abroad, could set the whole thing off.

More news: The brutal oppression of Indonesian dissidents went on, with police opening fire on a demonstration and killing twenty-two, mostly university students who had come out in support of striking bus drivers in Jakarta. In the United States, watchdog groups decried rising infant mortality rates, blaming the cutback in federal relief programs during the 1990s. Lynching of African-Americans was making a comeback in the South, the NAACP claimed. Another school shooting.

And so on and on and on, Ryan thought.

He almost dumped the paper, but then a special section caught his interest. The two-page spread concerned the rising conflict between religious groups in the United States. Tension was growing between traditional denominations and the rash of sects that had sprouted up in the last twenty years. The Justice Department was investigating a wave of bombings reportedly carried out by the Millennial Church against Southern Baptist and Church of Revelation and Redemption churches. Jared Constantine had flown back from Africa to calm his flock, whose members had threatened reprisals. An editorial warned that the United States risked being plunged into the kind of intersectarian warfare that had plagued the Middle East, India, Ireland, and Eastern Europe for so many years. Or, like so much of the Islamic world, a war between religious fundamentalists and the secular government.

Why is it intensifying now? Ryan wondered. *All over the world, fanatical religious fervor and mutual intolerance, suddenly blossoming. What's the trigger?* Jess's insights provided a large part of the answer, at least from a neurological and behavioral perspective. But what was the agent? Could it really be an ancient viral plague, rearing its head, or the bombardment of the brain by electromagnetic fields, as Nina Lafontaine's findings suggested? Then he wondered whether Hoague had found his beloved Nina that night. Poor crazy bastard.

Then he remembered to check his watch. Time to meet Karl.

They took a table that stood well apart from the others, toward the back of the hotel restaurant. It was a modern, chilly place, too much chrome and glass for Ryan's taste, but serviceable for the current purposes.

Karl threw himself into his chair, guzzled a glass of ice water, picked up the oversized menu, and looked at it disdainfully. On reflex, Ryan positioned himself so that he could observe the room, gauge the proximity of other diners or the waiters. Not too many customers yet, he was glad to see. This had to stay private.

"Listen, Karl, I need to get to business here. I'm running against the clock."

"The swordfish special looks good tonight, what do you think?" Karl pretended to be engrossed in the menu. "Or maybe the veal."

So Karl was going to play his fucking games even at a time like this. Abruptly Ryan had had it with him, and without thinking he backhanded the menu out of Karl's hands. It sailed to the floor, and for an instant Karl's face looked startled, exposed.

And then the sardonic mask dropped in place again. "Take a *pill*, dickhead! So you need something off of me. So now I'm supposed to come at your beck and call, do your royal bidding? And if I don't, what, you're gonna take me outside and duke it out with me? I don't think so, Ry. Act nice or I'll—"

"What's it *take,* Karl? How bad does it have to get before you can act like a human being? What do you live for, anyway? Seriously, what gets you out of bed every morning—just the opportunity to play the dirty nerdie and conceal your insecurities by fucking with people's heads one more time? My wife's in danger. Screw what *I* need, she's your friend, too, you little prick!"

Karl's face reddened, but before he could retort a waiter cleared his throat nearby. They both looked up, startled, tried to get themselves under control. Karl curtly ordered a piña colada, Ryan a diet cola. When the waiter left, they stared at each other, unsettled, wary.

"You know, you really look like shit," Karl said after a moment. He looked suddenly tireder, as if their fight had actually pierced him. "Or rather, you look like shit, but you also look focused. The look of burning purpose. So I guess it's true what Kafka said, huh? That which doesn't kill you makes you stronger?"

"Nietzsche. Nietzsche said it."

"Whatever." Karl waved the question away.

Ryan leaned across the table, lowered his voice. "Listen, Karl, I don't trust you. But right now I have no choice but to presume twenty years of friendship means something to you. You want to hear me out or not?"

Karl's eyes were flat, weary, and yet some part of him still seemed to be enjoying this. Enjoying the cloak-and-dagger dimensions of it, or Ryan's role as supplicant? Hard to tell. He tossed his head minutely, which Ryan took as an equivocal consent.

"Jess was taken because she learned things that someone wanted to know, or wanted to prevent others from knowing. She did something to catch the attention of the big gorillas you warned me about. Whoever took her didn't get all her notes, and we've rebuilt her files." That last was an exaggeration, but there it was, the hook that might catch the big bad fish. "So I have two favors to ask of you."

Karl bobbed his head, up and down and side to side: *Okay, maybe, spill it.*

"One is I need you to use whatever connections you have with whatever spook organizations you're affiliated with. Have you ever heard of a guy named Shipley? NSA black-acquisitions guy?"

"Nope. Name doesn't ring a bell."

"I need you to find out about him. I need to know if the NSA or any other agency was involved in this, if our scouting around the edges of behavioral-mod research made them feel threatened. Would any of your connections know about an operation like the raid on our place? Is that something you can find out for me?"

The waiter came with their drinks, and Karl thought about it, opening and folding the little paper umbrella, his scowl fading. At last he cleared his throat. "Back at Harvard, the CIA recruited openly, remember? Little tables in the corridors on career day, information meetings in the class-rooms? You weren't the only one solicited by the NSA and DIA, and you weren't the only one strapped for cash, Ry. So while you started your Geniuses Incorporated, or whatever you called it then, I took a different route to provide myself with some income." Karl stared at the pathetic yellow parasol, his face looking lopsided, a little nostalgic.

"So?"

"So, a deepening relationship, facilitating certain types of projects. Consulting, poking my nose into promising research. Never anything directly related to weapons programs, just the pure science, the founda-tion stuff. I knew it could have ugly applications in the wrong hands. I also thought it could have positive applications in the right hands, see? Only the right hands weren't providing the funding. So the sneaky boys got first dibs on the information."

Karl's confession had the ring of truth, Ryan thought. He had to fight a sense of dismay: that Karl's connections would be insufficient, useless.

"But," Karl went on, "I was in, one foot anyway, and I was useful. And it helped me—for example, I had a little outside help getting appointed to the Surgeon General's genetics panel. Fine. So now I consult on genetic engineering issues. Pure science. A lot of the 'defense-related' end of it I hear about is for crop manipulation—like genetically tailoring bac-terial pests that'll wipe out the Chinese rice crop, or Colombian coca. But for all I know, someday they'll put cheetah genes in human fetuses and raise them to serve as assault troops. The Agency's structure is com-partmentalized. I don't formally know what I don't need to know."

"Formally."

Karl lifted his beaded glass, chugged the piña colada like a beer. "Yah. In some ways it's not so different from any other organizational culture. Chance contacts, interdepartmental networking, personnel leaving one agency for another. Conferences where people get drunk, tell war stories, maybe exchange informal favors later. Twenty years down the road, I've done some favors, I'm owed some." He licked his lips, grimaced, craned his neck to look for the waiter.

When he'd signaled for another drink, Karl turned back and lowered his head. He whispered: "I'll ask around about your guy Shipley. I'll try to see if there's been an operation that sounds like the break-in. Best I can do. So will I at last win the unqualified respect of the great Ryan McCloud?"

This level of candor was unprecedented. Ryan wondered whether he had tipped a few in his room before coming down. For years, Jess had pointed out how much Karl admired Ryan, but he hadn't particularly seen it. But if Karl had been feeling unrequited admiration, yes, that would explain a lot. Envy—yes, it must have seemed back then that Ryan had everything: true love, lucky breakthroughs, fame, rich in-laws, even muscles. While Karl had made dubious loyalties and shady dealings his social stock-in-trade, and never gotten much mileage out of it.

"What else, Ry? You said *two* favors. What's the second?"

This was the one that would require real work on Karl's part—and real risks.

"Our house and offices were bugged," Ryan told him. "The FBI knows where the bugs came from, but won't tell me. Apparently the high-tech shop that produced them is a family secret, a resource for other cases they've deemed too valuable to risk by direct action. They learn a lot by watching it. The FBI isn't the only outfit who knows where it is."

"Oh Christ," Karl moaned. "Oh man."

"Yeah, I want you to find out where it is. Just tell me, Karl. I'll do the rest."

"What you're talking about isn't my bailiwick." Karl had begun to sweat, and he wiped his forehead with his napkin. "It'll be *noticed,* Ry! Me asking these questions, exposing assets. Especially if shortly thereafter you barge in on the shop I was just inquiring about—this could upset my apple cart big time. You're asking me to put twenty years' work at risk!"

"Yeah."

"Oh, motherfuck, why'd I even—Fuck me, you know? Fuck me up the ass!" Muttering to himself: "Fucking ingratiating myself to you—when do I get over this juvenile *shit?*"

"You get over it when you forget about that crap and think of it as helping a friend in his hour of need. The one and *only* time I've ever asked you for anything."

Karl was calculating, inventorying either his available responses or his resources, *tick-tick-tick*. Looking dubious.

At last Ryan couldn't stand the indecision. He whispered urgently, "You want something to even us up, Karl? Would that help? Okay, I'll give it to you. *Without Jess, I'm nothing!* Anything happens to her, I'll blow my fucking head off. I mean it. My life isn't worth *shit.*"

Karl snorted a humorless laugh. "Great! So now, on top of everything else, the life of the great Ryan McCloud rests in my hands? What do I get in return, Ry? A nice warm feeling?"

"How about *redemption,* you prick?"

Karl rolled his eyes. "Oh man," he said. He shook his head, incredulous at himself, laughing through a face that looked as if it wanted to cry. "Fuck me, you know? Huh? Just fuck me up the goddamned butt!"

This time, in the way he said it, Ryan could hear his assent.

Chapter 51

That night, alone in the house, Ryan labored to focus. Though details were missing, the arc of Jess's thoughts had taken full form. What he saw was breathtaking, and yet he could derive no pleasure from it. Because none of it brought him any closer to finding her.

It was now after midnight, November 5, and eleven days had passed since Jess was taken. She was due in six days, but realistically could give birth at any time. Bates had died during interrogation almost four days ago. What were the odds Jess was still alive?

Not good, he knew. But not quite zero, either. So you kept on.

Things had been set in motion. The Maywoods were leaving soon on their impromptu vacation, getting away to someplace where Abi would be safe. Presumably, Karl was at this very moment beginning to pursue the bug-shop, maybe getting some dope on Shipley. The first trial data exchanges with Ridder Global would start tomorrow, hopefully offering additional temptation for someone to hack them. Leap had finished building his homing pigeon and even now was down in the Catacombs with Wesley and Logan, installing the program, cocking the springs of the trap. Tomorrow they'd begin beating the gongs and waving the banners that said, *We've got it. Come and get it.*

That Jess had been followed in Germany as early as September 25, and that she'd been shadowed in the United States as well, and that she'd *known* about it, were details that had to be significant. Why hadn't she alerted everybody? Her inaction was a big hole in the doughnut, but what it implied he couldn't begin to guess.

Another hole, a detail that was surely trivial and yet wouldn't quit nagging at him: Jess's walking out of Weismann's lecture without talking to him, missing their lunch date. If he accepted that finding Jess required him, first and foremost, to understand *who is Jess McCloud,* this detail had to stand out: It was a discourtesy that was absolutely unlike Jess. *Why, Jessie?*

Another problem was that in his current mood everyone seemed suspect. Shipley was an obvious target for suspicion, but how about Karl?

How truthful was he, really, how much was bogus? Maybe Karl was more than he claimed, more devious and self-interested. Pathologically envious enough to hurt Jess, and, through her, Ryan. So maybe, back in May, Karl had told his superiors about Genesis's interest in military behavioral modification research. Or maybe one of the death-row test subjects had been an MKULTRA guinea pig. Or maybe Leap had done some hacking that he wasn't telling anyone about, and had drawn down somebody's ire. Whatever, a crack research team, idealistic as hell, going after their secrets, had to be seen as a security risk. They'd started following Genesis's progress back then, and when Jess had come too close—

And Burke: Was there more to his refusal to reveal the source of the bug? Was he using his sad, sincere face to protect some other knowledge—the fact that the whole thing was an intelligence community operation? Burke, a career domestic intelligence operative, given charge of this investigation not so that he could find Jess but so that he could wrap up loose ends, make sure forensic lab reports led nowhere, obstruct Ryan's inquiries—all in the interest of "national security." How far would a guy like that take it? How many murders?

And then a still more hideous thought came to him: Dagan. She admitted she'd been in love with him for years. Maybe it was more of an obsession, perpetually frustrated, growing until she decided she'd have to get Jess out of the way. Dagan had inherited a good chunk of family money, enough to commission a job like this if she really wanted to. The theft of the files could be a smoke screen; Bates's presence at the offices that night was an unforeseen inconvenience that regrettably had to be accommodated. And Jess had hardly been gone a week before Dagan had tried to get Ryan into bed!

No, no, part of him rebelled, *not Dagan, beautiful good Dagan, that near-seduction came from fear and shock, she loves Jess, she's our good friend, our, our—what?* Something more than a friend. An ambiguous relationship that she admitted tore at her. That night on the street in Geneva, when he'd been on top of the watcher, only to find himself suddenly flopping around on the pavement, knocked out by a blow he'd never seen coming: Maybe Dagan had hit him from behind. Maybe she'd staged the man's escape and her shooting to eliminate Ryan's suspicions, had feigned her shock and fear because it would propel Ryan and her toward each other—

Ryan pulled his hair, hoping the pain would stem the rush of thoughts. This was intolerable. Abruptly another thought came to him, and he found a sick fear sweat sticky on his palms, under his shirt. *The disease,* he thought wildly, *the Babel disease. Finally catching up after a life-time of exposure. Or maybe something in Kalesi.* He'd been seeing its symp-toms more and more in himself: the urge to violence, the pleasure of inflicting pain on that bastard on the street in front of Hoague's place. The distrust of everyone, the paranoia. All could be early warning signs. Indications of damage to certain modules in the brain, resulting in the subtle erosion of the sense of kinship with others, the loss of recognition of consciousness of others. *Can't see myself in others. Can't recognize Dagan as "like me."* The memory came back to him of Dagan and Mar-shall, walking ahead of him on the beach: Just a little shift in his percep-tive filter, and they had become two strangers, unfamiliar silhouettes on the shore.

He bolted up, groped in the liquor cabinet, found a half-gallon of something cheap, spun off the top. He took a snort out of the bottle, got it down the wrong pipe, coughed up a spray of battery-acid bourbon. Choking and swearing, he went to the deck doors, slid them open, and pitched the bottle out over the roof of the Catacombs below. It crashed on the shore rocks just as the motion-sensor lights came on, and immedi-ately one of the security men was there, crouched at the railing with gun leveled.

"It's me!" Ryan shouted. He froze, then turned so that the guard could see his face in the lights. He said again: "It's just me."

Just me. So true, so lonesome. And he thought, *This is the worst.* The guard relaxed slightly and lowered his gun. Ryan stepped back inside, thinking, *Please let this be the worst, let this be as bad as it gets.*

———

He awoke hunched on the couch, neck aching. Two hours had passed. The night was quiet, the shore dead still. He had fallen asleep with the contents of his briefcase spread around him: yellow pads, pocket recorder, calendar, CD player. And the disc of Weismann's lecture.

The tiniest movement, an itch, quivered in his subconscious. Without thinking about it, he put on the headphones and reviewed the last half of the lecture. Weismann's voice talking about cannibalism among lions. The echoing, shifting ambience of the lecture hall. The faintly heard students' questions, the laughter. Now he let the recording play on, as Weismann talked about the importance of evolutionary perspectives in human psychology.

And then, as Weismann paused, he heard it, very faint but audible.

His heart jolting in his chest, he leaped up and brought the disc to the stereo cabinet, put it in, forwarded to the same spot. He cranked the volume up until Weismann's words sounded like the thunderous pronouncements of some amiable New Jersey god, shaking the glassware in the kitchen. The lecture hall's ambient noise became cavernous. And in it he heard the faint sound of a cricket wheedling, *Brrrt-brrrt. Brrrt-brrrt.*

There was no mistaking it: the ringing of Jess's cell phone. The most discreet of the fifty optional tones of her old Nokia 6160, that they'd never gotten around to buying a vibrating battery for.

He checked the time reading on the CD player, calculating, then slapped off the stereo. *October 1, 11:29 A.M.* Washington, D.C. She wouldn't have talked in the lecture hall and distracted Weismann's students. She'd have cut the ringer and exited quickly. Or answered briefly, hung up, and left the hall to make an immediate call-back.

He fumbled for the kitchen telephone and dialed Leap's home number. It was three in the morning, but there was work to be done. Anyway, Leap would like this one.

Chapter **52**

He awoke Tuesday from three hours of sleep, refreshed enough to feel both excited and pissed off. Excited because today they would set the trap, call Marshall, and send some data to Brandt, pissed off because of what Leap had told him when he'd called back just before dawn.

It had turned out as Ryan hoped. Though the kidnappers had sabotaged the local UniOne cellular relay station, destroying records of Jess's Boston-area cell calls, they weren't so exhaustively thorough that they'd traveled to every city she'd visited and done the same. Which meant that although the overall billing records were gone, the calling information for October still existed in the databanks of the UniOne relays in the Washington, D.C., area. No doubt UniOne would provide the information voluntarily, but that would take time. So Leap had paid their computers a pre-dawn visit. What he found was that, yes, Jess's cellular number had received a call at 11:31 A.M., October 1. Call records didn't reveal the caller's number, only the time and duration of the call—one minute.

But Jess's outgoing call record did contain a number that she dialed at 11:33. The timing fit the scenario of her receiving a call in the lecture hall and leaving the room to return it immediately. She had dialed from the D.C. 202 area code to the 703 area code of northern Virginia, just across the Potomac River.

Ryan recognized the number immediately. Alex Shipley's number, at the NSA's DIRI division offices.

It was a four-minute call, long enough to suggest that she had indeed spoken with the Gray Ghost, short enough to tell him that they hadn't discussed anything at length. Almost certainly, just about the time required to arrange a meeting.

Unless he heard otherwise from Karl, *if* he heard from Karl, the fact that Shipley had met with Jess didn't prove anything. All he could think of, for now, was to meet with Shipley, ask him what Jess had contacted him about, and check out his responses. Apply some persuasion if he didn't seem forthcoming. He dialed the spook's number, left a message asking for a call back.

Then he did his best to put it aside. He talked with Logan and Leap, put the finishing touches on the first batch of files they'd launch later. At noon he called Marshall to confirm that they'd made big breakthroughs, recapitulating Jess's work and even advancing it. Speaking obliquely, he said it was not something he wanted to discuss over the phone, but he'd send some details over the wire. Convincingly encrypted but ultimately decipherable.

The material they sent was real data, a summary of some tests on the effect of endocrine disruptors on human neural metabolism, and another on electromagnetic field damage to the brains of monkeys, a hundred pages of dense scientific test results. It felt feeble, a message in a bottle tossed out into the cyberspace sea.

Karl, Karl, Karl, Ryan thought.

Thinking of Karl brought him around to another problem. Suppose Karl *did* come up with information suggesting the involvement of the NSA, or some other government agency? He drew a blank on what to do. Words from Jared Constantine's TV harangue came back to him: *Who're you gonna call when you're out there alone on the highway to hell?* When the Babel effect started breaking things up, trust of central authority was one of the first things to go.

Ultimately, he realized, *there is no recourse but your own action. Drunken Buddha. Your purpose is your only through-line.*

Or what if Karl did find a location for the illicit technology manufacturer? What was he going to do, walk in and beat up on whoever he found there until they gave him the information he wanted? The place would be guarded, have security systems, its records would be hidden and encrypted. He didn't know anything about how the criminal underworld worked. He was a scientist, not a spy, not a hit man.

But, it occurred to him, *I have* access *to a spy, a hit man.* Ridder had offered to lend him the lizard's specialized talents. Just the thought of working with Darion Gable gave him the chills, but...*Desperate times, desperate measures.*

He called Ridder's office, left a message requesting a return call. And that left precious little to do. Waiting for Shipley, for Karl, for Ridder, for hacks. He'd never been any good at waiting. For lack of anything better to do, he went up to the house, and on to the office. For the thousandth time he pondered the little collection of clues he'd pinned on the bulletin board. The doughnut one still gave him the itch, the tickle, and yet he couldn't figure out why.

He was still beating his head against that wall when the office phone rang.

"Call for you," Wesley said. "Some guy named Shipley?"

———————

How convenient that the Gray Ghost is in the Boston area again, Ryan mused suspiciously. He nosed the Subaru into a parking place, locked the car, and began walking back toward Harvard Square. Again, Shipley had chosen a very public spot for their rendezvous.

Wearing a dark-gray mackintosh over his gray bureaucratic suit, his fluorescent-bleached skin showing through thinning hair, Shipley looked out of place among the colorfully dressed students flocking to stores and restaurants. Again he carried a prop, this time a bright blue, string-handled shopping bag that he apparently thought helped him blend in. *Whatever Shipley is or isn't,* it occurred to Ryan, *his, what do they call it,* tradecraft, *isn't exactly impressive.*

Ryan gestured with his chin, and without saying anything Shipley fell in beside him as he continued walking.

"Jason told me about Jessamine," Shipley said after a time. "I'm very sorry."

"She met with you. October first, in Washington. I want to know what you discussed."

Shipley walked on, his face without expression. After a few moments he said, "We covered several topics, actually. She's a remarkable woman."

"Don't tell *me* what a remarkable woman she is!" Ryan snarled. A passing pair of young women looked at him oddly, and he brought his face and voice under control again.

"We discussed national security and patriotism and America's challenges in the twenty-first century. Among other things, how important it is for us to transcend our individual agendas in the interest of the common good."

"Meaning you told her to stay away from your nonlethal weapons programs, your behavioral-modification research projects. In the interest of the common good."

"Well, the subject did come up, yes. Suffice to say, she had her own ideas of what the 'common good' was." Shipley's mouth made a benign smile, as if amused at such human foibles. His eyes kept their dead quality.

Ryan turned onto Cambridge Avenue, where the pedestrian traffic thinned. After five years at Harvard, this was very familiar turf.

"Who took her, Shipley? You guys?" Ryan watched him carefully.

Shipley just shook his head and answered in a flat voice: "You give me too much credit, Ryan. I'm not 007. All I do is oversee contracts. I help coordinate general directions of research and I see that contractors fulfill the terms of their agreements. Yes, occasionally I deal with security-related issues. But it's hardly dramatic, Ryan, someone like yourself would find it very humdrum, very institutional." Shipley's voice hardened. "But I have to wonder why you are so suspicious of your own government. Your approach suggests that perhaps your government should reciprocate that suspicion. True?"

The hell with this, Ryan was thinking. This wasn't getting anywhere. Probably Shipley was what he said, a glorified clerk, a little cog in a big machine that ground along according to its charge, creating technologies intended to kill or harm or control people. The worst of nightmares inflicted on human beings had their origins in the blind, bland devotion of functionaries just like Shipley, or Adolph Eichmann. *Just doing my job.* One more dimension of man's evil, one more for the catalog.

"How do you justify what you do? How the hell do you sleep at night?"

The hard thing surfaced in Shipley's eyes. "I don't need to 'justify' anything! In case you hadn't noticed, it's not a nice world out there. We as a nation need these tools for our survival. And let me remind you, many technologies that begin as defense initiatives have been adapted to help and heal and serve. Your beloved cranial imaging machines, for example. The Internet, for another. So don't lecture *me!*"

They walked another block. Ryan steered their course onto a side street, and now to one of the meandering public alleys. For a couple of years he and Jess had lived nearby, and had explored the area while walking or jogging, finding shortcuts to campus, or looking for dark places to neck after late-night drinks. If memory served, this one dead-ended at the brick wall of a warehouse. And there were those stairwells descending to basements, well out of view of windows or the street. A good place to have a more focused talk.

Shipley took a few steps into the alley and then hesitated, seeing the dead end.

Ryan took his elbow and propelled him forward. "I really would like to know exactly what you talked about," Ryan said. "And if you know anything about my wife's abduction."

"This isn't the way—" Shipley began.

"It connects through," Ryan lied. "We can head back to Harvard Square." He put pressure on Shipley's arm, steering him around a Dumpster that partially blocked the way. "Now's the time for specifics, Shipley."

"Are you trying to threaten me?" Shipley's efforts to break free were feeble. His arm was bony, a paper-pusher's arm.

At the warehouse wall, the alley made a short jog to the left and ended at another wall and a pair of Dumpsters surrounded by stacks of crushed cardboard boxes. A stairwell descended from street level, and Ryan manhandled Shipley quickly down the stairs and against the steel-sheathed basement door. Shipley's shopping bag snagged on the railing and tore open, spilling some paperbacks and CDs onto the concrete.

"You're cutting your own throat," Shipley panted. "You can't do this!"

Ryan twisted Shipley's arm up behind his back, forcing the joint. "Who initiated your meeting? You or Jess?"

"Ow! For the—I did. I called her, asked for a rendezvous."

"So you could talk about what?"

"Let go and I'll tell you."

Ryan increased the pressure, restraining the urge to drive a knee into the Gray Ghost's backside. Shipley was bent forward now, his head against the concrete side wall of the stairwell. "Talk about what?"

"For God's sake—! She—I told her I knew about the test she ran at Sandia. I wanted to know what she had in mind."

"So she ran antisocial behaviors data on RAINDROP as a hypothetical outbreak. Which interested you because—?"

Shipley flopped and convulsed briefly, then gave up again. He was breathing hard, but from the side of his red face Ryan could see he was more furious than scared. "You're committing suicide here, McCloud!"

"You didn't like RAINDROP being used to plot behavioral symptoms. Why? Because you've got a technology that causes them? Because there've been accidents, and RAINDROP could reveal the epicenter and expose you? Because—what?"

"Because I wanted to know what she found, goddamn it! I thought *maybe* you guys had enough loyalty to your *country* to cooperate with—"

"Skip the political philosophy. What did she tell you?"

"The symptoms modeled as an epidemic," Shipley rasped. "She said she wanted my help. Said I could be a savior. If I'd help get her access to secret test data, military behavioral mod data, that she could put together with what she was finding, maybe make a cure."

"And you said—?"

"Let me up, goddamn it, this is intolerable!"

"And you said—?"

Shipley stiffened again and said nothing. This was taking too long, every minute increased the chance that someone would see them struggling here, intervene. Ryan brought his weight to bear, ground the blotchy gray-red face into the concrete. Surprising himself, he bent to whisper in Shipley's ear. "I'll kill you, right here. Beat your brains out on this wall. Give myself a few bruises and scrapes and toss both our wallets in a storm drain. Then run tell the police we were mugged. And you'll be dead, and I wouldn't mind that at all."

Shipley grunted, and at last the side of his face looked more scared than enraged. "I said I was worried that RAINDROP could be used to figure optimum dispersion patterns. I've *told* you this before! That your violence studies could be turned around, used to help create weapons technologies! That you people were vulnerable to terrorist action."

Ryan relaxed the pressure as Shipley talked, a little positive conditioning. "So to shut her up, you arranged the break-in and abduction—"

"Are you fucking *crazy?* You think we'd *bother,* take the risk of exposure an operation like that would entail, when we're going to get the information anyway?"

"From Ridder."

"From whoever, however. Who do you think you're working for, anyway? It goes the other way, too, you son of a bitch! Every nice idealistic scientific advance can and will be used for weapons and for all the things you hate, and there's nothing you can do about it. You and your wife have undoubtedly made many such contributions already. All I've ever done is try to make sure the good guys get it first. So go fuck yourself."

Ryan couldn't help feeling the Gray Ghost was being truthful—too much heat there, too much pressure, so out of character. Ryan let him go, went to the stairs, and sat.

Still cornered, Shipley straightened awkwardly, panting, holding his right arm tenderly with the other hand.

"You ducked my question. Did you tell Jess anything about the technologies? The agents? The neurological loci? You going to tell me, or do I have to break your head after all?"

Shipley was already getting cocky again. "I'm going to tell you *squat.* You know why? Because *I don't know.* We're compartmentalized. Not one of my project areas, and I don't need to know the details. Maybe weaponized, reengineered rabies virus? How about pulsed microwaves?

Take a guess, you're the goddamned genius!" When Ryan didn't come back at him, Shipley got bolder. "Go ahead, rip my arm off, you son of a bitch. Can't tell you what I don't know!" He offered his arm, revealing a flair for drama after all.

Ryan sat back against the concrete steps, aware of the cold, feeling suddenly dog-tired, emptied. Feeling sad. His instincts said Shipley was more or less telling the truth. In which case he didn't know anything that would help find Jess. He studied the spook, who composed himself by degrees, smoothing his hair, buckling his mac.

"So you ended with—"

"I told her to be careful. To institute strict security measures. To keep in contact with me. And she said not to worry, your company had installed new security systems and so on. That Ridder's people were keeping a very good eye out for your security, Ridder was just as paranoid as I was. As for RAINDROP, it was already too late, in the public domain, anyone with access to the right computers could repeat the test she'd made. Also that going after the military stuff wasn't the main focus of her research. 'At least not yet,' she said." Shipley's eyes flared, suggesting Jess's attitude had not endeared her to him.

Another question occurred to Ryan, one that he realized was very important. "Jess was being followed. Was that you guys?"

Shipley looked genuinely surprised. "Followed? Hell with you. As I said, why follow her when we're going to get the information anyway?" When Ryan roused himself threateningly, still skeptical, Shipley hissed, "You think we're *happy* somebody took your wife, with what she knows?"

"Did she mention to you that she was being followed?"

"No."

Ryan sighed, feeling despondent. He wasn't getting anything from this. It didn't look like Shipley's people were involved. "If you're so worried about who took her, why don't you help find her?"

"By 'you,' I presume you mean the United States government. Well, 'our' investigative branch *is* working to find her. It's called the FBI. And now I've about had enough of this. Either let me out of here, or get on with it—break my arms, kill me, whatever."

Yes, Ryan thought, *time to get back to work.* He stood and allowed Shipley up the stairs. The Gray Ghost stooped to recover his books and CDs, which he stuffed into his coat pockets.

They began walking back toward Harvard Square. Shipley's mouth clamped in a tight line. Ryan wondered just how badly the spook would try to fuck him over for roughing him up. Not anything overt, like bringing an assault charge: Shipley's professional instincts called for low profile, avoiding a fuss. Besides, Ryan would just deny it, and Shipley would have to reveal too much to claim the famous Ryan McCloud had a motive. No, it would be something subtler.

Part of him didn't care what the Gray Ghost did. As long as it didn't happen right away, didn't get in the way of finding Jess. At this stage there were too many other things to worry about. He thought wearily, *You want to fuck me over? Get in line.*

Chapter 53

Back at the Genesis offices, Ryan immediately checked with Leap. No sign of intrusion yet on their computers. No surprise there—it was only four-thirty, they'd sent out the first trick messages only four hours ago. But Wesley said Ridder's secretary had telephoned with instructions to call back this afternoon. He called immediately and was put through to Ridder.

"Ryan, I'm in a meeting," Ridder said gruffly. "I got exactly one minute."

"Do you have time to meet me later? At your office?"

"About?"

Ryan debated how much to say over an unprotected line. "An update on the status of our research. Also, I'd like to take you up on an offer you made earlier."

"Huh," Ridder grunted. Ryan could hear the gears shift in the billionaire's head as he adjusted to the idea of Ryan making use of Gable's services. The implications, the percentages. "Yeah," he said finally, "you're right, we need a face-to-face on this one. Okay. But it's impossible today or tomorrow. Have to be Thursday. Eight o'clock?" Anticipating Ryan's disappointment: "Sorry—best I can do. *Ciao.*"

"There's also this," Wesley said. He scratched his head, perplexed, as he handed Ryan a single sheet of paper. "Fax, came in, oh, an hour ago. I figured you'd know what to make of it."

Ryan took the sheet and scanned it quickly. Aside from the sender information at the very top of the sheet, the page held only a block of digits:

```
01000001 01010100    01000001 01010100    01000111 01000011    01000011 01000111
01010100 01000001    01000011 01000111    01010100 01000111    01000001 01010100
01000111 01000011    01000111 01000011    01010100 01000001    01000001 01010100
01000111 01000011    01000001 01010100    01000111 01000111    01000011 01010100
01000111 01000111    01000111 01000001    01010100 01000001    01010100 01000001
01000001 01000100    01000001 01010100    01000111 01000011    01000001 01000111
01000001 01000100    01000011 01000111    01000011 01000111    01010100 01000001
01000011 01000001    01000011 01000111    01010100 01000001    01000111 01000011
```

```
01010100 01000001    01000001 01010100    01000111 01000011    01000111 01000011
01000011 01000111    01010100 01000111    01000001 01010100    01000001 01010100
01000111 01000011    01000111 01000011    01010100 01000001    01000011 01000111
01000001 01010100    01000111 01000011    01000011 01000111    01010100 01000001
01010100 01000001    01000011 01000111    01000111 01000011    01000001 01010100
01000011 01010100    01000001 01010100    01000001 01010100    01000111 01000011
01000111 01000011    01010100 01000001    01000011 01000111    01010100 01000001
01000001 01010100    01000111 01000011    01000111 01000011    01000001 01010100
```

```
01000111 01000011    01000111 01000011    01000011 01000111    01010100 01000001
01000001 01010100    01000011 01000111    01010100 01000001    01010100 01000111
01000001 01010100    01000111 01000011    01000111 01000011    01010100 01000001
01000011 01010100    01010100 01000001    01000001 01010100    01000011 01000111
01000111 01000011    01000011 01000111    01000011 01000111    01000001 01010100
01000100 01000001    01000001 01010100    01000001 01010100    01000011 01000111
01000001 01010100    01000011 01000111    01000011 01000111    01000111 01000001
01000011 01000111    01000100 01000001    01010100 01000011    01000011 01000111
```

The fax was unsigned and came with a Mail Boxes Etc. address in New York. It took a moment of puzzling, but Ryan saw that the binary numbers became the digits 65, 84, 71, and 67. He quickly placed why their spacing seemed familiar: These were the ASCII numbers for the letters A, T, G, and C—which were the phosphate bonds that formed the nucleotides in DNA.

Genes. A message from Karl.

That each row consistently had only four pairs meant that this was not a real genetic message, its meaning somehow hidden in the implications of the genes themselves. Ryan scanned the digits quickly and immediately spotted the anomaly: There were errors in many of the lines. Adenine bonded only with thymine, guanine with cytosine. In the second row he saw a thymine-guanine bond, in the fourth a cytosine-thymine, combinations that could not occur in nature. Karl had encoded his message in a very simple way, but one that even a decent cryptographer would have a hard time deciphering unless he was enough of a generalist to know his organic chemistry, too. Hard to tell if Karl really felt such elaborate encryption was necessary, or whether it was just another way of rattling Ryan's chain.

Ryan scanned the larger body of digits, and more chemical errors began jumping out at him. Within seconds the pattern became clear: Karl had created a secondary binary code with the errors. After trying several possibilities, he found the solution. The first block had no errors in lines one, three, six, and seven, errors in lines two, four, five, and eight. That gave him 01011001: the letter *Y*. Following that system, he got an *E* in the second block, an *S* in the third.

YES, Karl had written. Meaning, Ryan assumed, *Yes, I'll do it*. Which further meant, he had to believe, *Yes, I CAN do it. Yes, I have the resources to locate the bug-shop.*

Good old Karl.

Chapter 54

Wednesday. Jess's synthesis hung in his mind like a cathedral, a construction of loft and elegance, luminous, beautiful. The long arcs, the convergences. But Ryan couldn't bear to look closely at it, not with the time ticking away and Jess gone and the sense of foreboding growing.

The first order of business was the daily download to Brandt Institute—credible scientific documents that implied rapid progress toward identifying the Babel agent. Second, they made calls to neuroscientists, psychologists, psychogeneticists, people the surviving phone bills showed Jess had spoken to. When Ryan called, he found himself talking in the slightly stilted way that came with knowing someone might be eavesdropping. *Hoping* someone was listening. Anyone observing the pattern of contacts, the transmissions, the cars in the parking lot and lights in the windows until all hours, would surely conclude Genesis was on to something.

When Wednesday afternoon came and there was still no word from Karl, still no call from Leap's homing pigeon, they began another phase: Mannie Skovanik. Ryan tasked Logan and Dagan to find everything available about the Skovanik murder, the criminal and civil trials, and GME, the power company whose security agent had been convicted of her murder. Scanning the printouts, he could see that Mannie Skovanik did not appear to be any kind of crackpot. A sound education in electrical engineering, toxicology, and workplace health issues. Married, two kids. Aside from her crusade to shed light on the mental-health risks associated with electromagnetic fields, she appeared to have lived a very normal life. During the criminal trial, the security operative's lawyers had tried to paint her as someone with psychological problems and shady associations that had gotten her killed. Neither judge nor jury had bought it, and Ryan didn't, either. It looked just as Hoague said: a good person, killed for knowing too much and for trying to let others know.

He made calls to Mannie Skovanik's husband and parents, who declined to talk with him. *Scarred,* he concluded, *and scared.* And with good reason. Had Jess contacted them, he asked. I'm sorry, Dr. McCloud, we don't discuss these things. We hear from every paranoid crackpot, every conspiracy buff. We don't know where Mannie put her safety files. We are trying to heal, to live normal lives. Don't call again.

So he instructed Logan and Dagan to cast a wider net, sift through the Web for data related to health effects of electromagnetic fields, radio, radar, magnetism. The printers began churning out reams of paper.

When night fell, he left all the exterior lights on: for security, and for the theater of industry that would impress a watcher. At 1:30 A.M., Dagan and Logan both stumped into the house. They nodded to Ryan, dumped a new stack of papers onto the pile of printouts he was reviewing. Logan called her husband and then trudged upstairs to the guest bedroom, too beat to say good night. Dagan put some water on to boil for chamomile tea and sat down numbly in the living room. When the kettle began to whistle and she didn't get up, Ryan looked over to find her sprawled unconscious on the couch. He shut off the gas, found a blanket, and spread it over her. Framed in the spill of dark hair, Dagan's face seemed pale, lost in a sleep so deep it seemed otherworldly. He turned out the lamp, repressed the urge to stroke her cheek, and went quietly upstairs. Through the open door to the guest bedroom, he could see that Logan had fallen asleep with her clothes on, the bedspread pulled haphazardly over her. He tucked her in gently, too, and then shut her door and went to the big bedroom.

He sat on the edge of the empty bed, toppled backwards, fell asleep with his shoes on and both feet still on the floor.

On Thursday the weather warmed suddenly as the remains of a tropical storm staggered north along the coast. When Ryan came out on the deck, tendrils of pink cloud grappled the dawn sky, but the system had lost all its moisture. Instead, a day of Indian summer, warm enough to work outside. At seven o'clock he situated himself at one of the deck tables with the coffeepot and extra cups for the overnighters. He continued reviewing the materials on EMFs. Peter and Dolores had culled out the most outrageous and had double-checked every report, footnoting each with references to supporting data. The resulting stack of reliable documents was a foot deep.

Out on the bay, a white sloop slid across the waves, tacked briefly upwind again, then crossed in front of the house a second time. Ryan watched it with the admiration he always felt for a well-handled sailboat, but then his admiration turned to alarm as the boat luffed and dropped sail directly out from Heart Cove. He could just make out movement on board, then a spark of sunlight reflected off some metal or glass on board. Ordinarily, totally innocuous. And yet. Something to keep one's eye on.

Back to the papers: The appalling thing was, if you wanted to look for a conspiracy, you could see one almost everywhere. If he didn't have a strong skeptical bent that he applied to pretty well everything, he'd say there was evidence of a nearly universal conspiracy to conceal the mental-health effects of EMFs, going back fifty years.

Example: *The* classic, universally accepted symptom of schizophrenia is that the subject believes he is being mentally influenced by electromagnetic fields, particularly radio. Maybe hearing voices, projected by radio. But, in fact, many studies had shown that radio frequencies *could* produce the sensation of audible sounds: Pulsed microwaves could cause rapid heating and cooling of the mechanisms of the inner ear, the thermoelastic properties of tissues creating surrogate sounds that only the test subject could hear. Probably the best explanation of the ubiquitous "Taos hum" that had made the news so much in the mid-1990s.

Back when he and other Project Alpha people had worked on schizoaffective subjects, *the* textbook symptom of the disorder was the subject thinks he *might* be being influenced by electromagnetic frequencies. Such a criterion should raise a red flag: *Might* was too broad. But what could better discourage a serious researcher from looking into the health effects of EMFs? Even *consider* the possibility, you've handed yourself the stigma of mental disorder. Your credibility: zero.

The myth of the safety of radio and magnetic fields had so permeated the mental-health establishment that even recent revelations of EMF weapons, developed specifically to influence the human brain and behavior, didn't change the old guard's resistance to studying the subject. Sure, everyone knew that the brain's natural electrical currents created tiny magnetic fields, routinely used to study brain activity. And yes, of course magnetic fields induced electrical currents, so exposure to EMFs should, *must,* induce mental activity of some sort.

But bring it up and you labeled yourself a borderline schizophrenic.

Ryan flipped though pages of dense technical data. Lab tests showing that beaming certain radio frequencies at chimpanzees could induce rage, fear, apathy, and avoidance behaviors. Tests on rodents, apes, and humans showing that exposure to certain EMFs reduced the blood-brain barrier, making the brain greatly more vulnerable to the effects of trace chemicals. Legitimate clinics successfully treating severe depression by exposure to magnetic fields. Neurologists pointing out the disorientation of patients who had undergone magnetic resonance imaging—like Hector Morales.

But, hey, let's not look under the rug for behavioral effects of exposure to EMFs.

Another flash of reflected sunlight drew his eyes to the white sloop, still rocking blithely a half-mile out. Only one figure on deck now, nobody seemed to be fishing. Bristling, Ryan stood and leaned on the railing, shielding his eyes with one hand. Couldn't really see anything. But one of the Peterson's guards, stalking the upper parking area, caught the gesture. He scanned the sloop, spoke into his lapel mike, and gave Ryan a nod: *We'll keep our eyes on it.*

Ryan waded back into the papers. According to reliable surveys, the level of exposure to electromagnetic frequencies had increased exponentially during the last twenty years, just as Nina Lafontaine's computer program had demonstrated. Innumerable new sources had appeared, all man-made: long-wave submarine-detection grids, short-wave radio, microwave communications, cellular-phone relays, vast satellite communications nets, commercial broadcasting, cathode-ray tubes in every home, radar from every passing jetliner and cop car, infrared to open the goddamned door at the grocery store. Cordless phones, global positioning, the great 'wireless revolution.' Not to mention the short-range but fierce fields generated by every home appliance, or workplace machinery. Adding up to daily exposures between four and eight *million* times natural levels.

But it was taboo to wonder if this *might* affect your brain.

How much of this stuff had Jess looked at? How central was it to the problem of her abduction? At the very least, she had to be aware of it as a potential Babel agent: She'd met Nina, she'd read over those first reports Leap had dug up.

Ryan thumbed through a monograph by an Israeli scientist who had mapped the convergence of radio waves, termed a *lattice effect,* on several continents. A lattice effect, the researcher explained, occurred when two or more radio waves overlapped, creating other, transient frequencies. He had shown a decisive correlation between transient radio conditions in the American Southeast and the fluctuations in violent crime rates there during the 1990s. The paper looked well researched, modest in its claims. Yet after it was published, Peter's footnote mentioned, the scientist had been booted from Israel's National Academy of Science.

Conspiracies: Ryan had long since decided that the whole human race—every family and government and religious group and corporation and crime syndicate, any three *kids* playing together—was rife with plots and collusions and little conspiracies of every sort. But a giant, all-permeating, all-embracing conspiracy was not a systemic possibility. The human race simply wasn't sufficiently organized. Too self-interested and too mule-headed, thank God—beyond certain numbers you couldn't get too many people to agree on *anything*. But how to explain the medical and scientific establishment's entrenched resistance to EMF behavioral research?

So maybe this was what Jess had meant when she'd scrawled *Ry— Doughnuts*. He could imagine her putting it all together when she heard them breaking in downstairs, suddenly deducing who had been shadowing her. She wanted to leave a clue for Ryan, but she couldn't leave anything important-looking. So she left a note only he would know was meaningful.

But Jessie, it's too broad. I can't get it. As Leap and Hoague had both suggested, *nobody* would be happy to have this stuff come out. Every broadcasting company and military communications spook, every computer manufacturer and electrical power provider: *Everybody* was a potential enemy.

And EMFs were only one of the three likely agents. Right now, down in the offices, the staff was accumulating material on brain trauma from viruses and prions, and on endocrine disruptors like polychlorinated biphenyls, phthalates, dioxins, furans, and phytoestrogens.

Ancient plagues or new nightmares? The viral agents looked like the best candidates for the ancient plagues side of it, accounting best for the long history of human violence and bloodshed: a pandemic, recurrent neural disease, detectable only with the most sophisticated modern medical technologies. One paper blamed the proverbial "curse of the Pharaohs"—the spate of murders and suicides among archaeologists that so often followed the opening of a newly discovered Egyptian tomb—on viruses locked in burial vaults for thousands of years. Not that weaponized or genetically engineered versions of ancient brain- and behavior-altering viruses couldn't account for some modern atrocities, too. As Shipley's comment had suggested.

The EDs fell in the middle. On the new nightmares side: Since the beginning of the industrial era, the world had become saturated with endocrine disruptors and hormone mimics, found in thousands of products and pollutants and known to produce brain and behavioral changes. On the ancient plagues side, there were also natural EDs, occasionally concentrated in foods like plums, peanuts, vegetable oils, rice, and cabbage, and in pollens and soils. Several papers reported unusually heavy concentrations of naturally occurring EDs in food grains and pollens at archaeological digs, prompting some scientists to speculate that ED-related syndromes caused the downfall of the ancient Mesopotamian city-states.

From just the sheer increase in number and variety and power of sources, the EMFs seemed the best candidate for the new nightmares category. And yet, historical variations in natural sources, such as the sun's field or cosmic radiation, could have—

He was startled to feel a pair of hands on his shoulders, gently alighting and then kneading the tense muscles there. He felt a moment of pleasure in the touch, thinking, *Dagan, she's gotten over it.* Then he looked up to see Logan, eyes puffy from sleep, grinning ruefully as she came around him and reached for the coffeepot.

"God, Ryan, it's almost nine! Why didn't you get me up?"

"I thought we all could use the sleep."

"Everybody but you, apparently." She squinted out at the day, the play of light on the waves. "What is this? August? What a day!" Then she saw the virgin-white sloop, bobbing on the bright water, and the slits of her eyes became suspicious.

"They're on it, Lo." Ryan pointed his chin to the side deck, where one of the Peterson's men watched the boat through binoculars. "I think it's okay."

She frowned at having to wake up to doubt and suspicion on such a beautiful day. "How're you feeling?" she asked. She looked him over critically, the breeze tugging at her hair.

Surprisingly, he felt pretty good. He'd slept for four hours. He hadn't been drinking, not choosing to avoid it so much as putting it off until he was so tired he just passed out without it. Maybe the absence of the aggregate sedative effect was beginning to do something to him.

He stood up. "I'm feeling pissed off! I'm feeling royally pissed off, Lo. I'm pissed off at having to be paranoid about boats coming into the bay on a beautiful morning. I'm pissed off because human beings are all stupid shits! I am royally *fucking* pissed off!" He swatted at a chair and watched it careen across the deck. Christ Jesus, it felt good to say it, to yell it, to toss a chair.

Dagan appeared on the deck, helped herself to coffee. The wind took her hair and plastered it across her face, and she had to set down her cup and use both hands to peel away the dark skein. Behind it, she was smiling grimly at Ryan's outburst. Logan was grinning, too, peering out at the sloop on the bay again as though she'd be happy to swim out there and bite a hole in its hull on suspicion alone.

Ryan faced the bay and spread his arms, felt the grim strength in his chest and shoulders, the bellicose optimism the warm day seemed to bring on. Being pissed off was the right way to be. Things were in motion. *Only four more days until her due date,* he remembered, a jab of panic piercing him. But if she was still alive, they were doing what they could to get her back. If she wasn't, they were at least on their way to doing something really fucking nasty to whoever had hurt her. Grim, yes. Revenge: the most desperate form of solace. *But there it is,* Ryan thought. *Your genes call out for the elimination of threats to your kind. You can't let people fuck with you or yours and get away without paying for it.*

Chapter 55

Ryan arrived at Ridder Global a few minutes
after eight. After hours, the building was quieter, the halls mostly empty
but for maintenance personnel manning floor polishers. A sense of chilly
somnolence.

Ryan waited as the elevator rose, wishing something had come their
way today. He'd found himself dropping in on Leap at regular intervals
all day, hoping for word that the homing pigeon had come back to roost.
Leap had finally told him firmly: "What, I'm going to sit on it? Trust me,
I'll let you know right away." But waiting was a strain. Realistically, the
fatigue-drunken, bitter optimism they had all felt that morning couldn't
be sustained long. Not without something to feed it.

Ridder's front-office staff on the fiftieth floor had gone home, replaced by
a pair of uniformed security guards who brought him into Ridder's office.

"Ryan! Good to see you," Ridder said. He was dressed casually in
khakis and a gray turtleneck. He gave Ryan a commiserating clap on the
shoulder and beckoned him into the room. "This must be a tough period
for you—I'm sorry. I hope we can help get Jessamine back soon. Get you
anything to drink?"

"No. I'm okay."

Ridder went over to his bar and began mixing himself a gin and tonic.
"I tell you I'm getting interviewed tomorrow night by your good friend
Diana Reese?"

"I heard, yes. Good luck."

Ridder chuckled, took a swig from his drink, and licked his lips appreciatively. "I watched you on her show last spring. She was really after the
dirt, wasn't she? Of course, you weren't entirely, uh, charming yourself.
But I can guess she'll come looking to provoke me, huh? I wouldn't do
it at all, but just between you and me, we're working on the public-
relations foundations of touchy takeover venture. Making me look accessible and pretty so as to improve my clout with stockholders and
boards."

"Listen, Mr. Ridder, I'd be grateful if we could just get down to business."

Ridder looked disappointed, but nodded in agreement. At his desk, he hit the intercom button and said curtly, "Darion, would you mind stepping down here for a moment?" Without waiting for a reply, he sat on the edge of the desk, sipping his drink and looking at Ryan speculatively.

After a moment Ryan heard an almost imperceptible hum from the far wall, which he deduced was an elevator descending. He wondered briefly if Gable lived here in the building, the centurion available at all times to do his master's bidding. Within seconds the inner door opened and there was Gable, a gliding silhouette against the big windows, the glittering lights of Boston's Hub. He gave Ryan a curt nod.

Ridder slipped on a casual silk sport jacket. "There's a new jazz club just opened up, I thought maybe we could catch the show as we talk about our business. Got a car downstairs to pick us up. But before we go, Ryan, don't take offense, but we've got a little ritual here—" Ridder nodded to Gable, who approached Ryan and gestured for him to raise his arms.

"Hell's this?"

"This is standard for certain kinds of conversations," Gable told him.

"I trust you completely, Ryan," Ridder said, "but I've found it best to let Darion have his way on these matters. This needs to be a private discussion."

Ryan let Gable pat him down, looking for a recording device. Gable's hard hands worked quickly up his back, armpits, inner thighs, calves, jacket pockets. When he was done, he caught Ryan's eyes and held them, as if his inspection had continued on into Ryan's thoughts, touching and sorting among his motives. "Okay," he said at last.

Ryan stifled his revulsion, reminding himself that at least Gable was on his side, the lizard's professional skills might have their uses. He'd deal with the ethical ironies of it later.

They took an elevator to a basement parking garage, where they were joined by two casually dressed but competent-looking bodyguards. After a moment a limo pulled up. The guards joined the driver in front, while Gable took the seat facing his boss and Ryan in the passenger compartment.

"Since my shooting incident," Ridder explained, tapping his chest, "I'm more cautious about my incognito outings. Much as I hate being shepherded around." When the car left the garage, he peered through the heavily tinted window, watching the street glide by with what Ryan saw was an avid hunger. The billionaire was in many ways held captive by his own power and importance.

After a time Ridder asked, "So where d'you want to start?"

Ryan glanced up at the guards and the driver, the heavy Lexan bulkhead that insulated the cab from the passenger compartment. "First, your friend Shipley."

"I take it you guys have not exactly started a mutual admiration society?"

"He's been interested in the Babel project from the beginning, because it cuts close to secret behavioral-modification research. He's warned me away several times, and he met with Jess while I was in Africa. Do you think he arranged the break-in?"

Ridder gave it a moment's thought. "No. He ain't the guy. Oh, his outfit would be interested. But they'd talk to me. And they wouldn't fuck up a project I was bankrolling—these guys need me, and they know I would be, shall we say, *unhappy* with any interference." Ridder's understatement was convincing. "But let's get on to the other thing."

"You offered me the loan of Darion's assistance. I'd like to accept."

Gable smiled thinly. "A matter of consultation, or of material participation?"

"I'm not sure."

"Comes down to the details, Ryan," Ridder said. "I take it you've made some progress toward finding your wife."

"Yes."

"And I further take it you don't feel the *federales* are doing an adequate job."

"Correct."

Ridder patted the breast of his jacket, found a golden pocket humidor, took out one of his long cigars. He sniffed it lovingly, then located his clipper and carefully sliced off the end. "You understand, this was maybe a rash offer on my part. Still, I won't back out if the details warrant a commitment of, uh, such resources on our part. Let's start with the Babel project—where you stand. My assumption has been that you've suspended your research operations pending Jessamine's safe return."

"No. Finding her has required we recapitulate her work, her contacts, her thoughts. Turns out she made enormous strides. What she put together is too important to let anyone derail progress. We're full speed ahead."

Ridder had obviously heard the rage surge in his voice. Now he paused with his cigar unlit, staring at Ryan with that keen light of savor and assessment in his eyes. "Nothing like an education on the streets of South Boston, huh, Darion?"

Gable nodded. He sat with his legs crossed, physically relaxed yet supremely focused on what they were saying.

"You gonna tell us what we're talking about?" Ridder prompted.

"My wife believes that a weakening of two closely related behaviors would account for the Babel effect. Kin-recognition and theory of mind are the instinctive foundations of all cooperative social behaviors. Kin-recognition is just that, and is the basis for altruistic behavior like food sharing and protection. Theory of mind is realizing that your mental perceptions are different from objective reality, and recognizing the same thing in others is the basis for creating social organization beyond just blood kin. The neural modules for both are localized in the same parts of the brain. Both manifest as feelings of kinship and belonging, and without those feelings you don't feel compelled to act with anything but self-interest. One person acting in complete self-interest can become crime and violence. A lot of people acting in complete self-interest is anarchy."

Ridder's cigar hovered halfway to his lips. "I like this," he said. "I really like this."

The car braked as traffic backed up. Thursday night, the early week-enders were heading out to bars and clubs and restaurants. Ridder turned to stare out through the dark glass at the world: people walking on the sidewalks, couples, a few families, some late commuters, moving among each other in an age-old dance. The dance was based on the deeply felt assumption of commonality, built into them from the molecular level on up, from the genes to the cells to the folds of the brain, embedded after millennia in culture and language and commerce. People going out to eat food made by chefs who could assume the preferences of their own palates resembled the tastes of other people. Going to plays or movies that told stories of fictional lives that their writers could assume would have meaning to strangers. Sitting down to an evening of music made by musicians who trusted that others shared the pleasures of tonal sequences. Families unthinkingly acting in concert as they held hands to cross the streets, discussed the choice of restaurant or movie with regard for each other's preferences, bickered and joked and teased. Partners walking and talking, reasonably sure they shared each other's feelings of attraction or attachment. All of them at best only vaguely aware that something was quietly gnawing away at the biological foundations of their ability to feel that way.

The side of Ridder's face as he looked out seemed hard, impassive. And lonely, Ryan thought. "I like this," Ridder said again, subdued. "It explains…a lot."

"Which brings you to the agent," Gable said. "What's affecting these parts of the brain? What's impairing these instincts?"

Gable's attentiveness to the scientific dimensions of the project surprised Ryan. It hadn't occurred to him the hit man would be interested in anything but his role, whatever nasty business he might be required to pull off.

"We've got several good candidates. But I don't want to go into it just now. The technical details are complex, and we've got other pressing stuff to discuss."

The intercom crackled, and the driver's disembodied voice spoke. "We're almost there, sir. Proceed as planned?"

Ridder grunted confirmation. The car stopped to let the two guards out, then went on for another block and pulled over again. The three of them got out and walked around the corner to the blue awning of the Sandlot. Ridder had lit his cigar and put on sunglasses, and now looked not so different from the other aficionados crowding toward the door.

It was a basement club, one big room with stone walls and dim lights, a long bar against the rear wall, a small stage lit by spots that threw tight circles around a piano, a trap set, an electronic keyboard cluster. The bodyguards had claimed a pair of tables close to one of the side walls in the front corner, and no one in the crowd gave their party a second glance. A haze of smoke already hung in a dense layer at head height. Ridder looked over the scene with satisfaction, a connoisseur's experienced assessment.

They sat down, ordered drinks. The loud hubbub of voices and piped-in jazz echoed in the room, making it a good spot for a secure conversation.

Ridder put his face close to Ryan's, and Gable leaned in to hear. "Okay," Ridder said. "Let's do the dirty. What do you need Darion's help for?"

"The bugs found at our house were manufactured at some kind of illicit high-tech shop. I believe I can find out where this shop is. I want to go there and find out who bought the bugs from them. But I don't have the resources to crash what I'm presuming will be a well-protected place, or to get the information I want from whoever runs it."

Gable's eyebrows arched skeptically. "How're you going to locate the shop?"

"I'd rather not say."

"I ask because this is a very tough proposition. Mistakes here could be costly. We need to be sure your information is accurate."

"I'm not in your line of work," Ryan told him, "but I am in the information business. I'll vouch for the accuracy of the information."

Ridder was frowning, absently opening and closing the guillotine blades of his cigar clipper. On stage, a blond woman in a slinky purple dress and net stockings had come out and was making adjustments to the bank of synthesizers. To her left, an older black man settled a tenor sax into a floor stand, and began wrestling with a mike on a long gooseneck.

Gable leaned toward Ridder. "On the face of it, I'd say we should avoid involvement. I'm sure Dr. McCloud wants his wife back. But this sounds very high-risk."

Ridder's scowl deepened. "Let me see if I've got this straight, Ryan. At this point you don't know where this place is, or how big it is, right? Could be a workbench in some electronics freak's basement, could be a big slick operation protected by thirty guys carrying violin cases. You don't know, right?"

"Not yet. But when I find out, I'll want to move fast."

Ridder pulled back to gaze at Ryan, heavy-lidded eyes seeming ancient, at once baleful and sad in the dim light. "You're getting glandular about this, aren't you? You don't give a damn how vulnerable caring about somebody that much makes you. So now you want to fuck somebody up pretty badly. Huh. Can't blame you. But are you sure you're being smart about this?" Then he turned to Gable, chuckling: "A funny question, huh, Darion—asking Dr. Ryan McCloud that!"

Gable just watched Ryan.

On stage, the piano player came out and took his chair, followed by the bass man and then the drummer, who perched on his stool and fired off a couple of rim-shots. He tapped his cymbals, brought them nearer, tapped them again, and found them just right. The crowd noise dwindled expectantly as the house lights went down and the stage spots turned into sharp cones of smoky light. The musicians caught each other's eyes and then the music exploded.

Ryan liked jazz as much as the next guy, but this was a demonic fusion of electric storm sounds from the vixen at the keyboards and screaming orgasmic sax and dive-bombing runs on the piano and the drums everywhere in scatters and clots like firecrackers at Chinese New Year.

He leaned into Ridder's ear to be heard. "I'll go after them with or without Darion's help. I thought I'd have better odds of success *with* it. Obviously, my continued work on your project may depend on the outcome."

The sound was too chaotic to think straight. He'd said all he could at this point. The rest was up to Ridder.

Ridder nodded, either to some beat buried in the avalanche of sound or in reply to what Ryan had said. After a minute he turned back to Gable. Ryan could just make out what he said: "Let's wait until we hear more from Ryan, decide when we hear the details. In the meantime, get your team on alert, ready to go. I'll take your concerns under advisement, but if the situation seems doable, I'm inclined to help Ryan out here. Are we clear?" For all his egalitarian informality, the Rat Pack hipster gloss on his CEO authority, when Ridder made a decision and issued a command there was no question who was boss.

Gable blinked almost laconically. "Absolutely clear," he said.

As Ridder went back to listening to the band, Ryan sat for a moment, buffeted by the music and aware that Gable was studying him, enjoying his discomfort. He bailed out before the drinks came, fleeing the war of sound and the flint-hard face of Gable and the suffocating tobacco smoke and the sense of time running out. Caught a cab back to Ridder Global, found the Subaru. Drove back toward Heart Cove feeling vaguely grateful to Ridder, feeling as if he'd accomplished what he set out to do, yet wondering what he'd really set in motion.

Chapter 56

It was ten-thirty by the time he got back to the house, which was bathed in lights like a goddamned movie set. He walked in to find Dagan stalking around the living room, rattling ice cubes in an empty glass. On the kitchen counter, a bottle of Glenfiddich. A practiced inventory told him a third of it had been poured.

"Decided I needed to take the edge off," she explained, holding up her glass. "Took the edge *way* off." She was wearing nylons and a businesslike navy blue dress set off by a string of pearls, but had kicked off her high heels, which lay toppled on the rug.

Dagan, drunk: Ryan had never seen that before. Despite his sense of alarm, his concern that stress was beginning to fray the team, he found himself curious.

"You do this a lot, right?" she asked him. *This* apparently meant the wobbly walk and the too-loose gestures, eyes widening in response to the uneven gravity of the floor. "What's it do for you, Ryan? Always wanted to ask. Like, cognitively."

"Not so much lately," he told her. "But, cognitively speaking, it usually makes me drunk and pretty goofy."

"See," she said, turning confrontationally, "I'm feeling very fucked up. You know what I'm talking about?"

"Why don't you have a seat and tell me?" he suggested mildly. He steered past her to the kitchen, where he took out the blender base and began rummaging for the top.

She followed him, braced herself on the counter, then climbed onto one of the stools, and Ryan thought maybe the recommendation to sit wasn't so good after all. Dagan unsteady on the tall stool. Legs crossed, fine shoulders held back and square despite her being so looped. She was wearing lipstick, and the whiskey had brought a flush to her cheeks. Her brows and chin were unusually mobile with emotion and drunkenness as she watched him find the blender top and open the refrigerator.

"You were going to tell me why you're feeling so fucked up," he reminded her.

"Right," she said. "Well, let's see. Science, politics, um, God, religion, human beings, belief, meaning, um, marriage, loyalty—"

"That's it? Nothing serious?" he joked humorlessly. Only an inexperienced drunk would get them all at once. With the additional topic of sports, the old Paddy alkies at South Boston pubs had the same set of concerns, but they tended to get hit with them only one at a time, or made a lifetime specialty out of just one or two. Poor Dagan. In the refrigerator he found the orange juice and a carton of eggs, set them out on the counter, and bellied up to it opposite her like a bartender.

"See, what Jess was doing," Dagan said. "What she was after. It's bugging me about five ways. I mean, you do see, right?" She laughed at herself, looking stricken. "That's stupid of me—of course you do. This thing of values having biological origins, it just is screwing my head around. I mean, I kind of *knew* all this stuff, I just never *looked* at it. All the things I deeply believe, they're just *genes?* They're just chemicals, they're just circuits? Just, the crazy games-theory guy, what'd he call 'em? 'Evolution'rily stable strategies.' They're like, like little math programs at work in genes, that's *it?* And this doesn't fuck you up, Ry?"

"I try to avoid letting it bother me." He moved the scotch bottle aside, out of her reach, and set up the blender in its place.

Dagan plunged ahead, groping her way toward the big, abstract pain she felt: "And the thing is, now I see it everywhere, even in myself, I'm just this programmed biological machine? I don't mean my, you know, hunger or thirst or being horny, that I can cope with, yeah, that's biology. But *loyalty,* or *love,* or *conscience,* or *sympathy,* or, or my commitment to social *justice?*" She made a big, loose gesture, lost her balance, and had to catch the counter to stay up.

Ryan poured orange juice into the blender, broke an egg into it.

"So then I think, what was Jess doing? She was making this bridge between science and values. Right? And my first reaction is, you're not supposed to do that. You've got, you're supposed to have empiricism over here—" With both hands she placed a large invisible object onto the left side of the counter. "And beliefs and values over here." Another double handful of air on the right. Again she lost balance, caught herself, frowned at the counter. "But Jess is saying, you can't have 'em separate. It's just a simple matter of scientific methodol'gy! You either decide that certain behaviors are relevant to a study, or they're not! But to do that you have to draw a line—what's normal, healthy, what isn't. Same as deciding what's right or wrong, and *poof!* You've just invented *values!* Can't keep 'em separate! Throws everything on its ear! Right?"

"You're a lot like me when I get drunk," Ryan told her, hoping it sounded reassuring. In the cabinet he found a jar of brewer's yeast, a good vitamin B spectrum, and tipped some into the blender, then peeled the last banana and dropped it in, potassium. And a pinch of salt to accelerate fluid uptake. Turning his back to Dagan, he found a bottle of aspirin, took out two tablets, and slipped them into the mix as well.

"Dagan," he said. "I'm just gonna run the blender for a second, okay?"

She looked at it with a frown, but he turned it on anyway, winced at the noise, watched the vortex suck the banana down and turn the whole thing into a creamy glop that would help dilute undigested alcohol and slow its absorption, hydrate her system, compensate for the booze-induced neuronutrient deficits, ease the imminent pain of hangover. When it had run long enough, he hit the button and poured her a tumbler full.

She ignored it. "When I was a kid, my father, he wanted me to know the basic tenets of Judaism? Taught me these foundation principles?" She was talking with the exaggerated precision drunks used just before their metabolisms crashed. Trying to, anyway.

"Drink," Ryan ordered.

She stared at the glass skeptically, resting her cheek on one hand and pulling her face into a lugubrious grin on one side. "I still rem'ber 'em. There's, let's see, *rahamanut,* that's compassion, or like, pity. Root word is *rehem,* that means 'womb,' so the basic idea is like 'mother love,' uncondition'l nurture. *Rahamanut,* you're supposed to love even those who have wronged you or don't love you in return."

"It's a beautiful word. A beautiful principle."

"And there's *gemilut hesed,* that's loving kindness, you're supposed to act with that even when no reward is expected? 'One of the three pillars of Judaism.' And what else. Oh yeah. *Kevod haberiyot.* Regard for human beings. Interpretation goes, man is made in God's image, so we're all of inest'able, ines*tim*able, worth. God deliberately made only one original human being, so we could all claim the same ancestor, we're all related, so we should act with loving kindness to all, regardless of kinship or race or whatever."

"Okay. I want you to drink this now." He pushed the glass toward her, and she tasted it dubiously. "All of it. Down the hatch. I mean it, Dagan, all of it."

She obeyed, gulping dutifully, then set the glass down and licked at the pale yellow mustache. A beautiful young woman, he thought, even in her most awkward moments. He poured the rest of the mix into her glass.

"So I'm supposed to go to my dad and tell him, Hey, Dad, you know those foundation princ'ples of the scriptures? Bunch of opportunistic fuckin' *genes!*" She frowned at Ryan as if he'd contrived the arrangement. But then her face brightened, she got a look of wonderment. "But at the same time it gives *validity* to those princ'ples, doesn't it? Proves they're anchored in...objective truth. Wow. And *that's* what Jess was doing, right? *That's* what she was really looking for, huh? Our ideas of goodness, we, they're, like, *provable!*"

"I think so," he said.

She got sad again. "But nobody'll separate the bullshit from the stuff we need so badly! Not the scientists, not the religious people. All these orthodoxies." She looked as if she wanted to cry, putting her face in her hands for a long moment. Then she brought her hands away and her cheeks were still dry. "But—I remember, I was going t'say—makes you have t'think about—you know. Where Jess is."

Ryan steadied her with a hand on her shoulder, and held the glass to her lips. She swallowed again. When at last he let go of her, she slipped abruptly off the stool, barely catching herself on the counter.

"Okay," he said, coming around the bar. "Let's get you sat down. Dagan? You listening? Let's go over to the couch."

She clutched his arms and he walked her to the living room, managed to get her seated. When she didn't let go of him, he allowed himself to sit next to her. She leaned her head against his shoulder.

"Y'know why I'm dressed like this?" she said miserably. "Didn't notice? Formal?" She swatted at her dress.

"I noticed. I always notice. But why?"

"Went to a job interview today. Presented myself, inquired, had conversation."

"Job interview? But you've got a job!" A pang of some new pain in his chest.

She pulled away from him, shaking her head. Her eyes brimmed. "I can't do this anymore. Y'know? Making me too sad, Ryan. God, it's making me so sad. Can't even be mad at you, I just fall into being along with you, moving next to you, I can't help it, like we're...like you and Jess are. And I was thinking about it, and I realize I love Jess the same way. Only not the, y'know, sexual dimension. So I've got to go away from you guys.

See?" She put her face in her hands and just cried. Little jagged sobs, still trying to hold back. "Just can't do this anymore."

He wanted to protest, but couldn't think of an argument. "It's going to be okay," he told her. "We'll figure it all out."

He put his arm around her shoulder. Her affect was crashing as the depressive effect of the scotch took over. Dagan made a lot of tears when she cried, a fountain flowing readily from her eyes. With Jess he would have comforted with kisses and caresses, gradually brought her out of it by the reminder of life's good things, their closeness, maybe the healing power of sexual intimacy. Now he couldn't think of how to hold Dagan, she was too female everywhere to touch her except most cautiously. The limited permissible repertoire of comforting contact.

"Know what my name means? *Dagan*—Hebrew word, means grain, corn—fertility. Good omen name. Abundance, lots of babies. Big joke, huh." The despondency in her slurred voice stabbed his heart, but before he could respond, she sat forward suddenly. "Oh!" she said, as if suddenly remembering something.

"What?"

"Think I'm gonna barf." She stood up and ran unevenly to the deck doors. Before he could get there to help her, she'd fumbled with the handle, jerked it open, and lurched out into the island of lights. He stood in the doorway, feeling useless, as she steadied herself at the railing and vomited over the edge.

Ryan watched her from the doorway, giving her space. When he was pretty sure she was done, he went to her and guided her back inside. She was trembling and shaky as he laid her down on the couch again. He brought a wet towel from the kitchen and wiped her sweaty face.

"'Nks," she said.

"You're welcome."

She opened one bleary eye. "You love me?"

"Very much." She was shivering, so he found the folded afghan and spread it over her.

She shut the eye again, pushed feebly at him. "'Kay. Go 'way now. Sleep."

———

He had thought to have a drink, but Dagan's misery and the smell of cast-up whiskey cooled him on the idea. Instead he went upstairs to the office and began going over his notes again.

Thinking, *Yes, Jess has really done it this time.* Built the bridge between the two great systems of knowing. She hadn't gone after the root of all evil. She'd gone after the root of all *goodness*. You could argue that goodness was "just" our program, the math, the chemicals, the circuits—and you could feel shitty and reduced and that life was without meaning. Or—what Jess was doing—you could build the case that goodness was built in, went all the way back, was provably natural law.

Or, if you were so inclined, divine law.

The desk clock beeped midnight, and the digits on the date slipped from November 7 to November 8. The sight brought a wrenching pain: Jess could go into labor at any time. If she was still alive. The odds that her kidnappers would be responsive to the needs of a woman in childbirth were slim. And what if there were complications?

A thought teased him: What had Dagan said? *Makes you think. About where Jess is.* Then she'd slipped off the stool and lost her train of thought. He'd have to remind her in the morning, ask her what she'd intended to say.

Chapter 57

Friday dawned clear and warm, another day of late Indian summer. Dagan was gone by the time Ryan came downstairs, and he assumed she had survived her ordeal by alcohol poisoning. Although he had slept for only two hours, he felt surprisingly energized. Some kind of anticipatory excitement, he decided, a sense of expectation. Something was coming.

The first inkling that he was right came when he walked into the front office to find Dolores at her desk, her radio tuned as always to the public radio station. From the speakers came the big, resigned cadences of Albinoni's *Adagio in g minor,* tragic and implacable. Dolores gave him a thin-lipped sideways glance instead of her usual matronly smile. Ryan wondered at it momentarily until he saw Logan and Peter in the glassed-in conference room, looking over spreadsheets and ledger binders. Logan beckoned him inside. From their faces he could tell this was a damage-assessment conference.

They confronted him with some of the hard facts that went with their current state of siege. It cost money to have round-the-clock security. In the past ten days, Genesis had spent over thirty thousand dollars for the guards alone. Purchasing new, state-of-the-art security systems in the house and the Catacombs, buying armored data-storage safes, improving security at all staff residences, making overtime pay for a staff working eighteen hours a day: They were running out of cash. The commission fee Ridder had advanced was in an escrow account that would take some legal finessing to release early.

"Bottom line," Peter spelled out, "I figure we can sustain another four days on our corporate accounts, and then we go into the red. We'll need to initiate negotiations with Ridder's lawyers for the escrow money, or start looking for loans. Right away." When Ryan just stared at him dully, he added, trying to be cheerful, "I'm sure our credit is good, though. But, uh, you know, how much do we borrow?"

Implying, *How long do we plan to keep this up? What's the long-term prognosis for this organization?*

"Another point, ultimately more important," Logan added, "is mental fatigue. We're wearing down, Ry. Probably everybody will insist that they're up for more of this level of work and tension, but the reality is our performance is starting to drop. Nobody thinks well when they're worn out. If we don't see…resolution…soon, we'll need to rethink our strategy here. Reposition ourselves, both emotionally and situationally." She watched him with wary concern, a good person facing into some hard stuff, having the guts to call it straight.

What she said was undeniable. The group wasn't accustomed to this level of fatigue and stress and uncertainty. Walking the halls in the Catacombs, listening in on talk at the cafeteria table, he'd felt the difference: people bickering, picking at small things, avoiding each other, indulging in depressed or complaining monologues. Wesley was conspicuously absent, and now Dagan was gone, too, maybe already embarking upon the new life that she needed and deserved. The team was starting to fray.

The Babel effect? he wondered. This had been a beautiful human system, an unusually cohesive team. Was it as simple as wear and tear pulling them apart, or was it something else—something clinical?

And implicit in what Logan had said was a disturbing truth: Everybody loved Jess, but they had lives of their own, this was their *job,* not their home. They were loyal to Genesis, sure, but they had their own husbands and wives and kids, who wanted them back. Who wanted them *alive.* At some point, if Jess could not be found, or if she turned up dead, they'd have to determine a future for the organization—without her.

Logan and Peter were waiting for his reply, but right now he couldn't imagine what such a future might possibly be. The tragic violins from the radio filled the silence.

The goddamned Albinoni score, he thought. *Not a sound track for a happy ending.* He realized he was jittery, morbid, the nagging sense of prescience making him look for omens everywhere.

He found Leap back in the data lab. For the last two days they had exchanged trial communications on the dedicated optical landline to Ridder Global, and now Leap was preparing to receive the first real data, formulae for pesticides and herbicides from one of Ridder's agricultural divisions. When Ryan stuck his head in the door, Leap just shook his head and went back to his terminal.

Where's the goddamned homing pigeon? Ryan bitched. They'd been waving around their availability for hacking for days, parading their red rear ends like female mandrills in heat. Why hadn't anybody noticed?

Ryan tried to work on various tasks, finding concentration almost impossible. Brain whizzing, multitasking and running out a thousand abortive lines, the growing sense of gloomy expectancy. Still no follow-up from Karl. And still no sign of Dagan; Peter said he had noticed that her car wasn't in the lot.

At eleven, he went to the front office and surprised Dolores and Peter and Logan, who were standing near Dolores's desk and talking. They turned to him with gray faces. Something gone badly wrong.

Logan said quickly, *"Not* about Jess. It's Karl Alexander. He's been killed."

"I heard it on the radio," Dolores said. "Eleven-o'clock news. I printed it up from our wire service, but I thought I should talk to Logan before—"

Before bringing you the bad news, Ryan thought. Strategizing how to cope with Ryan, with the whole situation. It was like a punch to the solar plexus, and he took the AP printout from Dolores feeling breathless, numb.

> Nov. 8. Police in New York have announced the death of Dr. Karl Alexander, who was pronounced dead of multiple gunshot wounds at New York's Roosevelt Hospital earlier today. Dr. Alexander was head of the prestigious Montgomery Genetic Laboratories and chairman of the U.S. Surgeon General's advisory board on genetic engineering policy. The elite panel was created to oversee policy issues on the biomedical ethics of gene research and the commercial and military use of genetically engineered organisms. Coming on the heels of the murder of another member of the advisory board, Dr. Elizabeth Kim of Stanford University's Genome Laboratory, just two weeks ago, Dr. Alexander's death has prompted renewed calls by members of Congress for a federal investigation into troubles within the Surgeon General's office and the genetic engineering industry.

For a moment Ryan was speechless. Then he said, "You're right, Lo. We need to rethink things." He said it calmly. Then he kicked a chair across the room.

He went outside and leaned on the deck railing. So they'd gotten to Karl. Who? The connection to Elizabeth Kim's death was suggestive. The sciences were so changing the world, so crucially important to all the various competing power structures, that the oversight of important information had become a battleground. Maybe Karl had died because somebody was determined to stack the genetic engineering committee, influencing policy by eliminating people with the wrong opinions.

But his gut told him otherwise. Karl had found out the bug shop, had somehow exposed himself in the process, and had been killed for it. *I'm sorry, Karl,* Ryan thought. *I prevailed upon your conscience, and sent you to your death. Here I thought you might be my Judas—and I turned out to be yours.* The thought sickened him, and he felt a wave of pity for Karl, for the life so used and wasted. The extent of his feeling for the bad-boy genius surprised him.

But worse was what it meant for their search for Jess. Karl had been killed before sending off the bug shop's address. Without a way to find out who had commissioned the device, they had only one initiative left: Leap's homing pigeon. Which so far had produced no results. It had been a long shot, predicated on the chance that the bad guys would be tempted to return for more data. Now it was the only shot.

And there were the concerns Peter and Logan had raised. Soon Genesis would simply deconstruct as people quit to protect themselves, or began getting sick, or became paralyzed by disagreements or indecision. Probably his first impulse had been correct. There wasn't enough forward momentum to justify continued risk. People were getting killed. The crew hadn't signed on for this. They'd have to disband, go home, call it quits.

He had just stepped back into the office to tell them so when the fax machine began the mutter of printing. When he picked up the first sheet, he felt a jolt, like an electric shock, at the sight of the blocks of ones and zeros. *Binary code, genetic information!*

Ryan grabbed the pages as the machine pumped them out. The sender's address was again a Mail Boxes Etc. in Manhattan—Karl had taken no chances here. But why was it arriving now, after his death?

Or *was* it from Karl? Maybe some subterfuge? His hands shook as he scanned the pages. It took him a couple of reads to be able to decipher it. *Found one decent bone,* the first sequence read. *At significant cost,* the next one spelled out. Then: *Big time gratitude in order, prick.*

Definitely Karl.

Then some long blocks that spelled out a street address.

Okay, Ryan thought, feeling his pulse accelerate. *All hands on deck. Action stations.* Time to alert the crew. Time to get in touch with Ridder and Gable. They had started down the waterfall, the wild ride toward the unknown destination.

Chapter 58

"This is a reasonably secure line, Dr. McCloud,"
Gable's flat voice said. "You have information?"

"I have an address in Manchester, New Hampshire. A few other details."

Gable didn't hesitate. "As Mr. Ridder instructed, we've been standing by. Our first step will be to observe. We'll act *only if it seems feasible.* Sound good?"

"Yes."

"Okay." Ryan heard the sound of paper folding, and assumed that Gable was opening a map. "Right. You're directly on the way to Manchester. We'll pick you up on the way. But you should know I consider direct action *highly* unlikely. So here are the rules. If, and note I say *if,* my team acts, you stay in the van. *I* decide what we do or don't do, not you. We need to be absolutely clear on this, or nobody goes anywhere. Do you agree?"

It rankled to subordinate himself in any way to Gable, but it made sense: Gable knew this business, Ryan didn't. "Okay," Ryan grumbled. "I agree."

"We'll need an hour to prepare, an hour to get to your place. So be ready in two hours," Gable ordered. And then the phone was dead.

Ryan finished off a couple of minor tasks and went up to the house. He changed into a loose-fitting pair of pants and what he thought was a nondescript green pullover sports shirt, and put on running shoes. Action clothing seemed appropriate, but he was increasingly aware he didn't have any idea how to prepare for something like this. He didn't know whether they'd have to stay all night, observing some building, or just case the place and come back right away, or what. Presumably Gable would have a grip on such things.

He ate a couple of granola bars and drank some orange juice, tending to his blood sugars. That left almost an hour and a half to wait for

Gable. Killing time, trying to find a purposeful calm, he sat in the upstairs office, staring at the bulletin boards, his private op-center. Pinned to the boards were the few little clues Jess had been able to leave, including that damned doughnuts note. It had irked him and teased him for two weeks. Jess didn't even *like* doughnuts. And the bad handwriting. And the vagueness: There was so much missing data associated with the Babel effect—how could anyone figure anything from the negative space?

Around and around. Thought ruts, going nowhere. He heaved himself up, unable to sit still, went down to the Catacombs. Still forty minutes until Gable and crew came for him.

———

Downstairs again, he ran into Leap as he was heading back toward the computer lab. Leap waved a sheet of paper in one hand, looking perplexed. "Just coming to look for you," Leap said. "E.T. called home, Ry. Sort of."

Ryan snatched the page. It was a print-off of a computer screen, a string of digits. "What is it?"

"It's the homing pigeon. Got an address for the originating network that activated it."

"What's the location? Jesus, Leap!"

"Ridder Global headquarters."

"What the—?"

"Hold on. Since yesterday, I've been exchanging material with them, checking our interfacing and encryption systems, establishing my superuser status. I wasn't planning to put the homing pigeon in the trial exchange files, but maybe I goofed, maybe my global insertion overreached. Maybe…" Leap went into arcane details that suggested he had mistakenly allowed the homing pigeon to get into Ridder Global's computer network.

"You sure that's it?"

"Or Ridder's testing us, slipping in a trial hack to see how secure we are before giving us full access. Can't entirely blame him, after all that's happened here. I'll straighten it out, Ry—I've got a call in to Zelinsky, Ridder's IT manager, trying to figure what happened."

"But the homing pigeon is activated when data is *sent*, right?—when someone forwards our files, downloads them to another destination. Why would Zelinsky be forwarding your trial data anywhere?"

"I was just going to mention that," Leap said. "It's a peach, ain't it?" A trace of a French accent had crept into his voice, *peach* sounding a bit like *bitch*.

Leap went back to the lab to work over his transmission log, but Ryan didn't join him. He was experiencing the discomfort that always came when some subconscious process was building pressure and urgency and was on the verge of demanding conscious attention. He frowned as he inspected the feeling. It was strongly laden with a sense of impeding danger. Maybe just Babel paranoia? But there was Jess in it, too, faint but definite, as if her voice were calling him from some faraway, dark place.

Back up the outside stairs, taking the plank steps slowly, only vaguely conscious of the warm day, the gently beating waves, the watchful security men. Up the inside stairs. Into the office.

Yes—the bulletin board. *Doughnuts.*

He'd figured out her thesis, remade her contacts. But one thing kept bothering him: Jess knew she was being followed—Freunde knew it in Munich, Father Connelly knew it, *Jess* knew it. Suddenly Ryan recalled her fax to him in Kalesi, that day of uplink problems and fragmentary messages: *nice to know our friends are watching out for us!*

She knew she was being watched as far back as September 18! And yet she and Bates told no one, and didn't think it was important enough to require any extra security precautions. The gaping hole, the missing datum. Even for Jess, with her independent working habits, too extreme an oversight, impossible.

And then it all shifted, clicked into place. *Oh, Jess!* he wailed internally. *I've been too stupid. It's so obvious!* He should have seen it in what she'd told Shipley: *Don't worry, Ridder's people are keeping an eye on our security.* He should have seen it the very first day.

He could visualize it clearly now. *Jess in the office, working at her desk. She hears a commotion downstairs, the intruders coming in and confronting Bates. Then she hears a voice she recognizes, or maybe Bates calls out a name before he's silenced. She's been aware that she and Bates have been being followed, and now she understands instantly what's happening, that she had missed the obvious. Footsteps pounding up the stairs, she knows she has only seconds to leave any kind of clue. She understands that if she leaves an obvious message, anything that looks useful or relevant, they'll take it along with all her other data. She knows Ryan, how he'll go about looking for her, how he'll recapitulate her movements, and she doesn't want him to make the same mistake she did: overlooking the most obvious aspect of the doughnut. She has just enough time to scrawl the note—thus the terrible handwriting—before she turns to face the intruders barging through the door. The clue is a long shot, a message in a bottle, but she knows her husband is a smart guy, trusts him to put it together.*

And he fucks it up, Ryan thought, tearing the hair at his temples. The thought that his stupidity might have killed her made him sick with self-loathing.

It was no mistake that the homing pigeon returned from Ridder Global. Jess had seen her watchers, recognized one of them. But she'd seen him as an ally, keeping an eye on her for security's sake, a slightly bothersome but not entirely unwelcome intrusion. No need to mention it. Until she heard the clamor from downstairs, his voice or Bates shouting his name. The man who had toured the house earlier, recommended the new security system. The security system that *had* been armed that night, but had been shut down to admit someone Bates recognized.

Gable.

Which, Ryan thought numbly, *leaves another little problem to be solved.* Gable, on his way to Heart Cove with a crack team of hard guys, aware that Ryan has located the bug shop, that it could all unravel on him unless he acted immediately. Gable, feeling suddenly exposed and desperate. Only fifteen minutes until he arrived.

Down the house stairs, then the outside stairs three at a time. On the Catacombs deck he encountered one of the Peterson's men, who looked at him wide-eyed. "Get three men up to the driveway entrance," Ryan commanded. "Other three down here, forget the house. Tell them we may have a hostile intrusion."

He burst through the doors. "Get on the intercom, get everybody up here, right now," he told Dolores. He charged past her to Logan's office, dragged her out of her chair. "Front office," he told her. "Got to get everybody, quick. No dawdling." Dear fabulous Logan, not a word of questioning, just action, down the hall and into the other offices. People coming out of their doors, quizzical glances. It took ninety seconds for the crew to assemble. Everybody but Dagan.

"We've got a situation. Leap, go save whatever, back up, lock our data in the new safes, then lock the door to the lab and shut down everything.

Lo, call the police, tell them there's been a traffic accident right out front, end of our driveway. People hurt, send cruisers and ambulances and whatever. Everybody else, shut down your desks. Anybody comes in, give them whatever they want, don't be heroes and get hurt. Probably nothing will happen. I'm outta here right now, but I'll be back. *Call the Beverly Police only,* just for the traffic accident. *No other calls, no state police or FBI!* This is imperative. Everybody understand?"

Dazed nods, then they scattered.

Racing back up the stairs, he felt almost bodiless, in such a heightened state of cognitive function that the physical world seemed almost unreal. How quickly a plan shaped itself once a few details came clear. Some expansive cognitive process, paradoxical, not easily replicated in a clinical setting. Something they'd missed at Project Alpha. Felt good.

He got to the parking lot, jumped into the Subaru. Gable was due any moment. Two of the Peterson's men arrived at a run, and he yelled at them, "There are people coming who *must not* come into this driveway. No matter what they say or who they are. There's going to be a problem out front, on the town highway, the police will be here. Tell anybody who asks that I've been hurt, that a staff member has taken me to the hospital. That's all you know. But *nobody* comes in. Don't leave your positions for any reason. Get on the radio and tell the guy up front what I just told you."

He floored the car, careened out of the circular drive spitting gravel. At the end of the driveway, the lone Peterson's guard was holding his ear-piece with one hand, nodding, and when he saw Ryan barreling toward him, he stepped aside.

Ryan took a left onto the two-lane town road, drove as far as the first neighbor's driveway, and yanked the old Subaru into a U-turn. He pulled over to let a car go past, waited until it rounded the next bend, checked the rearview mirror, and then floored it back toward Genesis. *Dagan was right,* he was thinking, *this job is tough on cars.* And then there it was, the big oak at the corner of the driveway and the town road. He brought the up car to forty, then slammed on the brakes enough to leave diagonal streaks on the pavement.

The crash threw him against the seat belt and his head whipped forward, smashing his nose against the steering wheel. When his vision cleared he could see the hood crumpled nicely around the tree, steam rising around the twisted metal. But the damned windshield hadn't quite broken. He wrenched the door open and staggered out, recovered, and then drove his fist into the windshield until a big circular web of breaks appeared.

He glanced up the road and was relieved to see that nobody was coming. Leaving the door wide open, key in and alarm buzzing, he loped off into the field and dove through the ragged hedgerow fifty yards from the wrecked car.

For a moment he lay on his back in a sumac-sheltered niche behind the tumbledown stone wall. Catching his breath, gazing at the freak summer sky through the wizened purple leaves. Mottled sunshine moving over thin branches. Very nice effect. A paradoxical oasis of momentary calm that he accepted gratefully. He felt like a kid in a fort, safe and secret. Then body parts started complaining: fist, face, something in the shoulder, a knee. But nothing irreparable, he decided. He was almost euphoric, which felt wrong until he traced the origin of the feeling: *At last to be acting, moving, doing something. At last to find the starting place back to Jess.*

When he heard the first distant sirens, he rolled over and rose up on his elbows to peer through the foliage and over the fallen stones of the wall. From this vantage point he had a good view of the end of the driveway, the three tense Peterson's men at their car, with which they'd thoughtfully blocked the drive, and the steaming Subaru in its forlorn embrace with the big oak. He could just hear the wavering buzz of the car's key alarm. A couple of cars had pulled over, their occupants standing around uncertainly.

And then around the far bend came a black Land Rover followed closely by a big white van. They slowed as they approached, and pulled into the very end of the driveway. Gable and his bully-boys.

Like clockwork, you fucks, Ryan gloated. *Welcome to* my *agenda.*

One of the Peterson's men approached the Land Rover just as two Beverly police cruisers roared down the road, an ambulance behind them. The Peterson's guard gestured to the driver of the Land Rover. Gable got out on the passenger side and began explaining something to the Peterson's man, who shook his head, shrugged, pointed off in the general direction of town. Gable took off his sunglasses to look over the wrecked Subaru. Then the cruisers and ambulance pulled up.

All in all, not a good moment for Gable to make any kind of move. Better, the accident offered a nicely misleading idea of Ryan's whereabouts, his condition. Gable would have figured, correctly, that Ryan's knowledge of the location of the bug shop could unravel his game. Gable couldn't afford to leave any lines leading back to him. So Ryan would have gotten into the black Land Rover and then either disappeared or had an accident. Or something.

But now two of the Beverly cops had begun directing traffic, a third was quizzing the Peterson's man, another stood in his cruiser's doorway, talking into his handset. Even from this distance, Gable looked miffed. After a few more minutes he got back into the Land Rover, and the two vehicles eased out and headed back toward Boston. *This is almost fun,* Ryan rejoiced darkly.

Once the little convoy had passed out of view, he hunched and ran quickly back to the house. *A lot to do,* he thought. *On to the next phase. Probably it won't stay fun for long.*

Chapter 59

Leap piloted his BMW deftly through Cambridge traffic as Ryan checked his equipment. ETA at Diana Reese's hotel, about ten minutes. So far so good.

The staff had done what he'd instructed, although no one had looked too happy when he burst through the door covered with dirt and leaves and blood, torqued wild on the strange murderous glee that came with finding the beginning place. He'd told them briefly about Gable, the need to be vague if anybody asked where they'd taken Ryan for medical treatment. When he'd asked Leap to join him for the next phase, he'd agreed enthusiastically. Thank God for Leap.

The plan had emerged full-blown the instant he'd deciphered Jess's doughnuts note. No, he didn't know how to do any of this. But there it was again, the power of the original solution, the offbeat approach. The unpredictable moves made by someone who didn't know the rules and so didn't play by them. Drunken Buddha. He'd absorbed Gable's first strike, and now it was time for an offensive of his own. Find the flaws in Gable's system, come at him from the unlikely angle.

First, a call to call Diana Reese. Her producer's office forwarded him to her suite at the Four Seasons Hotel, and he was relieved to hear her warm, microphone-savvy voice over the line: "You egotistical bastard! Why don't you return calls? You know I'm in Boston now, right? I'm taping an interview with Jason Ridder at eight tonight." It was an opening—practically an invitation. "Actually," he admitted, "that's why I called." She agreed to see him before the interview.

With that crucial piece in place, Logan had called her husband, Walter, at the Franklin Park Zoo, to relay Ryan's request. Leap had redlined the BMW through the Hub and South Boston, and they'd arrived at the zoo to find Walter alone in the large-mammal clinic, the equipment packed and ready. "If push comes to shove," he'd told Ryan, "I'll report this as having been stolen. Just so you know." Meaning, *I'll go this far, but won't take a fall for you.* He'd handed Ryan a small stainless-steel case, and then spent a few minutes discussing the chemical makeup of the kit and familiarizing Ryan with the apparatus. The crucial element was the dosage, which Walter had carefully calculated for typical human blood volume. Large-mammal dentistry required some highly specialized knowledge of tranquilizers and anesthetics. Ryan had once brought Abi to see Walter in action, bringing down the polar bears with well-placed shots before he entered their cage. They said *woof!*, looked around at the darts in their haunches, began to wobble like drunks, and then fell over lazily with a stupefied glaze stealing the fierceness from their piggy eyes. Walter and his assistant had kept a stopwatch nearby as they worked on an abscess in the mouth of the big male, because you didn't want to be in the cage when the tranquilizer wore off. Timing was everything when dealing with big predators.

Packed in egg-carton foam, the kit contained a CO_2 pistol, two small syringe darts containing premeasured doses of tranquilizer, and a third loaded syringe of antidote to be used if the patient had an undesirable reaction. The airgun was larger than the CO_2 pistol he'd had as a kid, but it was still small enough to pack inconspicuously among other equipment. If they got that far. Walter stressed that Ryan should expect ten to fifteen seconds before the drug began to incapacitate the patient, fifteen to twenty minutes of torpor from a single dose. *Timing, timing, timing. Those first ten to fifteen seconds could be hard ones,* Ryan reflected. Even if he could somehow keep Gable from using the gun he no doubt carried, the hit man would be lethal with his hands and feet.

"We're almost there, Ry," Leap said. "Better put the goods away."

They crossed over Harvard Bridge and turned onto Boylston, only a few blocks from the Four Seasons. Leap was chewing his gum like a gnawing rodent, adrenaline and nicotine goosing his metabolism, and Ryan hoped his aroused state wouldn't draw attention to them later.

The last stop had been Dr. Ackerman's office at Harvard Medical School. Ryan had asked for a favor that caused the old doctor's white eyebrows to lift. But after only a momentary hesitation, Ackerman had left the office, returning several minutes later with a small plastic case the size of a pack of cigarettes. Inside were another syringe and two capped, sterile vials of clear liquid. Dr. Ackerman had handed them to Ryan with a hard stare, but hadn't asked for details.

Thanks, Dr. A, Ryan thought. *Thanks, Walter.* He'd prevailed hard on people who trusted him, and they'd come through. Something to be said for having a reputation as an upright guy. Not that he'd have much of it left after tonight.

Leap pulled the car over just as Ryan tucked the equipment into his briefcase. Six-fifteen, and they had come up to the portico of Diana Reese's hotel. This was the hard part, Ryan knew. For an instant he looked at the façade of the hotel and felt the impossibility of what he was trying to do. Then he thought, *Hell, it's all the hard part.* He got out before the doorman arrived, went inside, leaving Leap waiting at the curb.

Diana hadn't yet dressed for the Ridder interview, but even in the loose beige tunic and pants she looked stunning. She had changed her hair for the new series, a more controlled, coiffed style that despite the vibrancy of her features made her look older, sober and journalistic. At the door, she gave him an air-kiss and brought him into the living room of the suite, a large room with big windows, white drapes, furnishings in elegant hotel-colonial. She shut a door to another series of rooms, closing off the voices of her production crew on the other side.

She turned and faced Ryan with her arms crossed. "This better be good."

"It's not just good, it's necessary."

"Okay, that's provocative. Go on." She was disconcertingly self-possessed, lovely, skeptical.

"I know I've got no right to ask a favor, but I'm—I'm desperate. And I think you're a person of sufficient courage and integrity to see the urgency of what I ask."

She chuckled, her mouth sarcastic. "Well, the flattery part's pretty good. Hey, why not? Look what your moral guidance did for me last time! I've been made over. Now I'm no longer a sleazy gossip-show host, I'm the Barbara Walters of the new millennium. All thanks to your barb about intelligence and substance and such crap. Also to my PR managers."

"I never intended—"

"Go on, Ryan. What's the favor?"

"I want to be part of your crew tonight. Myself and one of my staff. To come with you when you interview Ridder. He knows me, I'm working with him, and I need to see him tonight."

Diana's frown turned doubtful. "So why not just schedule a meeting through regular channels?"

"Because this visit needs to be a surprise. And it has to happen tonight, not tomorrow or the next day." *Before Gable could reasonably expect me, in a setting he'd never anticipate. To catch him before he can regroup and make his countermove. To pin Ridder to the wall and get to the bottom of this, after hours when his secretary won't wonder why he isn't taking calls for a while.* Ryan swayed on his feet, unable to contain the nervous energy inside him. A burst of muffled laughter came through from the crew's suite, and suddenly, amid the room's beiges and burgundies, the tasteful but sterile furnishings, he felt the impossibility of his request. Judging from Diana's expression, she was seeing it that way, too. The paucity of his plan was now apparent. Also the lack of a Plan B.

Diana strode away and then wheeled back to face him. "It isn't *done,* Ryan. You don't just bring unexpected guests to an interview! It's a violation of journalistic ethics! Really, I was looking forward to *grudgingly* doing you this exotic favor you were going to ask, but *this—*"

"—is important enough to make an exception."

She put her hands on her hips, defining her hourglass shape. Her hard grin had returned. "I was going to say, *This* will take some extra persuasion—a lot. Let's be frank. What's going down? And what's in it for me?"

"What's in it for you is you'll have made a hard choice, against the grain, and you'll come out of it knowing that you've done the right thing. For whatever that's worth."

"Son of a bitch!" She rolled her eyes. "I'm not a fucking *philanthropist,* Ryan! I don't measure myself by whatever idealistic, late-baby-boomer *bullshit* yardstick you do. I'm a climber, okay? Gen X. I want material goodies and money and status and—"

"You'll get a terrific scoop. You'll be on the scene with cameras and mikes when some real news is made." He took her shoulders so he could look into her face. "You know me well enough to know I'm always straight up, even if it gives me grief. *Trust me.* Please."

"So what's this great scoop going to be?"

"Either I go down in flames or someone else does."

For a long moment, she bounced his direct look right back at him. Again Ryan was startled by the unmistakable electricity around her, his responsiveness.

Finally she shrugged free of his hands and went to a dresser, rummaged among her toiletries. She watched herself in the mirror as she brushed her hair with perfunctory, distracted movements. "Last spring— I was stupid. I was lonely, I'd just ended an important relationship. I was vulnerable, I was attracted to you and I got aggressive. But it's not like that now, I've got a boyfriend in L.A.—"

"Forget it."

"And," she said turning back to him, "the thing that really pisses me off is how goddamned...*accessible* I still feel." She shook her head in self-disgust. "Makes me sick. You infuriate me."

He just waited.

She glared at him for another second, and then her features softened slightly, a little anxious now. "Is it going to be illegal?" she asked.

Diana's interview format required, demanded, only a small crew: Too much intrusion of people and equipment could destroy the sense of spontaneity and intimacy she sought. Typically, she told Ryan, they came in with an entourage of a production supervisor, Diana's wardrobe and makeup artists, two techies, a secretary and general gofer, and two camera operators who managed their own lights and sound during the interview. But the goal was to produce a candid, informal glimpse of an important American, on his or her home turf, so only Diana and the two cameramen, both expert at unobtrusive filming, actually worked in the room when the interview took place. The plan tonight was for everybody else to remain in the outer offices during filming. A good arrangement for the purposes at hand, Ryan thought.

He'd told her nothing of his plans, and though she remained suspicious Diana put a light face on it when she explained it to her crew. They saw it as some sort of prank between fellow celebs, and took the whole gambit in stride. It helped that one of the cameramen had worked Ryan's earlier show with Diana. Only the production supervisor was skeptical, but he was familiar with Ryan from his media appearances, and deferred to Diana's well-acted enthusiasm.

They left for Ridder Global in a big van and two cars, Leap and Ryan bouncing around in the van with the tech crew. With Leap blocking the others' view, Ryan slipped the airgun into one of the bulky aluminum camera cases, between the thick foam padding and the case wall. He put the small case carrying syringe and vials into his jacket pocket. Leap wore a grin as subtle and predacious as Sneaky Pete's.

Everything had gone perfectly. And yet it all still hung by the slenderest of threads. So much that could go wrong. Ridder's security people might recognize Ryan and suspect something screwy was happening. Or they might search the equipment and find the airgun. Or Gable might not even be there. Or—

Or, he thought with horror, he'd called it all wrong. Jess's doughnut message could have meant something else entirely, the apparent hack from Ridder Global could have an innocent explanation. He'd go in there, wired tight and mean-hungry for revenge and answers, and make a big mistake, fucking over himself and Diana and Genesis and not coming one step closer to Jess.

And even if he was right about everything, and Gable was there, and Ryan got a dart into him, there was still that time lag before the drug began to take effect. A man like Gable could accomplish a lot in ten seconds.

The cars pulled up at the main entrance to Ridder Global and everybody disembarked. Ryan borrowed a New York Yankees cap from one of the tech crew, pulling it low, slung a black nylon bag over his shoulder, and carried two large aluminum cases. The producer began to bitch about getting footage of the façade of the building and the soaring entry lobby, but Diana cut him short: "Ben, we'll get the B-roll on the way out, okay? Don't get your knickers in a twist." She had changed into a burgundy suit with a conservatively cut skirt, and swept toward the security desk cloaked in the aura of easy confidence that accompanied her stardom. Leap looked his part perfectly, carrying a tripod jauntily over his shoulder, bags swinging around him, looking around with professional interest. Ryan bumbled along, head down, aware of the security cameras on the walls.

The downstairs guards sent them straight to a pair of elevators. Packed into the confined space with the others, it seemed to Ryan that he could smell his own fear sweat. It got worse when they got out on the fiftieth floor and were met by a group of security men, some in uniform and some in dark suits.

"Ms. Reese, welcome to Ridder Global," said one of the men. "We're all big fans of yours. I hope you won't mind our standard security precautions here—times being what they are. If you gentlemen and ladies would just open your cases for us, this will only take a moment." He gestured toward a pair of large tables that had been set up for the inspection. The uniformed guards stood back, and three of the humorless suited men came forward.

Leap flashed a look at Ryan.

Ryan crowded toward the tables with the others. He set out his suitcases, unslung the nylon pack and set it on the table, aware of the syringe and vials against his chest.

Diana began to chat charmingly with the men, asking them about their jobs, how interesting and difficult it must be to provide security for an important man like Ridder. Did they ever have, you know, *trouble?* She was doing a terrific job of distracting them. Without appearing to be deliberately provocative, she threw out one hip as she chatted, and Ryan could see a ripple of sexual interest pass through the men.

Every little bit helps, he thought gratefully. *Thank you, Diana.*

One of the men opened the first of Ryan's cases, lifted and inspected the cameras, opened and groped in the inner compartments. Then the second one, with the gun hidden in the foam. Ryan's lungs stopped, empty.

And then the guy was done, snapping the cases shut again. But just as Ryan was about to lift them off the table, the same guard held up his hands.

"Sorry, sir. Just one more formality." He passed a metal-detecting wand over Ryan's chest and legs, his back, his armpits. When he was done he patted Ryan's pockets and immediately located the case containing the syringe and the two vials.

The guard stepped back—casually, but with very alert eyes. "Sir, may I ask what's in the jacket pocket?"

Ryan dug out the case, opened it on his palm, held it out for inspection. "Insulin," he muttered. "I'm a, uh, a diabetic."

The guard looked it over, nodded, pointed down the hall. "Thank you. If you'd like to step over there, we'll bring you in to Mr. Ridder in a moment."

Ryan gathered his gear and joined the other members of Diana's crew. Only when he'd gotten safely away from the flat eyes of the head security man, the too-bright lights, did he remember to inhale.

As Diana greeted Jason Ridder, Ryan hesitated just inside the door, turning away from the group and pretending to check his equipment. The tech assistants began setting up the lights. Ryan found the pistol, loaded it, and tucked it into his waistband beneath his jacket. Diana was radiant, deferential yet authoritative, easily charming Ridder.

Diana explained the interview format to Ridder, and after adjustments to the furniture and some last touches to Diana's makeup, the others left. Ryan quietly locked the door. It was heavily soundproofed, probably lined with steel plate between the walnut panels, he saw with pleasure:

Ridder's office was enclosed like a safe. At last he turned to face the center of the big room. Ridder's staff had opened up one of the conversation clusters, set a fine silver coffee service on the table in front of a long couch, and Diana's techs had arranged for a bright but homey sphere of light to fall on the arrangement. Against the side wall, Ridder's Patton shrine stood in its halo of light, the general's portrait gazing cryptically down on them.

When he saw Ryan, the billionaire's face went quizzical. He turned to Diana. "Hell's this?"

"Hello, Jason," Ryan said. "Surprise visit."

"Ryan, what're you doing here? I have to say, this is one hell of a time for—"

Ryan approached him. "Sit down, Jason. I need you to answer some questions. Like why Darion Gable kidnapped my wife and killed my friends and tried to wreck our research on the Babel effect."

Ridder's face turned livid red, pressure building so that his veins stood out on his neck. A look of incredulity and contempt. "I'm going to have your ass on a platter, Ryan. And yours too, Ms. Reese. Both of you can get the fuck out of my office."

"Ryan—?" Diana looked at him wide-eyed, her confidence faltering.

Ridder had stepped toward his desk, the intercom, but Ryan cut him off. "No. Sit over there. On the couch."

Ridder ignored him, came forward and tried to push him aside. A meaty push with weight behind it, full of the arrogance of status and physical strength. Ryan hit him with a tight left cross to the side of the jaw, catching him by surprise and dropping him to the floor. *Sack of potatoes,* Ryan thought. Jesus, it felt good to see Ridder on his ass, his look of shock and quickly covered shame. Leap had moved to Diana's side, ready to restrain her if she interfered.

"Sorry," Ryan said. "This is very serious. Go sit on the couch."

"I'm gonna punch your goddamned lights out—" Ridder began getting to his feet.

There really wasn't time for this. Ryan gave Ridder a shove as he came up, hurling him off balance backwards onto the couch, then drew the airgun from his waistband. "Jason, let's cut the macho stuff. We can resolve this quickly and I'll be out of here. I want to know where Jess is, and why you guys have done this."

Outraged, Ridder sputtered but stayed seated. "How would I know where she is? What is this? You've gone fucking nuts!" Ryan couldn't tell

whether he was telling the truth or just bluffing with the practiced coun-
tenance of the lifelong, high-stakes poker player.

Diana burst out: "Mr. Ridder, you have to believe me, I never
intended—"

"Diana," Ryan interrupted, "you'll understand better in a few minutes. Jason, you want to open up your computer, or should I? We're
going to check something out."

"Fuck you. Your ass is cooked, McCloud—"

"Leap, would you do the honors?" Ryan tilted his head toward
Ridder's huge desk, which held both a desktop workstation and a notebook computer. As Ridder glowered, Leap switched them both on,
waited for them to boot up. Diana took an uncertain seat on the edge of
the couch, interested despite her fear.

"They're both locked down," Leap announced. "Need passwords."

"Can you break it?"

Leap pecked around. "Yeah. But it could take longer than we've
got here."

On the couch, Ridder had regained some of his smug look.

"Jason, would you like to tell us your password?" Ryan asked.

"Fuck you. Nobody does this to me, McCloud."

Ryan went over to Leap, looked at the screens, where the cursor
blinked nervously at a password blank. Ridder Global's mainframes
would be protected as well as any in the world, but it was unlikely Jason
would have installed extreme security into his personal computers. He
was too impatient for complex protocols on a daily basis, arrogant
enough to believe that his key-coded elevators and security staff and
vaultlike door were defense enough.

"Okay," Ryan said after a moment. "Try 'Old Blood and Guts,' Leap."

Leap pecked. "Nope."

"Nah, right. Bad idea. You'd aim higher, right, Jason, give your ego
more of a thrill. A little more historical resonance—'man of destiny' and
all that. Try 'Alcibiades,' Leap."

"What's that?" Leap's hands hesitated over the keyboard.

Ryan spelled out the name. "Alcibiades, the great Athenian general,
born around 450 B.C. As smart and ruthless and impetuous as our friend
here. Got Athens into all kinds of trouble. Ridder's idol Patton claimed
he'd been Alcibiades in a former life. One of his many reincarnations."

Over on the couch, Ridder had turned red again.

"Smart boyo!" Leap said admiringly, Irish himself now. "That's it.
We're in."

"Look for your watermark. I want to know if our files are here or have ever been here."

Leap slipped in one of the discs he'd brought, and his fingers attacked the keyboard.

"These guys have gone crazy," Ridder was telling Diana. "I mean, listen to this. Certifiable. Jesus, they *work* for me. I'm paying them a fucking fortune, and this is what I get."

Ryan crossed his arms against his chest, leaned against the side of the desk, watched Ridder as Leap worked. He felt contempt for the transparent bastard. Also pity. What could you do about a guy like him? How could you fix him? There was no way.

"You know what my wife's computer password is?" he said. "'Gandhi.' She really admires the guy. Mine's 'Mandela.'"

"What's that supposed to mean?" Ridder snapped.

"Just something to think about."

"Uh, Ry," Leap said, and Ryan's heart plummeted. "Uh, Ry. Nothing here. Not our files, no Kilroy. Pigeon didn't fly from computers on this subnet."

Shit, Ryan thought. The fear of a mistake sparked through him. Ridder gloated, gathering his power again. Ryan did his best to look unimpressed. "Okay, then. Jason, is Darion Gable upstairs? I'd like you to invite him down here."

Ridder hesitated, wanting to resist. But then a glint of satisfaction lit his eyes, as if he thought having Gable join them wasn't a bad idea. He stood up, walked stiffly to the desk, began to reach for the intercom.

"One additional favor," Ryan said, grabbing his wrist. "I want you to say these words exactly: 'Darion, would you mind stepping down here for a moment?'" When Ridder balked, Ryan held the airgun to the older man's temple. "Those words exactly." *No point in risking Ridder's warning Gable through some code hidden in the wording of his call. Need to surprise him. Timing is everything for big predators.*

Ridder did as he was told, still looking too confident for Ryan's comfort. Simply faith in Gable's skills, or had Ryan overlooked something? Within a few seconds Ryan heard the familiar faint hum in the far wall. Gable's private elevator.

"Thank you," Ryan said. He jerked Ridder away from the desk, pushed him across the floor and down into the couch again, then yanked a lamp cord out of the wall and looped it around his neck. "Leap, would you come around here and hold this? I'd like Mr. Ridder to remain seated. Diana, I need you to stay sitting, no matter what happens here. If

I have to forcibly restrain you, I will." *Sorry for the tough tone, Diana. But it'll help get you off the hook with Ridder if this all goes screwy.* She glared at him, but the presence of the gun seemed to have paralyzed her. *About five more seconds until the inner door opens.* When Leap had come to stand behind Ridder and taken a firm grip on the lamp cord, Ryan leaped quickly back to the desk. He crouched behind it, checked the air pistol, and leveled it over the smooth ebony surface. Aimed at the door, maybe twenty-five feet away, thinking, *Ten to fifteen seconds. Got to last just ten to fifteen seconds.*

Chapter 60

It took Ryan an instant to see the shape of Darion Gable against the dark hallway behind him. He waited a half-second for Gable to emerge into the better light of the room, the gunsight dancing on the chest of the black collarless shirt. *Neck shot gets it into the blood-stream fastest,* Walter had told him. *But you go for center mass if you're at all unsure of your shot.* Ryan went for center mass. The gun went *chug!* but when he looked to see if he'd landed a dart, the doorway was empty.

Instinctively, Ryan lunged sideways, around the desk toward where Gable had been. *Drunken Buddha. Got to keep him too busy to draw his gun for fifteen seconds.* He turned just as Gable landed on the desk like a bird of prey striking for a kill. Ryan saw the black shoes hit the surface, and he lunged back toward the desk. Suddenly Ridder's desk chair was airborne, upside down and gone, and then Ryan was shooting forward, propelled by an explosion of pain between his shoulder blades. Face driven into the carpet. He scrambled nearly upright just in time to take another kick that just missed the vulnerable base of his neck. Gable's feet were as hard and sharp as trenching spades.

Ryan rolled and in the split second of free movement he realized he still had the airgun in his hand. He rolled again and managed to get his hands and knees under him before Gable was there and a blunt shock hit him in the forehead, knocking his head back, nearly breaking his neck. Gable's knee. Some part of his mind announced dully that maybe two seconds had elapsed since he'd shot the dart. Eight more to go, minimum. If he had even managed to hit Gable. Had to keep him preoccupied enough not to draw his gun.

Another knee to his forehead knocked him over backwards and suddenly he found himself tangled in something hard-soft and complicated. Ridder's chair, sent spinning by Gable's first kick. With one hand he pulled it over on top of him and felt it absorb a shock and then he flung it forward, skating on its five-wheeled base. It skittered at Gable, who kicked at it to get it out of the way. This time the chair seat and back spun and came around in front of Gable again, and the hit man had to use both hands to toss it aside. The extra second allowed Ryan to get to his feet.

Gable feinted with a left jab and then drove in a right so fast it was invisible. The callused knuckles of his hand missed Ryan's solar plexus but knocked the breath out of him anyway. Ryan rocked back, swung a punch of his own that seemed to float in slow motion toward the space where Gable's face had been. Then a sweeping kick took his feet out from under him. He struck out with the gun as he went down, hitting something, then landed on the floor again. Good view of Gable's shoes, and again he struck with the gun at one ankle. Then Gable's heel drove into his nose. He heard a breaking sound inside his head, like chewing on ice cubes, and he couldn't see very well, there seemed to be explosions and collisions in the room, big faraway blossoms of fire and darkness. But after an instant he opened his eyes to a view of Ridder's executive carpeting. Oddly tranquil view, nicely planar and smooth. He was supposed to do something, he knew, but couldn't remember what it was. Partly he was distracted by the sight of Gable's face, also lying cheek-down on the carpet, two arm's lengths away. Gable kept arching his neck to look down at his own chest. One leathery talon plucked at his shirt front. Ryan saw the dart lodged near the top button of his shirt, snagging the gold chain and cross. A little circle of wet stain. Gable's hand kept plucking around the area, never quite finding the source of the prick, and then he looked at Ryan with eyes that pulsed a white spark of fury. Then the spark iced over and the eyes stared past Ryan. Blinked slowly. Stared. Blinked.

Ryan got onto on elbow, then onto his ass and then onto his feet. He wanted to give Gable a boot in the chops just for the hell of it, but he felt too sick. Shock. Concussion. Nausea. Hypoxia. *Oh, hell,* he decided, *just a little one.* But it wouldn't do to damage the bastard. Had to be able to talk. Ryan drew back a foot, almost losing his balance, and drove it into Gable's thigh. The force of the kick rolled Gable over onto his back, but otherwise he was unresponsive. Dull stare, slow blink. Stare. Blink.

He found Gable's gun in its armpit holster, fumbled it free, flung it across the room. His kidneys stabbed him with pain, but after a few tries he found he could almost straighten his back. He was swallowing blood that trickled down the back of his throat, but when he touched his upper lip he found only a little red there.

This was great. Everything was going like clockwork.

"Okay," Ryan said. "Thank you all for coming."

The humor was lost on Ridder, who sat on the couch with wrists tied behind him, and on Diana, who watched wide-eyed, barely restrained by his threats and assurances. Even Leap was looking nervous. Gable was sitting in one of the chairs with his wrists taped around the back, his ankles taped behind the chair's hydraulic column, neck bound to the stem of the headrest, and he wasn't laughing a lot either. *That's the problem with the world today,* Ryan thought grimly, *nobody has a sense of humor anymore.*

They'd found rolls of silver duct tape in one of the equipment cases. After they'd immobilized Gable, as they waited for the tranquilizer to wear off, Ryan had gotten some ice cubes from Ridder's bar and now pressed them against his own nose.

"How you doin', Darion?" he asked.

"F'ck y'," Gable muttered. His eyes rolled wildly.

"Darion, I'm going to give you one chance to answer my questions, on your own volition, and then I'm going to have to compel you to answer. Do you understand me?"

"Fuck you," Gable said, more clearly now.

Ryan put down the ice to hold Gable's cheeks in both hands. "Ready? Listen carefully. One chance. First question: Where is my wife?"

Gable's expressionless face stared back, defiance rising as the tranquilizer ebbed.

"Why did you install surveillance devices in my house and offices?"

No answer. Ridder, though, looked interested.

"Why did you steal my wife's data on the Babel effect? Who are you working for?"

"This is nuts," Ridder barked. "Darion works for me. No reason he'd steal data I'd already paid for."

Gable's thin lips managed a smirk. Ryan felt his control waver, the sense that he was again in territory he knew little about. Already half an hour had elapsed, and there was a great deal more to do. How long before Ridder's security people got concerned? What if Gable *didn't* crack? He turned away, swung his arms to relieve the tension gathering around the pain in his shoulders, then turned back.

"Earlier today," he began again, "you relayed information you hacked from our computers. Who'd you send it to?"

"Fuck yourself," Gable said again. But his cheek twitched microscopically, and Ryan took it as a good sign: Gable was surprised they'd caught the hack.

"You sure this is how you want to do it?"

Gable was coming up to speed, confidence flowing back into him. "Give it up, McCloud. You've shot your wad. You think we don't know who you are? You're a famous nonviolent egghead pussy-ass. You aren't going to do anything to me."

The enormity of Gable's lack of comprehension struck him, and abruptly Ryan reared back and roared, laughing until the convulsions in his chest almost became sobs. It was outrageous, hilarious, a big pile of hilarious shit. He wiped at the tears streaming down his face, trying to find one word that would even *begin* to explain. One word that was anything but an understatement so preposterous as to be obscene.

"Oh, Darion." He shook his head. "Oh man! I have to tell you—you have no fucking *idea.* You know what? Before all this happened, I'd have done anything to be with Jess. To protect her? *Anything."* Abruptly the anger came back, searing, ugly. He put his face into Gable's and let the anger stream out of him, a beam that he focused on Gable's eyes. "So you can imagine how I feel *now,"* he hissed. "After all you've done. What I'll do to get her back."

Gable just stared back at him with a face impassive as a preying mantis's. "Yeah? Well, I've got a high pain tolerance, McCloud." He said it as an understatement of his own, and Ryan couldn't doubt it was true. The hit man's scar-seamed hands had been forged and annealed as weapons through a lifetime of impact training that had to have caused a great deal of pain. He had probably conducted interrogations and tortures himself and knew well the art of enduring as well as causing pain.

So we're really going to have to do this, Ryan thought sadly.

"A high pain tolerance," he repeated. "Yes, I thought you might. So for what comes next, I'm going to give you a little chemistry lesson. I want you to pay close attention. Do you know what endorphins are?"

Gable gave him a Bronx cheer. He was flexing his wrists, testing his restraints. Good—it meant that he'd returned to almost full alertness. Gable had to be receptive to verbal communication for this next stage.

"Endorphins are chemicals your body releases to overcome pain or stress. Natural opiates. Guy like you, high pain tolerance, has a metabolism that produces a lot of them, and that's how you can take a lot of pain. The way they work is, the cells of the body have receptors for endorphins. Think of the receptors as locks, and the molecules of the endorphins as keys that fit into these special locks. When your body is injured, your bloodstream floods with these natural opiates, which go to sensory nerve cells and fit into the little locks. Once in the lock, they cause chemical changes in the cell so that it can't transmit the pain signal."

"Skip the lecture. Get to work. Give me the pain. When you're done, go fuck yourself."

Ryan took out the little case Dr. Ackerman had given him, opened it, showed the contents to Gable. "I used this stuff back when I was doing research on the brain and central nervous system." He lifted one of the vials. "It's a variant of nalaxone, a compound developed during the 1970s. A hormone mimic—your body thinks it's one of its own endorphins. When it gets into your bloodstream, all these keys fit into the endorphin receptors on all your cells. Problem is, it *can't kill the pain.* Think of a key that's broken off in a door lock—doesn't open the door, just prevents the real key from fitting in. You getting the idea?"

Gable's eyes inadvertently flicked to the bottle.

"So with this inside you," Ryan went on, "you have no defense against pain. None. In our experiments on animals, those with the highest pain tolerances were the ones *most* affected by this stuff, because they were so unaccustomed to physical pain. I have to tell you, I personally stopped doing those experiments when one of my test monkeys tore off his own skin, literally half his own hide, trying to attack the sense of pain. And that was just from the increased sensitivity—we weren't hurting him yet."

"Jesus Christ, McCloud!" Ridder said. Diana looked as if she were going to be sick.

"I'm going to inject it into you. I'll give it five minutes to take full effect, and then I'm going to ask you my questions again. If you don't answer, I'll start hurting you. I don't have time to screw around."

Gable swore again, and strained against the tape. For a moment, as Ryan loaded the syringe, the whole chair vibrated with his effort. Beads of sweat broke on Gable's forehead as his own fear chemicals flooded his bloodstream. Ryan tore away Gable's gold chain and cross and ripped open his shirt front, revealing his sectioned chest and stomach. He ripped off the left sleeve, then slid the needle into Gable's vein and pumped the fluid in.

Ryan stood back. "Within a few seconds you'll feel a tingling just under your skin over the entire surface of your body. Your skin will flush red and will itch. I've heard that the itch alone can drive someone insane. And it doesn't stop. You'll feel hot, and then after a few minutes you'll be ready. You'll feel every nerve in your body—and that's before I start to hurt you. How're you doing, Darion?"

Gable didn't say anything.

"Oh yes." Ryan held up the other vial. "This is the antidote. It clips off part of the nalaxone molecules, makes 'em so they don't fit into your endorphin receptors anymore. Within a minute you feel the agony subside, a sweeping feeling of relief that's euphoric. It's yours when you tell me where my wife is. Feel anything yet?"

Gable didn't answer, but checking his watch Ryan knew that his skin sensation was increasing. The sense of heat, the prickle as the chemical started to reach the most sensitive nerves of the body—not so much Gable's hands, probably, but his temples, eyelids, nipples, genitals. Gable worked at his restraints again.

Giving it the time it needed, Ryan went to Ridder's desk, rummaged in a drawer. He found the box of Hoyo de Monterreys, a lighter, and the platinum end-clipper. He put the end of the cigar into the clipper and slid the blades together, finding that the tightly rolled tip offered no resistance to the double razor edges. When he was done he lit up, puffed several times, then left the burning cigar on the desk ashtray.

Gable had a blotchy red rash on his chest, his face and ears had turned neon red. He was breathing fast, squirming slightly with discomfort.

"Listen, Darion. That itch is something, isn't it? I'll bet even the pressure of the chair against your back is getting very difficult to ignore, right? Now, one more time: Will you please answer me now?"

"Screw you."

Ryan turned to Ridder and Diana. "I just want it on record that I asked nicely first," he said, as levelly as he could.

But the ice-cool act was getting hard to sustain, and abruptly he'd had enough. *Hey, you got a problem with high androgen levels, maybe? I can fix that.* He bent over Gable and undid his belt, ripping it free and then tearing open the button and fly. With one hard pull, he yanked the pants down to the knees, then tore the underpants away. Gable sat exposed, his entire skin blotched brilliant red, his penis shriveled against his thigh.

Ryan snorted and he looked down at him in contempt. "That's it? That's all? Why, you pathetic little overcompensator!" He had to laugh. "This explains everything!"

Gable was obviously losing control. "Yeah? Well, your wife liked it. She couldn't get enough of it. I never knew a pregnant woman could be so horny."

And now you've given me what I wanted, Ryan thought. *The first admission.* Over on the couch, Ridder's face had changed. While Diana was studiously keeping her eyes averted, Ridder was watching with heightened interest. A baleful, shrewd look. *Jesus,* Ryan thought, *if Ridder isn't in this with you, Darion, I'm the least of your worries.*

He went back to the desk, took a few puffs to revive the cigar, fingered the clipper, then came back to Gable. A look of understanding came over the hit man, and he mustered another derisive laugh. "That's what's going to make me talk? Burn me with a cigar? Take a lot more than that." The words were there, but the bravado was unconvincing. Little tremors were shivering the surface muscles of his body.

Ryan took the cigar out of his mouth and looked at it in surprise. "Hadn't occurred to me," he said truthfully. "I was thinking of this." He showed Gable the cigar cutter. A little flat oval of platinum, hole the diameter of a quarter, spring-loaded guillotine blades that slid across the hole, *snick-snick.* Gable shrank away as he bent forward with the tool, but the chair didn't allow much movement.

His hand had barely brushed Gable's rash-inflamed thigh when the hit man screamed, and an instant later he was talking, blurting, babbling. "Okay! All right! Jesus Christ, get that away from me! Jason, tell him to back off, Jesus Christ, get him off!"

Ryan didn't straighten. "I figure that at about a quarter of an inch each time, you'll get maybe eight chances to answer before—"

"She's in Africa! In Kisangani!"

"Why'd you send her there?"

"Constantine's there! The Church of Redemption and Revelation."

"That's who you worked for?"

"Yes, okay? Yes! My orders came from Constantine. Okay?"

Of course, Ryan thought. All the parts slid into place, the pattern obvious. *Doughnuts.*

From the side of his eye, Ryan watched Ridder's response. No mistaking the real outrage, the imperious anger at his centurion's deceit. A rage noise rumbling in his chest, Ridder began straining at his bonds as if he'd like to get at Gable himself.

"Exactly where is she now?" Ryan asked.

"I don't know. Constantine's headquarters, I haven't had anything to do with that end of it, I don't hear everything! Jesus, give me the antidote. After we sent her, I don't know, I wasn't there, I didn't decide."

"Who killed Bates?" Ryan snicked the blades of the cigar cutter, a reminder.

"Accident! We overdid it, just an accident. Believe me, that's it, that's all I know—"

Ryan knew from the sudden slide of Gable's eyes that he was lying, had taken Bates's life with his own hands, probably with pleasure. "Did you also kill Karl Alexander?"

"That wasn't us! We thought maybe we'd have to, but the electronics guys, or maybe it was somebody in his own shop. Not us, okay?" Again the sliding eyes, a lie. "Christ Jesus, give me the antidote! Somebody give me the, somebody—Jason, tell him to—"

Ryan reached under Gable's jaw and slammed his mouth shut. "The more you babble, the longer this will take. Now I need some details."

It took a few more minutes to wring the necessary information out of Gable, and then Ryan clamped his jaw shut again, deadly sick of the sound of his voice. Yes, it would be interesting to know whether he did it all for money or just because he was a true believer. What motivated a creature like this. Or precisely why Constantine had needed Jess and her data on the Babel effect. But ultimately it didn't matter, because the next steps would be the same. And there wasn't time.

"Leap," Ryan said, "will you untie Mr. Ridder? I'm sorry, Jason. That we had to do it this way."

Speechless, Ridder stood up, rubbing his wrists, face blackening like a thunderhead.

"I have to go now," Ryan told him. "Diana, you're the greatest. You're fabulous. I owe you, and I won't forget it. Now you better get your cameramen in here, here's your scoop. Citizen's arrest by prominent scientist. Kidnapping and murder. Corporate espionage, a scandal for Constantine—I'm sure your spin guys'll find the right angle for it."

The instant Ryan let go of Gable's jaw, he gasped again: "The antidote!"

Ryan tossed the vial onto the floor, crushed it with his foot. Gable's eyes popped wide, and he began to moan.

By the time Ryan and Leap got to the door, Gable's moan was mounting, his mouth frothing with wordless anger and fear. Ryan turned back to him. "Relax, you dumb fuck. I injected you with niacin—a B vitamin. Over-the-counter nutritional supplement. The itch, all that skin sensitivity will wear off in half an hour. Jason, I hope you'll do the right thing by Darion."

Ridder nodded, preoccupied. You had to admire the guy: He'd regained that look, the hard look of pleasure and savor and curiosity as he approached Gable, who writhed in his chair.

Chapter 61

MONDAY, NOVEMBER 11

Ryan waited on the sidewalk in front of the Hotel Wagenia. On Route de Buta, the traffic of Kisangani rushed and lumbered past—beat-up Fiats and Volkswagens, bicycles, military trucks, motor scooters, pedestrians. At the crumbling curb nearby, an emaciated man in rags cooked something in a can over a fire of street refuse, filling the air with an acrid stink. It was eighty-five degrees and threatening rain. The mood in Kisangani was a mix of panic and wild opportunism as another turnover loomed, another period of anarchy. The belly of Africa ripped open once more.

Ryan tried to repress his impatience, only barely holding the pressure inside. Waiting badly as always. Everything dammed up, waiting. So close, yet so much indeterminacy. Nineteen days since Jess was taken. He couldn't help feeling that if she was still alive he'd be able to *feel* her, through some psychic radar or intuition or quantum fold in space-time. He tried to grope forward into the architecture of this system, but there was no data, just hope and heat and speculation, a knot of vague darkness as murky as the sky above the battered city.

Half a block away, a panicked goat appeared suddenly and skittered through the traffic and the sidewalk pedestrians, chased by several men. It broke left and right until its hooves slid on the buckled pavement and it went down jarringly. Its piteous bleating was stifled by the pursuers, who piled onto it and began killing it then and there. Ryan looked away.

He'd thought hard on how best to approach Constantine, but in the end it had been simple. Using numbers Gable had given him, he'd called the Church of Revelation and Redemption's North American "bishop," the man who had apparently supervised Gable's operation. "This is Dr. Ryan McCloud," he'd said. "I need to see Constantine. I've got information he will find useful. Also, I'd like my wife back."

It had proved not as hard as getting an audience with the Pope. More like setting up a business meeting with a mafia don. They almost seemed to be expecting his call, to welcome it.

Before leaving, he'd debated on how to support his mission. Burke seemed the obvious person to enlist, but he'd had second thoughts. He still wasn't sure he could trust the FBI—what was the extent of Constantine's influence? Had Burke or his superiors deliberately deflected the investigation? In the end he'd decided to call the ASAC, only to find that his concerns were all moot. Burke had explained that Ryan had insufficient evidence Constantine personally had committed the crime, and thus the FBI couldn't act, especially on something that concerned a religious organization. And FBI action on foreign soil was problematic in any case, and anyway, the legal attaché in charge of American interests in the DRC was back in the Paris office, evacuated like all the other American federal personnel. "Don't go, Ryan," Burke had concluded wearily. "We don't have any resources for you there. We can't support you. Too many things can go wrong."

The thought had already occurred to him.

Trying not to be impetuous, he set Logan and Peter to work contacting various agencies—the State Department, Interpol, the Red Cross. But just getting the ball rolling would take days. And the outcome was dubious in any case: *Nobody* had any resources in the anarchy of the eastern Democratic Republic of Congo.

Ridder had arranged for him to fly on a company jet as far as Addis Ababa, but even his clout hadn't offered a way to Kisangani. Heavy bribes and some scary moments led to a bumpy flight on a cigarette-smuggling plane that dropped him in Kisangani. The pilot more or less agreed to return in three days to see if Ryan wanted a lift out.

And so back to Africa, alone. Appropriate, Ryan thought. A kind of pilgrimage.

A nearly new Lincoln pulled up in front of the hotel, and for a moment it looked as if his guide had come, the ride to Constantine's secret headquarters. But the car let out a solitary, frightened-looking Japanese businessman and then pulled quickly away.

From what Gable had told him, and other intelligence he was able to piece together, he learned that Constantine had originally set up his African headquarters in Bukavu, the city on Lake Kivu that was practically the epicenter of the last twenty years of crisis. But it had all fallen apart on him there, his missions and offices destroyed, staff killed, equipment stolen, and he'd retreated to Kisangani. Constantine's handlers insisted that the secrecy about the location of the reverend's current headquarters had nothing to do with Ryan personally: Except for his heavily guarded media appearances, his whereabouts had to be kept secret. He was the target of two Islamic fundamentalist groups; he was a thorn in the side of several warlords, military juntas, and insurgent leaders, who wanted his interfering ass out of their turf. The handlers didn't mention the church's mounting legal problems back in the United States.

Which meant complex terms for this rendezvous. Burke had urged Ryan to do it on Constantine's terms as much as possible. Standard hostage-release negotiation protocol: Give the hostage taker what he needs to feel secure, avoid spooking him into a mistake. Above all, don't back him into a corner, scare him into disposing of his hostage. He had urged Ryan to soft-pedal his intentions, to frame his visit as a request for Constantine's assistance in finding Jess: "Most important, *give him a safe exit strategy.*"

Ryan came abruptly out of his thoughts when a beat-up Fiat van rattled to the curb. The back door slid open as it rocked to a halt, and a white man called out, "Hop in, Dr. McCloud." The moment he was inside, the van tore away, toppling him backwards into the rear seat.

The man in back with Ryan wore iridescent sunglasses and baggy khakis and had biceps that strained the sleeves of his T-shirt. With the gaps between his yellow teeth, he had the reckless, white-trash look of a Serbian paramilitary. As soon as they had turned down Avenue d'Eglise, he leveled a gun at Ryan and handed him a strip of dark cloth. "Put this on over your eyes," he ordered. "When you're done, lie down on the floor."

Ryan did as he was told. The van's floor was filthy with grit and food garbage. Constantine's aides had warned him he'd be blindfolded for part of the drive, but somehow he'd expected a more ceremonious approach. As befitted an important meeting.

Of course, he thought suddenly, maybe this wasn't supposed to be a meeting. Maybe this was just an execution.

The thought brought a spike of fear, and he blurted, "Who are you guys?"

The guy in the back with him called to the driver, "Who are we again?"

"We're Islamic militants. Terrorists."

"That's right. We're Islamic militants. You got kidnapped by Islamic terrorists." They laughed at that. "Yeah, there's a car from the church waiting for you at the hotel, wondering where you are," the guy in back told him. "But you were abducted by fanatical Islamic fundamentalists."

They laughed hard again. The driver practically had hysterics. Ryan could feel the van weaving as he pounded the steering wheel and belly-laughed.

———

They rocked on for another ten minutes, the men joking sourly about Brother Michael, whom Ryan deduced was their boss and an intimate of Constantine's. Then the van slowed to a stop, Ryan heard the rattle of a big door, and moments later they pulled slowly forward. From the sound of the engine he could tell they were inside now, a garage or courtyard. One of the men helped him out of the van, and a third man joined them, giving curt orders to the others. Brother Michael.

"Undress, please," Brother Michael said. A quiet but firm voice. "Including the shoes and socks."

"This isn't necessary," Ryan began. "I don't have—"

Abruptly Ryan felt his arms gripped and the front of his shirt ripped away, but then Brother Michael spoke again, sternly: "Gently! We're not animals!" More-respectful hands continued the process until he stood for a moment wearing nothing but the blindfold. After another moment a pile of fabric was put into his hands, and Brother Michael ordered him to get dressed. He put on a pair of pants and a short-sleeved shirt of some rough fabric, and then was led to a new vehicle, a sedan. The drive began again.

No doubt they'd removed his clothes to eliminate the possibility that he carried a homing device by which he might be followed, and they'd switched cars so that no one would put together the car he'd left the hotel in with the one he was in now. At first it seemed like excessive secrecy. But the quip about Islamic militants, the car waiting at the hotel, put it all together: If Ryan had to be disappeared, Constantine could claim he'd never seen him. Sorry, but Dr. McCloud must have fallen victim to the chaos and conflict that was all around. So unfortunate.

No wonder it had been so easy to arrange seeing Constantine. They had covered every contingency. It occurred to Ryan that if Constantine was covering his ass so thoroughly, it didn't bode well for the outcome of their impending meeting.

Chapter 62

Constantine on a tirade. *In person, up close: both better and worse than on TV,* Ryan thought. *Both weaker and more powerful.*

The flunkies had finally removed the blindfold, and Ryan at last saw Brother Michael. He'd expected a hard-mouthed man, another Gable, but though Michael had Gable's whippet-lean body, he was a black man with a round, soft face, a head shaved nearly bald, sober and cautious brown eyes. Tough, well-disciplined, deeply religious, deeply troubled, Ryan saw at a glance: Constantine's factotum was a modern-day warrior monk.

From an interior courtyard, Michael led Ryan into a large, decaying mansion that had probably once belonged to some wealthy colonial in times past. Inside, the building was a bustle of activity, hushed and urgent, as men and women came and went. Many were armed, all had a chastened, anxious look. *An organization in trouble, on the defensive,* Ryan decided.

He followed Michael up a broad staircase and at last to a long room with high ceilings and parquet floors, probably once the mansion's ballroom. Now it was set up to serve the several functions of Constantine's nerve center. The big table surrounded by chairs suggested a corporate conference room, but the raised dais and thronelike chair suggested a ceremonial audience chamber. And the steel-shuttered French doors, along with the map tables and communications equipment along one wall, gave it the atmosphere of a military field headquarters. As did the armed guards who stood in pairs at the door and on either side of the dais.

Brother Michael stopped, held up his hand for Ryan to wait.

Constantine was raging, pacing back and forth across the length of the dais as a half-dozen men and women stood submissively, absorbing his wrath. "I want those people *found!* I don't care if someone has to *walk* on *foot* to Kigali! Brother Titus, this was to be *your* responsibility!" He stabbed a finger at Titus. "You have failed your responsibility, and I want to know, right here, right now, *why!*" Touch of a southern accent: *Rot here, rot now.*

Brother Titus muttered a reply as Constantine listened, shaking with rage. He was dressed in crisp white slacks and a white, long-sleeved shirt that showed up the red flush of anger on his skin, the taut tendons and swelling veins in his neck. He was gaunter now, his cheekbones sharply hollowed, and bandages covered his right ear.

Titus was dismissed, and Constantine moved on to the petition of an older woman wearing a pinstriped business suit and carrying an attaché case. "Sister Elaine!" he interrupted her. "Sister! What did I say last time? What did I say? *Can you tell me what I said!* Very good! So now go tell that pack of carrion-eating lawyer colleagues of yours that I am unavailable, thank you. That you can't find me. That I'm sick! Do I have to spell it for you?"

It went on for another twenty minutes, Constantine haranguing his staff with all the power he used to chasten sinners at his revivals. One by one his aides confronted him with the hard facts of missing supplies, failed communications, church members lost in war zones, legal problems, money running out. *An organization in crisis,* Ryan confirmed. But why would Constantine have allowed him to witness this? Maybe because he wasn't expected to live long afterwards.

When the last of the group had gone, Brother Michael brought Ryan forward. Constantine was still breathing hard, his eyes still wild. He watched Ryan with ferocious attention as he advanced the length of the room.

"Michael," he said, "I'd like you to bind him so that we can converse without having to worry he'll do something violent."

Ryan bridled, but Brother Michael put a hand on his arm. "There will be no point," he said quietly. "Please." Four guards came forward, and Ryan realized that Michael was right, this wasn't going to be about physical conflict. If it was, he'd already lost—he was on enemy territory, surrounded, unarmed. The struggle that was coming would have to take place on a different level.

As the guards held Ryan's arms, Brother Michael brought over a heavy wooden chair. The guards pushed him into it, and Michael took his arms behind the back of it and clicked on a pair of handcuffs.

Constantine had stood with his back to them until it was over. "Now y'all get out of here," he told the guards. "Wait outside. Brother Michael, of course, will stay."

When the guards shut the door behind them, Constantine walked up to Ryan, looking him up and down. Ryan returned the inspection. This close, he could feel Constantine's charisma, a heat that moved with him, inexplicably compelling. The strong nose and brows and resolute chin spoke of enormous confidence, but they were compromised by the line of the mouth and the wrinkles of his brow, telling of narcissism and ruthlessness and opportunism. Something else in those blue eyes, too: desperation, no, *devastation*, a huge sorrow or—or what? *Fear*, maybe.

Ryan's own eyes must have widened at this unexpected revelation, because Constantine smiled ruefully. "You see how it is," he said quietly. *My power, my burden.* "I'm glad. Because you and I have a lot to talk about." Again the accent, the hint of laconic Dixie chivalry.

"Like what? Just let Jess go."

"Well, now. Unfortunately, it can't be that easy, can it? Anyhow, you said you had information that would be useful to me, and I fully agree. I am very anxious to hear it."

"Let us both go, and you have my word we will not prosecute you. I'll tell you what we know about the Babel effect. Everything."

"If you mean Jessamine's theories of neurological deficits, or maybe the idea that we're being irradiated with magnetic fields and so on? Thank you, no, I think I've gotten the gist of those. No—the information you can give me has to do with *God*, and what it means to *believe*. A frank exchange of views could mean a great deal to us both."

Ryan shook his head, incredulous. "What, you want to *convert* me? Hey, you can believe anything you want to. Fine with me, seriously— just leave me and my family out of it."

"*You,*" Constantine shouted, suddenly livid again, *"will indulge me!* Do you for one *moment* think you would be here if I had not wanted you to come? You are made of *clay*, Dr. McCloud, and right now your clay is in *my* hands. You *will* do as I say. Do I make myself clear?"

Ryan lunged forward, straining his arms against the chair back, wanting to rip Constantine apart. The chair rocked, lifted, but the heavy wood was too strong to break.

Constantine watched until he gave up. "Good. I'm glad we've settled that. Now, I am going to tell you a story, and afterwards I am going to ask you a couple of questions. Just two questions, and I want you to use your fabled intelligence to answer as truthfully as you are able."

"You've already talked to my wife. If she can't answer it, I can't."

"Oh, actually, no. I assure you, there are two questions only *you* can answer. But we will get to that. First we need to put the issue in context."

Constantine began to pace, revving up to address his audience of two. Brother Michael stood to one side, his hands folded in front of him, just waiting. In the moment of silence, Ryan could hear the rumble of heavy vehicles moving past in the street outside the shuttered windows—by their weight and clank, they had to be tanks or half-track armored personnel carriers.

"You are looking," Constantine began calmly, "at a man who has been *humbled.* Yes—deeply humbled. When you came in, you saw what I have to deal with, the stupidity and bumbling, the lawyers, the banal concerns. I wanted you to see that—to witness the frustrations of my position." His voice was reasonable, gentle, insinuating.

"I saw a lousy administrator blaming other people for his own failings."

Constantine didn't break his stride. "Oh? Well, I assure you, I blame myself more than anyone, more than you can imagine. I abhor my own failings most of all. You see, just as you were a precocious child, I was precocious. I was given an outrageous talent. Where you could decipher your, whatever, scientific mysteries, I could *move men.* I found that gift when I was a boy, I learned that I could move people's feelings, that I could direct them. That I could change people! And so I knew what my calling would be."

Constantine's voice was rising as his enthusiasm grew. His affective lability, Ryan decided, was more than a revivalist's technique at work. It was borderline schizophrenia. Or maybe the compartmentalization that went with Syndrome E, or the Babel effect.

"I looked at the world, and I saw suffering and confusion and sorrow everywhere. I saw a world mired in misery—*unnecessarily,* Dr. McCloud! Unnecessarily! And I saw that the world needed a person to move mankind in the right direction. The world needed a *savior!*" Constantine stopped in front of Ryan's chair and bent so that they were face to face. "Surely you agree that this world *desperately* needs a savior?" A *save-yuh.*

Ryan stared back at him. "Is that one of the two questions?"

Constantine straightened, looked to Brother Michael. "He is a hard one, isn't he, Michael? Gonna pop my balloon every time. No, that is not one of the questions! But you go ahead and answer it anyway."

"Personally, I think what the world needs is a whole lot of people to behave a whole lot better. Not just one."

"Okay—okay, I'll agree to that. But, see, how you going to get them to behave better? That's where the savior comes in! *And I wanted to be that savior!* I knew I had the gift to see into men's minds and hearts, and to persuade them." Constantine held up his hands, warding. "Now I know what you're going to say, you're going to tell me I ain't him, I couldn't be him in a million years. But I *know* that. I know that, very very *very* well." He looked genuinely crestfallen now, chastened. "Maybe I knew it fifteen years ago, too," he said quietly. "But I knew I had the gift. And I felt *somebody* had to *try* to be him. You see?"

His sadness was so genuine that for all his hatred of Constantine Ryan was struck with pity and couldn't answer. Best to let him go where he needed to, see where it led.

"So that brings this poor country boy's story to the last few months. During which I have been *humbled.* Humbled by the world, by the *scale* of man's evil. The depth of cruelty and stupidity—before this, truly, *I had no idea!*" Constantine shook his head as if incredulous at the things he'd witnessed, and Ryan saw that a dot of blood had seeped through the bandages over his ear. *"Humbled* by the fact that I cannot find the miracle that will unite mankind. *Humbled* by the fact that I cannot even lead my own *church,* cannot control my own *bishops,* or my *flock,* who *commit* every form of *abomination* in *my name!* Humbled," he shouted, "by what I have myself done! By what I have found in myself, yes, and what I have *not* found!"

Constantine had slipped into the repeated crescendos and staccato emphases of the revival harangue. Ryan stared at him, fascinated, repulsed but also feeling the power there, the charisma, the passion.

Beginning quietly again: "Now, before all this, what I have loved about God is not the sheer majesty of His creation—formidable as it is, awesome as it is—but that His creation is informed with *moral order.* Right? But my faith in this fact has been *wounded,* dealt two devastating blows! First, by what I have witnessed during the last few months. I have labored mightily, I have prayed for understanding, I have reminded myself that the Creator's designs may be difficult for a weak, mortal man to discern. But I have seen too much wrong. I have seen children's *bodies* used as *sandbags* to keep flooding off the road! I have seen women with their bellies opened and their unborn babies exposed. I have seen men *eating* each other! And I have discovered my own weakness in the face of such images. Can you understand why I have become desperate?"

Constantine paused, looking for sympathy in Ryan's eyes. Not finding it, he went on: "And then, when I was already wounded, crippled, your wife came into the picture. And she explained that even all the good things, human kindness and charity and mercy, everything I have always taken as proofs of God's moral design, were just accidents of probability, or strategies of opportunistic replicating chemicals, or mathematical patterns that were resistant to change. Have I got that right? And she is very persuasive! In the light of what I have seen, what she said, I have had to ask, *Does God have a moral design for the universe?* These are terrible things to contemplate, Dr. McCloud! *Crushing* for a man raised in the religious tradition! Crushing!"

He looked at Ryan beseechingly, tears rimming his eyes. "So I lay all this before you, asking for your understanding. Your compassion, your sympathy."

Talking about his existential problems, under the circumstances—the egotism, the narcissism of the man was appalling. Didn't he see it? Or was there something else behind all this, some reason for the performance and its rhetorical logic?

"Okay," Ryan said. "You have my condolences. So now please bring me my wife."

Impatience flared in Constantine's face, and again his affect changed. "Before we get to Jessamine—a little carrot-and-stick thing here—I want your opinion. Tell me whether *you* think God has a moral design for His creation."

"I think it's the wrong question. The question you ought to be asking is whether you've got a moral design for your life. The rest isn't up to you, and so, as you've said, is pretty irrelevant. So now bring Jess here."

For an instant, Constantine looked as if he were going to hit Ryan. Then he pulled away, his eyes taking on a calculating look. "Brother Michael. Dr. McCloud appears determined to be difficult. It may be that he needs more incentive to participate in our dialogue with full enthusiasm. Would you be so kind as to bring our other guest here?"

Ryan's heart leaped. *Jess is alive! She's okay!* Abruptly he felt weak, stunned. Dizzied with relief.

Brother Michael seemed to hesitate, but then went quickly to the door and disappeared.

In the moment of silence after the door shut, Ryan could hear a new sound from the street—a steady, rumbling rustle. At first he took it to be heavy rainfall, the laden clouds breaking at last, but then he recognized it as the tread of many feet. Some large body of infantry was passing. Constantine heard it, too, cocking his head to listen with his good ear.

"Troubled times," he said confidingly. "Oh, the trouble I have seen. We had to pull back, you know. We had to retreat. I prayed to God for a victory in His name, but we were beaten. I prayed for Him to grant me the power of miracle, and I was denied. And now it looks like we'll lose this beachhead, too. My advisers tell me we must retreat again soon, there are armies converging here. And still I pray for a miracle and am rebuffed."

"That's why you took Jess? You wanted a miracle, and you thought she could provide it?"

Constantine bent close to Ryan's face again, fixing him with the mad blue eyes, the tragic eyes. "That strikes you as hypocritical? Then you don't comprehend the degree of motivation here, Dr. McCloud. I would accept the miracle from any quarter, yes. Absolutely."

"Even if it meant kidnapping, and killing, and—"

"At *any* price, yes! But, in fact, *I* did not initiate the abduction of your wife. One of my church officers did, in his zeal, in his love for our church. First he heard of your desire to inspect the brain of our Brother Hector, at the prison. Then he heard from one of our most devoted soldiers, Darion Gable, that you and your wife were embarking on a quest that was so very much like our own. So we began to monitor your offices. At some point, impatience ruled the day. As I told you, I cannot even control my own flock! And once the deed was done, we could not very well back away, could we? I felt we might as well see what benefit we might derive. And then, at first, the more I heard of her ideas, the more I agreed that, yes, my people had done the right thing in taking her. Why? I began to hope that perhaps your wife held the key to the miracle! To save mankind! To save my church! Yes, to save my leadership, I won't deny it! Yes, I wanted the miracle!"

The knowledge that Jess was near, was soon going to be here with him, washed Ryan almost clear of other thoughts. Still, the idiocy of what Constantine was saying appalled him. "But developing her neurological hypothesis will take *years* of research! And to isolate a cause—years and years of lab work! You were *years* premature, she was nowhere near—"

"Maybe so." Constantine stood up again, his brow showing that this line of talk troubled him. "Maybe so. But my people are not *scientists.* They are *faithful,* and they are *fervent,* and they feel as I do that time is short. They observed your wife. She gave every evidence that she had made a breakthrough. We wanted it. And the world could certainly not wait! Be frank, Dr. McCloud—even though you knew your research would take years, didn't you and your colleagues cherish a secret, niggling little hope that by some luck you'd find a quick cure? Maybe in time to prevent this crisis in Turkey and Greece from exploding? Or the next crisis, assuredly just days or weeks down the road? Didn't you wish you could spare mankind that misery?" Chiding.

Of course we did, Ryan acknowledged. *And of course you knew we did— you were eavesdropping on everything we said.*

Constantine had barely paused to see the answer in Ryan's face. "Yes, you did. And so did we! We *needed* the miracle! We could not wait and allow Ridder Global to own the miracle! And my church needed the miracle sooner, not later! Yes, we were mistaken. Only one mistake of many, many, as it turns out."

His sadness lasted only an instant, and then he whirled back to face Ryan, his face a mask of anger. "But there is another reason we had to take your wife," he hissed. "Your wife took great pains to explain it to me in my own terms. 'All men are brothers'—in your language, evolutionary psychology language, that's 'Generalize kinship, recognize and treat everybody as if they're kin, altruistically and cooperatively.' Right? How about 'Love thy neighbor as thyself,' or 'Love thine enemy'? That's 'Behave altruistically toward generalized kin,' and 'as thyself' is the theory-of-mind thing, seeing yourself in others. 'Love thine enemy,' that's games theory, meaning 'Choose nice strategies, forget quickly about the hostile actions of others.' As is 'Turn the other cheek.'" Constantine's rage was a red blaze behind his eyes. "Am I getting this straight, Dr. McCloud? Have I got the science about right?"

"Why does this make you angry?"

Constantine ignored him. "Let's see, what else? 'The meek shall inherit the earth,' that's an observation of the end result of cooperative games strategies, pure and simple, right? Then there's 'Do unto others as you would have others do unto you.' Oh, that's a real good one, yeah, that's 'Recognize self in others,' it's 'Generalize or extend kin altruism,' it's 'Don't initiate hostile or uncooperative transactions.' That's just the best! Oh, that Jesus, he was just one hell of a scientist, wasn't he!"

In one sense, yes, Ryan realized, feeling himself toppling at the edge of deep time. *Like the Hebrew prophets who observed the meta-patterns, the encompassing systems, of* rahamanut *and* gemilut hesed. *The brilliant desert shamans returning wild-eyed with their revelations, with the magic they knew would allow their tribes to survive, to thrive.* But he knew he dared not say it to Constantine.

"You and your wife would replace religious belief with a scientific definition of values! She would take our message from us, and offer a cure for the body when what's needed is a cure for the spirit! These are desperate times, people cling to any answer. Jessamine posed a mortal danger to our church. We couldn't allow her to continue, take from us what is ours, supplant our truths with her lies. *She was a danger and we defended ourselves!*"

Jessie, Jessie, Ryan was thinking. *So that's what it was—Constantine was afraid we'd market a product too similar to his own, cut into his business. Another hole in the doughnut, you told me and it was there all along but I was too stupid to see it: Everybody wondered what was at the core of Constantine's church, what was his prescription to avoid the days of Babel. And the answer is, Nothing. A hollow theology, a lot of people all worked up but nothing at the center. A man winging it and hoping the answer would come in time, he'd be the savior after all. Jessie, my Jessie, together we'll find a way out of this madman's grip.*

As if in reply, the big doors swung open. Ryan's heart lurched, and he craned his neck to see Brother Michael coming into the room. With another guard, leading a woman whom at first he didn't recognize. Then he saw it was Dagan.

Chapter **63**

Constantine got himself under control again, ratcheted down his righteous anger. "Dr. Rabinovitch," he said with ironic formality, "I believe you have already met Dr. Ryan McCloud?"

Speechless, Ryan watched her enter the room. Dagan looked at him as if frightened of him, a *guilty* look, saying nothing.

Constantine chuckled humorlessly. "You see? I'm not the only one who can't control his people, am I?" He bent his face close to Ryan's again, watching him keenly. "So many emotions. Disappointment that it isn't your wife, yes. But don't I also see a sense of betrayal? You guess that she helped us—that you could not trust this person who you hold in such affection, who you have worked so closely with? Now you have a taste of what I live with every day, Dr. McCloud!"

"Dagan—" Ryan croaked.

"I'm sorry!" Dagan said. "This wasn't how it was supposed to turn out!"

He couldn't respond. Beautiful Dagan, heart-shaped face, dark sincere eyes, all the trust and closeness: complete deception.

"It got all screwed up!" she went on. She started to approach Ryan, but the guard stopped her. "See how we missed the obvious? We dismissed the ethical resonances of her research, thinking it was just her personal quest, her desperation. So we didn't put together the motivation to abduct her. We asked all along, *Who* is Jess. If we'd answered that right, we'd have seen who would most want this information, who would feel most threatened! So obvious!"

Ryan heard it with great relief. Other details that should have told him the truth immediately: the bruises on her face, the sprung shoulder of her jacket. Dagan was no voluntary "guest."

"So that morning after I got drunk I was sure I was on the right track about who had taken her. I went to the church's Boston center. I was going to just feel it out—maybe bluff them, sort of scare them with what I knew and see if I got a response. They brought me right to the bishop—"

"Why didn't you tell anyone where you were going!?"

"Ry, I walked into their storefront church in Scollay Square! I mean, I was in the same *building* as the FBI offices, I was ten feet from a busy sidewalk, I never thought they'd—"

"With what she had figured out," Constantine said, "we felt it best to invite Ms. Rabinovitch to visit me here. I wanted to ask her certain important questions, but she has proven to be completely unhelpful."

"I know it screws everything up to have me here," Dagan moaned. "But—"

"But I need," Constantine continued, "to press on. Your presence may help persuade Dr. McCloud to answer my questions." *Puh-swade. An-suh.*

"I said I'd tell you anything!" Ryan shouted. "Anyway, you don't like the answers I give you. Just tell me where Jess is. Let us go."

Constantine was about to answer when the door opened suddenly. Brother Michael intercepted the pair of men who came in, conferred with them briefly.

"Jared," Michael said. "This is urgent. The west side mission dormitory has been—"

"I am occupied!" Constantine exploded. *"What* does it take to convince you to follow the instructions I have given you? I am *busy! Do I look busy?* Do I?"

"Please, Jared. We have a crisis that—"

"You men leave this room!" Constantine bellowed. "I am about the *Lord's work!* We are engaged in matters of the *utmost* importance, compared to which the most urgent earthly concern is entirely *beneath my notice!* Do not interrupt me again! Are we clear on this? Are we *clear?"*

The men exchanged glances, mumbled their assent, and left the room.

Constantine returned to Ryan. As if the encounter had emptied him, he was quieter now, sorrow engulfing his anger. He dragged over a chair and sat in it, knees almost touching Ryan's. "We were about to get to the crux of the matter. We had gotten as far as whether God does indeed impose moral order on the universe."

"Jess told you! Our sense of right and wrong springs from the, the ancient shape of the world, the foundations of life—you can call it whatever you—"

"Oh yes! That she did. And here we come to the heart of it. You don't really want to deal with me, but as you can see, I am a desperate man. Look in my eyes! What do you see? *Tell me what you see."*

Ryan looked. The too-wide eyes, the fear and sorrow, the madness. The darkness and the wisdom. And that metaphysical devastation.

"Yes," he said. "A desperate man."

"So," Constantine went on quietly, "let's make a bargain. You know something I desperately want to know, and I know something you desperately want to know. So I will tell you where Jessamine is—*if,* if you will now inspect your soul and answer me in complete honesty. Look me in the eyes, Dr. McCloud. A man's soul hangs in the balance here—no, two souls, yours and mine. Now, to summarize what Jessamine explained in great detail, science tells us that we are just biological machines, vehicles for genes, evolved through chance. Our emotions are chemicals, what we call our conscience is just a cost-benefit-calculating computer in our brains, and our attachments to each other are nothing more than selfish survival strategies. I am reluctant to accept all this, but your facts are very persuasive. So I wish to bring the issue directly home to you. I wish to hear it from you, one of the world's great thinkers—who now has a very personal reason, need I remind you, to answer honestly. Answer this question: *Can you honestly say that that is all there is to your love of Jessamine?*"

Ryan started to answer, then paused. He had never really put it all to that test. All the ideas Constantine had mentioned constituted a separate system, a world completely distinct from the feelings he had for Jess. Like everything else, he'd wadded the implicit contradictions up in the middle and mustered by, avoiding looking too closely at it. *What do you really believe? What do you really live by?* The truth of it was something he barely grasped, a meta-meta-pattern too vast and yet too personal for anyone else to understand.

"It's not that simple—"

"Answer me," Constantine whispered. "Let me add another life to the balance—Ms. Rabinovitch. Her life now depends on your answer as well."

Ryan's thoughts stuttered, but there was only one honest answer.

"No," he said at last. "All that...it doesn't...it's not a sufficient explanation." *And so much has to unravel if you accept that one fact,* he realized dimly.

Constantine shut his eyes, crossed his hands in his lap, leaned back in his chair, blew out his breath slowly. "Thank you. Your answer means more to me than you can ever know."

"Now tell me where she is."

Constantine stood up, walked away thoughtfully. "Yes. Well. Your wife posed a danger to me. She could have exposed me, the church, put us in jeopardy."

"*Where is she!?*"

"But that *earthly* jeopardy—that she might accuse me, might bring me trouble with police?—*that* was not enough to seal her fate. She was *Eve*, she tempted me, I ate of her apple of knowledge, and thus she destroyed me. And so I *hated* her! And so I had to destroy her! Surely you can understand! Surely you can sympathize with me! She took away that which I *depended* upon for my *life!* She put my church in *danger!* I had an obligation to defend that which was mine! Yes, now I regret it. It was sinful and wrathful and arrogant. But your wife is dead. I ordered her killed eight days ago. Brother Michael took her to the countryside."

Ryan had no words, no breath. Dagan settled quickly, weakly, to the floor.

Constantine was sorrowful, grieving. "So there is your answer. Which brings me to my final question. Tell me, Dr. McCloud, *What has become of the faith that sustained you?* Now that you know she is dead? Can you sympathize with me now? You and I are in the same boat, aren't we? *Tell me what sustains you*—this is what I must learn, you see. If I am to go on."

Ryan stared at him, too devastated even to hate. Unable to claim any underpinning at all, any source of sustenance whatsoever. *Nothing, nothing, nothing at all.*

Still Constantine watched, his head tipped back, eyes squinted half shut, as if gazing at Ryan from very far away. Then he said sadly, "Yeah. I thought as much." He turned and walked slowly back past the dais and to a door at the back of the room. At the door, he turned to call wearily over his shoulder, "Brother Michael. Dr. McCloud has honored his end of our bargain. I take some comfort in knowing he shares my, uh, my predicament. Deal with them as we discussed. And then don't bother me until I call for you."

The door shut behind him. Outside, the rain had finally started to fall, a deadening thrumming that resonated in the big room, blotting out all other sound.

Chapter 64

Brother Michael and four guards brought them to the courtyard again, where a windowless van and two more guards waited. The guards manhandled Ryan inside and shackled his handcuffs to a flange on the van's wall, then shoved Dagan in after him and slammed the doors. Brother Michael instructed them to lie down, and they did, Dagan crying quietly, pathetic and beautiful as a broken butterfly, Ryan still numb, half wishing himself dead.

But the other half was looking for an opportunity. Getting away was unlikely, but he'd be damned if he'd let the killer of his wife and his unborn child go without paying back some grief, if he'd be passively led to slaughter like some sheep. Michael deserved a taste of pain. No chance here, he decided, but no doubt they'd cover their tracks, switch vehicles again. Maybe then.

They drove for five minutes, taking many turns, Michael and the guards watching them grimly, rain drumming on the roof. No one spoke until the van slowed and they heard the rattle of big doors. "Watch him carefully," Brother Michael ordered. The van doors opened, and the guards dragged Ryan out and dropped him on the packed earth floor.

The garage was long and narrow, littered with car parts and other trash, lit only by small windows above double doors at each end. In the center of the room, a heavy engine hoist on a pulley hung from chains at head height. Beyond, in the shadows, a tall black man waited next to a battered Land Rover. Their hearse.

Dagan shuffled ahead of him, downcast. Ryan followed slowly, appraising the junk on the floor. He still wore handcuffs, but the guards had moved them to the front before throwing him in the van, giving his arms some freedom. *Big mistake, fuckheads.* As they came to the engine hoist, Ryan lunged forward and grappled it with his manacled hands, swinging it at the knot of guards. They dodged, but the distraction gave him an instant to stoop and grab a length of rusted iron pipe from the floor. He straightened, swinging it awkwardly at Brother Michael. It glanced off Michael's shoulder, and immediately Ryan plunged forward, using his weight to drive the warrior monk against the wall. The pipe twisted out of his grip, but he drove his clenched hands into Michael's face and followed through by ramming a shoulder into his chest.

"Stop!" Michael shouted.

Like hell, Ryan thought. He bulled Michael, pushing him and swinging his hands at him, mostly missing as the warrior monk deftly stepped aside and ducked.

"Stop!" Michael screamed. *"Do not shoot!"*

It took him another instant to realize that Michael was not yelling at him but at the guards, who held their guns ready to fire. He pulled up, panting, feeling wobbly and crazed. For a moment the room was silent except for the creaking of the engine hoist as it swung back and forth. Michael stood watching him with those sober eyes, so wide and deeply troubled. At last he said, "I didn't kill your wife."

———

Brother Michael ordered the guards to leave, and when they had gone he closed the doors behind them. The tall man still watched silently from the open door of the Rover.

"I am going to release you," Michael said quietly. "But don't mistake me for a friend. I abhor what people like you have done to the world."

"Then why release us?" Ryan panted.

"It is not for you but for Reverend Constantine. Jared is unstable. Until he is himself again, I must prevent him from betraying himself."

"What happened to Jessamine?"

"Jared told me to see to her execution. I told him that I was not the best person for the assignment. That I have been wrestling with a cruel paradox, that absolute belief in absolute truths seems to force one into the most ambiguous moral decisions. That I am troubled by...much that we have done."

"So what did—"

"He was angry. He told me that simple obedience would solve my dilemma." Brother Michael's eyes looked ancient. "So I drove her into the countryside, torn between my commitment to serve as a perfect instrument of Jared's intention and my desire to avoid making worse the tragedy that surrounds him. But in the end, the choice was made for me. Not far from the city, we were stopped by some faction's troops, the jeep stolen. I returned here on foot, and your wife went into the tide of refugees on the Bunia road. I lied when I told Jared I had done as he had ordered. But it was not much of a lie. She is probably dead."

Michael apparently saw the hope blossoming in Ryan's face, because he paused to shake his head. "Don't hope. She was very burdened by her pregnancy. Eight days—so many die on the refugee roads, in the fighting, in the camps."

"If she lived, where—?"

"Perhaps at the big refugee camp on the Bunia road—on this side of the Lindi River, just below Bafwasende. A hundred and thirty miles from here. Many thousands are trapped there, between the armies, unable to go east or west."

"Can you help us get to the camp?" Dagan asked.

Michael gestured toward the Land Rover, the waiting man. "Brother Joseph will drive you. He is from a village on that road and knows the region. He wants to search for his family, so I have given him permission to drive with you. You should know it is a difficult drive, maybe sixteen hours at the best of times. Now—maybe impossible."

"Why would you help us this way?" Ryan asked suspiciously.

For a moment sorrow poured into Brother Michael, filling his brown face as if he were a clear pitcher filling with dark liquid. "Once I felt that Jared had, he *was,* a strong conscience, and was lacking only an equally strong right hand. I strove to be that right hand. But more and more it seems it is his conscience that is lacking. And so I have tried to become that conscience. As I said, many of his own actions…betray him. And I wish to save him from betrayal from any source. We must remedy…the wrongs we have caused. We must atone."

"Why do you stay with him?" Ryan asked. "He's insane. He's dangerous."

"Yes, the man I chose to follow ten years ago is gone. Perhaps this one is insane. Perhaps what our church has become is insane. It is all coming undone, all the good we hoped for. And yet I cannot abandon him, can I?" Michael faltered, rallied, checked his wristwatch. "Now you had better go."

The Route de Bunia headed east out of the ruined city of Kisangani, quickly becoming a track gouged into ruts by the heavy traffic of refugees and military vehicles. Not far from Constantine's headquarters, the buildings of downtown gave way to tin-roofed shanties, uneven streets bordered by open sewer ditches. Just outside the city, the land near the road was cleared for scabby vegetable gardens and the red earth yards of mud-brick houses, but as they went farther the jungle began to close in.

The Land Rover had an aluminum body so battered that Ryan was at first skeptical it could take them as far as Bafwasende. But the engine seemed strong, and the tires had good, knobby tread. He was grateful for the mud-smeared windows: From outside, it would be hard to see whether there was anything worth stealing inside, how many occupied the car, or how heavily armed they might be.

Joseph, the man assigned to accompany them, wore a mechanic's coverall with a pistol shoved into one pocket. He spoke little English or French, and seemed to have little to say anyway. The rain poured down, raising a murky humidity, obscuring the landscape, and driving required all his attention. Ryan sat next to Joseph in the front seat, thinking, *Ten miles an hour, thirteen hours.* Then they slowed to a crawl behind a clot of walking people, and he thought, *two miles an hour, sixty-five hours.* The Rover wouldn't have enough gas, even with the safety tanks, to make it at that speed.

Dagan sat in the backseat. For a time she leaned forward, resting her forehead against the back of his neck and shoulder. He took only a wary comfort from the contact.

"Help me figure this out," she said quietly, near his ear.

"What?"

A couple of beats passed. "I—I want to be of use, of help to you. But you can hardly *look* at me, you can't take anything from me because you can't admit or say or think anything bad has happened to Jess. I can't say *Don't worry,* because that's crazy. And I can't say *I understand what this must be like, I feel the same,* because it could never be the same for me. And I can't say anything like, like, *I promise you won't be alone,* because that's presumption and it's almost like admitting she's…and maybe you'll think I'm, I'm opportunistic or something. But at the same time… this is when we, when people need each other. So what am I supposed to do? I can't find a way to be here with you."

He didn't know the answer to any of it. So he just sat there, silent, stony, paralyzed. Later he glanced back to find her sprawled across the ragged leather seat, asleep.

He thought: *Eight days. Where are you, Jessie?* An American woman, black of skin and with a face that strongly resembled the appearance of the regional tribes, but not speaking the languages or having any local connections or allies. Not accustomed to local bacteria, unused to the appalling hardships of war and anarchy. No knowledge of this landscape, little or no food available. Very pregnant, maybe going into labor. Soldiers and bandits and desperate people everywhere. How could she possibly live through all this? Maybe they'd already passed her, just one of the many anonymous, bloated bodies in the ditches. And yet Jess was in excellent physical condition, had more body fat to sustain her than the average Congolese or Rwandan refugee, and had had a wide range of vaccinations. The burdens of pregnancy came with the advantage of better circulation and disease resistance. Jess was very, very smart and adaptable, sensible about sanitation. A brown belt in aikido, a will of hardened steel. Those things had to count, too.

Seeing the dynamic array of factors, he knew that at best her survival was only a marginal possibility. Every moment counted, every delay reduced the odds of her living through this. *Jessie,* his thoughts cried. *Jessie, guide me to you.*

He must have drowsed, because he awoke suddenly when the Rover hit a particularly jarring hole and bucked violently. His head struck the window and he came awake to hear Joseph swearing in Lingala. Something pounded the Rover's undercarriage and ground along beneath.

"So muddy this road," Joseph explained. "Armies put logs. Logs come up, make worse sometimes."

The rain had stopped, but the mud remained. It was nearing evening. Ahead lay a stretch of corduroy road, trees laid side by side across a shifting base of earth. Some had seesawed up as one end sank, rising like uneven hurdles to bar the way. Still, the road was better than the tangle of brush and earth and wreckage on the shoulders.

"Where are we?" Ryan asked.

"Soon Bafwaboli."

Ryan's heart sank. According to the map Brother Michael had showed him, Bafwaboli was only a third of the way to the refugee camp.

"How much more of this kind of road?"

"Maybe fifteen kilometers. Better after Bafwaboli."

Ryan watched the darkening road. After a few minutes a shape loomed ahead, and Ryan saw that it was an armored car, listing sharply and partly blocking the road. Joseph cursed and slowed. Two men in muddy military fatigues stood in front of it, automatic rifles in their hands. They waved the Land Rover to a stop.

"Very bad," Joseph whispered.

The men came one to each window and looked inside. The one on Joseph's side spoke in Lingala, and Joseph answered. The one nearest Ryan just began pulling the door handle. Ryan held the inside handle down.

"He say we get out," Joseph said. "Maybe they kill us. Take truck."

The soldier on Ryan's side had stepped back a pace and was looking into the back window at Dagan, who had just begun to wake up. He grinned and made a phallic gesture with his rifle.

Ryan saw it all through a haze. His metabolism kicked into some sort of overdrive, the pent-up rage and frustration welling and obliterating even his fear. He opened the door, stepped out. He took one quick step toward the soldier and grabbed the rifle, yanking it toward him and pulling the man off balance. In the same move, he broke the gun out of his hands and swung the stock into his head. The soldier dropped into the wet earth, and Ryan felt flash of pleasure. *No grip, no reflexes. Stupid fuck.*

He turned just as the other soldier shouted and raised his weapon. Ryan fumbled with the rifle, pulled the trigger, got nothing, flung it at the other soldier, ducked. A shot exploded as he scrambled on all fours around the hood of the Land Rover. The second soldier had lost his weapon and was reeling backwards, looking down wide-eyed at his own arm. It had exploded into a blown rose of bone and blood just below the shoulder. From the window of the Rover, Joseph shot again but missed.

Ryan dove onto the soldier, knocked him down, straddled him, beat at his face. The round head rocked left and right with each punch. After a moment Ryan groped for the pistol on the soldier's belt, yanked it free, shoved the barrel into his contorted face. *Blow you away, motherfuck.* When he was done with this piece of shit, he'd go finish the other one.

And hesitated, shook his head. Panted. The soldier moaned, his body twisted feebly. Looking down now, Ryan saw a starved, scared teenager. The bony body that arched between his thighs had no strength, was so hungry it had started to consume its own tissue.

"Jesus," Ryan whispered. He paused, horrified. Defending himself was one thing, but he'd wanted to *kill* these guys. He'd felt pleasure in his own bloodlust, in their pain. Now it sickened him. *The Babel effect!* he thought with horror. *Worse and worse. Each time a little closer to completely forgetting. Not recognizing common humanity.* Abruptly he remembered the moment Dagan had entered Constantine's audience room: the strangeness of her, his struggle to recognize her. Maybe because he'd been expecting Jess, didn't match the face. But, no, he pieced together "Dagan" from the jacket, the jeans, the explosion of dark hair. And then there was his distrust, his immediate assumption that she was in league with Constantine.

"Oh Christ," he moaned. *The Babel effect.*

Dagan had come up behind him. "Ryan, it's okay now. It's okay. You can get off him."

Ryan stood up, covered with mud and blood. The soldier gripped his shattered arm, looking up with round eyes, his breath coming in little gasps.

"Yeah," Ryan panted. "Right. Okay." Though it was anything but okay.

Later, he drove as Joseph slept. The road in one yellow headlight. The warm, bitter night, the wounded night, of the refugee road. In the higher land beyond Bafwaboli, it had not rained as much and the driving was better. Ten miles an hour, except when other vehicles or clots of walkers slowed them.

Midnight: the scene of a recent battle. The night lit by smoldering trucks, wrecked half-tracks. Humped corpses strewn and making long shadows in the erratic firelight. Near one burning jeep, a grove of stakes stuck into the earth, a round strange object perched on top of each. Heads. Ryan's eyes fled the sight, but were drawn back to the stake nearest the road, the head that still wore an ornate field marshal's hat, vaguely familiar. He didn't place the tight-skinned, grimacing face until he'd driven another mile. *General Weasel,* he thought, his stomach rising. *Live by it, die by it, you poor son of a bitch.*

Later: a village of dark doorways, gutted walls. A dull glow in the darkness ahead, a fire. A cooking-meat smell in the air momentarily stirred the hunger in his empty stomach. Until, closer, he saw that it was a pile of human corpses. Glowing embers, little flames licking around human shapes, easily a hundred or more. A sudden flare as a man tossed more kerosene onto the pyre, illuminating another man swinging the body of a child onto the pile.

Much later he was able to push away the thought that Jess could be in that pile. Unthinkable. But he couldn't contain the perseveration, his mind replaying the fight with the soldiers, with Brother Michael, Shipley, the watcher on the street in Geneva. How easy it had become to be violent. Yes, and the paranoia about Burke, Dagan, Karl, everyone. And the sudden unfamiliarity of Marshall, and of Dagan—some variant of face agnosia? *The Babel syndrome.* And then the thought occurred to him: *If I do find her, will I know her? Will I even recognize her?*

That was the worst. That had to be the worst of all.

Chapter 65

The muted morning sun was just above the hills as they mounted a rise and at last saw the refugee camp at Bafwasende. Spread for two miles along the road and the banks of the Lindi was a ragged human horde, stopped by the river and the hostile factional armies on the other side. Like locusts, the refugees had stripped most of the forest here, using the trees for firewood and rough shelters, and in the open spaces individuals and families crowded on the beaten earth. Tents, makeshift scrap-wood huts. Fire pits, columns of smoke. A few animals, a few vehicles. Plastic jugs and bottles, bundles of possessions, suitcases. Carts, wheelbarrows, bicycles. Muddy pools from the rains. Bright plastic tarps stretched between poles. Laundry spread on propped-up dead branches. Mainly, just people and beaten ground. Near the middle of the vast human desert, Ryan could see the stretched white nylon of much larger shelters, and a row of canvas-covered heavy trucks marked with red crosses.

Twenty thousand people? Ryan wondered, despairing. *Thirty?*

"It's good the Red Cross is here," Dagan said. "Would there be a, a registry or something? Where people sign in?" She gestured at the expanse of land, the teeming bodies. "I mean, how're we ever—" She stopped, looked away from Ryan's anguish.

They had driven through the night, eighteen hours straight, and at dawn had dropped Joseph at the track that led to Opienge. He had walked away to look for his family in a nameless hamlet a few miles down. "We'll come back for you," Dagan told him. "After we find Jess. We'll drive you back to Kisangani."

Joseph shook his head. "If I find, I stay," he said. "If not find, don't care." His eyes had told Ryan he meant, *If I can't find them I don't care what happens to me—come, go, live, die, all the same.* Ryan understood completely.

Dagan drove as they slowly descended into the camp. Woodsmoke mingled with the smell of human sewage. People watched them with apathetic curiosity as the Rover went past. *The faces!* Ryan thought, terrified. He could make out a range of characteristics of many tribal groups, but most appeared to be Tutsis and Hutus. Or probably many were Banyamulenge, a populous regional tribe closely related to the Tutsis. *The faces. They look like Jess.* How pleasing it had been, only six weeks ago, to discover Jess's resemblance to these people. How disastrous now.

He looked at women. The women nearest the road, the middle distance, the far distance: He scanned the faces, beginning to panic. *So many.* Women with dark chocolate skin, good cheekbones, flashing ivory teeth. Pregnant women, women with tiny babies. So similar in their common ancestry, their shared look of hunger and fatigue and desolation, the patina of dirt on faces and clothes. As far as the eye could see in all directions. Here was Jess, there was Jess, everywhere and nowhere was Jess. His heart seemed to be fibrillating in his chest, feeble, not beating so much as shaking or shivering. A dying bird.

"Dagan, I don't know if—" he began. "I'm not sure I—" He gave up.

She manhandled the big vehicle carefully between potholes and walkers. "Let's get to the Red Cross people. Maybe Jess is already there."

That brought a surge of hope. After another ten minutes they made it to a small Red Cross tent and a cluster of trailers, the administrative center of the refugee relief effort. White-helmeted armed guards stopped them.

"Qu'est-ce que vous voulez?" one of them asked Ryan. *What do you want?*

"S'il vous plaît, nous cherchons une Americaine, Jessamine McCloud," Dagan explained.

"Americaine?" The guard looked skeptical.

"M'épouse," Ryan said. *My wife.*

The guard's face took on a perplexed expression. *"Attendez,"* he ordered. He spoke into a walkie-talkie for a moment, and before long a white man emerged from the tent, wearing khakis and a Red Cross armband. Late fifties, hair going white, a compact athletic build. He squinted dubiously at them, but approached and came to Ryan's window.

"I am Pierre Marineau, chief administrator of this mission. You are looking for an American woman, your wife?"

"Yes," Ryan said. "She was last seen on this road and we believe she may be here."

Marineau shook his head. "I'm sorry. We have only just arrived, and have not yet established a roster. But I can tell you that we have not seen any white women among the refugees."

"She's not white. She's, she's black...African-American."

Marineau's eyebrows went up. "Then your problem will be much greater to find her—I am so sorry. But no, no American woman of any color has come forward. You must understand, we are not yet fully organized. We are understaffed and stretched very thin just to see to the most seriously ill or injured. I have little help to offer you."

"Can we look for her in the camp?" Dagan asked.

"Who would stop you?" Marineau shrugged. "But there are twenty-five thousand displaced people in this valley. The odds of encountering her—" He spread his hands. It was self-explanatory.

They refilled the Land Rover's tank from the emergency cans, and then Dagan began to drive slowly through the camp, navigating with a rough map Marineau had sketched for them. The camp had grown up along a branching series of lesser roads and paths, and Ryan had plotted a route that would more or less take them to every part of the main refugee concentration. Now he sat on the roof, swaying with the roll of the truck, calling her name. Shielding his eyes against the rallying sun, looking at the people.

The faces. The shapes of bodies, the bend of necks, the jut of elbows. Was he looking for a very pregnant woman? A woman who had already given birth? A woman carrying a baby in her arms, or a woman who had lost her baby? And what was Jess wearing? Here were women in sweatshirts and shorts, in woven tribal robes, in polyester slacks. Secretaries from the offices of Goma and Bukavu and Kisangani in cotton blouses, women in coarse print dresses, in wrapped skirts. Brown skin on long limbs, like Jess. Jess's dark, kinked hair. From one and then a dozen and then fifty faces, some feature of Jess's face jumped out at him: her lips, her cheekbones, the upward tilt of her chin, her eyes. Bringing an electric jolt of hope and then a sagging letdown.

He almost called down to Dagan: *Dagan, I can't see her, I won't recognize her. I have caught the sickness of our age, I cannot know her. Dagan, she's everywhere, she's nowhere. My brain is damaged, I have an illness, I have lost the knowing of my wife.*

The sun picked up heat. Ryan's voice gave out and he searched in silence. Dagan turned the truck down another track, another aisle between the huddled tents, the hunched groups, the piled possessions. Another hundred faces turned to his, dully curious, dully suspicious. The faces. Jess here, Jess not here. The common face of humanity. The legions, all familiar, all strange. There were women bent to children or to cooking fires, women carrying water in plastic jugs. There were women whose bodies had the right length, or the swell of hip, or the rhythm in their walk or the movements of their arms, but who did not follow him with their eyes, did not smile or call out.

And there were women whose faces he couldn't quite see: women who didn't look up, women too far away, women almost invisible in tent shelters, women asleep with faces turned away. *You could drive this same route ten times and still miss her,* he realized.

Another turn, a small grove of trees, people packed into the partial shade. A woman in a blue cotton shirt straightening from a small fire and sending an arrow into his heart and then she was not Jess, too short and far too young. Another turn, the slow, remorseless motion of the Land Rover. A woman in a brown shift turning as if someone had called her name, a bolt in his heart, and her face strange, too wide, too defeated. The metal of the roof began to burn his hands.

Another hour, the endless slow parade through the strewn landscape. A pretty, blanket-wrapped woman standing straight and shading her eyes as she looked back at him and he felt the explosion of hope. She turned away, revealing the great swell of her pregnant belly, and he almost called out, and then he saw the decorative scarring that ringed her bare arms in traditional designs.

The features of faces scrambled, inverted, rearranged like the pieces of a puzzle with no solution. *Dagan,* he almost called out, *Dagan, I don't know what makes us individual, I can't see it. I don't even know what it means. I can't see Jess. Dagan, which family does she belong to—to this, her genetic tribe, or to the McClouds of Heart Cove, Massachusetts? Can there really be a family of the heart?*

After two more hours he lost his balance and almost fell off the roof when the Land Rover turned again.

"Dagan," he croaked, finally. "I can't. I won't be able to."

Her voice came up: "You want me to take a turn up there?"

He almost leaned then, not with the roll of the truck but toward the succor of her voice. *I promise you'll never be alone.* In a flash he felt the gravitation of a system, the basin of chaotic attraction, that resolved without Jess at all, at all. *Dagan.* A life without Jess could claim him, carry him away. *Dagan: Is that how all this ends?* His own weakness appalled him, and he changed his mind: "No. I guess a little longer." But there was little energy left.

A pregnant woman in dirty white, drinking water from a jar: the way of her wrist, the momentary jut of her breasts, the shock of recognition hits him and then she puts down the jar and she is a stranger. And there a woman with her leg splinted, head bandaged, and some familiar defiance in her posture as she sits unmoving, waiting, enduring. Closer, he sees her too-large front teeth, her weak chin, and the resemblance vanishes again. Dizzy now. Maybe dehydration, no water for how long? Heat. The puzzle faces shifting. And there a woman wearing a loose purple dress, sitting cross-legged as she mends a sandal or shoe, pulling a thong taut and clipping it with her teeth. And then she's looking up at him and he feels the stab again and then the denial again and then she's standing up to look at him and yes she's very pregnant. And he finds he's fallen off the truck roof and he stands quickly to keep looking at her. That self-possession shining like a deep light through the fatigue and dust and anxiety, and he thinks, *A woman who has very much found what had been lost.* He takes one hesitant step, unbelieving. The woman does, too.

Oh, most beautiful of all, he is thinking, *in her eyes, her mouth, the smile of recognition. The recognition of recognition, the infinite mirror of that dark face.* He's barely aware of walking toward her. *Of course you would,* he chides himself. *Oh faithless. How could there have been a doubt? Of course nothing could prevent this.*

And then Jess was in his arms and there was only that.

Chapter 66

TUESDAY, NOVEMBER 26

A day at home at Heart Cove. Ryan half sat, half lay on the couch, just enjoying the play of light in the living room. Through the north-facing windows, he could see Jess and Abi meandering, far up the shore.

He had started the day determined to get a lot done, but he'd found himself easily distracted. A nice kind of distraction. After Abi had caught the bus to the last day of school before Thanksgiving break, he and Jess had caressed each other, very gently and for a long time. The tenderness and frustration of postpartum lovemaking. With the baby asleep, they'd luxuriated in the privacy of their house, the time, the quiet, the big bed. He had rubbed the loose skin of her belly with oil. And after that, as he'd made coffee downstairs, just the spaciousness of the room seduced him, with its views of late-November seascape: sky like watered milk, bright yet austere. Water gray-blue and busy at the shore, trees bare now and waiting for snow. He'd put on a CD, cello filling the air with the great golden auditory cathedrals of Bach.

They'd had phenomenal luck getting out of Bafwasende. Dagan and he had spent a few days assisting the Red Cross team before Jess went into labor and delivered Liam, a beautiful son whom Ryan received from her body and held as he took his first uneven breath. And after two more days a temporary cease-fire was arranged, allowing food and medicine to be brought to the refugee relief mission. Also allowing the four of them to hitch a ride with a convoy heading for a supply dump at Bunia. From there, planes to Nairobi, to Rome, to Boston.

Coming back to the United States, they'd been stunned, culture-shocked. They had walked wide-eyed through the gleaming concourse of Logan Airport, with its restaurants and shops and newspaper stands, the plastic and neon, the orderly crowds. It all seemed unreal, impossible. Or, no, more like *fragile,* or *transitory.* Which, of course, it could very well be. If they didn't find a way to deal with the Babel effect.

While Jess and the baby had spent a few days in the hospital, one of Ryan's first tasks had been to check in with Ridder. Some lingering questions to resolve.

Ridder had welcomed him into his office with a bash on the shoulder. "Hey, lemme show you something." He led Ryan to the desk, where a new objet d'art was displayed—a Lucite block with Ridder's cigar cutter suspended inside.

"See," Ridder said, loving this, "I tell my staff the story of this item. I tell them I'll use one just like it on *them* if I don't get quality work. Lemme tell you, this little visual aid has improved job performance around here one hundred percent!"

Someone behind them chuckled and Ryan wheeled quickly. But it wasn't Gable.

"This is Nick Wolfe," Ridder told him. "He's not a new employee, but he's been, uh, recently promoted. Shake hands, gents, I'd like you two to be good friends."

Wolfe was a broad-shouldered man wearing a crisp suit, power tie. Early forties, dark short hair, a rocky jaw. Physically very different, but something much the same in the eyes: Gable's replacement.

"You're wondering what happened to Darion," Ridder said, frowning. "An unfortunate story. Had to call the police, of course. Our friend Diana Reese filmed the whole thing. After that—well, you tell him, Nick."

"Mr. Gable was held down at Boston PD lockup, pending his hearing," Wolfe said. "He was apparently full of remorse. Hung himself in his cell."

Ryan looked back into Wolfe's unwavering eyes, thinking, *Right, a suicide.* But of course Gable was chock-full of secrets about Ridder Global. Wouldn't want to risk him trading loose talk for lenient sentencing.

"I see," he said.

"Unfortunate," Ridder said again, pouting. "Seems his guru had a bad bout of suicide, too, over in Africa."

Ryan had heard the news: Constantine had died in Kisangani from a self-inflicted gunshot wound. Remembering the hollow man who had left the audience chamber, he didn't doubt that this was a real suicide. They'd flown the body home to his birthplace, a small town in Missouri, and video clips showed legions of faithful kneeling around the funeral bier, the body of Constantine pillowed in flowers. Ryan had felt nothing but sorrow, a sense of waste. A rare creature, tangled in his own talents, torn by the warring parts of himself. So close to what he wanted to be, and so far from it.

"Yeah, suicide, I heard," he told Ridder. "Maybe it's catching."

"Catching, yeah, I like that. Which brings us to business. You going ahead with the Babel project, or you going to back out?"

"First I have a question," Ryan told him. "Your friend Shipley is trying to invoke some national security legal bullshit to obstruct our further research. Can you do anything about that?"

Ridder grinned. "Oh, Alex. I'll smooth his feathers. I'm, uh, pretty good buddies with his boss, too. Consider it done." He made a dismissive gesture.

Ryan didn't say anything for a while, just looked at Ridder, who looked back at him, waiting for his answer: *Continuing the Babel study, or not?* Ryan had talked with the crew about it, then had spent a long afternoon working over it with Jess. Last, he'd talked frankly with Abi. He hadn't been able to dissuade any of them, not one.

"We're going ahead with our part of the project," he said, shrugging. "I wasn't as enthusiastic as the rest of the staff—but then, I have to deal with *you,* and they don't."

Ryan had grinned his shark's grin. "You gotta love this guy, huh, Nick? I like your moxie here, Ryan," he had said. "I like this a lot."

Abi burst through the door, bringing with her a gust of cold air. Behind her Jess moved more cautiously, protecting the baby, a swaddled lump in the blue sling.

"How was it?" Ryan asked.

"Freezing!" Abi hollered. She was wearing a brilliantly colored sweater of some Scandinavian knit, and her skin was shiny from the cold.

"It was, shall we say, *brisk,*" Jess confirmed. She smiled at her own understatement. With her lost weight, the cold would hit her hard. Looking at her Ryan realized with a jolt something that had been nagging at the edge of his awareness since their return. A big difference about Jess. *The smile,* he thought, *the uncovered smile, no hand coming up to hide it.*

Abi approached the couch with her hands behind her back. "I found a really neat specimen. Ma says it's some kind of squid." Abruptly she brandished it in his face, rubbery arms waggling, wrinkly yellow-white body, and he recoiled.

Abi doubled over with laughter. She thrust it at him again. A rubber kitchen glove, a piece of sand-scoured beach litter. Abi dropped it and collapsed into his lap, laughing, inviting tickling.

Ryan complied. "Squid! You goofus. Rodent goofus rat. Total goofus! Jesus."

Jess admired them together. After a moment Ryan pulled her in, too, gently tugging her into his lap and protecting the baby from Abi's flailing feet, thinking, *This is good. This is balm. This is the one safe redoubt.*

Ryan followed Jess up the stairs to Dagan's apartment, carrying a bottle of Moet & Chandon, Ryan feeling distinctly uneasy. Between her ordeal, Liam's birth, travelling, Jess had been sick, weak, sleeping a lot, hard put just to cope—he'd tried several times to talk with her about the complexities with Dagan, but every time he'd wavered, not wanting to impose it on her yet, and ended up talking in stilted generalities that probably meant nothing to her. But it was all still there inside him, a knotty wad that would sooner or later have to be explored.

They had dropped Abi off at her grandparents' for an hour or so. She swore she didn't mind: It had been a week since she'd seen them, and she actually missed them.

Dagan opened the door, gave Jess a sideways hug, kissed the baby, and stood aside for them to enter. She wore workout sweats and had bare feet and looked much better now, fourteen days after the ordeal in Kisangani. The apartment had floors of oak parquet, high ceilings, Dagan's watercolors on white walls.

"Liam, Liam, Liam," Dagan cooed, unable to take her eyes off the baby. Liam looked back at her, round vague eyes in a café-au-lait face, and grunted quizzically.

"Brought you this," Ryan said, handing her the champagne.

"Oh! Should we open it now?"

"Absolutely," Jess said. "That's what we're here for. To celebrate your launching. Unless you'd like us to break it over your head."

Dagan patted the faint green bruises on her cheekbone. "No, thanks. I'll get glasses."

They sat in the living room in front of a pleasant gas fire burning in the little hearth. Dagan raised a toast to the baby and Jess. Jess toasted Dagan: "To being your own boss. To getting away from the McCloud madhouse."

They touched glasses and sipped. Ryan felt anything but celebratory. Dagan's leaving Genesis felt like a blow. And there was the reason for it. He felt clumsy and wordless, and was sure Jess would notice his awkwardness. He should have tried harder to talk it through before now.

Jess seemed perfectly happy. "You sure you don't want to subcontract some of the Babel work? We'd be good clients!"

Dagan gave it a moment's thought. "Well, I have to admit the archaeo-epidemiological side of it is tempting. I've got some friends at a dig in Iran, turning up some interesting ancient viral forms in a village they've been excavating—"

"It's yours if you want it," Jess told her, smiling.

Dagan shook her head. "I think I'd better...wing it. At least until I'm established on my own."

They were silent for a moment. "Dagan," Ryan said uneasily, "we came here tonight partly to make you an offer."

"Uh-oh—"

"Hang on," Jess said. "All we want you to do is remember what you yourself said so eloquently, D. The idea that murder and genocide and war truly is a 'sickness,' a plague that has shaped our history and our sense of ourselves—so much promise there. So much hope. Right?"

Dagan raised a skeptical eyebrow. "And so many dangers. As you have both so eloquently pointed out."

"Absolutely. Working on this, we'll get vilified, ridiculed, sabotaged by both religious and scientific fundamentalists. We'll be at risk from every quarter. And yet sooner or later someone will have to stick their necks out on this. Who better than us, D.? Our necks are apparently made of tough stuff."

"By 'us' you mean Genesis. But I'm no longer part of Genesis."

"That's where our offer comes in," Ryan said. "The Babel hypotheses will take years of research to validate, to clarify. But five years, ten years—sooner or later, it'll be time to think about a cure. A remedy. We'll need you then."

"As a peer, not as a research assistant," Jess put in. "There's no one better. You've...come a long way. You know you're ready for it, Dagan."

Dagan looked at them both, her face changing. At first flattered and inspired by the prospect, then growing wary, and then sad. At last she said, "You know nothing could excite me more, and you're unashamedly exploiting my idealism—you're worse than Ridder!" She chuckled unhappily. "I'll consider it. But right now I can't promise. I'm sorry."

Jess nodded, serious again. "Well. I can understand the need to keep your distance."

Ryan tried to look engrossed in the bubbles in his champagne.

But for the moment that was as close as it got. They drank in companionable silence for a time, then talked about other things.

"Oh—Logan told me to tell you," Dagan said after a while, "she was following up on a couple of details."

"Such as?" Ryan asked.

"Karl Alexander. Logan wanted to know why his fax came after he was killed? It's pretty sad. She learned from the place where he faxed the messages that he'd dropped it off with instructions to hold it until a certain time. If he didn't come back by then, they were to send it out. He didn't come back, so you got the fax."

"Why'd he bother with the fail-safe?"

"Lo thinks he knew he'd been found out when he looked into the bug shop. At the last minute, knowing they'd catch up with him, he set it up so that the unsent message could be used as a bargaining chip—'Let me live and it'll never be sent, kill me and it will automatically be sent.' Gable killed Karl anyway. He knew you'd just call him when you got Karl's message."

One decent bone, yes, Ryan thought sadly. Reflexively, he swigged some champagne and then caught himself and set the glass down again. Since coming back, he'd been trying to put the brakes on. No big proclamations, just quietly trying to get hold of it. Though she hadn't said anything, he was sure Jess had noticed and approved.

They chatted on about other things, comparative trivia that was a welcome respite from dire considerations: The news was full of the standoff between Turkey and Greece. For the moment, the rush toward war had hesitated, right at the brink, thanks to desperate last-minute diplomacy. Greece had agreed to give the vaccine to Turkey, Turkey had agreed to monitoring of nuclear sites by an international team that would include Greek weapons engineers. But the peace was fragile, the situation volatile. One incident between angry, stressed, desocialized individuals, one assassination or mob attack, could set it off. Far too likely for comfort.

Even in the most clearly territorial or political conflicts, Ryan realized, *the Babel effect plays a crucial role. Like the trigger of a nuclear bomb. The thing that sets it all off, pushes it past the threshold of all restraint. If only—*

Jess broke into his thoughts: "This is the first booze I've had in a long time. Jeez, I've had about one tablespoon, and I'm completely *gone!*" She looked it: beautiful, eyes sparkling. She caught Ryan watching her and said to Dagan: "He *is* cute, isn't he?"

"Terribly," Dagan agreed, looking at him critically.

"Ryan, you've been walking on eggshells and looking hangdog all night. Relax, okay? Dagan and I long ago agreed that if anything were to happen to me, I would *hope* she would take care of you—if she were so inclined."

They were both observing him with unruffled amusement, perfectly at ease with the topic. Clearly they'd talked about the whole thing. Two imposingly beautiful and self-possessed women, enjoying his discomfort. "Take care of" sounded condescending, but, yes, after all, that was what it was all about.

"Uh-huh," Ryan mustered.

———

An hour later, Liam slept in his car carrier in the backseat as Ryan drove to pick up Abi. Jess leaned tiredly back in her seat, eyes shut.

"That said," she went on, as if they'd talked about nothing else since, "if I ever catch you so much as *looking* at another woman, I'll draw and quarter you, dear. I'm no goddamned saint. Just so we're clear on this."

He looked over at her face in the dark car. Yes, there was a smile at the ends of her mouth, but it was a particular species of no-nonsense smile he'd learned not to probe.

"Uh-huh," he said. Feeling awkward but not minding.

———

Later they sat on the couch, facing the big windows that overlooked the bay. Abi had gabbled and stuck her face into Liam's and played with her mother's hair and kicked at Ryan and finally fallen asleep. They'd carried her up to her room. Now Liam snored with gusto, still in his car carrier. After a while Ryan reached over and turned out the lamp. As the room went dark, the big windows came alight with a crisp November night sky, full of stars, a few distant ships, a rising chip of moon that bled blue-white light into the whole sky. They observed it with satisfaction for a long time.

He hadn't probed Jess on what she'd experienced, how the synthesis she'd come to had changed her. Best to let her find the beginning place to tell him. Now she was little more than a silhouette against the night sky star field, her but he heard her intake of breath, her slow exhalation. An intimacy grew around them in the half-light.

"Constantine," she began.

Ryan turned to face her and moved closer.

"I couldn't reach him, Ry. I tried. I said what I had to tell him should *help* him, *confirm* his beliefs." Trying to explain, she had unconsciously held her hands in front of her chest, as if cupping a candle there, protecting the flame or warming her hands on it. "He just…couldn't see it. He saw everything I said as a threat."

Ryan was thinking: *Yes.* At first it seemed to undermine everything, to rip you to shreds. But then suddenly you glimpsed the pattern stretching down, reaching back, built into every living thing, a deep corridor into the most ancient past. You pulled back, terrified and awestruck, but then you had to look again. *How big, how rainbow-hued it is, Jessie. How long its building has been going on. How small we are, and yet how completely we're a part of all the rest.* And then you felt embraced by it. The child of it. That's how Jess saw it: science and spirituality, the great ways of knowing, converging at last. Reverence and curiosity becoming a single impulse, as they should be. Breathtaking.

But still he stayed quiet, wanting to hear her tell it.

"The funny thing is," Jess went on, "I didn't understand it myself, not really, until afterwards. Until the Bunia road."

She explained: The soldiers who took the jeep were a platoon of scared, heavily armed boys, in such a hurry that they didn't stop to kill her or Brother Michael. The moment they pulled away, she ran to join the stream of walkers shuffling toward Bafwasende. She'd looked back to see Brother Michael watching her indecisively. To her relief, he turned back toward Kisangani.

In the towns she passed through, she could see the results of the fighting, why people would sacrifice so much to flee. One warring faction was slowly retreating from another, falling back along a wide front that engulfed first one town and hamlet and then another, leaving them gutted and ransacked. When each new army came into a town, their first act was to round up those they considered enemy sympathizers. Some were decapitated so that their heads could be displayed as object lessons to others. Another favorite method of killing was to put a car tire around the victim and set it on fire—the slow-burning, melting rubber caused an excruciating death, certain but not too fast. Others were given the choice of "short sleeves or long sleeves": having their arms hacked off at the wrist or above the elbow.

Jess stopped and looked over at Liam with concern, as if afraid he might hear and understand. She reached to stroke his forehead before going on.

She knew her clothes, her hair, just the well-fed American *shine* of her, would attract attention that could be fatal. She had to look as though she possessed nothing of value, as though she herself were valueless. So she rubbed dirt into her hair and skin, hid her watch, turned her jacket inside out. Later she saw a dead woman in a doorway, wearing a loose purple dress of too little value for anyone to have stolen. Undressing the corpse was difficult because the old woman's limbs were stiff with rigor mortis. Worse was having to look at her: She had been struck so hard in the temple that one eye had been driven out of its socket. But the dress was clean of blood or putrefaction. Jess thanked the body, rolled her own clothes into a rag, and rejoined the throng.

"Oh, babe," Ryan groaned. "I'm sorry—" *That you had to see that. To do that.*

No, no, the dead were the least upsetting. Seeing the leathery, scabbed bodies of poor farmers, or the plumper, smoother corpses of wealthier urbanites, she realized how egalitarian death is. And even beautiful. Even when they had disfiguring injuries, or bloating, their repose almost always seemed somehow gentle. Innocent, without burden.

No, it was the living that most disturbed her. The family that had walked until the sick mother fell, leaving the father and two young children sitting with her, faced with the impossible dilemma of whether to stay with her or to flee. Family members stripping the clothes from their own fallen. Babies who had no food and cried without stopping, or went beyond crying into leaden torpor. People clawing at each other to make space to cling to passing vehicles. Mothers who refused to stop carrying children who were clearly dead.

Ryan listened, wondering how, after all she'd been through, she'd preserved her will, her desire to keep living. But he couldn't find the right words to ask.

She went on: After two days without food, walking ten or more hours each day, she began to feel herself starving. The baby was drawing everything out of her. But she did eat four meals during those eight days. The first was from a dented can of condensed milk, miraculously overlooked by other scavengers, that she found in a demolished troop transport. She managed to puncture the can, poured a little puddle of the thick fluid into her palm, and carefully licked it up. And then another round white pool. Her body screamed at her to gulp the whole can, but she knew that the milk would come right back up, and that she'd make best use of the nutrients by rationing it. So as she walked she held it carefully in her bundle of rags, occasionally leaving the road and secretly tasting another half-dollar-sized white puddle. By nightfall she still had half the can left, and she felt confident the remainder would see her through the next day.

That night she took shelter in a stick barn with enough roof to shed some of the sifting rain. She settled herself on the ground and was about to have some of the milk when she saw that the shadow against the other wall was a person. Two people, actually: a woman with a child maybe three years old, a shawl draped over their heads. Jess could just make out their faces, turned toward her. They looked at her, and they looked at the can of milk.

After a time the child fussed, and the woman bared her breasts. The child suckled at first one, then the other, a few seconds each. Then rooted at the first again. Then gave up. Then child and mother turned their faces back to Jess.

She was careful not to let them drink it too fast. A puddle in your palm, she showed them. Lap it. Wait a while, then another puddle. As her eyes adjusted to the dark, she could see that the mother was very young, sixteen perhaps, very frightened. Another circle of milk in each palm. By the time the can was empty, she could hear the squelching noise of their stomachs digesting it. She fell asleep to the sound of the child's raspy breathing, distant gunshots, rain.

For an hour or so the next day, she walked near the young woman, who in daylight turned her shawl into a sling to carry the child. The child was very orange, sickly, listless. The young mother knew no French or English, Jess knew no Lingala or Kinyarwanda, so they couldn't converse. The starved, burdened mother walked more slowly. After a few hours Jess lost sight of them among the other refugees.

Sitting on the couch, Jess was silent for a long time. Then she rallied and went on.

"When I got closer to Bafwasende, I had three more meals. There hadn't been as much fighting there, there was more food available, and I traded first my watch and then my jacket for bowls of manioc porridge. But before that, in the middle—that's when I almost died. I was too hungry, too weak, I couldn't walk anymore. I had drunk water from streams and pools and I had diarrhea and it was emptying me. Liam was so heavy in my stomach. On the sixth day I started falling down. Every little rut and bump tripped me. That afternoon I got off the road and just lay at the base of a big tree. I couldn't even get far from the road, I was too exhausted, I just lay and stared up at the leaves as night came on. I didn't have any thoughts. I could hear the voices of people walking on the road. I kind of assumed I was dying. Hardly enough energy to breathe.

"Then I heard footsteps, and I looked up to see someone coming close by. It was half dark by then. I wasn't scared—too tired, too numb. And then I saw it was the young mother. I recognized the print of her shawl. She sat down against the tree. I don't know if she had seen me or just had accidentally stopped at the same place I had. She didn't have the child anymore."

Jess's voice fell into a hypnotic rhythm of recollection, soft, persistent, stark yet full of wonder: "She looked at me; I could tell she recognized me from that night in the little barn, three days ago. I looked back at her, but I couldn't sit up. So then she came over and lifted my head and shoulders and held me against her. She opened her dress. The child must have died the day before, because she had milk, Ry. Her poor breasts were still making a trickle, turning her own flesh into milk, and they had filled. Maybe they were uncomfortable. She let me drink from her. I drank milk from the breasts of a woman young enough to be my own daughter. And that's what saved my life."

Ryan held his breath.

Jess waited in the starlight. After a time she finished: "In the morning, we started walking again. I lost her in the crowds as we came near Bafwasende. I think she maybe made it to the camp, but I don't know."

More minutes of just moon and stars. Then she leaned her face against his. "Ryan," she said quietly, "I will never forget the moment I saw you riding along on that Land Rover. I will never, *never* forget that feeling. It was like my heart…*exploded.* And yet, this sounds strange, I wasn't really surprised. All along, I had complete trust in you—I had complete faith in *us,* actually. In us having more to do together."

"I'm glad," he said. An insufficient reply. But she'd know what he meant.

For a moment he wanted to tell her, to unburden: *We're such badly flawed beings, Jessie. The world's in such terrible trouble. There's been too much wounding, too much sorrow and misery. Jess McCloud has reached a grand, marvelous synthesis, but you can't prescribe it for the world's ills, at best it's a personal revelation, your personal way. Not even your husband can go there with you! I can't see beyond all the pain and loneliness. I'm not there yet, Jessie. I'll try to get there, but I can't promise it.*

But there was the other side, too: He couldn't deny the new strength in her, either. The freedom she'd found in relinquishing her hatred for those who had harmed her. Couldn't deny the fire and certainty her synthesis had given her. Nor that where one person had walked, others could follow. In a sense, they'd already found the cure for the Babel effect. Part of it, anyway.

Yes, a lot more to say. But she was tired. Not just now. He consoled himself: With any luck, there'd be time enough.

They watched the sky together. Big bowl of light and space, stars rolling slowly up the sky, moon casting slivers of blue light on the water. Liam snored gently, in sync with the waves outside. The sky struck Ryan as full of designs, imaginary creatures in the constellations, geometries of every sort, energies abounding in the depths of space. The three powers within the atom, and light, and magnetism. Mother Gravity, Father Time. If you looked closely and long, it all interlocked, design within design, the endless mandala.

The Babel Effect is based on true science and true history distilled from three years of intensive research—a project that transformed the way I think of myself, of human beings, and of our future.

The book's neuroscientific elements are all real and offer great promise. But they also pose great risks. The knowledge gained threatens to take a wrecking ball to our values and beliefs. As I considered questions like "Are we intentional personalities or just biochemical machines?," my deepest beliefs seemed to deconstruct. Worse, I realized that, like other technologies, neuroscientific discoveries can be abused. This book recounts real military neuropsychological projects intended to develop programmable assassins and large-population mind control. The suspicious deaths of scientists working on EMF weapons projects are a fact. The MKULTRA experiments are real. Arthur Shawcross is a real serial killer who is almost certainly a "manufactured personality." These facts—and others like Interpol's statistics on children sold for organ harvesting—offer a disconcerting glimpse of humanity's darkest side.

The idea that large-scale violence results from a brain disorder was first proposed by Dr. Itzhak Fried. But Fried's Syndrome E is only one way that mental disorders might affect large populations; it is far more likely that subacute, but widespread, impairments shape the way whole societies function. We are increasingly recognizing the possible causes of such "neurological plagues," which include, ironically, many of the same advances that offer so much hope. Though we have long known about disease-causing bacteria, we've only recently discovered the pervasiveness of viruses and prions, capable of causing brain disorders as catastrophic as "mad cow disease" or as insidious as depression, and all the more dangerous in our era of genetic engineering and bioweapons. Endocrine-disrupting chemicals really can upset brain function and cause violent behaviors; the Center for Disease Control is, in fact, currently researching 15,000 common endocrine disruptors. The World Health Organization is conducting a major study on electromagnetic fields, which are known to induce avoidance behaviors, remediate depression, and cause memory loss, confusion, and anxiety.

The *Sin Nombre* outbreak of 1993 is one of the many real cases in which epidemiologists relied on tribal oral histories to solve a medical mystery. Such occurrences give credibility to the Babel-like folk tales—groups of people suddenly losing their ability to communicate or cooperate—that occur throughout the world. Modern neuroscience also supports these oral histories by showing that human social behaviors originate in specific brain regions and neurochemistry, and they can be impaired by disease or injury. Face agnosia and autism are real examples of isolated neurological decrements that affect highly specific behaviors. Kinship recognition and social cooperation likewise originate in specific neural systems and are the basis for all animal and human societies. Our might civilization is thus built on the most fragile of foundations: those microscopic networks of soft stuff between our ears.

But the convergence of modern science and ancient wisdom may save us. Ultimately the most important true science in *The Babel Effect* concerns the idea that our behavior stems from genetic programs, that values have biological origins. While this at first seems to undermine our moral commitments and mystical yearnings, it can also *affirm* them. Games theory and recent discoveries in microbiology and animal behavior do indeed echo the revelations of the ancient seers and the core tenets of the world's religions. I'm not claiming that "science proves the Bible right"; rather, that both science and spirituality stem from the same origins: our passionate hunger to understand and the mythical awe we experience when we discern the universe's grand designs. And that, if we acknowledge this, there may be hope for us after all.

Before becoming a writer, DANIEL HECHT spent twenty years as a guitarist, a musical career that included albums on Windham Hill Records, concerts at Carnegie Hall, and international performance tours. Today, he lives with his family in Vermont.